Mulberry Hill

Copyright

Copyright © October 2015 by Josephine Booth

First Printing: October 2015

ISBN 978-1-326-44819-6

Chapter 1

Walter and Gracie were huddled together in the doorway of St Michael's church in Leeds on a bright, gusty, spring morning in early April 1944.

'Where is Sylvia? Where the ruddy…bloody….hell is Sylvia?' Walter was spitting out his words through gritted teeth. He ran his finger round the starched collar of his best shirt, trying to loosen it.

Gracie looked at her father with curious amusement. She had never seen him so agitated. His easy going nature had momentarily vanished and he was actually starting to hop from one foot to the other in irritation. She looked down to see his fists were clenched and his lean face was quite flushed.

She put her hand gently on his shoulder.

'It's alright Dad. I am certain she will turn up any moment now. After all it is the bride's prerogative to be late on her wedding day.'

'I know that lass but the prerogative is for the bride not the sodding bridesmaid.' muttered Walter.

They smiled at one another and Walter started to relax, soothed by Gracie.

'Sorry Gracie, swearing like that in front of you.'

Walter flashed a comical look of guilt up at the cross adorning the entrance to the church.

'In front of Him, too.'

He looked lovingly at his daughter.

'Look at you, always so calm, just like your mother. Let's give Sylvia one minute more, eh?'

They had been waiting outside the church for twenty minutes for Gracie's errant bridesmaid, Sylvia. The large wedding party inside the comparative warmth of the old church was looking cheerful, if slightly drab in their austere post war suits. They had been smiling indulgently at one another, looking at their watches in a light hearted manner, agreeing that brides were always late. But now the hard pews were beginning to cause discomfort on the collective bottoms and the shuffling had begun.

Gracie and Walter pushed themselves further into Church doorway ineffectually protecting themselves from the inclement weather. Gracie had started shivering violently. The lively Northern wind was biting through the French lace of her wedding dress. Her fearsome sister-in-law, Dorothy, had insisted, in her usual bossy manner, Gracie borrow a white wool bolero jacket. It was a kind gesture and Gracie, ever the peace maker, had accepted graciously. Once she had climbed into the back of the hired Rolls Royce though, she discreetly slipped it off. There was no doubt in her mind that a hand knitted cardigan would spoil the elegance of her beautiful dress, even if it was practical.

Gracie held tightly onto a bouquet of red and white roses which cascaded almost to the ground. Her black hair was being constantly blown round her neck but the rolls at the front remained firmly in position thanks to her foresight to use at least fifty hair pins to hold the style. Gracie's teeth were beginning to chatter and she kept rubbing her tongue across her front teeth in case any Ruby Rose lipstick went astray from her lovely mouth.

Walter took out his pocket watch.

'We can't keep the vicar waiting any longer. Let's have one last look at you.' Walter's voice had suddenly become loud and hearty to detract attention away from his eyes that had started to glisten with tears.

He stood back on his heels and whistled.

She really did make a beautiful bride. Tall and slim with thick shining hair and sparkling brown eyes. Her pale olive complexion was complimented beautifully by a touch of blusher and mascara, her wide smiling mouth emphasised by the crimson lipstick.

Gracie took his arm and they entered the church together, their eyes struggling to adjust from the bright sunlight to the holy gloom of St Michael's. The organ launched into the wedding march, gloriously off key, Mrs Jameson had been at the communion wine again.

The wedding party gave a collective sigh of appreciation at the sight of lovely Gracie and proud Walter with his chest puffed, both grinning happily.

'Oh yes, straight out of Vogue' agreed Frieda and Janet, two of Gracie's more genial sisters- in- law. Dorothy, Gracie's third sister-in-law, immediately noticed the lack of cardigan and registered the snub. She tried to quiet the sharp stab of jealous energy that had shot through her stomach. She looked down at her feet, consoling herself by admiring her new suede shoes from Schofields department store, feeling sure they would have cost the same as Gracie's dress. With a herculean effort she smoothed out the scowl and set her face to a pleasant neutral, reminding herself that scowling, after all, encouraged lines.

Sylvia's mother Amy looked uncomfortable when she realised her daughter was conspicuously absent. Practically the whole of Westridge village knew how much fuss Sylvia had made about being the bridesmaid. She had been very trying, being particularly difficult about her dress. Sylvia and Gracie had made endless trips to Lewis' haberdashery department. There was of course a shortage of fabrics after the war. Gracie had quickly settled on a piece of white lace and purchased it before another eager bride snapped it up. Sylvia had in mind a particular shade of pale lilac in duchess satin which they had great difficulty in finding, finally opting to dye a piece of fabric as best they could. Gracie privately thought that peach would have been more of a complementary colour choice. Sylvia at her most glowing had the all the colouring of a washed out dishcloth and lilac would certainly drain any vibrancy. Gracie kept that thought to herself because Sylvia could become very difficult when challenged.

Sylvia had also accompanied Gracie to every single one of her dress fittings. The dresses were being made by Mrs Mary Goldstein, a Jewish German refugee, in her tiny workshop above a chip shop in Leeds. Mrs Goldstein, along with her daughter, little Mary, were remarkably brilliant seamstresses. They had been extremely lucky to escape Hitler's Germany in the early 1930's and had taken sanctuary in England. Mr Goldstein had not been so lucky.

Gracie enjoyed her visits to the little flat. The Goldsteins were so friendly and warm. They effusively complimented Gracie's looks and figure and made her feel wonderful. They were endlessly patient with Sylvia when she insisted her dress be adjusted unnecessarily at each fitting. Sylvia was embarrassingly brusque in her manner and bossed the two Marys around sharply. Gracie found Sylvia's behaviour very uncomfortable and told her so on the way home on the bus. As soon as Sylvia was out of the door of the little flat the seamstresses would roll their eyes at one another in amusement.

'That Sylvia.' Mrs Goldstein would say shaking her head.

'For such a drab girl to make such a fuss. Why does sweet Gracie bother with her? A jealous girl like that will come to a sticky end, you mark my words.'

Little Mary would nod her head in vigorous agreement, unable to vocalise her thoughts as her mouth was full of pins.

Amy wasn't particularly surprised that Sylvia hadn't turned up. Amy knew she could be a spiteful girl when she chose to be. She loved her daughter but she often didn't like her very much and found her to be utterly unapproachable. Amy felt for the reassuring shape of the gin bottle nestling within her best velvet bag. At least she would be able to cope with the reception and ignore all the reproachful glances she would surely get from her neighbours. She hoped her friends, the Atwell family, would not be too upset by Sylvia's behaviour.

She didn't bother trying to catch the eye of her husband Bill. He had turned his back on her anyway and was deep within a silly conversation with Ella, another of Gracie's friends. Ella was a curvaceous bubble curled blond. Bill was extravagantly complimenting her rather snug fitting dress and she was giggling in shocked delight. Ella was no fool though. She knew exactly what kind of man Bill Jenkinson was and would be avoiding him and his wandering hands on the dance floor later on in the day. She had also noticed his frail, nervous looking wife with the trembling hands and felt sorry for her.

Down at the front of the church stood Gracie's fiancé. Tall, straight backed with a serious handsome face. He turned as Gracie walked slowly down the aisle and looked at her. His face registered approval, she was perfect. He was not particularly a man given to rushes of emotion but for a split second he felt almost winded with happiness, tinged with relief that she was finally going to belong to him.

Chapter 2

1922

Amy Bright was a house model at Sables, an exclusive ladies fashion boutique situated bang in the centre of Knightsbridge, London. The emporium stocked the very finest couture. They also had their own in-house designers. They were almost as famous for their accessories. A large selection of hats, gloves and scarves made from wonderful cashmere, silks, velvets and kid leathers. The name Sables would be spoken in hushed, almost reverent tone, by the majority of the inhabitants of the capital city, unable to even get past the enormous door man into the opulent store, let alone afford the luxuries ensconced inside.

The models were housed on the third floor which was used for the private viewings of brand new collections by the wealthiest clients. By appointment only, naturally. The large warm room was luxuriously decorated in the manner of a French boudoir with great swathes of soft creamy fabric draped around the walls and rich Aubusson rugs on the carpeted floor. The lighting was soft and golden. There were a number of large ancient mirrors leant artfully against walls away from harsh sunlight, chosen particularly for their flattering reflections.

She spent her days diving in and out of clothes, holding various graceful model poses and ignoring a rumbling tummy. She didn't mind the job even though it was very boring. The store could be rather fun and the other models were quite friendly. Amy had always loved fashion from being a little girl and never ceased to be thrilled when the new lines arrived. She adored the feel of expensive fabrics, silks and satins in particular and would always give the dresses a surreptitious rub with her hands, sometimes even holding them against her cheek if no one was looking. She never tired of looking at the array of beautiful colours and deciding, to herself, which colours would suit the clients best. The sight of a magnificently hand sewn beaded frock could almost take her breath away.

Amy sported a look which suited the current fashion perfectly. Her fine straight golden hair was cut in a razor sharp bob and her large blue eyes looked enormous when outlined in black kohl pencil. Her body was naturally very thin, verging on fragility. Her head almost looked too large to be supported by such a slim neck and her legs were birdlike. She also held her body in a slightly louche position, a look so popular with the young upper class London smart set. She narrowly avoided looking childlike through her height and she often rounded her shoulders to disguise her full chest.

One hot sticky August morning Amy was thoroughly fed up. Along with two other girls, she had been parading up and down the showroom for three hours for the delectation of a select group of older wealthy ladies under the ever watchful eye of Miss Haddock, the huge mistress of the wardrobe. Amy usually found Miss Haddock's sycophantic chatter with "her ladies" amusing. Miss Haddock had a loud ringing plummy voice which delivered endless compliments used to charm and cajole her ladies into purchasing much more than they had intended.

Amy found Miss Haddock fascinating, such was the force of her personality, her customers took her word on fashion as absolute gospel, even though she resembled the back end of a large bus.

Amy was feeling particularly tired. She had her monthly visitor and was terrified of getting blood on the gowns. She also had a large spot on her chest that Miss Haddock repeatedly glared at, affronted by the temporary imperfection. Amy looked over at the overfed self-important figures of the morning's clients and felt slightly nauseous imagining their plump bodies squeezed into the restrictive taffetas and satins. Even though the more forgiving drop waist was currently very much in fashion, a lot of the gowns were sleeveless and this collection of society ladies all had arms like sides of ham.

Eventually the ladies were exhausted from the punishing toil of gazing upon selections of dresses, blouses and suits and were about to be guided solicitously by Miss Haddock to the delightful French bistro next door. Sables paid the luncheon bill, all part of the deluxe service for their very best clients. The ladies were clucking in excitement, the anticipation of a large lunch with plenty of delicious wine being a very stimulating thought.

Miss Haddock led them towards the large golden lift. Amy gave them a good five minutes, dashed down the back stairs and out of a side door. She looked up and down the street cautiously then scurried up the road and dived into a dark, sophisticated bar. Amy was starving but she only allowed herself a black coffee with two sugars. She fancied a gin but didn't dare as Miss Haddock was a staunch Methodist and could smell the booze on an employee's breath a mile away.

Amy had kept her current gown on. It was a light whispering dress made from layer upon layer of gossamer fine silk. It was a beautiful pale grey which was iridescent in the light. It had the latest drop waist and was held up by thin beaded straps. Amy felt absolutely wonderful in it. The thought that other people outside the store could believe the dress belonged to her was very empowering. She ordered her coffee and the spotty young man behind the bar brought it to her table. His eyes were fixed upon her and his mouth was slightly open. She looks like a fairy from a book, he thought to himself.

Amy was enjoying the boy's admiration and wished the bar was busier. She drank her coffee slowly savouring the bitter-sweetness and the jolt of energy that now ran through her blood. She thought vaguely that she must keep an eye on the time. If she was missing when Miss Haddock returned she would be for the high jump. Anyway, she thought, I should be able to hear when the old bitch leaves the restaurant, her whalebones will be creaking under the pressure of that big body.

The door of the bar swung open and in strode Bill Jenkinson bringing with him a blast of hot fetid London August air. He was very tall with broad shoulders. His dark hair was swept back from a fine forehead with the aid of Macassar oil. His cheek-bones were very high and he had a firm chin with a shallow cleft in the centre. Amy had turned eighteen the previous month and she guessed this wonderful man, who looked as if he belonged on the stage, was a only a couple of years older than herself. Amy also thought he was the most handsome man she had ever seen.

He didn't look round to take in his surroundings rather he marched directly up to the bar and snapped his fingers at the barman. The boy behind the bar jumped slightly as he was rudely yanked out of a very pleasant daydream involving himself, the fairy and a picnic rug behind a haystack. Bill ordered a whiskey in a snappy confident manner. Amy detected a northern twang in his deep voice.

Bill was also employed within the luxury clothing industry. He was a very successful salesman for Silverbond of York, producers of very fine hand finished shirts. He had just closed a very lucrative deal with Julian De Vere, the chief buyer for Lamparts, situated on Saville Row. Lamparts was probably the closest to Sables for luxury items for menswear. Bill had just ensured Lamparts would stock Silverbonds' shirts for the next three years. It was almost always the case that when Lamparts stocked a brand the other lesser department stores would inevitably follow.

Bill attributed his success as a salesman to his ability to read his customers and apply the appropriate flattery or pressure depending on their personalities. He carefully researched personal details appertaining to his clients prior to his meetings. He achieved this in a number of ways. Often visiting a particular store the day before if possible, pretending to be a customer, and chatting to the shop floor boys and girls. It was worth his while to make one or two small purchases whilst gently encouraging any snippets of useful information about their managers.

Another very useful source of gossip was through the network of fellow salesmen. Their jobs required travelling around the county. They had their favourite guest-houses and hotels and met up regularly. When their paths crossed and they were staying in the same place it meant they could go out on the town, when they had finished their working day and go for a couple of ales. Otherwise the life of a travelling salesman would be very lonely indeed. They would swap the gossip they had gleaned and share useful information about their clients, who was married to whom, who was spending late evenings with their secretaries, political and religious views. Sometimes Bill would meet up with a chap who was in the same line as him. He would still be genial and go for a drink, but would then keep his cards very close to his chest. It was every man for himself after all.

Some of the younger, unmarried salesmen would also recommend the beds of certain welcoming landladies to one another. Bill sometimes would take advantage of a warm embrace from an older woman. It required minimal effort on his part and they were always so grateful.

Bill had a justified reputation of being a ladies' man. It was rare for him to have a steady relationship though. To share a bed with a female who understood it was only to be for a night or two, before he moved on, suited him nicely. He enjoyed the company of women and took a lot of pleasure in making them laugh and feel good about themselves. He was very skilled in the bedroom, he had had a lot of practice. He never admitted though, even to himself, that his favourite part of a shared night was the comfort of cuddling in the aftermath.

His father was stationed in India with his mother for most of his childhood and he grew up in an austere, sometimes violent, private boarding school. In the holidays he and his older brother stayed with grandparents who had firm Victorian values on how to bring up children. Bread and water and beatings were a regular feature of his life. Comfort and love were sadly lacking. His mother died of malaria when he was eight. He didn't cry. He barely knew the woman.

That morning, after Bill had extracted himself from the plump lavender scented embrace of a Mrs Landsbury of Ash Lodge, Brixton and used all the Lodge's hot water in a deep morning bath, he hailed a cab and headed off to Lamparts. He had dressed particularly carefully. He was wearing his best double-breasted navy suit with the subtle pinstripe and he chose a golden tie that he knew enhanced the light flecks in his hazel eyes. He changed his cologne from his usual dark musk to a light almost floral scent and tucked a silk paisley handkerchief in his suit top pocket. On leaving Ash Lodge he pinched a white iceberg rose from the garden and popped it in his buttonhole.

The previous day Bill had had a rather informative chat with Jeffery, one of the boys who worked in the warehouse at the back of Lamparts. Bill had dressed rather differently for this errand, wearing a rough work shirt and a cloth cap pulled over his eyes. He loitered outside the loading bay doors until inevitably one of the boys came out for a gasper. He fell into easy conversation with Jeffery after offering him a cigarette and a match. Jeffery was used to men loitering outside the big heavy double doors, they were usually discharged soldiers from the Great War hoping some work was available, however temporary. Jeffery was an affable young man of fourteen who was happy to chat with anyone who offered him a smoke.

Bill was shown into the office of Julian De Vere by Julian's twittery arthritic secretary, a spinster named Miss Maddox.

The men shook hands in greeting and Bill allowed his hand to remain in Julian's for a split second longer than necessary, and smiled directly into his eyes.

From Jeffery, Bill had learned that Julian was very fond of Pekinese dogs and still lived with his mother at the age of forty-five. In under a minute Bill had gently directed the conversation towards the responsibilities of caring for aged parents, suggesting untruthfully that he had just picked up an early Christmas present for his own mother, who was ailing. He then sat back and listened to Julian's effusive and lengthy response. Bill also admired Julian's little painting of his beloved dog Fifi, and was able to discuss the merits of having a canine companion.

Finally, Bill smoothly guided the conversation back to the matter of shirts and took out his samples from his attaché case. He laid them out with a flourish across Julian's enormous Queen-Anne desk. As Julian bent slightly over the desk to examine the sample shirts, Bill put a light supporting hand on Julian's rather bony back. Bill felt Julian give a slight shiver at his touch and Bill felt hopeful. Another five minutes, concentrating on the quality of the workmanship paired with the modern style of the shirts and he had secured the huge lucrative order. He shook Julian's hand once more and left the room swiftly leaving traces of scent that reminded Julian of the winter hyacinths his mother kept on their grand marble fireplace in January.

Julian slumped his slight frame down into his study chair and let out a large sigh. He poured himself a large restorative gin. He was very pleased with the deal they had struck and he knew the shirts would sell very well indeed.

'What a beautiful boy,' he thought and continued to think for the rest of the day. Just outside his office door Miss Maddox was thinking the very same thing.

Bill was also aware of the importance of establishing a rapport with buyer's secretary. Miss Maddox thought Bill absolutely charming. He had given her a Bullseye and a friendly wink on his way out. She also thought he had taken a lingering look across her blouse which made her feel quite faint.

On leaving the store Bill was deep in thought as he totted up his commission. A very satisfactory morning's work.

He decided to treat himself to a large expensive whiskey. He could certainly afford it. He knew other stores would be slavishly following Lamparts so he would be in for an easy ride for the next few weeks that he was based in London.

Amy admired Bill's broad shoulders and long legs in his expensive suit. His strong neck was lightly tanned and contrasted well against his crisp white collar. She cleared her throat a number of times but Bill didn't turn around. He was busy working out which approach he would use at the next store on his list.

Amy decided to take matters into her own hands and approached the bar to order another coffee. Bill turned and watched her, finally becoming aware of her presence. Amy then turned prettily on her heels and sashayed self-consciously back to her table, a smile playing on her cupid bow lips. That ought to do it, she thought in glee.

Bill was transfixed. Everyone Bill had met that morning seemed to be struggling with the roaring temperature of the summer's day. Faces were pink and damp with perspiration. Clothes were clinging unpleasantly. Amy, by contrast, looked ice cool in the fierce heat of the day. Her hair was pale gold, shining almost white under the dim lighting of the bar. Her long slender limbs were smooth ivory. The silver dress enhanced the almost translucent quality to her skin. He threw his whiskey back in a careless manner and came and sat with Amy at her table. He pulled his chair very close to hers. He lit a cigarette and stared into the distance, silently.

Bill continued to smoke leisurely without making any eye contact. Amy found his stillness intoxicating.

Finally, just as Amy thought she couldn't bare the tension any longer, Bill turned his head.

'Hello' he drawled. 'I think you are very pretty. Do you mind if I share your table?'

Amy was about to feign distress in a coy, playful way, fluttering her eyelashes like a starlet and protest that there were plenty of other tables for him to sit at. As their eyes locked though she found she couldn't speak so she just nodded, aware her cheeks were reddening as her body was filled with a rush of heat. He was quite simply the most handsome man she had ever seen. He was sitting so she could catch the scent of whiskey and tobacco on his breath but there was also another smell, less tangible, very male and it was making her senses reel.

Bills' eyes, which were an unusual dark hazel, topped with strong dark brows, wandered unabashed up and down her body for a moment.

'You're a model aren't you?' Such was Bill's self-assurance he often spoke in a series of statements.

Amy nodded again, disappointed that this man had seen through her disguise so quickly. She felt unable to protest, or lie, she was transfixed by his gaze. She felt like a butterfly trapped in a web.

'That dress doesn't belong to you,' he said mildly, still assessing her body. 'I can see where it is pinned to improve the fit. Where do you work? Sables?'

Amy smiled miserably, embarrassed at being caught out.

Bill looked thoughtfully at her, then smiled back at her, gently.

'You almost pulled that trick off. The rich socialite having coffee in her new designer frock in an uptown bar. Do you know what else gave you away? The rich socialites hunt in packs, like hyenas. You were almost a clever girl.'

Bill nodded over to the young spotty barman with his goggling eyes and receding chin.

'Is that your boyfriend?'

Amy giggled, cheering up suddenly. 'Absolutely not.'

'Do you have a young man?'

'No.' said Amy beginning to smile properly so pretty dimples appeared at each cheek.

'I think that might be about to change, don't you? Would you like to have dinner with me tonight? I will meet you outside Sables when you have finished work.'

'I would love that, thank you.'

Amy suddenly noticed the large golden Art Deco clock on the mirrored wall of the bar. She jumped up.

'I have to dash. I finish at 6 o clock.' Amy stood up and held out her hand.

'I am Amy by the way.'

Bill had remained seated and took her hand in his.

'Good.' he said.

Amy scuttled out in her ill-fitting shoes and headed down the rubbish strewn side-street which lead to the back entrance. She got back into the sparse dressing room just before Miss Haddock and her ladies arrived, well fed and slightly tipsy. She sat down on the floor for a moment to catch her breath, something else Miss Haddock absolutely forbade her girls to do in the sample frocks. Amy realised she didn't even know Bill's name.

For Bill and Amy that chance meeting was the beginning of two months of whirlwind romance. Amy fell very quickly in love with Bill. He was funny, charming and generous. When he met Amy, that evening outside Sables, he was carrying a large black box tied with a gold ribbon. Amy recognised the packaging. To her delight and amazement, he had bought her the silver dress she had been wearing in the bar. No one had ever bought her a gift like that in her life.

They met almost every evening after work and Bill took her to the theatre and restaurants. He was very fond of dancing and they would whoop it up in the clubs, making temporary friends for the evening with other revellers. Bill always had plenty of money and would buy champagne for all and sundry. He was very tactile but never invited her back to his lodgings.

'A perfect gentleman.' thought Amy hugging her new mink stole.

Although Bill was treating Amy with the upmost courtesy, he was still lodging within the cosy welcome of Ash Lodge for the two months of his stay in London. He had no intention of disrupting his pleasant arrangement with the ever accommodating Mrs Landsbury by introducing another female to Ash Lodge.

Amy never mentioned her own home to Bill and he was shrewd enough to realise that Amy was ashamed of her birthplace. Although Amy looked the part, it was clear to Bill that she had very little experience of the finer things in life. She was very nervous in restaurants and observed Bill continually in matters of etiquette. Bill found her gauche ways rather beguiling. Bar the time she stuffed herself with so much caviar and foie gras and she vomited in the doorway of the Ritz.

He once enquired after her mother but Amy pretended not to hear his question, so he let the matter drop entirely. Bill wasn't interested in Amy's past. He always gave her money for a taxi to take her to the doorstep of her home, where ever it was. Amy would often instruct the driver to drop her at the nearest tube station after she had waved Bill goodbye and she would pocket the money.

As the summer nights began to close in and the leaves on the Plane trees began to turn, Bill told Amy he had to return up North. He would be heading up towards Scotland for a month. Amy was very upset. They were sitting in the elegant Simpsons restaurant and she started to cry quite loudly. Bill looked round panicking slightly. 'God Amy please shut up, we are out in public.' Amy proceeded to cry even louder.

Bill was irritated. He disliked scenes of any kind. He could see out of the corner of his eye the maître de and a couple of waiters all moving silently towards their table in a sort of pincer movement. Bill loved Simpsons and fully intended to return at some point. He daren't go back to the Ritz after Amy's over indulgence had had such embarrassing consequences.

'I can come and see you again. You are my girl but I have to go where the work is, this is my job. I don't live in London, you know that.' Bill was speaking urgently, willing her to shut up.

Bill said rather desperately Amy, 'Look why don't you come up to Leeds with me?'

Amy stopped crying suddenly with a large hiccup. Her big eyes filled with hope.

'Are you asking me to marry you Bill? Yes, yes Bill I will marry you.'

Bill nodded cautiously, relieved she had stopped making the awful racket and thought quickly about the surprising turn the conversation had just taken. Perhaps it was a good idea. It was probably time for him to settle down. He liked her, she was quite quiet really but she was a lot of fun when she had a few gins inside her. They made a very handsome couple indeed and heads turned where ever they went. Surely that was enough for a marriage, he quickly convinced himself. She had certainly cheered up.

They married the following month. They had a simple ceremony witnessed by two strangers from the street. Amy wore an expensive navy woollen suit with a red velvet cloche hat, all bought by Bill. Her face was aglow with happiness and the new gorgeous string of pearls, another gift, added to the illumination.

Bill had just bought, outright, a large detached house in the little Northern village of Westridge, close to Leeds. His father had died the year before and he and his brother had inherited their family's small fortune. It would have provided Bill a small, comfortable income for the rest of his days without him needing to work but Bill was a very driven creature and he thoroughly enjoyed his job.

They travelled by train the same day of the wedding up to Leeds. Amy left everything behind, only bringing with her the presents from Bill and her best coat which was the first item she had bought with her first wage packet. She left her mother a short note on the kitchen stove at home.

Amy was brought up in the slums of the East End of London. Her father had left his wife, at least Amy had presumed they were married, when Amy was two years old. Her mother, once a pretty woman, quickly fell into the cosy cradle of the gin bottle. The streets of the East End were very poor but the families looked out for one another as best they could. For a few years Amy and her mother survived on kind charity from neighbours and the meagre wages Vera brought home from her job in the printing works. After a few very sparse years Vera Bright began to invite gentlemen callers into her home on an evening, after a boozy session in the 'Duck and Dog'. Their decent, generous neighbours soon cottoned on to how Vera was supplementing her income and withdrew their charity, and avoided her on the street.

Vera often shooed Amy out of their tiny damp house into the streets with the other children. She would have to shut her ears to the mean things they would say about her mother. She would never rise to their baiting, preferring to remain silent. Besides she knew their chants were true, her mother was a tomcat.

She never found making friends particularly easy. Often, she would watch the children playing and feel that she would like to join in their games but was unsure how to approach them. An overwhelming feeling of helplessness would fill her little body and so she would just watch. Amy was a very beautiful child. Sometimes beauty can be a curse even in childhood. Her strange ethereal looks with her white hair, huge staring blue eyes and tiny body were unusual, which both attracted and repelled the other boys and girls in the same measure. It was her capacity for silence that would unnerve even the older children so she was mainly left alone.

As she grew older she retreated even further into her own quiet world. She found the other children tiresome and unsophisticated. She would read discarded newspapers and magazines out of the dustbins in order to study the latest fashions, desperate to find clues on how to make her escape from the life she was born into. If her mother was entertaining in an evening, Amy would push her mattress against the door of her tiny grim room and push softened candle wax into her ears to block all of the sounds containing within the four damp walls of the house she shared with her mother. Her mother's guttural cries could still sometimes be heard. She would stare at the images of elegant laughing women, arm in arm with handsome men with kind faces until her eyes hurt.

She did reasonably well at the poor school she attended, but left at fourteen. She grew tall. One or two of Vera's regulars had started to take an interest in her and Amy was under no illusions as to what they wanted from her and knew it was only a matter of time before something very unpleasant happened. Vera would be no protection. She had been fired from her factory job years before for being drunk and spent her days in a thick alcoholic stupor. Amy no longer felt safe in her own bed. To leave the slums she would need money and that meant getting a job. Amy worked hard to smooth out her East End twang and she always lied glibly at job interviews, particularly about her age. She worked for a while in a factory, still living at home, putting decent food on the table for her and Vera. Part of her wage given to Vera for her gin, just to keep the peace.

When she was sixteen, she presented herself for her interview at Sables attired in an immaculate dress coat, hiding her own threadbare clothing underneath. She had stolen the coat the week beforehand from a church jumble sale. It fitted her perfectly. She had borrowed the shoes from her drunk mother and filled the ends with newspaper to ensure they stayed on her small feet.

Amy had no qualms about going to Leeds and leaving Vera, her feckless mother, behind. She could drown in her own vomit for all she cared.

Bill and Amy were blissfully happy that first year of marriage. Amy was dazzled by Bill. He was perfect, just like a hero in a book. He was kind to her. The romantic rescue fantasy of her lonely teen years had come true.

Bill worked away most of the week but he made sure he returned home at the weekend. They had wonderful times together full of rowdy dinners with Bill's friends and their wives. Leeds was a lively little city and Bill always seemed to know where was the best place to eat, drink and dance the night away. He had boundless energy. He was very generous with the housekeeping and would often come home on a Friday evening with gifts of flowers, perfume and satin lingerie.

After one or two attempts at inviting friends over to their house for dinner Bill quickly realised that Amy was not a natural hostess and was frankly an appalling cook. She tended to panic if she was responsible for the cooking and would knock back the wine. Bill was a little disappointed. Having clients to his home for dinner parties was something Bill would have liked Amy to take care of, he had always presumed that was what a wife did. He neatly sidestepped the problem by always taking clients or indeed their own friends out to the best restaurants in Leeds and footing the expense himself.

Bill admired beauty in others and was enchanted by Amy. Her slim figure was so fashionable and her hair, in its neat bob was always perfect. She epitomised 1920's chic. She was quiet and agreeable.

He liked to accompany her on shopping trips. He was very generous with money but liked to dominate her clothing choices. He would suggest soft wool suits and blouses made from silk and chiffon. For the evening he would direct her to the heavily beaded backless dresses and impractical satins. Amy would nod happily at his suggestions and blossomed under his admiring gaze. Bill never considered that Amy's frame was very slight, the Northern climate was very sharp and she might actually feel the cold. He dressed her like a life-sized doll. Amy was a very pretty young woman and under Bill's direction she had become the very essence of elegance and poise.

Bill loved parading Amy in front of his friends. He would get a whip crack of pride through his stomach when he observed his male friends and colleagues look her up and down appreciatively. He especially enjoyed watching their wives fawning round her, complimenting her dress or giving her sharp jealous glances.

Bill found Amy fascinating. He knew he was good at reading people but with Amy he found he had absolutely no idea what she was thinking. He would stare at her inscrutable, flawless face and wonder what was going on behind those big blue eyes, if indeed there was anything going on at all. She tended to agree his opinions. Yet she wasn't a complete doormat. Bill knew she must have an inner strength to manage her escape from the slums. Bill had slowly pieced together the sad story of her childhood over the year. Sometimes on their many nights out on the town, Amy would accidently let her accent slip or let her guard down and drunkenly reminisce. Bill never reminded her of these shared hazy memories the next day because he knew she wasn't confiding in him because they were close, she was just drunk. Amy would also be quiet for long periods of time. Bill rather liked the quieter side of her personality, it gave him space to think.

Chapter 3

Westridge was a busy, friendly village. The church was very much central to the lives of the village's inhabitants, providing plenty of social entertainment in the form of jumble sales, dances and scout troops for the children. It also provided much needed spiritual guidance and solace to those trying their best to recover from the losses of their husbands and sons in the Great War. It had its own busy little high street with a post office, bakers, butchers, grocers and other shops selling everyday requirements. There was a tiny train station and decent bus route into the city of Leeds, which was only ten miles away.

Amy loved her new home. The four bedroom, redbrick Victorian house, was set back from the road within its own private garden. The house was one of many built upon the steep Mulberry Hill which led down to the centre of the village of Westridge. The house was sparsely decorated as Bill hadn't been interested in the interior since his purchase. Bill had a wardrobe, bed and two leather club armchairs. The floors were bare and there were no curtains at the windows. To Amy, though, already it was an absolute palace. There was a large kitchen with a range and a Yorkshire stone floor. It even had an inside lavatory and separate bathroom.

Amy lost no time in securing a generous budget from Bill and furnishing the whole house from top to bottom. She found an absolute treasure of a handyman and decorator in the village, who was thrilled to be working for such a glamorous couple and dropped all his usual business in favour of the Jenkinsons and their extravagant plans, backed up by their seemingly bottomless purse.

The progress of the Jenkinson's house was a topic of much discussion in the Fox and Hounds on an evening and Mr Drake the decorator suddenly found himself the focus of much attention. The villagers all listened agog to Mr Drake's tales of burnt orange, heavily lacquered walls. Shiny parquet flooring topped with zebra-patterned rugs. He had to employ a small team of young men to help with all the carpentry work. Amy had read that free standing furniture was no longer fashionable so had ordered them to fill the plentiful fireside nooks with shelving to house brand new books and displays of cocktail glasses and enamel cigarette cases. The pub gasped in delight to learn that he was painting the Jenkinson's bedroom in black and white and one wall was actually going to be covered with mirrored tiles. The vicar's wife bristled slightly at this, strangely excited by the idea.

Amy remained determinedly distant from her friendly neighbours. Her exotic looks and stylish dress caused a lot of interest in the village at first and Amy was inundated with invites to suppers, bridge evenings and WI meetings. She firmly refused them all, claiming she was far too busy organising her new house for her husband. The villagers were confused. Bill was such a genial chap, always ready with a joke or good for a round of drinks in the pub. His wife seemed very standoffish.

Amy had always preferred her own company and was quite happy to wander round from room to room, trying on various outfits, flicking through the latest copies of Vogue. She would lounge upon her huge angular sofa which had been upholstered in a wildly expensive oriental-patterned silk. Her latest gift from Bill had been a gramophone and radio set, which she absolutely loved. In the afternoons she would pour herself a hefty gin and dance the hours away. She had to go to the village for provisions of course but she chose to get up early and shop first thing to avoid tedious chatter when the shops became busy later on in the morning.

She really looked forward to Bill's return on Friday night, which always meant evenings out with fun, glamorous people, from the city. Drinking and dancing with wild abandon. Amy found socialising in a noisy club environment much easier than speaking face to face with eager villagers in the butchers shop or sharing gossip over a cup of tea at some parish meeting.

Friday night also inevitably meant sex. Amy was not fond of activity in the bedroom. She found Bill attractive. He was a very handsome man and she enjoyed kissing him but she thought the act of making love was suffocating and brutal. Amy found Bill to be distastefully animal-like. She hated the heat they generated together, the grunting, most of all the loss of control. She would dutifully lie back and try to make appreciative noises, keeping her eyes shut tight and waiting for him to finish.

Bill had been pleasing women since the age of fifteen. He had always liked and admired the fairer sex and thought himself to be quite an accomplished lover. He was puzzled as to Amy's reticence in the bedroom. He quickly perceived she wasn't keen on sex. He patiently encouraged her and tried his best to ensure she had a wonderful time but she remained resolutely cold and unresponsive. Bill didn't understand it. She was affectionate enough with their clothes on. She would sit on his knee and kiss him on the cheek. Blow him kisses and squeeze his arm when they were shopping. Gradually though he felt the demonstrations of affection were posed as if she were modelling again, rather than expressions of genuine love.

She was a splendid wife in many ways, laughing at his jokes, beautiful to look at, always running down their drive on his return from work dressed in her finest. The house looked wonderful and was greatly admired by visitors. She wasn't really a homemaker beyond the fun of furniture purchasing and choosing paint colours to match curtains but Bill didn't really care about a bit of dust and they always ate out when he came home. She could certainly hold her liquor now and he loved watching her become animated as the alcohol infused her blood. She would become more chatty and confident. It was an attractive transformation, he wished it would help with shedding her inhibitions in their bed.

After about six months of trying to please Amy, Bill decided he was getting bored with it. He had never doubted his own sexual prowess and wasn't about to now. He thought she was obviously flawed in some way. She never actually denied him his conjugal rites so he told himself perhaps she enjoyed it quietly. He was a little disappointed in her.

Amy fell pregnant in 1923. She was absolutely horrified. She would stare at her flat belly for hours in the mirror in disgust, imagining how bloated it would become in a few months. She also quickly became victim to dreadful morning sickness that lasted for the whole day. She vaguely toyed with the idea of trying to find a woman to help her out with her problem but she had no idea how to locate such a woman. She didn't have any close female friends up in Leeds that she could confide in. She wasn't particularly close to anyone down in London.

The people they socialised with in the city were really Bill's friends. Although Amy quite enjoyed the company of those women she always remained on her guard and never really indulged in shared indiscretions, drunken or otherwise. She was filled with the dread of any of them seeing past the perfect presentation and viewing the girl from the slums with a prostitute for a mother.

Amy had no idea how to approach the subject with Bill.

The matter was taken out of her hands. One Saturday evening Bill was getting ready to go to the local pub. Amy had locked the bathroom door and vomiting copiously in the sink. Bill rattled the handle impatiently and kept rapping on the door and shouting for her to hurry it along.

'Go away.' Amy wailed pitifully.

Bill was starting to get irritated. Amy was turning sour. So miserable all the time now and so snappy. She was no longer looking at him with the adoration he felt he deserved. Bill pushed against the door with his large shoulders and the old lock gave way with a snap. Bill marched into the bathroom.

'I only want to brush my teeth. Carry on with whatever you are doing. I said I would meet the lads at eight and that is exactly what I am going to do.'

Bill paused when he saw that Amy had her head over the sink.

'Oh gippy tummy?' he asked with interest.

'Yes.' mumbled Amy thickly.

'Must have been something I ate.'

Bill turned away and put some powder on his tooth brush. 'Not pregnant are you, doll?' he laughed.

There was a long pause. Amy did not respond.

'Amy?'

Bill gently lifted Amy up to a standing position and turned her to face him. He was grinning widely.

'You are.'

Amy nodded miserably.

'I shall get fat,' she said listlessly.

'Don't worry about that doll, we will soon get you back into shape after he arrives. This is great news I can't wait to tell the fellows. Come on let's get you into bed.' He put his hand gently on her back and guided her solicitously towards the bedroom.

'Right, anything you need? Do you want me to bring up your magazines and a nice glass of wine?'

Amy shook her head faintly.

Bill helped Amy to undress and get into her nightdress and lifted her into bed. He smoothed her forehead. Suddenly he whipped up her nightdress and gave her flat belly an enthusiastic kiss, thinking she would giggle. Amy flinched and tried not to pull a face but she failed to hide her disdain. Their eyes met for a split second. Bill felt a brief flash of anger but stepped back and took a deep breath.

'OK you two.' he said in a pleasant voice. 'I will see you later on. I love you Amy.'

He gave her a cheery wave and disappeared to the Fox and Hounds for the rest of the evening.

When he had gone Amy snuggled down under the candlewick bedspread and felt a little happier. Perhaps Bill will still love her when she is fat.

When Bill married Amy he vowed to remain faithful to her for the rest of his life. As Amy's pregnancy progressed though he felt increasingly distant from her. He continued with his endless round of drinks parties and dinners. Amy valiantly tried to accompany him but found it impossible as she continued to be sick well into her second trimester. She lost a lot of weight and her fine golden hair lost its lustre. Her face took on a sickly, almost skeletal look. She became really short tempered and snapped at Bill all of the time. She seemed irritated by his very presence. He solved the problem by ensuring he was out of the house almost all of the time.

Bill was actually enjoying his newly found freedom. Amy didn't want to be in his company at the moment. He had forgotten how nice it was to have a quick kiss and a cuddle with an attractive girl at a party or with one or two of his lovely landladies. He controlled himself though and never ended up in anyone's bed. He always thought a little squeeze never did anyone any harm in the long run.

He stuck resolutely to his own particular brand of faithfulness to Amy, until he met Violet Pinkerton.

Bill had been invited to the Limewood hunt ball. It was a magnificent occasion held in the ballroom of Limewood House, the enormous country seat of a minor member of the aristocracy. Bill wasn't interested in country sports but he played poker with the local JP so had wangled an invite. Bill never let a business opportunity slip by and he knew the ball would be crammed with useful members of Yorkshire society. The ball would be Bill's own hunting ground.

Just before he left, he and Amy had an almighty row. She was going to accompany him but had a crisis of confidence just before they were due to set off. She ended up crying and throwing a large vanity case at his head when he dared to suggest she hurry along and get ready. Bill had looked at her in disdain and ordered her to stay at home. He would be glad when this baby business was over and she would go back to normal. He had spoken to his brother who had reassured him that women went funny when they were pregnant and he had to ride it out. His brother hadn't fully grasped the gravity of the situation though. His pleasant wife had sailed through her recent pregnancy. The only change Bill's brother had noticed was that she had eaten chutney with absolutely everything and refused to cook fish.

When he arrived in the ballroom, Bill immediately cheered up. The drink was flowing freely and there was a noisy hum of chatter almost drowning out the band. The dance floor was busy with red hunting coats and colourful ball gowns all jostling for space as the dancers were attempting many versions of the Charleston. Bill made his way around the room making small talk. After a while though he grew tired of being pleasant. The hunting set were not open to discussing business. They were all absolutely horse-mad and their chatter was relentlessly revolving round upcoming races, shows and meets. Bill was rather out of his depth and had hence become rather bored.

He grabbed himself a couple of glasses of wine from a silver tray held aloft by a haughty looking waiter and found himself one of the tables that surrounded the dance floor. He gazed round the room, enjoying the excellent Chardonnay. He caught a waft of very strong perfume, turned his head and was confronted with a magnificent bosom barely covered by artfully draped silk satin. Bill choked briefly on his wine which made his brown eyes water. He managed to clear his throat and looked up. Staring down at him from quite a height was the handsome, predatory face of Violet Pinkerton. She smiled at Bill and licked her full bright red lips slowly with a pink tongue.

'May I sit down? I have been dancing for hours'.

Her voice was rich and deep. She spoke slowly as if each word was significant in some way.

'Of course.' said Bill regaining composure quickly and pulled up a chair for her with a flourish.

Violet leaned towards Bill.

'Do you hunt? I don't think I have ever seen you at a meet. I would have definitely remembered you.'

Bill shook his head. Honesty was the best policy here. Violet was clearly no fool.

'No I have never even been on a horse. I know Major Edwards from the pub, that's all.'

Violet seemed unperturbed.

'Really?' she drawled. She ran her eyes up and down Bill's long thighs. 'You look like you would be an excellent rider.' She smiled revealing small pointed teeth leaving no doubt in Bill's mind to what she was referring.

There was a charged pause.

Bill felt a familiar rise of excitement.

Violet took a deep breath which enhanced her chest splendidly. Bill could not help taking an admiring glance.

'You simply must try hunting. There is nothing else like the thrill of the chase.' She raised one perfectly groomed eyebrow suggestively.

Bill stared back at her for a moment.

'I know all about the thrill of the chase,' he said in low voice.

'Oh yes' breathed Violet, leaning closer towards him.

'Yes,' said Bill.

'I am in sales.'

Violet let out a bark of laughter.

'Wonderful,' she said loudly clapping her hands.

'Would you like to dance?'

Violet and Bill were very good rhythmical dancers both having been taught at their respective boarding schools. As a boy, Bill absolutely despised dance lessons especially as he always seemed to be partnered with Jefferson minor, a revolting hulk of a lad with questionable personal hygiene and warts. He was rather glad of his lessons now though. Violet was an absolute handful. She was brimming over with energy and life. Her body was full and strong and she constantly fought to take the lead. Bill enjoyed dominating her, using his own strength to gain control.

In the slower dances she would hold herself almost indecently close to him, not caring one jot about the disapproving glances coming from the more staid members of the Hunt. Her family was so rich no one would ever dare say anything to her anyway. Bill was very much aware of her persistently undulating body and was finding it increasingly difficult to concentrate on the dance steps.

After a particularly strenuous tango that attracted quite a lot of attention. Violet murmured in his ear.

'I am tired of drinking this cheap plonk. I know where his Lordship keeps his whiskey, are you up for a spot of pillaging?'

Bill had just about managed to get his breath back.

'You naughty girl,' he said in delight 'of course I am.'

'Better not leave at the same time. I will go first. I will meet you in the Butler's pantry in five minutes. It is in the back of the kitchen. Just head down the main corridor and turn left at the end. Down a few steps. Let's hope it's empty.'

Violet slipped away. Bill waited a minute or two, knocked back another glass of wine, which he thought was rather good. His pallet clearly wasn't as finely tuned as Madam's. He then coolly exited the hot noisy ballroom.

When he reached the main corridor he couldn't help breaking into a trot towards the kitchen. He was in no doubt of Violet's intentions and it would certainly involve a lot more than just sampling some rare scotch. The long kitchen was virtually in darkness. There was a very large window at one end through which a pale moonlight provided a ghostly illumination. There were a multitude of copper pots and pans all neatly lined up on the long oak shelving which ran down one wall and an enormous scrubbed oak table which dominated down the centre. On the other side there was a huge range standing solidly, gleaming with black lead polish.

Bills' dress shoes were making a loud clicking noise on the stone floor as he made his way to the end of the kitchen towards a set of double doors which Bill could only presume lead to the Butler's pantry.

There was no sign of Violet. Bill almost giggled in excitement. He was reminded of the thrill he used to get from games of hide and seek he used to play with his brother in his grandparents' garden.

'Violet' he hissed 'where are you, you little minx?'

He almost jumped out of his skin as one of the large pantry doors creaked slowly open in front of him and a long leg, encased in a black stocking, curled round the door. She ran her foot up and down the side of the door. The leg then disappeared and was replaced by Violet's bare arm sliding round the door, her finger beckoned Bill towards her.

Bill needed no further encouragement. He jumped forward and flung the door open. Violet was standing in the middle of the pantry completely naked apart from a pair of black seamed stockings held up with a black lace suspender belt. She was coolly sipping a cut glass crystal tumbler full of his Lordship's whiskey.

She was a magnificent sight. Her skin was white and glowed like a pearl in the moonlight. Her muscular arms and thighs were softened by curvaceous hips and breasts. Her face was a still mask of desire and she was looking at Bill though half closed eyes. He felt his knees almost give way.

Violet gave him a slow pussycat smile.

'So William, would you care to dance?'

Bill only realised how drunk he had become when he made his way outside into the garden for a breath of fresh air an hour later. He lit up a cigarette and vomited copiously into a large hydrangea. He finished his cigarette and decided to go home rather than return to the ball room as Violet had casually suggested.

He drove the four miles home cautiously. He was looking over two steering wheels and his stomach was churning violently. He was also aware of a very uncomfortable feeling of guilty disquiet in the back of his mind. He was a weak man he told himself sternly. When he got back to his house he managed to knock the aspidistra from its stand in the hallway. Its brass bowl landing with a tremendous crash on the polished Parke flooring. Amy appeared at the top of the stairs looking angry. Her skinny frame was emphasised by her massive round pregnancy belly.

'Oh it's you,' she said, without any warmth.

Bill was instantly defensive.

'Well, who did you think it was? Perhaps you were hoping for the milkman to drop in to give you a bit of rough, a bit of early morning pleasure?'

The drink was making Bill vicious. That and his guilt regarding his own early morning pleasure.

'Don't be disgusting,' she spat back at him.

Bill shook his fist behind Amy's skinny departing back and decided to sleep in one of their spare rooms.

Although Bill saw Violet at various functions they never repeated their glorious hour of unbridled passionate sex. She would always wink in a conspiratorial way at him from across a room and they would both be transported back to that moonlit scrubbed kitchen table, but she never approached him again, even to talk. Bill understood perfectly that sex was a game to Violet and she was never interested in him personally.

Bill put his infidelity to the back of his mind and told himself that everything would be alright when the baby was born. He never particularly thought about Violet again unless he was occasionally feeling lonely whilst taking a bath.

He became very busy at work. Silverbond of York had just launched a brand new line of slightly more affordable shirts, still very much high end quality and they were proving to be very popular with the more thrifty Scots. Bill was based around Aberdeen during the week and sometimes didn't bother to come home at all on a weekend. The baby was due anytime. Amy was moaning all day long complaining of backache, headaches and non-existent swollen ankles.

Bill had planned to take a few weeks leave when the baby was born. He was really looking forward to the birth. He hoped it would be a boy. He didn't want another whinging female on the premises. He wanted to be a good father. They bought a lovely white painted crib for the baby's room and the nursery itself was painted a very modern Nile green with navy gloss work. They had delivered the latest Silver Cross pram from Harrods. Sitting in the pram was a teddy which gave a realistic growl when it was tipped forward.

Chapter 4

Sylvia Jenkinson was born at home after a lengthy and exhausting delivery. Bill was absent. Amy was in the excellent hands of Enid Green the local midwife, a large ugly woman with a permanently stern expression and more than a suggestion of a moustache. The new mothers in the village would joke that you would bloody well force the baby out as fast as you could to avoid a telling off from that old cow. Enid was very experienced but stood for absolutely no nonsense from her mothers.

Enid was tough as old boots but was rather concerned about Amy throughout the labour. Amy had struggled through a very long night and by the time dawn was creeping in she seemed to be dropping in and out of consciousness. Enid called the local doctor. The doctor came immediately. Just as he was shrugging off his coat and removing his Homburg hat Amy let out a wolf-like howl and forced Sylvia out into the world with one last desperate heave.

Amy lay back on the sweat-soaked sheets of her bed with her eyes closed. Dr James and Enid gave Sylvia a quick once-over. She was a very large baby with a bright red angry face. She immediately started to cry with surprising rancour.

'Sterling work as always Enid. Didn't need me after all. Marvellous.' rumbled Dr James.

He nodded over to Amy. 'Mother looks a bit thin. Keep an eye out will you. Any worries, give me a call. Playing bridge on Tuesday at the vicarage? Bloody good rubbers last week. Keeps us on our toes, what?'

Dr James whacked Enid across her beefy shoulders and gave a hearty laugh.

'Right ladies. I am off back to bed.' Dr James shot out without a backwards glance at Amy or Sylvia, in a hurry to get back to the cosy pleasantries of a morning in bed with Gertrude his agreeable wife.

Enid washed the baby and swaddled her tightly. She handed Sylvia over to Amy but Amy didn't cuddle her.

Amy immediately laid Sylvia down next to her in the bed and turned her back on her. Enid looked sharply at Amy but decided not to say anything.

'I am going home now dear to get some sleep. I will look in on you later and we will see if baby can have a nice feed.' Enid had already established there was no one else to stay with Amy. She decided to have a firm word with Mr Jenkinson, whenever he deemed it fit to put in an appearance.

Bill was working away in Aberdeen the night of Sylvia's arrival. Amy left a message with one of the Silverbond secretaries at the office so they could try to contact him. Bill was staying in a hotel in Aberdeen. He was over the moon to hear the news that he had a daughter and that evening he bought everyone in the hotel bar scotch and cigars. He got very drunk and missed his morning appointments the next day. It was going to take him a couple of days to get back home so Amy would be on her own until then.

Amy was very weak after the birth and was having trouble feeding the baby herself. Sylvia had severe colic and screamed constantly. One side of her little tummy distended at regular intervals and her nappies were full of bubbling green sludge. Enid was not the monster the village woman made out. She was very bossy but she also recognised a new mother floundering. She dropped in to see Amy and Sylvia every day for their first week. Amy had slid into the dark pool of baby blues and was crying virtually non-stop.

Enid was very comforting and encouraging for the first couple of visits. She sat with Amy and listened to her wail. She ran Amy a bath but Amy refused to get out of bed.

On the fourth day Enid had had enough. Amy was sitting in the bed with tears streaming down her face. She still hadn't taken a bath and smelt most unpleasant. Sylvia was lying in her cot in the corner of room yelling her head off in a soggy nappy. Enid wasn't even sure if Amy had eaten at all over the last couple of days.

'Amy,' she said briskly, clapping her hands to get her attention. 'This baby is failing to thrive we are going to have to try much harder here. We might need to employ the services of a wet nurse. I am sure your husband can afford it.'

Amy's cries amplified to a long drawn out hysterical scream.

Enid stared at her for a moment then stepped forward and gave her a sharp slap across the face.

Amy looked up from her bed with wide eyes, shocked into silence. Enid sighed. 'I am sorry about that dear, but this is not about you, this is about baby. She needs you to pull yourself together, she is losing too much weight. You cannot sit there screaming like a banshee.'

Amy gulped back a couple of sobs but remained quiet.

'Now, do you think you are up to trying to feed her again because baby is hungry? You have plenty of milk dear. It is all over these sheets for one thing.' tutted Enid.

Enid lowered her considerable bulk so she was face to face with Amy. She smiled encouragingly. 'Amy you can do this. I know you can.'

Amy rallied. 'Yes, yes I can, can't I?' she said in a brave slightly wobbly voice.

Enid nodded relieved. 'Good girl. We will give you and baby another couple of days and see if she can get the hang of it. Now I will take baby for a minute. I have something in my bag which might help relax this little tummy.' Enid took a yelling Sylvia next door and laid her gently on a blanket on the floor. She drew out a small bottle of brandy from her cavernous bag. She dipped her finger in the bottle then put her finger in Sylvia's mouth. Sylvia sucked hard on her finger and a faint look of surprise pass across her round face.

Enid brought Sylvia back into the bedroom and the fractious baby seemed a little quieter.

'What did you do?' asked Amy, suddenly interested.

'Just a little trick.' Enid waved her big hands dismissively. There was no way she was letting her new mothers into that secret, far too risky.

Amy took Sylvia and the baby latched on straight away.

'Right. Amy you can share my ham sandwich with me and we will have a cup of tea. If you are going to successfully get weight on this baby you need to keep your own strength up. Afterwards you will take a bath and change the bed sheets. Absolutely no more of this nonsense. Where is Mr Jenkinson?'

'He is on his way home tonight.' Amy smiled for the first time in a long time.

Amy valiantly continued to feed Sylvia herself and Sylvia began to put on enough weight for Enid to nod in approval. Her colic continued though and Amy was driven to distraction by the screaming. Many of the village women found Enid's uncompromising ways irritating, but Amy felt so weak that she drew strength from Enid's direct orders.

On Enid's last visit to the house. Amy was thrown into a complete panic. She clung onto Enid's large grainy hand and begged her to keep visiting every day. Enid firmly untangled herself. 'Don't be silly dear. Baby is coming along splendidly. You will be absolutely fine on your own. Why don't you take a walk into the village and have a word with one or two of the other new mothers?'

Bill had actually tried valiantly to return from Scotland as quickly as he could but his journey home was plagued by delayed trains. When he finally arrived back he bounded up the stairs to get a first look at his daughter. He was delighted with Sylvia. He tried to give Amy a cuddle but she pushed him away violently. Bill backed away from her with real hurt in his eyes.

He picked Sylvia up out of her crib straight away and held her at arms-length for a moment to get a proper look at her face. He stared at her in wonder.

'She is perfect Amy. I can't believe she is here. Do you think she looks like my mother?'

'No I don't.' snapped Amy.

He sat on the side of the bed nestling the baby in the crook of his arm.

'Get off the bed,' ordered Amy 'I want to go to sleep before she starts yelling again.'

'All right.' said Bill affably, still mesmerised by his new baby daughter. 'I might take her downstairs. I will light the fire and sit with her for a while.'

Amy shrugged not looking at them. 'Do what you like.'

For the rest of the evening Sylvia slept peacefully up against his chest, dribbling gently down his shirt. Enjoying the warmth and security of being held. Her aching tummy was eased by the gentle pressure of their cuddle.

Amy lay in bed unable to sleep despite her exhaustion. She stared at the wallpaper with a bitter expression on her face. How was Bill able to love so easily? She thought of the two of them all cosy downstairs in front of the fire and felt very much a stranger looking in from the outside.

Bill remained at home for a couple of days then decided to go back to work. He was returning to London and loved the busy capital.

He always looked forward to coming home to see Sylvia though. He seemed to be oblivious to Sylvia's screams. Amy noticed that Sylvia actually perceptually was more settled when Bill was around. Probably because he would pick her up so often.

'If you pick her up all the time you will spoil her,' she would say spitefully.

'Rubbish.' Bill would snap back.

'She is the only one in this house pleased to see me. She only cries because of the colic. She can't help herself. Enid told me.'

'Oh.' said Amy angrily, 'So you have been chatting up Enid now have you?'

Bill looked at Amy as if she was crazy.

Bill had spoken to Enid and not just about Sylvia. He told her Amy was also crying all the time and asked her what she thought he should do.

'Just a bout of baby blues Mr Jenkinson,' boomed Enid looking over her half-moon glasses. 'Nothing much to worry about. It will pass. Try to jolly her along a bit. There's a good chap.'

For the first couple of months Bill tried really hard to cheer Amy up as best he could. He bought her the same gifts that used to delight her when they were first married. Amy would refuse even to look at them. She rarely spoke to him and would retire to bed very early. If Bill tried to put his arms round her thin shoulders or give her a perfunctory kiss she would shrug him off immediately and dissolve into tears. Bill was at a loss. She was exhausting him.

Eventually he gave up trying. He would come home on a Friday evening. Play with Sylvia if she was awake and as there was no meal ready for him, disappear to the pub for the rest of the night.

When Sylvia was four months old he was sent to work in Kent for three weeks. He had an absolutely gruelling schedule of appointments so he decided to stay down there for the whole time.

He told Amy.

She muttered 'Why don't you just stay down there. We don't want you here.'

Bill stared at her. 'We don't want you here'. He couldn't believe words could hurt him like that. He did not understand how she could reject him like that. He knew he was popular with his work colleagues and he had plenty of good friends. He knew he wasn't a bad man. He didn't understand why she had turned against him.

A thought crossed his mind. When he was a child, he was also very popular at school but even so, his mother never wanted him enough to send for him to be with her in India.

Bill felt a wave of sadness crash over him. He thought of the photo he had of his mother. She was standing in a sunlit field of wheat, dressed in a long cotton dress and was peering out from under a wide brimmed hat. She was smiling slightly as if she was sharing a joke with the camera man. She looked like she would have been a fun, loving mother, Bill would have liked her to laugh at his jokes. He looked at Amy, she was spitting out words but he had lost track of what she was saying.

Suddenly Amy ran at him across the room screaming and scratched his face. He grappled with her skinny arms trying to hold her back. Sylvia let out a long wail from her pram.

He managed to take hold of Amy's wrists and pin them to the side of her body.

'I hate you', she was yelling. 'I wish you were dead. I wish you were dead'. Spit was flying from her mouth. All of a sudden her rage died down and she let out a long shuddering sigh. Her eyes seemed huge in her tiny pale face.

'Do you have other women?' she asked in a matter of fact voice.

Bill let go of her arms and stepped back, he felt almost frightened by her flip of mood. She stood very still and fixed her gaze somewhere on his chest. It was eerie. Bill panicked for a moment or two. He doubted she had found out about Violet, Violet wasn't the kiss and tell type, she was supremely self-confident and never felt the need to share the stories of her exploits. Amy must be referring to the barmaids at the Fox with whom he sometimes had a drunken fumble, but who cares about that? He certainly wasn't in their beds. His thoughts were cut short as he realised Amy was speaking again.

'You need other women don't you? You need to be surrounded by them to make you feel like a real man.'

Bill took a deep breath, he had never been spoken to like that before, by anyone.

Then Amy said it again, deliberately, slowly,

'We don't want you here.'

Anger rocketed through Bill's body, making it difficult to breathe. He lashed out at her catching her across the side of her head and knocking her to the floor.

He looked down at her in horror. He was shocked at what he had done. He couldn't believe he had just struck her. He didn't want to be that kind of man, he had always thought men who beat their wives were cowards.

'Don't ever speak to me like that again. Sort yourself out you stupid bitch.' His voice was shaking and he felt near to tears. He shoved his hands into his trouser pockets to make sure he didn't take another swipe at Amy.

Bill left for Kent the next morning. They didn't say a single word to one another and Bill had slept on the nursery floor to be near Sylvia. Bill said goodbye to Sylvia and gave her a squeeze. Sylvia gazed at him and gave him an approving smile. He smiled back.

When he left, Amy became lost in thought. She hadn't been particularly injured by Bill but she had been very surprised. It was the first time he had ever struck her. She realised there had been a damaging shift in their relationship. She knew men sometimes beat their wives. She had a very vague recollection of her own father taking a swing at her mother. If she walked out though, where would she go? Back to the East End slums to end up like her mother. She could try to model again, perhaps shop or secretarial work in the city but with a small child in tow that would be difficult. Bill was very handsome and earned a lot of money. He was generous with it too.

Perhaps it wasn't so bad that Bill enjoyed the company of other women. Perhaps it was only natural. She didn't want him anywhere near her so what was he supposed to do? She must be useless. She started to cry. From the moment Sylvia had been born Amy was filled with an oppressive darkness within her stomach which was making it so hard to be happy, in fact hard to feel anything at all.

Chapter 5

Bill was driving himself down to Kent and it was a very long drive. All his anger had evaporated as his car ate up the miles and he was left feeling very sad indeed. Being married was very difficult.

He was booked into the appropriately named Sea View guest-house in Margate. He had never stayed there before. On arrival he was overjoyed to find a couple of his fellow travelling salesman friends were also staying. John Wells, handmade shoes and Alexander Jones, briefcases.

For the first couple of days they had a jolly time. Working hard during the day and whooping it up on an evening in the pubs round the seaside town.

The Sea View was a large Victorian villa, each room was crammed with appropriate heavy Victorian furniture. There were thick velvet drapes at all the windows and faded luxurious rugs on the floors. It may have felt oppressive but for the high ceilings and many of the large windows which had a vista that looked out across the sea. The Sea View guest-house was run by a Mrs Rosie Frost. A pretty widow of twenty nine who had lost her husband in the war. After Richard Frost had died, Rosie had to open her own home as a guest house to pay her way in the world. She had been hesitant to invite strangers into her home at first, then necessity had forced her hand. She could have sold up and bought something smaller after her beloved husband had been killed but she found she couldn't let go of all the happy memories. The sensible thing to do then was to join the masses of widows in England's coastal towns and open up a guest-house.

She quickly got used to it and began to take pride in her new business venture. She found she liked meeting new people and was friendly without being intrusive. She was also an excellent cook.

Bill was extremely busy in his first week. During the day he was driving all over Kent and was working very long hours. He was finding selling his shirts to the Gentlemen's outfitters in Kent far more challenging than the big department stores of the capital. After the Great War the whole country was suffering from a punishing economic downturn. Bill, John and Alexander all pooled their strategies over pints of ale on an evening. They each had their own technique but could all detect interest a mile off.

Bill was very tired. He worked hard and the tensions at home were sapping his energy. He also wondered if he was drinking too much.

One evening he was preparing to go out into town by having a wet shave and re-applying his oil to his dark hair when he got a sharp pain in the back of his head. It came on suddenly and ran down the back of his neck and into his shoulder blade. He looked at himself in the mirror and found his reflection was distorted by sparkling white lights. He sat down on his bed and shut his eyes for a minute or two. The flashing lights had gone when he opened them again but the headache had intensified and he felt very sick indeed.

There was a loud rap on the door.

'Come on Bill, old man we are in need of liquid refreshment,' yelled Alexander.

'Sorry fellows I can't make it tonight I have got some paperwork to catch up on.' His voice sounded weak and trembled a little.

Alexander rapped a lively tattoo on the door, each loud knock rattling Bill's aching head.

'All right old fruit, see you later. We will drink your share.' Alexander and John made a cheerful, noisy exit. Bill got up slowly. He was seized by a panic. His health was usually excellent and he never suffered from headaches. He was frightened.

He crept downstairs, it was just past 9 o'clock. He made his way to the kitchen in search of some aspirin.

Rosie Frost was washing up, humming to herself. She had served her guests an excellent mutton stew followed by a delicious apple and blackberry crumble with thick custard. Unfortunately the food had welded itself to her large unwieldy cooking pots and she was working up quite a sweat trying to scrub them clean. Bill stood in the doorway for a minute or two enjoying the sight of Rosie's bottom swinging from side to side as she added an extra burst of energy to her vigorous scrubbing. Bill cleared his throat. Rosie jumped and dropped her brush with a clatter. She turned round and put her hand to her throat.

'Goodness me Mr Jenkinson you made me jump out of my skin.' Her round cheeks were flushed and her dark curly hair was escaping her loose bun.

'Oh dear me,' she exclaimed with a giggle as she realised the top buttons of her flowered cotton blouse had come undone through her exertions. She blushed becomingly and hurried to do them back up. Bill tactfully averted his eyes. Rosie giggled again.

'Now I am fully dressed, can I help you at all Mr Jenkinson?'

'I just wondered if you had any aspirin? I have got a terrible pain in my head, in my eye too,' said Bill rather feebly.

Rosie dried her damp hands on her wool skirt and looked at him with concern.

'Your eyes, little bright firecrackers in them?'

Bill nodded miserably.

To his surprise Rosie stepped forward and put her hand gently on his forehead.

'There is no temperature,' she said reassuringly. 'It sounds very much like a nasty migraine, you poor old thing. Let's get you settled in the front room with an aspirin and a nice cup of tea. I will get you a cool cloth for your head.'

Rosie led Bill into the front room and pulled an armchair close to the fire. He sat down and rested his aching head against a clean white antimacassar. As she headed back towards the kitchen she said 'I can send for Dr Johnson if you like but I think you are going to live.'

Bill shook his head feeling slightly foolish. He had heard of migraines of course.

It was very cosy in the room. The coals were glowing red in the fire grate and the heavy velvet curtains were drawn against the strong spring wind that was blowing straight across from the sea. There was a large Tiffany lamp on the piano which cast a gentle, colourful light.

Rosie came back into the room with a tray. She had brought as promised the aspirin, tea and a damp cloth.

She set the tray down on an occasional table by Bill's chair.

She pulled a rug from a small chaise longue which was positioned under the window to allow her guest to stare out across the bay in comfort. She tucked the rug around Bill's legs. Bill was again slightly startled by her familiarity but didn't protest.

'There now. I need to finish up in the kitchen. I will come back and check on you if you like and we will see how the land lies.' She patted Bill's hand. 'My sister suffers dreadfully from neuralgia so I know how frightening that kind of head pain can be, especially when you are far from home.' She gave Bill a final sweet smile and disappeared back into the steamy kitchen.

Bill felt close to tears again and it wasn't just because he felt ill.

He was a charismatic confident man. He usually evoked some kind of emotional response from people, often admiration, sometimes jealousy or outright dislike. He was friendly with a lot of people but most of his friendships had a surface quality to them. Offers of genuine kindness or sympathy were few and far between. Most people presumed as he was blessed with good looks and money then he must be very happy. He needed love from his wife but the distance between him and Amy was now so great she might as well be living in another country.

The room was peaceful. He could hear the wind howling outside but the sound was muffled by the solid walls of the old house. There was the regular tick from the overlarge grandfather clock in the corner. Rosie had a superior looking ginger cat called Marmalade. He was also spending his evening in the front room in the warm and was sound asleep on the piano stool snoring majestically.

Bill felt the pain in his head and neck beginning to ease and found himself relaxing properly and drifting off to sleep. He awoke with a jump when some hot coals tumbled forward in the grate as the fire settled itself. Rosie popped her head round the door. She looked searchingly at Bill.

'Do we still need to call the doctor?'

Bill shook his head. 'No thank you I think I will live.'

'Good he is a terrible old quack, doesn't know his arse from his elbow. Probably prescribe you an enema.'

Bill laughed then looked shrewdly at her for a moment.

'You have a very good bedside manner...' He wasn't being suggestive rather he was referring to the efficient kind way she had just looked after him.

'Ah well, yes. That is probably because I was a nurse in a previous life. Old habits and all of that. Nursing auxiliary towards the end of the war. I worked at the respite care home on top of the Mount. Looked after boys in a much worse state than you.' She smiled sadly and shook her head. 'We patched them up and sent them straight back out into the fray.'

'Are you still nursing?' asked Bill, interested.

Rosie gulped for a second. 'No, well when I lost my Richard, that's my husband, I continued to nurse through the war and for a while afterwards. When Richard died I was left with this house. It was his old family home. A lot said I was lucky to inherit such a fine home but it is an absolute bugger to heat and I wasn't even earning enough to feed me and Marmalade. I began to think I had better sell it. I was nursing a nice old man for a while called Major Blenkinsop. He was old Indian army. He had gone out into the field in an advisory capacity but he took a lung full gas and he was ruined. He was quite chatty and told me that he didn't want to go back to London with all the smog and smoke and he really liked Margate. It didn't take a genius to see that if he took board with me it would solve a number of problems for both of us. He was a very nice polite gentleman and the house was big enough for us to rattle around without getting in each other's way. He offered me a very tidy sum each month if I would cook for him as well. He stayed for a year, then contracted pneumonia, his lungs just couldn't cope. So that was that.'

'Then one day, after Major B died, I set off to work for my shift as usual and when I got to the door I found I couldn't go in. I just couldn't go through the door. I was stood frozen like a ruddy statue. Someone sent for Matron but she couldn't shift me either. They sent me home and gave me a couple of weeks leave to sort myself out but I seemed to have lost my nerve completely. I don't know why. I suppose there is only so much suffering you can surround yourself with and well, I don't know, I missed my Richard so much. So the only thing to do was open up Sea View as a guest-house.'

She rubbed her eyes vigorously as if to dash away the memories and took a deep breath.

'I'm sorry Mr Jenkinson. I don't know where that all came from. I will be giving you another headache. That is quite enough about me. It is a funny old thing being a landlady you are surrounded by people in your own home but you never get the chance to talk properly.'

'It is alright really,' said Bill.

'I think my head is going to remain attached to my body for the foreseeable future. You haven't got any cocoa have you? Let's celebrate.'

Rosie didn't usually sit in her own front room with her guests on an evening. She would retire to her own bedroom after cleaning up after dinner. This time though, after she brought his cocoa through, she agreed to stay and sit with Bill awhile.

They spent a very pleasant evening together. Bill wasn't a particularly introspective man but he found Rosie very easy to talk to. He found himself telling her about Amy and Sylvia. Rosie listened carefully without interruption occasionally nodding or smiling when he described his baby daughter. Eventually Bill stopped talking and they sat in relaxed silence in the warm room and watched the dying embers of the fire.

Bill felt as if his troubles were a hundred miles away. He turned to look at her properly. She wasn't his usual idea of an attractive woman. She certainly was not elegant. She wore no make-up on her round face and her simple home-made skirt and flowered blouse did nothing in particular to enhance her figure. Her brown wool stockings were practical but made her calves look quite plump. There was something undeniably attractive about her though. When she smiled her whole face lit up and she looked out upon the world through intelligent green eyes that sparkled with life. Her cheek bones were high and flushed with a delicate pink and her lips were plump and inviting.

Bill leaned across the tea tray and took her hand.

'You are lovely,' he said simply.

Rosie shook her head gently, 'and you are married Mr Jenkinson.'

She didn't move her hand away though. The wind was still howling outside.

She realised that this was the first time anyone had held her hand since Richard had left her, to die in six feet of foul mud somewhere in France. It was a small token of affection but it felt wonderful. She shut her eyes.

The spell was broken by the frantic rattling of the front door and Alexander and John fell noisily into the hall. Rosie snatched her hand away and jumped up.

For the rest of that week Bill stayed in on the evening, claiming he had too much work to catch up on to go with them to the pub. John and Alexander exchanged knowing glances and jabbed Bill in a jocular way but didn't press him any further. Bill and Rosie liked each other immensely. Bill was full of stories about the village at home and all the characters he met on his travels. He made her laugh. She, in turn, entertained Bill with tales of her houseguests and stories from the hospital. They parried gently, Rosie teasing Bill when sounding conceited and he, embarrassing her by complimenting her pretty smile. They talked about their childhoods. Rosie had always lived in Margate and had a wonderful childhood, most of it spent playing on the beach with other children in the sunshine. Bill found himself briefly being able to vocalise some of his darker memories of his childhood for the first time, predominantly how much he missed his mother and how angry he felt towards his father for taking her away. Rosie listened with empathy. He also told her funny stories of the tricks he and his brother used to play on their cruel prefects at school, a flour bag balanced on the top of an ajar door being a particular favourite.

It was worth risking the chance of six just to see the fabulous powdery explosion.

When the weekend came they decided to take a leisurely stroll along the beach together. Rosie was reticent at first feeling sure she would get some raised eyebrows in her direction. Bill was the kind of man that attracted a second glance from both men and women. He had a glamour to his looks that stood out. If she bumped into any of her friends or neighbours around the town, they would sit up and take notice immediately. Bill convinced her that she was being silly and jollied her along into agreeing to walk out with him. He felt carefree for the first time in a long time and wanted Rosie to relax with him.

It was a fine sunny day. They took off their shoes and socks and felt the sand between their toes. They even paddled for a while at the edge of the sea, which was very cold.

They found a spot to settle and sat down, sharing a tub of cockles, which Bill thought were absolutely vile.

'Oh,' said Rosie. 'By the way I got a booking for Monday from your firm.'

'Who is coming?' asked Bill, interested. He had been very busy and had been working hard but hadn't managed to procure as many orders as he would have liked. He didn't mind Silverbonds sending someone else to join him, he got along well with most of the other salesmen and it would mean that by sharing the workload he could slow down a little bit, maybe spending a bit more time on the seashore in the evening.

'It is someone called Marcus Simpkins.'

Bill threw his head back and let out a huge dramatic groan.

'Friends are you?' joked Rosie.

'Not really, well not at all, actually I hate him.'

'Goodness me, what on earth has he done?'

Marcus Simpkins had done a good many things to irritate Bill in his time at Silverbonds. He was a sly unpleasant man. Marcus would try to undermine Bill in their business meetings, a couple of times he had taken the credit for large orders which Bill had done all the groundwork. A few years previously Bill had a lovely secretary called Molly working for him. She was very efficient and pretty in a large eyed innocent way. She was also very young and shy. Bill was polite and very courteous to her and looked out for her to make sure she was treated decently by everyone else in the office, which she was for a time.

Marcus Simpkins spotted her and was irritated that Bill had such an attractive girl working for him. He bided his time and started to pop into Molly's office when Bill was away, often bringing her little treats from the nearby bakery or sweets from the little shop round the corner. Molly thought he was marvellous, she was only fifteen, an only child and had lived a sheltered life with caring, very vigilant parents. Bill was working away for a couple of weeks and on his return he found Molly had left the company. No one seemed to know why. She just failed to turn up on the Monday morning and had not contacted the company since. Bill didn't think too much about her disappearance, he was furnished with a new secretary immediately and went about his business.

Later on in the week though, Bill was busy ploughing through his paperwork when Marcus dropped into his office on the pretext of borrowing some ink for his fountain-pen. Bill looked carefully at him. Marcus never just dropped by and his own secretary could have got him the replacement ink. Marcus chatted about the weather for a few minutes then casually dropped into the rather strained conversation that he had taken Molly out at the weekend.

He gave Bill a challenging stare and Bill's heart sank. He had heard a couple of whispers of Marcus' aggression towards some of the landladies when he had a drink.

'Right,' Bill had replied neutrally. 'Molly is a pretty girl.'

Marcus' face stretched out into a grin, almost a leer.

'Yes, lovely. Not as friendly as you would have thought though. With a wiggle like that you would have thought she would have been game.'

'Why hasn't she come back into work? Do you know?'

Marcus shrugged.

'No idea Bill mate. Probably still crying.'

Bill felt anger surge through him. He waited until Marcus had left, strutting out of his office.

Bill shot out of the building. He knew where Molly lived, in a little blue house close by to the river. He knew he would be able to find it easily enough.

He knocked on the door and it was answered by an older lady. Bill was surprised and wondered if this was Molly's grandmother for a moment. It turned out to be her mother.

Bill introduced himself and said he had been concerned that Molly had not turned up to work for a week.

Molly's mother looked angrily at him.

'Molly won't be coming back,' she snapped. 'That place, that big posh office. It is not safe for a girl like her, not safe at all.'

Molly's mother looked as if she was going to burst into tears, she began to shake. Molly appeared at her side.

'Mr Jenkinson, hello,' she said politely, giving him a small smile.

Her little face looked pale and drawn.

'Molly,' said Bill, deciding it might be best to ask Molly a straight question. Her mother was already trying to close the door.

He spoke urgently 'I need to ask you something, did someone hurt you this weekend? Did Mr Simpkins hurt you?'

Molly nodded, she held her wrists out towards Bill and he saw they were covered in small bruises.

Bill clenched his teeth.

'He stopped though, I told him I was fifteen and he stopped before, well before...' Molly's voice trailed off, just as her mother slammed the door in his face.

Bill returned to work in an absolute rage. He stormed up to the top floor where the managing directors were housed.

He chose to speak to a Mr Brown who he knew was a staunch family man with daughters himself.

Mr Brown listened carefully, drawing on his pipe.

'Understand your rage. That Simpkins needs to control himself. Trouble is with this my dear boy, is we have no proof.'

'What about the bruises on her arms?' countered Bill.

Mr Brown shrugged, they both knew Marcus would lie and lie. Bill knew he was fighting a losing battle.

Marcus' father was second cousin to the proprietor of Silverbonds, an enormously wealthy entrepreneur, who Bill had never met, as he spent all of his time playing roulette in the casinos of Monte Carlo.

Marcus had never met his powerful relative either but it didn't stop him from using his vague family connection to put pressure on his superiors if any decision didn't suit him. Although Marcus was working as a salesman at the moment. Mr Brown knew he would soon rise in the ranks, probably taking Mr Brown's job.

'Hands are tied I am afraid Jenkinson from my point of view. A great shame, terrible thing for a girl to be frightened like that.'

Mr Brown cleared his throat and looked directly at Bill.

'My hands are tied but I don't believe yours are.'

Marcus, sensing trouble, decided to take a week long holiday that he was overdue. He decided to take it that very afternoon. After that he would be on the road for a couple more weeks, then Bill would be away. Their paths didn't cross for a good long while after that and Bill didn't get the opportunity to confront Marcus. Mr Brown thought that was a great shame.

Bill told her the story. Rosie was suitably concerned.

'Just be a bit careful round him won't you, he can be a nasty piece of work.' Bill advised.

'Look I know how to handle Marcus, don't worry about it.'

Marcus arrived late in the afternoon. Rosie felt a little nervous about his arrival after all Bill had told her and was surprised, when she finally met him, to see he was a slight man, not much taller than her, with receding blond hair and a spoilt-looking expression on his face.

He was polite and went straight up to his room, saying he was very tired and didn't want to be disturbed.

Bill came in later on in the evening. He looked cautiously round, making Rosie laugh.

'He has arrived,' she whispered dramatically, laughing.

The next couple of days ran smoothly and Marcus remained fairly quiet, treating Bill distantly and seemingly not even noticing Rosie.

He had been sent down to Kent to work independently from Bill. Seeing clients individually, so their paths were not crossing.

Bill started to relax. Out of the office, Marcus no longer seemed interested in wielding any power over Bill.

On the Thursday night Bill was working late, taking some clients to dinner.

Unusually the guest-house was empty. Rosie had gone out to play bingo with friends and was returning at eight. In the meantime Marcus had returned to the Sea View after a particularly trying day at work. He couldn't wait to stop this sales lark and get himself a comfy desk back at the headquarters. He felt he was due to be promoted anytime. His Father had ensured a small matter of the disappearance of some petty cash had been swept nicely under the carpet. He had bought himself a small bottle of whiskey and intended to drink it that evening and have a nice lie in the next morning. He would claim his car had broken down and he was unable to reach his clients. A clever little ruse he often put to good use.

He sat on his comfortable bed with his shoes on and began swigging from the bottle. As the level dropped Marcus began to feel restless. He idly mused whether Rosie was the kind of generous land lady who was willing to earn a bit extra. He didn't think she looked the type if he was being honest but as he had continued to drink he decided he might as well go downstairs and ask.

He heard the front door bang shut and hoped it was Rosie. He shuffled ungainly off the bed, staggering slightly. Lascivious thoughts were now flooding his brain. He made his way downstairs. He found Rosie putting the kettle on in the kitchen.

Rosie turned to face him, noticing his pale face was flush. As he began to speak, she thought she could detect a very slight slur.

She smiled brightly, pulling her cardigan round her body tightly in an unconscious defensive movement.

'What can I do for you Mr Simpkins? Do you require anything before retiring? ' she asked pointedly.

'What can you do for me, now there is a question, the oldest question in the world, I think?'

'Mr Simpkins. After dinner has been served I usually retire to my room and am no longer available.' Rosie spoke firmly and turned the gas off on the stove, leaving the kettle to cool.

She felt uncomfortable, there was something about Marcus' smiling face. He looked like he was laughing at some smug private joke, one that she wasn't privy to. He was also stood in the doorway that led out of the kitchen. He was leaning against the doorframe and she wasn't sure how to pass by without touching him if he chose not to move.

This was the first time Rosie had ever felt threatened in her own home. Since the Major had first arrived, all of her guests had been without fail decent and polite.

Marcus was still smiling, a little like a crocodile.

'I heard you were a widow, must get lonely. I'm a little lonely too this evening.' Marcus rearranged himself in his trousers and then stretched his arms above his head, reminding Rosie of a cat.

Rosie had had enough. Even if she hadn't known about poor little Molly and the stealing and untruthfulness, she could recognise a very unpleasant man.

She marched past Marcus who didn't move from the doorway.

He reached out and grabbed her wrist as she shoved her way past, determined not to show she was now unnerved.

'Let me go immediately.'

There was a charged pause as Marcus brought his face close to Rosie's. She turned her head away but she could feel his hot breath on her cheek. He slowly pushed his groin against her.

They both jumped as the front door opened. Bill was standing in the hallway. Quickly taking in the scene, he leapt forward.

Marcus let go of Rosie's wrist and was surprised to find himself instantly flat on his back, sliding unceremoniously along the polished floor of the hallway.

He had been shoved hard, not by Bill but by Rosie.

She walked over to him, he was still laid on the floor, arms and legs spread out rather in the manner of a starfish. He was slow to get back on his feet, partly from the whiskey swishing round his blood stream and partly because he had banged his head on the wall and he was seeing stars.

'Go to bed Mr Simpkins, you are drunk,' ordered Rosie.

As she turned away from him she deliberately stood on his fingers, for a brief moment, causing Marcus to howl in pain.

'That's for Molly,' she muttered under her breath.

Marcus scrambled to his feet, the shock of the pain in his hand sobering him up slightly.

For a moment it looked like he was about to retaliate, but rapidly changed his mind as Bill took a step towards him.

Rosie disappeared into the sitting-room. Bill made sure Marcus had gone upstairs and bounded into the sitting-room to join Rosie. She was stood by the window with her back to him.

'Jolly good Rosie, you showed him. I thought I was going to have to give him a smack in the mouth but you took care of the little rat yourself. Bloody marvellous.'

He scooped up Marmalade the cat and did a silly joyful jig round the room. Marmalade hissed violently at him, very irritated to be disturbed in such an unruly manner.

Bill put Marmalade down gently and joined Rosie by the window. She was shaking and there were tears in her eyes.

Bill gathered her up in his arms for the first time. His only thought was to comfort her.

'Come on Rosie, you were really brave. I am proud of you, you were like a ….'Bill searched for a good word. His face cleared. 'Like a Valkyrie.'

Rosie gave a slightly shaky laugh.

Bill looked down at her still in his arms. His body flooded with heat. He was in love with this woman. He knew at that moment he had never really been in love before in his life.

He relaxed his hold on Rosie and she smiled at him and retired to bed alone.

Marcus left the Sea View without a word the next morning, claiming he had stomach flu and he would see Bill back at the office some time. Bill made a mental note to find another position if Marcus ever moved up in the company. Bill didn't expect any trouble from him in the foreseeable future but if Marcus gained any real power he would probably make it his business to pay Bill back in some way.

The following night Bill ended up in Rosie's bed.

Rosie had never taken a lover before. In fact, a few years ago she would have actively disapproved of relationships outside of a marriage. She had seen enough suffering in her twenty nine years of life though to now feel that perhaps one should take comfort when it was offered. She thought she may have very quickly fallen in love with Bill too. She recognized that Bill was needing love and warmth, just like herself and it seemed almost inevitable that they would end up together in some way. She put the fact that Bill was married, with a child, out of her mind. Besides, Amy sounded like an absolute horror.

Bill returned to the Sea View guest-house regularly. Even when he was working in London he would make the drive across to Kent. Rosie was always delighted to see him and welcomed him with open arms. Although she always knew when he was going to stay she never made any special effort to dress up for him in anyway. In an odd way, Bill found that very fact very comforting and if he was honest, arousing. Her simplicity and warmth was effortless. They didn't always end up in the bedroom and sometimes, especially in high season Bill barely saw her on his visits. There were times in the winter months when they made love for hours. They had a wonderful time. Her soft curved body was responsive and always smelt deliciously of rose soap. Her kisses were enthusiastic and tasted as pure as spring water.

Every so often as they lay in her large bed, sated, relaxed and laid with their limbs entwined, Bill would declare that he would leave Amy and move down to Kent to be with her.

Rosie would always shake her head gently.

'Bill you must never leave Sylvia. She needs her father. Your parents were a thousand miles away from you. You don't want to do that to your own sweet baby do you?' Rosie never spoke of Amy.

'Go home and live the life you have made for yourself. I will still be here a while longer and I will still love you.'

Chapter 6

Sylvia was now coming up to eight months old and Amy was struggling. A cold frost had set hard in the Jenkinson household. When Bill returned home from work Amy wouldn't even acknowledge his arrival. Bill seriously resented her. Her rejection constantly hurt him but he was used to rejection after all. What hurt the most though, was that Amy didn't seem to have very much affection for Sylvia. Sylvia was healthy, clean and well-dressed but Amy never seemed to pick her up and always spoke very dismissively of her.

As the love and friendship with Rosie Frost had deepened he recognised the stark contrast between the two women in his life. He watched Amy as she mainly ignored his baby daughter with growing rage and despair. How could she not love her own daughter? He could reconcile himself to her dislike of him, after all he was an unfaithful husband. He wasn't sure how much Amy knew but his own guilt was enough to make him feel uncomfortable. They were adults though. Sylvia hadn't done anything so why was Amy blaming her for her own unhappiness.

To escape to the coast was a wonderful idea when he was cossetted within Rosie's warm safe embrace, his head lay upon her chest and she would stroke his hair. They would share a cigarette and giggle about some of Rosie's other guests. The fact that they had to always keep quiet gave Bill an additional thrill. Her room was small and very plain and she slept in an old iron bed. The larger bedrooms being given to her guests.

To Bill, this tiny room represented the sanctuary he had been needing throughout his life. It was the very opposite to his own glamorous bedroom with its sharp edges and bold, almost aggressive colour schemes. He had finally found a place of love. The walls were painted a delicate pink and her eiderdown was a faded floral chintz. The curtains were a thin white muslin through which the strong coastal sunlight shone, softened. There was an old white painted rocking chair where Rosie's old beloved doll sat, with a worn china face and a lacy dress. On her dressing-table there was a collection of shells and bottle of perfume with only one or two drops left in its cut glass container. There was a photograph of her husband Richard, not the usual uniformed army snap. He was stood by the seashore. His shirt sleeves were rolled up and the wind was blowing his hair about. He was laughing, the laughter of a man enjoying his day in the sunshine, enjoying the company of his family and friends. Bill would sometimes catch Rosie staring into the photo and the light would dim in her eyes. Bill would want to reach out to her and hold her but he didn't dare interrupt her private moments of loss.

When he returned to his own home, returned to work, returned to his own life, he knew it wasn't possible to leave. If he left Amy he would damage his excellent reputation within the clothing industry. Quite a few of the store owners and captains of industry had series of mistresses but all staunchly disapproved of divorce.

Amy was in a very bad way. She felt her whole body was full of darkness. She had great difficulty eating and often suffered from bad bouts of indigestion. When she awoke in the morning she always felt exhausted and full of gloom at the thought of enduring another long boring day. She looked after Sylvia's physical needs well enough by making sure she was clean and well fed. When she picked her up and stared at her sweet chubby face though she still felt nothing, not even the slightest twitch of affection.

The house had taken on the musty smell of dust. In fact during the week Amy herself developed a musty smell. She simply didn't have the energy to bathe. The bathroom was so cold. Amy was always cold. On a Friday afternoon she knew that Bill would be putting in an appearance so she would run a deep hot bath, when Sylvia was asleep, and sit in it for an hour or so. She would drag herself out when it had cooled and attempt to brighten her wan face with mascara block and blush. Sometimes when she had overdone it with the gin, dark thoughts of ending it all would creep into her tired brain. She sometimes wondered if Bill had got himself a woman, to take care of his needs properly but couldn't even be bothered to challenge him anymore. Just as she thought she was about to lose her mind, the Atwell family moved in next door.

Amy had taken up her habitual position on the seating by the large bay window to watch the world go by and listlessly watched the hustle and bustle of a large family moving in. Pleasant spring weather had heralded their arrival. As the weather improved Amy found her mood was lifting slightly. Sylvia had finally begun to sleep during the night and the frantic screaming of the daytime was gradually being replaced by the happy burbling as her colic finally began to ease. Amy hadn't called round to welcome the Atwell family to the road.

Amy began to sit out in the garden when the sun came out, her skinny frame always wrapped in a huge ugly brown cardigan. She could hear the low buzz of chatter from the Atwell family as they organised themselves in their new home. There were three boys, quite close together in age and seemed to spend a large amount of their time playing football and cricket in the garden. Their games would regularly descend into good natured arguments. Occasionally they would become overheated and their games would devolve into wrestling matches and Amy would hear their mother's voice raise slightly in remonstrations.

One such morning, in early May, the sun was shining brightly. Amy was sitting in her wooden deck- chair nursing a cup of black coffee. Sylvia was sleeping peacefully in her Silver Cross carriage. There was a breeze which carried the gentle scent of the bluebells from the wood nearby. Although Amy's garden soil was bare awaiting the planting of summer marigolds, the lawn had taken on a brighter shade of green.

She felt her shoulder muscles uncoil pleasantly for the first time in months. She took a deep lungful of spring air and relaxed further into her chair. All of a sudden a football sailed over the tall beech hedge which divided the two houses. It narrowly missed Amy's head. Amy remained still and stared at the heavy leather football. Then she heard a frantic rustling coming from the bottom of the hedge. A small boy erupted unceremoniously from within its leaves. He jumped up and dusted his shorts vigorously. He marched up to Amy and offered out his grubby hand in greeting.

'Good morning', he piped in a friendly fashion. 'My name is Ian. From next door,' he added helpfully. 'Could I have my ball back?'

He paused then said deliberately.

'Please and thank you.'

He peered out from under his tousled light brown fringe.

'I am five,' he informed Amy importantly.

Amy couldn't help smiling. He had such a cheerful face with his snub nose and rosy cheeks. He was staring at Amy completely unabashed.

'Hello Ian. Of course you can fetch your ball. In fact you can come and get it whenever it lands in my garden. I don't mind at all.'

Ian nodded solemnly.

'That is good. Thanks. Our old neighbour never used to let us get it. We had to wait until he went out. Do you know what he did once? He popped my best blue ball with his garden fork because it had accidently broken a window in his greenhouse.'

Ian's face turned red and he clenched his fists. The memory was clearly causing great agitation within his small soul.

'I don't have a garden fork or a greenhouse for that matter, so I think you will be alright. Come in when you need to, you don't have to ask.'

Further encouraged to continue his tale Ian moved closer to Amy, looked round furtively and said in a loud piercing whisper. 'Our Robert said he is a mean old sod. I am not allowed to say that,' he added as an afterthought whilst looking highly delighted that he was quoting his older brother.

Ian looked seriously at her. 'My mother says I always have to ask and always have to say please and thank you, so I had better do that.'

Amy shrugged.

'What is that?' asked Ian pointing down the garden at Sylvia in her pram.

'It's a baby,' said Amy indifferently.

'Can I go and see it?'

'If you like.'

Ian trundled down the lawn. Beech leaves were stuck to the back of his hair. He peered into the pram at the sleeping Sylvia. He carefully pressed one finger against her plump cheek and nodded in approval.

He walked back up to Amy, ball under one arm. 'Bye', he said briefly, turned and disappeared back through the hedge.

After that, Ian made it his business to launch his ball into Amy's garden on a daily basis. He would squash his sturdy frame through the hedge and check on Baby Sylvia. He always obediently requested permission to fetch his ball. If the weather was bad and Amy was inside he would knock on the door persistently until she answered.

Amy knew it would be Ian and would fling the door open dramatically and pretend she was about to come outside and burst his ball with a knife and fork. Ian would roar with laughter every time and scuttle off home, ball tucked under his arm.

Ian was Amy's only visitor. Enid the draconian midwife had requested, or rather ordered, one or two of the new mothers in the village to drop in on Amy and invite her to their mothers' meetings at the Parish church. They obediently tried a number of times, if only to take a look round the Jenkinson's famous home. Also they didn't dare ignore a direct order from Enid. The women were pleased to have the opportunity to visit Amy and her baby. The combination of her exotic glamour and disinterest fascinated them. They all openly admired her handsome husband with his dark looks, expensive clothes and witty banter.

They were to be disappointed though. Amy would hide in her house and refuse to answer the door. The ladies of Westridge Village tended to do their daily shopping in the mid-morning so Amy would now deliberately head to the shops around 5 o' clock. With Bill away so much she didn't have the same time constrictions of having to have dinner on the table by 6 o'clock. She tended to eat much later in the evening or not at all.

One sunny morning in June, Amy heard Ian rapping loudly on the door. She flung it open and shouted in a deep voice, 'Too late you scallywag. I put that ball in the oven and cooked it for my breakfast and...'

She stopped midsentence as she realised Ian was standing hand in hand with a pleasant looking woman of about forty. She was small and neat.

Amy wrapped her brown cardigan around her skinny body protectively and looked at the woman with a guarded expression.

Ian's mother seemed unperturbed and introduced herself.

'Hello there, I'm Ada from next door. I hear you have been visited by this young man already. I'm sorry I haven't introduced myself before but we have been ever so busy settling in.'

Amy said nothing. Sylvia was in her usual place in her pram and it was parked in the kitchen. She let out a wail. Amy sighed and rolled her eyes. She went to pick her up.

'Oh may I?' cooed Ada. 'I love babies. I would love to have one.' Amy looked puzzled for a second but then couldn't be bothered to enquire further.

Ada sensed quite quickly that she wasn't particularly welcome so handed Sylvia back and said 'Well it has been nice to finally meet. If you ever fancy a brew then you know where to find us.'

'Yes, we live next door,' clarified Ian.

Ada said 'I think Ian may have forged a path through the hedge so you could go that way for convenience and to save time.'

Ian looked highly delighted at the thought and even Amy managed a small giggle.

'Thank you,' she said. 'Actually that might be nice.'

Amy suddenly became very defensive again. 'I have been very tired too, the baby screams.'

Ada nodded sympathetically. 'Life is not always easy.'

Chapter 7

Ada Atwell felt distinctly queasy. She heaved the shirts out of the sink onto the scrubbed kitchen table. They felt much heavier than usual. She eyed up the mangle which seemed to be staring balefully back at her. Ada shook her head in defeat and flopped down into the wooden chair by the Aga. She considered making a cup of tea but immediately changed her mind as her stomach churned at the thought.

There was a languid knock on the door.

'It's open,' said Ada weakly.

Amy wandered into the kitchen, looking around vaguely. She was dressed in a lovely silk kimono-style blouse with a matching scarf knotted artfully round her tiny waist. It was navy blue and covered in bright orange pansies. She had paired it with very modern wide leg trousers. Her face was immaculately made up.

Sylvia was trundling along behind her but Amy pushed her back out of the door. 'Go play in the garden a while darling.' Sylvia started to wail but Amy shut the door firmly on her. Sylvia was no longer a baby but had grown into a particularly strong willed toddler. She wasn't an attractive child. She had a constant runny nose and her thin mousey hair hung down in rats tails no matter how often Amy combed it. She had a very quick temper and would often kick and bite Amy in her many moments of frustration.

'It is fine for her to come in Amy,' said Ada.

Amy shook her head. 'God she had driven me up the wall today.' Sadly, Ada thought, Amy never said anything nice about Sylvia.

Amy let out a long draw out sigh. 'I was wondering if I could borrow a pie flute. Bill is back tonight and I thought I might make a pie of some kind.'

Amy often popped in to see Ada if she was going to attempt a meal more challenging than baked beans on toast. It was always under the guise of borrowing a kitchen utensil but really it was a way to ask for Ada's help.

Ada would often end up going round to the Jenkinson's kitchen and preparing the meal herself whilst Amy poured herself a restorative gin and gossiped casually about the village families. Amy was always very grateful for Ada's help. She would watch as Ada deftly rolled out pastry or fit a lamb joint snuggly into a roasting tin and pack it round with onions and rosemary. Amy would shake her head in amazement and look fondly at her friend.

'You are just so clever.'

Ada and Amy had gradually become friends as the months passed. Ada had an air of calm and steady presence that Amy warmed to and found very reassuring. Ada was gentle and never intrusive.

Amy's dark viscous gloom after having Sylvia had eventually lifted, by the time Sylvia had turned one year old. Still Amy wasn't a natural mother and found Sylvia very irritating at the best of times. In turn Sylvia picked up on her mother's lack of attention and became whiney and bad tempered.

Amy looked like her old self again. Well put together and always glamourous. She popped the old smelly cardigan on the fire one night to symbolise a new start. She bought a whole new wardrobe of clothes and asked Ada to donate some of her old items to the church jumble sale. It caused great excitement and almost a riot at one point when a couple of ladies, who had been the best of friends, actually started fighting over a cashmere coat, never to speak to one another again. The vicar had been briefly manhandled, as he tried to separate them and was very upset.

Bill registered the change in Amy and was relieved. At least he no longer felt ashamed at what she looked like and people had stopped asking him if she was quite well. He no longer accompanied her on her shopping trips though. She seemed to be dressing for herself and wasn't interested in his opinion anymore. When he sensed a lightness of mood Bill would cautiously attempt to reconcile with her. The adoring fairy girl he had married was gone forever but so had the desperately depressed wife. Amy was now stronger but her mood swings were unpredictable. She would be giddy with delight one day, followed by violent rages and finally longer periods of gloom. When

Bill returned home from work and entered his home he would approach with caution, any one of Amy's kaleidoscope of moods could greet him on a Friday night.

Sometimes the dark sticky anger would fill Amy almost entirely. She didn't understand it and she couldn't bear it. Amy began to drink more to ease the stress that filled her delicate body. She would pounce on Bill as he came through the door. Deliberately starting fights and her unhappy venom spitting out of her in violent physical rage. Bill would have to fend her off and try desperately not to lash out back at her, sometimes on occasion he would end up hitting her back, which he would instantly regret. Amy would cry and cling to him, afraid that he would leave her. The rages would pass and she would become friendly and loving towards him. Bill treated her with caution.

She no longer joined Bill on his social evenings, claiming they had no one to watch Sylvia. This wasn't true. Ada had volunteered on many an occasion.

Amy was now painfully aware that Bill was seeing another women or maybe more than one. If they took a walk through the village as a family Amy would notice a few giggling women giving Bill the eye, whilst freezing Amy out. Bill would smile back or give them a wink. If Amy asked who they were, Bill would mutter something dismissive about meeting them in a pub or restaurant. Sometimes Bill would arrive home very late indeed from his travels. He would climb into their bed, thinking Amy was sound asleep and so wouldn't even do her the courtesy of having a wash before he got in between their sheets. Amy would pretend to be asleep but through the whiskey fumes she would recognise a deeper disturbing scent.

Without Bill's adoration, she no longer felt comfortable at dinners and dances. She would scan the room and wonder exactly whose dress Bill had been eagerly rummaging through. She also was very perceptive to looks of pity that came from other women and couldn't stand that.

Their marriage was damaged beyond repair.

Amy had returned to her former elegant glory visually, but her confidence was in tatters.

Ada on the other hand enjoyed Amy's company. She was such an exotic creature with her unsuitable glamorous clothes, heavy make-up and air of vulnerability. Amy didn't want to make any other friends within the village and always managed to maintain her distance but she was quite a keen observer of human nature and always made Ada giggle with the gossip she would hear. Amy made a massive effort to hide her depression from Ada.

Ada couldn't fail to notice the change that came over Amy when Bill returned home at the weekend. She could see the tension in Amy's skinny body. Her voice took on a shrill tone and her hands would tremble ever so slightly. She would also drink a lot more to soothe herself. She had noticed faint bruising on Amy's cheek a couple of times, under the pancake make-up. Amy never discussed her marriage with Ada in any depth. Any enquiries to her happiness were always brushed aside and the subject was changed. Ada never approached the subject of the bruising but she knew that helping Amy out here and there with cooking or some other little domestic chore would help to make Amy's life run a little smoother.

Amy took up an elegant position leaning slightly against the table, a bird like hand resting on top of the sopping wet pile of shirts. Amy appeared not to notice the damp. She was humming a little tune under her breath. She stopped and finally focussed on Ada.

'Oh are you quite well? You look a little something....' She finished lamely.

Ada smiled brightly at her friend, jumped up quickly and vomited noisily into the sink. Amy patted her ineffectually on her back.

Ada collapsed back down on the wooden chair with a bang, wiping her mouth.

'Must be something I ate, I suppose.'

Amy reassumed her pose by the table.

'Hmmm the last time I threw up like that I was pregnant with Sylvia. You're not pregnant are you?' she asked neutrally.

Ada sat in silence for a while. 'I suppose it is possible but I am 42. I can't be.' Ada said to almost to herself, her voice filling with hope as she dared to consider the wonderful possibility.

'Lovely I suppose.' murmured Amy with as much enthusiasm as she could muster. 'Children are lovely, it's just they are so noisy and can be a bit....selfish.'

Ada looked up at Amy trying so hard to be happy for her friend and giggled.

'Right.' She nodded towards the paper bag that Ada had slung casually on the floor. It was oozing red juices onto the stone tiles.

'What is in that bag?' asked Ada innocently knowing full well Amy had brought pie filling ingredients with her.

Amy fluttered her eyelashes comically at Ada.

'Pie filling. If you wouldn't mind knocking it together for me? You really are an absolute marvel. I always make a frightful hash of pies. I will be eternally in your debt.'

'Go on then, what is this marvellous pie going to be?'

'Steak and kidney.'

Ada turned bright green at the thought and immediately vomited again, this time onto the hearth.

Amy returned home and sat at her kitchen table, tracing circles in the flour that she had artfully sprinkled on the table, giving the impression she had been baking. Her eyes strayed to the pie that Ada had bravely made for her. Amy smiled fondly at the thought of her good friend.

She jumped as she heard the front door open then close with a loud slam. She looked up to see Bill's large frame filling the doorway. He looked at her uncertainly, trying to gauge her mood of the evening. He looked very tired. His brow was heavy and his hair was uncharacteristically out of place.

Amy stood up quickly and began fluttering round the kitchen, needlessly arranging the pans on the stove. She sensed he was in a very bad mood. His jaw was set and his eyes were radiating tension. She smiled slightly nervously at Bill.

'Good trip?' she chirped.

'No, not really.' He had been working the South Coast and had had a hellish journey home. 'These bloody seaside towns. I don't know why they send me. There is no bloody money there. They would cut a ha'penny in half. Where is Sil?'

'She's next door playing.'

Bill nodded. For some reason Amy was already irritating him, the least she could do was look after her own child. He was already paying for a cleaner and another woman to do the laundry.

Bill loosened his tie from round his strong neck and ran his eyes up and down Amy's frame appraisingly. He had a petulant expression on his face and was drumming his fingers on the table. Amy felt herself tense up. He was definitely in an explosive mood. This was quite unusual for Bill and Amy didn't like it.

'You are putting on weight,' he said. 'You're not up the duff again are you? Or have you been sitting on your arse all week? The punishing world of being a housewife eh? You must be exhausted.' he said sarcastically.

Amy felt her cheeks redden. He could be mean when he was in a bad mood. Amy almost protested that she was exactly the same size as when he met her, even though she had carried a child. She decided not to retaliate.

Suddenly he stepped forward and stood directly in front of her. She could feel the heat radiate from him and actually he could have done with a bath. She fixed her eyes on the floor and flinched very slightly when he raised his hand. Bill smoothed a few strands of hair that had escaped the lacquer on Amy's perfectly smooth bob.

'Don't let yourself go Amy or I will trade you in for a new model. Where will you live then? On the slagheap? I don't want a fat wife.'

He turned away and sat down at the table.

Amy cleared her throat and swallowed down the panic. Bill knew exactly how to hurt her just as she knew how to hurt him.

She decided to ignore the jibes and smiled brightly at Bill.

'I have got a bit of news. Ada, from next door, is going to have a baby.'

Bill didn't have much time for the Atwells. He would sometimes chat to Walter or the older boys about football or cricket but he couldn't really see the point of Ada.

Bill didn't say anything for a minute, he looked as if he was thinking. After a minute he smiled and said 'Good old Walter eh, still life in the old dog yet. Well that is a nice bit of news.'

Bill's demeanour changed. He shrugged off his mean mood as if shedding a jacket. His scowl softened and his face relaxed. He looked at Amy in a hopeful way.

Amy watched his expression with growing horror. She knew exactly what he was going to say from the look on his face.

Bill's tone was consolatory. He stood up and came close to Amy again.

'Sorry about earlier. It has been a rotten week. You look pretty today.'

Amy felt her body stiffen.

'You know I think it might be time for Sylvia to have a little brother, don't you Amy? We could try for a little boy this time. Syl is getting to be a bit of a madam, it will do her good to have her edges knocked off.'

Amy absolutely did not want another child. She had only just started to feel herself again, whoever that might be anyway. The thought of going through it all again filled her stomach with a cold fear.

'Amy?' Bill's voice had taken on a hopeful tone.

Amy glanced down at his trousers. He was clearly enamoured with the thought.

Amy considered refusing but felt herself deflate with resignation.

She looked at Bill who was looking back at her with a tenderness that definitely had not existed a moment before.

Bill was beginning to thicken round the middle slightly but his jaw and cheekbones were still as flawless as ever. He was the best looking man for miles around. They were the best looking couple for miles for that matter. It was inevitable that Bill would want another child. She thought briefly about her own wreck of a mother, after her father left, she never found another man to cherish her, in fact quite the reverse. Vera spent her miserable days being used in the worst possible way. The men in her life were like animals. Bill could be aggressive but Amy knew that, if she was being honest with herself, usually she started the rows. She strongly suspected he went with other women but what on earth could she do about that. At least he never taunted her with that, his own guilt in that respect kept him in check. There was so much about their relationship that was wrong but he had always been her escape from the slums and from poverty. If she left him there was no way she could stand on her own two feet, even if he provided for Sylvia, she certainly wouldn't be able to live in the style she had become accustomed to. She knew she had a number of admirers in the village. The men tended to watch her from a distance though and she hadn't managed to connect in a real way with any other men.

At least when she was carrying a child, Bill wouldn't badger her for sex for a good long while. She had better get it over with.

She nodded in agreement.

Bill scooped her up in his arms and whooped in excitement. Amy couldn't help laughing. Amy didn't particularly enjoy herself that evening. Bill was gentle and tender, treating their lovemaking with the reverence he felt it deserved. Amy did try to relax but any pleasant twitching of desire was disturbed by the faintest whiff of rose soap which arose from Bill's warm body.

Ada was definitely pregnant and she and Walter were thrilled. She managed very well. The boys rallied round their mother, fetching and carrying the shopping, hanging out the washing and generally jumping up to assist her whenever she needed a hand. After Walter had given them the hard word, Sid and Ian valiantly tried to rein in their filial battles, but you can't fight human nature, particularly between high spirited brothers close in age.

Amy fell pregnant almost straight away, she was very sick again but somehow things didn't seem as bad as the first time. Ada's quiet reassuring presence helped to soothe her mind and give her strength. Ada tried to teach Amy to knit, to make the new baby's layette. Amy couldn't fathom it out at all so Ada ended up making two layettes. Amy paid Ada generously from her housekeeping for the tiny clothes. Ada refused the money at first so Amy popped it secretly in the tea caddy on the way out, to be found later when Amy had returned home.

Gracie Atwell arrived a whole two months before schedule, weighing just three pounds. Enid had only just managed to dismount her huge bicycle and scrub her hands before Gracie shot out onto the new towels Ada had bought the day previous in preparation. She was tiny but very strong with an excellent pair of lungs. Gracie spent the first three months of her life slotted down the front of Ada's cardigan in a makeshift sling so as to keep warm. She thrived and progressed nicely becoming a fat contented baby with a ready smile and enormous brown eyes, like Ada's. Her brothers were all blonde with blue eyes but Gracie had a shock of black hair. She was the apple of Walter's eye. Her three brothers were also very fond of her, especially Ian, who liked to wheel her about in his wooden cart.

Amy and Bill's baby followed a couple of months after. They named him Joe. He was a sturdy little chap who slept very well from the off. Bill was absolutely thrilled to have a son.

Ada encouraged Amy to come for long walks with her, pushing the babies, swaddled in crochet blankets, in their respective carriages. They also attended the church mothers group which Amy found she rather liked as long as she had her friend by her side, although the coffee was foul.

Amy managed to stave off the darkness of her previous post-natal days and found Joe was manageable.

Sylvia was not so keen on Joe and would take every opportunity to pinch or scratch him. To solve this problem, Amy paid a Mrs Land who was a kindly but very poor member of the village to take Sylvia off her hands on a daily basis. Mrs Land had two sets of twins, born a year apart, aged six and five respectively. She looked after other children to supplement her husband's inadequate income. When Amy dropped her off at the little cottage Sylvia would scream the place down just to punish Amy for leaving her. As soon as Amy had disappeared down the little lane with Joe, Sylvia would joyfully get on with playing with the other boys and girls. On her first day Sylvia quickly realised she couldn't bully any of Mrs Land's robust children. Any attempts at shoving or biting were swiftly dealt with, by a retaliating swipe from one of the Land brood or sometimes even Mrs Land. Mrs Land observed Sylvia's behaviour and was completely unsympathetic to her wails and told her 'if you hit 'em they will hit thee back'.

Chapter 8

Gracie screamed with excitement. She clung on to the sides of the old perambulator that she was sat in with all her might. She wedged her feet into the bottom corners to try to prevent being bounced clean out. The wind streamed through her black glossy hair, which had escaped the neat plaits Ada had done that morning. Her eyes were watering. Her cries of 'Stop you beast' only made Ian push the pram faster down the long steep hill of Mulberry Hill. Ian's skinny legs pumped and he yelled lustily. Gracie shut her eyes tight as Ian skidded to a halt in front of the gate of their family home half-way down the hill. Ian wrenched the pram round and pushed it through the gate. He sped along the drive.

'To the coal shed,' he bellowed at the top of his voice.

In one smooth move he flung open the shed door and tipped Gracie unceremoniously out of the old pram straight onto the coal heap and banged the door shut.

'Ian you brute, let me out,' shouted Gracie.

She pushed against the ancient wooden door with all her might. It was stuck fast. She sat back down on the coal, plump sun-tanned arms folded and a smile on her face. This was all part of their favourite game.

It was nice and cool in the shed. It provided shelter from the fierce July sunshine outside. The large cracks in the door let in little shafts of sunlight which highlighted the swirling coal dust that Gracie had disturbed. She watched the dust dance a while. Just as she was starting to get bored Ian flung open the door and Gracie squinted against the bright light.

'Brilliant,' grinned Ian.

'I almost let you go at the top you know Gracie, next time I will and we will make the old pram really fly.'

'You always say that and I don't believe you.'

Gracie scrambled out of the coal and aimed a lazy punch at her older brother.

Gracie was now seven and the tiny premature baby had grown into a splendid sturdy little girl. Her brown eyes were still huge and her hair had remained very dark and shone like a polished conker. She had soft olive skin which enhanced her white even teeth. She laughed loud and often, especially when she was with her brothers.

Ian was fourteen but didn't particularly look his age yet. Ian and Gracie got along very well despite their age difference. Although Ian was a popular boy and had plenty of friends his own age he would always make time for his little sister. He was very small for his age and slim. What he lacked in stature though, he made up for with his vivacious personality and a "voice like a fog horn" according to his older brothers Robert and Edward. His tousled blond hair still stood up wildly no matter how much water he used to slick it down. He had a cute snub nose which he hated. He and Gracie had the same wide smiling mouth.

'What should we do now? Another spin in the pram?'

'I don't think I could take the pram back up to the top of the hill again, it is too ruddy hot.'

'Should we make daisy chains?' asked Gracie tentatively.

Ian pulled a face and rolled his eyes. 'Not on your Nelly Gracie,' he replied. 'I am not a ruddy girl.'

Gracie quickly tried to think of something Ian might want to play. She knew that Ian might go and join his friends in a game of football on the street if she didn't hold his attention and she loved spending time with him. He could make her laugh until tears streamed down her face.

'I am starving,' he groaned clutching his stomach dramatically. 'Let's go and see if lunch is ready.'

They wandered into the large kitchen. The door was open but the stone floor was keeping it nice and cool. Ada stood by the stove surrounded by a most delicious aroma. She stirred the beef stew that was bubbling gently in a huge pot.

'Out,' she instructed the two children mildly. She brushed a few strands of hair out of her eyes and stretched her arms upwards. She had risen early to get started on the washing. With a family of six to keep clean and tidy, washing day was the time of the week she enjoyed the least. It was a manual job which made her back ache for the rest of the day. At least when the weather was as hot as this, the sheets would dry nicely.

Ada never complained. She often said there was enough noise in the house without herself joining in. She really loved her family. She was at her happiest sat around the table at meal times, listening to the chatter, jokes and inevitable good natured arguing.

Edward and Robert were now both out at work but they came home on a lunch time along with Walter for a cooked lunch.

They were to have an extra guest for lunch that morning. Ada's older sister, Clara.

Edward, Robert, Ian and Gracie absolutely adored Aunt Clara. She was a frequent visitor to the Atwell household. Clara was a heavy imposing woman with an efficient bossy manner and a loud booming voice. She wore heavy tweed clothes and sturdy boots no matter the weather. She spent most of her spare time with horses and smelt ever so slightly like sweet manure. She taught the Atwell children how to smoke a pipe, wolf-whistle and to win at poker.

Ada had met Walter later on in her life, when her youthful bloom had begun to fade and had been replaced by a graceful maturity. Ada and Clara had lived together for almost forty years when Walter came into their lives.

Ada and Clara had lost both their parents when they were ten. They were cared for by an elderly aunt who owned a tobacco shop on Kirkstall Road in Leeds. They lived quite happily together in the cosy flat above the shop. The aunt subsequently died and left the flat and shop to Ada and Clara. The shop had a steady stream of clientele and provided the young women with a small income.

Neither Ada nor Clara married. There was a sad shortage of eligible young men after the Great War. Clara had once had a beau. A beautiful boy named Arthur, he was killed at Ypres aged 17. Clara and Arthur had been childhood friends and they had fallen in love in the long hot summer of 1913. Arthur had immediately joined up and Clara was full of youthful pride. She felt sure the war would be over swiftly and they would begin a wonderful life together full of children and travel. The day Clara got the news of Arthur's death the pain had seared through her heart and left such a scar that Clara knew she would never love another man again.

Time passed by, as it tends to do and Ada and Clara had reached the respective ages of 38 and 43.

Clara had embraced spinsterhood and had become a formidable, efficient woman. She had thrown all her energies into ensuring the success of the shop. She enjoyed travelling down to London to source the more exotic imported tobaccos every so often. She involved herself with parish work and was forever raising money for charities. Their local vicar thought she was absolutely terrifying and allowed her pretty much free rein at the parish council meetings. She loved riding. She had her own horse which she kept at a local farm, the farmer willing to stable her horse in exchange for a steady supply of cigarettes and a small fee. She hunted regularly and was known for her fearless riding and strength. She could also drink most men under the table.

In contrast Ada lived her life quietly.

Clara had a sharp dismissive tongue and could be very brisk if she felt she was being crossed but she had always cared about Ada's well-being. She sometimes worried about Ada and her sheltered life working in the shop. Ada had always been content to live in Clara's shadow. Clara would try to encourage Ada to meet new people. Ada was a romantic soul and spent her spare time reading and taking long walks by herself, thinking. She had a great love of learning and enjoyed the radio. At 38 she was still a pretty woman with a heart shaped face and a dreamy look in her dark eyes. There had been a few gentlemen callers in the past and she would take walks round Kirkstall Abbey ruins and along the river, but as soon as they started to show signs of adoration she would gently wave them away. She found their attentions clumsy and their conversations lacking. Clara began to despair of her younger sister.

When challenged by Clara, Ada would say quietly 'I am happy here with you and the shop. Why complicate matters?'

Walter had dropped into the tobacconist's one day to pick up some Old Holborn as a gift for his friend Bert who was recovering from a bout of whooping cough. Walter was a chief engineer at a factory that produced springs and axles for road vehicles. The shop was a little out of Walter's way but Bert was a good pal and he didn't mind picking him up a tin of his favourite baccy on his way home. He pushed open the door and inhaled the heavy scent of leather and tobacco. There was an air of reverence in the little shop not dissimilar to a library. The walls were lined with heavy oak shelving. There were glass jars on each shelf filled with the shrivelled, toasted leaves in their many shades of brown. There was also neat displays of pipes, leather pouches and wallets on the counter next to a grand ornate till and large copper weighing scales. It was a Friday evening and the shop was busy with customers all stocking up for their weekend smokes. As he stood patiently in the queue he admired the neat figure of Ada moving assuredly amongst the jars. Her face was lit with multi-coloured lights by the low evening sunlight that streamed through the stained glass window above the door. Although the shop was busy, Ada seemed unperturbed by the queue of men respectfully waiting their turn and served each customer in an unhurried manner. She moved gracefully and exuded a sense of calm. When it was Walter's turn to be served he thanked Ada with his most dazzling smile. Ada returned his smile politely and looked away with disinterest. Walter was now very interested.

Walter was a genial man. He was popular at the works and had a reputation of being a very fair boss. His sunny nature had been shaded somewhat when his first wife passed away unexpectedly, years previously, leaving Walter and their three young sons.

Walter had always enjoyed the company of women and usually never had any difficulty in asking them if they would care to accompany him for a stroll or for a meal, but there was something about Ada's inscrutable demeanour that made his easy patter dry up somewhat. He increased his own smoking threefold just to keep returning to the shop. As he established himself as a regular both Ada and Clara began to look forward to his visits. He was very chatty and full of gossip about the factory. His face was not classically handsome but he had a wide smile which showed all his teeth. He had a noisy infectious laugh which always made Ada smile, even if she hadn't quite caught the joke. He was very open about his life, he had lost his wife to the Spanish flu just after the war. He regaled them with tales of his three mischievous young sons, Edward, Robert and Ian. Ian was an absolute scamp and was driving Walter to distraction.

Ada recognised the love in Walter's voice when he spoke of the boys. He was always cheerful and looked very much on the bright side. Sometimes they would be alone in the shop and Ada found herself revealing her own thoughts on life to Walter under his gently probing questions.

Gradually Ada began to open up to this kind, funny, quick witted man and gradually fell in love.

It took Walter a while to pluck up the courage to ask Ada if she would like to court. She was difficult to read. If he extravagantly complimented her on her dress, as was his want, she would blush and wave him away and retreat into her shy shell. Yet when they were alone and chatted so easily and honestly he felt he had known her forever.

Ada knew she had finally found a man she could love.

Clara was absolutely over the moon. She thought Walter was a super chap but more importantly she could see the joy in Ada's eyes.

They married soon after and Ada was thrown in at the deep end, moving in to a large detached house filled with a ready-made family of three lively boys.

The boys took to Ada easily. The older two boys missed their own mother terribly and appreciated the gentleness Ada had brought to their home. She eased her way into their lives quietly and consistently, always in the background but there when they needed her.

Walter asked Clara if she would like to move in with them also. Clara was moved at his kind offer but opted to stay in the little flat. She and Ada amicably arrived at a satisfactory financial arrangement.

Clara continued to run the shop herself and missed Ada very much but she was always, without exception, welcome at the Atwell home, so she visited regularly.

Clara hoped one day she would meet her very own Walter and play out her own romance to the scent of cigarettes and pipes but it wasn't to be. Clara resigned herself to life as a spinster but was greatly consoled to be part of a warm loving family.

If Amy knew Clara was visiting she would avoid her. She found Clara's abrupt mannerisms and shrewd observations of human nature very unnerving. Likewise Clara thought Amy feckless, without backbone and was utterly unsympathetic to her plight. Clara always referred to her as the 'flibbertigibbet.'

Ada wisely kept the two relationships separate. Amy would crumble if Clara got the bit between her teeth and started dishing out her own brand of advice on how to handle Bill, however well-meaning Clara was trying to be.

Lunch wasn't ready yet Gracie and Ian obediently reversed back out of the kitchen door into the large messy garden. The lawn was in need of a haircut, dotted with clover, daisies and dandelions. There was a large border which was crammed with pink foxgloves, jostling for room with poppies and soft blue cornflowers. The children flung themselves down on the grass, thankful for the shade offered by the ancient gnarled apple tree. Gracie used to imagine fairies living amongst the tree's twisted branches, especially when it was covered in the soft white blossom in spring. She felt at the age of seven, almost eight, she should let go of childish imaginings but the tree still held a fascination for her. How could the ugly lichen covered branches produce apples of such a sherbet sweetness in the autumn? In winter the Atwell family had their own supply of mistletoe to hang over the door at Christmas, another gift from the old tree. Fairies might no longer exist but nature was still truly magical.

Gracie and Ian laid on their backs in companionable silence, listening to the bees hard at work in amongst Ada's flowers. 'Nice feeling being at the beginning of the hols eh Gracie?'

'Oh yes,' agreed Gracie 'absolutely anything could happen.'

She was a natural optimist. When she woke on a morning, she looked forward to each day, feeling sure something interesting was bound to happen.

'What are you up to?'

A round moon face, topped with a mop of curly brown hair appeared through the hedge. It was Joe. He arrived into the garden through the beech hedge. Walter had cut a proper gap into the hedge because Ada was getting tired of mending torn shirts and jumpers. The children always used the hedge to go next door so Walter solved their problem with a grin.

Ian blew a dandelion clock into Joe's merry face.

'Not much Jenkies. How about you?'

'I've been working on my bike all morning and I have to say it is stumping me why the dashed brake pads keep sticking on. Come and have a look Ian will you?' he pleaded.

Ian and Gracie groaned.

'Joe why don't you just ride the new one your father bought you. It is brand spanking new and must have cost a packet?'

Joe's face went red.

'A couple of weeks ago I was riding it round the village and some bigger boys followed me, they chased me and ruddy well knocked me off and threw it in the pond. He rolled up the sleeve of his shirt and showed the children his forearm which was purple with bruising. They said I was a spoilt little rich boy.'

Ian looked thoughtfully at little Joe.

'What did these boys look like?'

Joe described them to Ian.

A pair of real mean village boys who had no business picking on a seven year old, especially Joe who was bright and breezy and never had a bad word to say about anyone.

Ian jumped up. 'Never mind eh Joe just you give them a bloody nose next time. Let's go look at this old bone shaker of yours again for the hundredth time.'

Joe's broken old bike was a perennial problem. It was ancient, he had found it in the woods close by, apparently abandoned. Joe was very interested in how things mechanical worked. The only trouble was when he took them apart he had great difficulty putting them back together again. He hardly ever saw Bill so he sought out the advice of the Atwell boys. Ian was actually enjoying trying to fix up the bike but would always tease Joe.

Ian had another hobby, he had taken up amateur boxing and was proving to be very useful in his featherweight division. He knew exactly who the older boys were who had attacked Joe. He decided to make use of his lightning right hook the very next time he saw them.

Ian was further tempted to help work on the bike that morning because Amy Jenkinson was beginning to hold a fascination over him. Gracie liked her because she never minded how many biscuits the children pinched out of the larder and Gracie was always hungry.

Amy was dressed beautifully as always in an expensive chiffon blouse and tight fitting linen pencil skirt in an elegant shade of cool pale blue. She had already drunk her first gin as it was past 11 o' clock. 'Not quite over the yard arm but very close,' she would wink at Joe.

Amy had become happier in years that followed Joe's arrival. She still spent most of her time planning her wardrobe, making changes to their house and spending plenty of Bill's money. She drank daily and rather heavily. She had become a little more involved with the events of the village. Ada had taught her the game of bridge and Amy found she rather enjoyed card evenings, as long as there was plenty to drink. She was cautious enough to control herself at the games though, saving her heavy drinking for her return home. Amy and Bill had found a reasonably stable equilibrium at home so rows were much fewer. Bill was absolutely in love with Rosie Frost and spent his time, when he wasn't in her company, thinking about her.

After a couple of years though, another man came into Rosie's life. He was a quiet, intelligent doctor who was based at the hospital on secondment. He stayed at her guest house. Rosie was very fond of Bill. He made her laugh a lot but she had started to wonder if their relationship had run its course.

Bill was heartbroken when Rosie gently told him that they could no longer share a bed. She told him that she had made a new friend in Alec, the doctor, and she wanted to give this new friendship a chance to blossom. Bill became angry as was his want when he was upset and kicked over the white rocking chair in Rosie's room, smashing the face of her childhood doll.

Rosie remained calm and stayed sat on her bed, twisting the fringe of the flowered bedspread, the only clue to her own agitation.

Bill flung himself down onto the bed next to her and cried softly.

'I can't live without you Rosie, you are the only warm thing in my life. I need you.'

Rosie's own green eyes filled with tears and she smoothed his thick dark hair.

After a while, she said quietly 'Bill we have to end this. I really like Alec and he is a good man. I have to have a chance for a normal life. I want children and I want them to have a father that comes home at 6 o'clock to his tea on the table. I want to go on holiday. I would like to train again in my nursing and do some good in this world. We have had a wonderful time and I will always love you but you don't belong with me and you never have. You know that deep down.'

Bill nodded unhappily. They made love for the last time that night their tears mixing with their kisses.

Amy smiled fondly as Joe appeared through the hedge followed by a scrambling Ian and Gracie. The Jenkinsons' garden was immaculate as always with its marigolds in straight rows and a lawn that would have been perfect for a game of bowls. Bill employed a gardener twice a week. It was very neat and an absolute contrast to the pretty wild garden of the Atwells. Ada allowed weeds to mix in with her flowers if she found them pleasing to her eye.

'A weed is plant in the wrong place after all,' she was fond of saying quietly to no one in particular.

Gracie knew exactly which garden she preferred.

Amy was sat on the step of the back door, her skirt hitched up to her stocking tops sunning herself. She angled her finely drawn face towards the sun with her eyes closed.

'Everything alright darlings?'

She opened her big blue eyes and looked directly at Ian. Ian was staring at her long slim legs. He gulped and hiccupped slightly.

'Yes thank you Mrs Jenkinson.' his voice boomed out startling little Joe beside him.

There was a long pause. Ian was transfixed, unable to avert his eyes. Amy moved her legs apart a fraction whilst still holding Ian's gaze and he caught a miniscule flash of the white silk of her French knickers. Ian's mouth dropped open. Amy smiled knowingly at him but then looked over his shoulder into the distance and became vague again.

'Run along then darlings,' she said dismissively 'I need some peace.'

Ian hesitated desperately trying to think of something to say to hold the attention to of this miraculous woman who was beginning to appear in his dreams but his mind was blank.

Joe tugged at his arm. 'Come on in for a minute first,' he said impatiently and Ian and Gracie obediently followed, Ian still in a daze.

It was quite dark in the kitchen as Amy had forgotten to open the curtains. Some of her more uncharitable neighbours suggested it was to hide her visits to the drinks cabinet. This wasn't true. Amy couldn't care less what they thought and imposed her own limits on her gin consumption, just sufficient to take the edge off the day and no more.

The Jenkinson's house smelled very strongly of the lavender beeswax polish that Amy's treasure of a cleaning woman applied to almost every object in their home with incredible industry. There was also an undercurrent of a musty smell which belonged to the damp that ran through the house. This damp, that no one could be bothered to try to remedy became the downfall of little Joe who went on to develop rheumatism in his teens.

'Is Sylvia in?' Gracie addressed the back of Joe's head, which was sticking into the pantry looking for goodies to eat.

Joe came out of the pantry with a whole apple pie, rolled his eyes and snorted

'Oh her. She is sulking in her room, you can go up if you like but I have to warn you she is in one of her sulks. She threw a shoe at me this morning.'

The children laughed at his comical hurt expression, imagining Sylvia's Start-rite sandal landing smack in the middle of Joe's merry round face.

'Or Gracie, you could help me with my bike? I think I made some progress with the chain yesterday.'

Joe had a little crush on Gracie but would deny it vigorously. His apple cheeks went red and he quickly shot back into the pantry to hide his blushes.

'Maybe later Joe. I will just have a word with Syl.'

Gracie climbed the stairs enjoying the feel of the deep luxurious wool carpet between her toes. It was held in place by brass stair-rods which Gracie thought were possibly made from gold. The stairs in the Atwell's house next door were still bare, wooden boards. Walter had sanded them but their budget wouldn't stretch to a stair carpet for a long time. She greatly admired the Jenkinson's home and vowed to live in a palace such as this when she grew up. Gracie gave a tentative knock on Sylvia's door. Silence.

'Syl are you there?'

Gracie pushed the door open. Sylvia was laid flat on her pink candlewick bedspread staring at the ceiling.

'Alright?'

'Yes thank you,' snapped Sylvia apparently very irritated to have her lounging interrupted.

'I hear you threw a shoe at Joe's head this morning.' Gracie smiled tentatively. Gracie watched Sylvia trying to see if she was in a good mood. Sylvia had the back of her hand across her forehead in the manner of a film star in the depths of despair. She managed to carry it off rather well Gracie thought, considering she was only nine. After a pause that felt like forever to Gracie, she smiled and turned to Gracie.

'Ruddy well nearly knocked his block off. He drives me mad, that boy.'

Gracie was relieved and moved into the room. Sylvia was a puzzle to Gracie, who was pretty even tempered.

'Can I sit on your bed?'

'Alright,' shrugged Sylvia. 'But mind my best doll.' she added sharply. Her eyes narrowed. 'Have you got a new dress Gracie?' she asked with accusation in her voice.

Gracie looked down guiltily at her little red and blue plaid cotton sundress with its sweet puff sleeves.

She replied quickly, knowing Sylvia's predisposition towards envy. 'Mrs Anderson made me a new one, I had grown out of my others. I needed a new one.'

The Jenkinsons were far and away better off financially than the Atwells. Sylvia had plenty of her own new dresses which would always be bought from Schofields department store in Leeds. Gracie's dresses were efficiently run up on Mrs Anderson's machine, a popular dressmaker in Westridge. The fabrics were often plain cotton and Ada favoured a simple smocking across the front. She chose bright colours whenever possible which contrasted nicely with Gracie's black hair. Sylvia was not blessed with Gracie's vibrancy. She had inherited Amy's wan colouring and her virtually lash less eyes were the colour of mushroom soup. She often had a disgruntled demeanour which added an almost unpleasant ugly element to her face. Some of the village boys were starting to notice Ian's little sister and Sylvia was acutely aware of that fact.

Sometimes Gracie wondered why she bothered trying to be friends with Sylvia. Her brothers referred to her as the moody mare next door. When she was feeling agreeable though she could be a lot of fun and she didn't mind playing dolls with Gracie. She had quite a good imagination and they would make up a little world under her bed which contained pirates, wizards, princesses and all manner of mythical creatures. They made miniature gardens on plates and hunted for ladybirds to live in them. She could also be generous when it suited her, lending Gracie books and sharing her plentiful sweets.

Even at the tender age of seven Gracie was aware that Amy Jenkinson was not a particularly attentive mother and she felt sorry for Sylvia. Unfortunately this morning Sylvia was not feeling agreeable and eventually Gracie gave up, muttering a vague excuse about helping her mother with some baking and beat a retreat out of Sylvia's bedroom.

Gracie decided it was too nice a day to try to untangle Sylvia's mood so headed outside again for the decidedly more cheerful company of Joe and Ian. They split the apple pie and feasted without worry, safe in the knowledge that Amy would not even notice it had gone, let alone care. They spent a very pleasant hour taking the brakes of Joe's bike apart and cleaning and oiling, ever hopeful that it would solve the rather inexplicable issue of the brakes jamming on for no apparent reason.

They heard Ada's voice drifting over the fence, calling Gracie and Ian in for lunch.

They scrambled back through the hedge giving Joe a perfunctory wave. Ian dared himself to take one last glance at Amy's ballerina legs, hoping to get one final look at her stocking tops.

They ran upstairs for a lightning change of clothes, they had both got rather a lot of oil on their things. Gracie felt a bit guilty, as her dress was new. She decided to show it to Ada after lunch and offer to try to scrub the oil out herself. Ada never raised her voice to any of the children but she did have a way of looking over her reading glasses with a disappointed expression, if they had caused some mischief, which Gracie couldn't stand.

They both jostled for the carbolic soap in the bathroom to wash their hands, then shot downstairs. Every ready for more food.

The dining room was quite compact. It was cheerfully decorated with wallpaper covered in pale pink peonies on a soft gold background. It contained a large fireplace which rather dominated the small room. Ada displayed her few best bits of china on the mantelpiece. The family ate in the kitchen during the week but Walter liked to use the dining room at the weekend. Edward, Robert and Walter were already seated round the table, as was Clara, much to the joy of Ian and Gracie. It was a bit of a squash round the old dark table but no one minded. Robert had left school and had become a trainee plumber, he boxed along with Ian and played the trumpet. His main preoccupation was girls and he had quite a following. He was currently sporting a black eye he had received from a fight the previous week where he had been surprised by his opponent's very sneaky left jab. Ian had teased him about it mercilessly but Robert didn't really mind because it had generated a lot of tender sympathy from his girlfriends.

Edward, Walter's oldest son was sat quietly at the table alongside Walter. They were speaking in hushed tone about the disturbances in Europe. Edward was a deep thinker and was beginning to seriously worry. Edward had always been a sensitive boy and didn't have the lightness that the rest of Walter's children had inherited from him. Walter knew that the only way to relieve his worries was just to listen and let Edward talk and reason for himself. Edward never responded to comforting platitudes. As a child he was old enough to remember the morning his lovely mother Stella died from Spanish flu. He was sitting in their kitchen eating his porridge, telling her about the tadpoles he had found in the little stream close by their house. He watched in surprise as she suddenly fell to the floor in a crumpled heap dropping the mug of tea that she was nursing. He sat for a while staring at the tea as it spread across the stone floor and ran into Stella's beautiful russet hair making it damp. Her face had taken on a frightening grey tinge, leaving no doubt in Edward's mind that his mother was very ill indeed. Baby Ian's cries from his pram broke the spell. Edward gave Robert stern instructions not to move from his little stool at the breakfast table, which Robert had obeyed, staring at Stella with big fearful eyes. Edward had run as fast as his legs would carry him to the house of their village Doctor.

Edward was heartbroken and carried that sadness through his young life. Subsequently he had always observed the world with caution, knowing that bad things really did happen to good people.

The serious mood was broken by Gracie and Ian erupting into the room, still jostling with one another. They were still sporting a fair amount of grime from their morning's activities, despite their best efforts. Walter smiled indulgently at his two youngest.

Ada came in staggering under the weight of an enormous lamb casserole with rosemary and dumplings. There was already two steaming bowls of peas and carrots on the table. She began ladling it out onto plates. The room was filled with the fragrant warmth of onions and gravy.

'Mmmm,' sniffed Edward appreciatively. 'That looks smashing mother.'

Ada gave him a smile and felt pleased she was appreciated.

Robert flashed a quick glance at Ian 'I'm not sure about the peas, they look distinctly shabby. It is as if they haven't been properly popped.'

'Oh,' protested Ian, taking the bait immediately. 'Me and Gracie podded those peas and they are just fine aren't they Gracie? It took us ruddy ages. You say we had done them nicely mother didn't you?'

'Robert give over, Ian no swearing,' said Ada automatically.

Ian punched Robert on the arm.

'Ian,' warned Walter.

'Gracie look there is an aeroplane. Look, look,' said Ian urgently.

Gracie looked out of the window into an expanse of empty sky. Ian had taken the opportunity to plunge his fork into Gracie's stew and pop a large piece of her lamb straight into his mouth.

'Laddie,' said Walter again in a much sterner voice.

Ian looked uncomfortable for a moment. Then smiled his most charming wide grin at Ada. 'This is lovely mother.' Ada tutted at him in admonishment but couldn't hide her own smile.

Clara ruffled Gracie's hair affectionately. 'You need to sharpen up Gracie,' she boomed. 'Don't let that little beast get the better of you.'

Clara was tucking into a huge pile of stew and making appreciative noises as she rapidly dispatched it, spilling gravy down her shirt.

Walter said 'Honestly Clara I bet your horses eat with better manners than you. You are not in the stables now.'

Clara winked at Gracie who was gazing at her in delight.

Suddenly Clara put down her knife and fork and looked intently at Gracie.

'What on earth is that behind your ear?' she asked Gracie dramatically.

Gracie looked slightly worried. Clara stretched out her hand and magically produced a penny from behind her ear.

Gracie was amazed.

'How did you do that?' demanded Ian.

I travel round the world hunting for the most powerful tobaccos and I met a mystical shaman who taught me many, many magic tricks. Now eat your dinner before I turn you into a frog.'

Edward cleared his throat.

'Could you put the water on at three please mum? I'd like to take a bath, I am taking Dorothy to a dance tonight.'

'You are taking Dorothy, are you sure Dotty is not taking you?' chipped in Robert.

'Don't call her Dotty I told you she hates it,' protested Edward.

'All right, all right,' said Robert with his hands up. 'I wouldn't dare cross Lady Dorothy I would end up with another black eye for sure. Here have another potato to keep your strength up.'

Dorothy was Edward's new girlfriend. A statuesque, haughty looking blonde. She worked at Schofields department store in the haberdashery department. Dorothy was the same age as Edward but such was the force of her personality, she had already been promoted to manageress of the busy section. She dressed in the very latest fashion, always in the very brightest of colours. She was a little plumper than she imagined herself to be so her clothes were always on the tight side. Nevertheless she cut an impressive figure.

'Is Dorothy coming round here first?' asked Gracie hopefully.

Gracie admired Dorothy tremendously.

The family had first been introduced to Dorothy a couple of months previously. It was in fact the first time Edward had ever brought a girl home. The family were sat in the front room politely eating Ada's scones and drinking tea from their best china. Walter was dressed uncomfortably in his best suit and Ada had made two kinds of cake. Dorothy seemed very much at ease and was staunchly ignoring both Gracie and Ian who were staring at her, unabashed. Edward seemed a little nervous and kept jumping up and pouring more tea into already full cups.

There was only one awkward moment when Gracie piped up 'Oh I think I have seen you before, on the bead stall.'

Dorothy looked pained and said imperiously. 'I think you are referring to Schofields haberdashery department dear.

Gracie went red, feeling she might have upset Dorothy but not really knowing why.

'Oh yes that is exactly what I mean, sorry.'

Dorothy looked down at Gracie and quickly relented.

'Well we do stock an excellent range of beads I suppose. Come and say hello next time and I will show you the new stock.'

Gracie was delighted.

Chapter 9

1940

'Dad, Dad,' yelled Ian in his customary way. 'Come into the front room, me and Gracie have composed a little song, it's quite good if you want to hear it.'

Walter was in the garden trying removed the big puddle that was filling the floor of their Anderson shelter.

Walter made his way back into the house, shaking off his muddy wellingtons at the door. All three boys still lived at home, Edward and Robert were both saving madly to get married and move out to start new lives with their respective fiancés. Dorothy had bestowed Edward the honour of graciously accepting when he asked for her hand in marriage. Robert had been courting a lively, fun loving girl called Rita. They made a very cheerful couple and were managing to live life to the full despite the onset of the war.

Walter sat down cautiously in the front room, he was beginning to have a bit of trouble with lumbago. He hated getting older.

Gracie sat down at her piano. Walter and Ada had saved hard for a year to buy her this wonderful instrument. Gracie had to remind herself of that fact when she gloomily bashed out the scales in her daily practice. She was taught by a Miss Harbour, which wasn't much fun either. Miss Harbour did sometimes make her laugh though because she would dreamily keep time with her baton often dropping it when she got carried away with a tune. Miss Harbour would bend down to retrieve the stick and reveal red lace trimmed bloomers just above stout wool socks. Gracie and Ian would laugh about it.

Gracie began to play the jaunty tune they had written and Ian was playing his trumpet as softly as he could so as not to drown out the piano. Robert and Edward appeared at the door of the front room to listen.

They ran back up to their rooms to fetch their banjo and violin and joined Gracie and Ian. The family went on to play all old favourite tunes together for a good hour. Ada and Clara had joined them. Clara was tapping out the rhythm on her solid tweed clad thighs and was singing lustily.

After one last rousing tune of Roll out the Barrel they decided they had had enough. The family sat round the fireplace on an assortment of mismatched chairs. Gracie sat on the floor at Walter's feet, leaning against his bony leg.

Ada stood up.

'Cocoa everyone, it is getting a bit chilly out there? See if you can get the fire going again Ian will you love?'

'Mother, can you sit down for a moment...please? Me, Robert and Ian need to have a word with you and father.' Edward's voice was serious and stopped Ada in her tracks. She exchanged an anxious look with Walter.

'Of course, what is it?'

She sat down. Her legs felt weak. She knew what they were going to say. She found she was holding her breath.

Edward cleared his throat.

'Mother, father, we have decided to join up.'

Ada and Walter absorbed the announcement in silence. Ada put her hand to her mouth and found she couldn't speak. Clara stood beside Ada and put a large comforting hand on her shoulder.

The clock ticked loudly. Gracie stayed perfectly still, not daring to move for fear of disturbing the tension that had filled the room.

Eventually Walter sighed deeply and said 'All right boys if that is what you need to do, then we won't stop you. You mind you be careful out there. It is not a game, I have been there myself.' His voice cracked ever so slightly and he turned away and took hold of the poker and prodded the fire roughly.

Ada stood up again and hurried out of the room, not trusting herself to speak. She wanted to grab each boy and howl. She went into the kitchen, ran a bucket of water and began scrubbing the already clean floor on her hands and knees.

Walter looked back at his three sons. So young, full of life and hope. He had served in the First World War and the thought that his boys would experience even a fraction of his time served in the British army broke his heart.

He repeated, almost to himself this time.

'If that is what you need to do then we won't stop you.'

Gracie was also staring up at her big brothers.

They are going to be soldiers. She thought. She smiled up at their handsome faces. She was so proud of them. All at once a rush of emotion filled her chest and she burst into tears. Walter gathered her up in his arms, as if she was small, and rocked her against his chest.

'There now lassie,' he said gently. 'Don't take on so.'

The boys quietly left the room together, understanding their parents might need a moment to absorb the news. Ian was a little perturbed, he thought they would be cheering at their bravery. Edward and Robert understood, they both remember losing their real mother Stella, they had experienced loss, they also knew that when you went to war, you didn't always come back.

Walter and Gracie stayed clinging to each other watching the fire die slowly in the grate.

Gracie soon found herself standing at Leeds station, at the age of thirteen, clutching Ada and Walter hands. Clara was standing next to Ada and Ada was leaning slightly on her shoulder as if she was trying to draw strength from her older sister's presence. Clara was silent, almost overwhelmed by the memory of waving off her only love, Arthur, from this very same station.

It was incredibly noisy in the station and the people were jostling like ants. There was lots of jocular, forced laughter which rose up along with the hot wet steam released by the great powerful trains. The Atwell family stood quietly amongst the hustle. Walter and Ada both sporting smiles that didn't quite reach their bewildered eyes. Clara, Robert and Ian had been valiantly discussing a comedy show they had listened to on the wireless the night before but eventually their conversation dried up.

A train had pulled up at their platform and somehow its magnificent solid presence reassured Gracie. At least they would be safe on the very first leg of the journey of their trip away from home. The huge train would look after them for a while.

Gracie hugged them each in turn. Ian picked her up and spun her round until she squealed, laughing.

'I will miss you Gracie,' he said looking into her eyes, suddenly serious. His voice was gruff with emotion.

Dorothy and Rita had come along to wave their brave men off, bright smiles plastered on their faces and fear in their hearts.

Robert put a gentle hand on Ian's shoulder.

'Come on, our kid, it's time to go.'

The train let out a deafening screech and made them all jump.

The Atwell sons boarded the train. Robert with his arm still round Ian's shoulder to steady him and Edward in the lead, his serious mouth set in a grim line as he searched for space in the crammed carriage.

Walter, Clara, Ada and Gracie stayed on the platform and watched the train depart. Gracie had been waving madly and when the train disappeared round the bend of the track, found she couldn't stop waving.

Clara caught her wrist and enveloped her in a tight hug for a moment. Gracie's face itched against the rough tweed of Clara's jacket.

'Here Gracie, love, I've brought a quarter of sherbet lemons. I thought we might need a dose of sugar.' They walk slowly along the platform of the big station. Gracie still hand in hand with her mother. Walter and Clara dropped behind and were talking together in hushed tones. Gracie had always loved sherbet lemons but she found she had lost her taste for them that afternoon.

The house was very quiet that summer and Gracie missed her brothers unbearably. She went to school and knocked about with Joe and Sylvia on a weekend. Sylvia had taken on the role of Gracie's absolute best friend and was making a sterling effort to be kind. They spent a lot of time riding round the village and up through the woods.

Often taking picnics, although rations were strict and so the feasts were sparse.

Sylvia and Joe both loved the cinema. They would often pay for Gracie to come along with them, if she had already spent the little pocket money Walter gave her on a Saturday morning. Sylvia and Joe seemed to have plenty of their own money. They would dip constantly into Amy's purse and take her housekeeping. This arrangement fascinated Gracie.

'Doesn't she mind?' Gracie would ask.

Joe and Sylvia would shrug and say they always ask her and she just tells them to take what they want.

'Sometimes, I am not sure she cares what we do, you know Gracie.' Joe would look sad.

Sylvia would often mimic the starlets she had watched on the big screen, pouting and flicking her hair around, sometimes even adopting an American accent for the day. She took herself rather seriously, to Gracie and Joe's amusement. Sylvia would irritate Gracie at times because she sometimes would moan that she didn't have any brothers to worry about as if she envied Gracie's situation, as if Gracie were a tragic heroine in one of their Saturday matinees. She once asked Gracie what she would wear to the funeral if they died and Gracie got so upset she gave her a great shove and knocked her off her bike. They made friends a couple of days later.

Clara came round often and she, Ada and Gracie would sit round the kitchen table on an evening, playing cards. She continued to practice her piano every day to please Walter but she didn't feel like singing along. Walter tended to leave his girls to it and sit in the front room nursing a small whiskey. They all stayed resolutely cheerful and even tempered but their worries had a ghostlike presence, always hovering above them.

One night Gracie was too hot to sleep and she crept downstairs to get a small glass of milk which was kept cool on the larder floor. As she past the front room she heard the old rocking chair creak. She pushed open the door cautiously. Walter was sat in chair staring unseeingly into the empty fire grate with an empty glass held loosely in his hand.

He was muttering to himself.

'Stella, my Stella, my boys.'

Gracie reversed out of the doorway and ran lightly back to her room, forgetting about her glass of milk.

A couple of weeks later Gracie was sat with Clara having a rousing game of knock out-whist. She could hear the birds trilling and the sunshine was streaming in through the open kitchen door. She hoped the bright clean sun was shining on her brothers. Ada had her hands wrapped round a hot cup of tea watching their game quietly.

'Gracie, love,' said Ada in her steady voice.

'I need to talk to you.' She took a large gulp of tea, as if it were medicine.

'We live near the airport as you know.'

Gracie nodded enthusiastically. She loved the airport and she and Joe had taken to riding up there on an evening. They couldn't get close of course but they could just about make out the grass covered roofs topped with pretend cows. A foxy ruse to confuse the Germans if they made it over in their planes.

'It has been decided that the children of Westridge might not be safe, so you might all be sent on a little holiday to Ripon.'

'Do you mean I am going to be evacuated Mum?' Gracie's voice trembled a little.

Ada nodded not trusting herself to speak. Her face was pale and she was shaking a little.

Clara put her hand over Ada's. 'It will only be for a while Gracie and it will be marvellous fun. A little holiday. Ripon is a pretty little town, you will like it. I expect Joe and Sylvia will be going along too.'

Gracie stood up straight to her full height, took a deep breath and said 'if that is what I need to do, then you won't stop me,' in a funny echo of Walter's words to her brothers.

'Good girl,' said Clara in loud approval. 'What a brave lot you are, makes me proud. It won't be for long dear I am sure. I have heard we are giving that Hitler a damn good thrashing.'

Chapter 10

Gracie was rather enjoying being evacuated. On the day of their departure Walter had agreed to drive Sylvia and Joe to the station. Ada wasn't going to accompany them because she had woken up with a blinding headache, no doubt with the stress of her young daughter being sent to goodness knows where to avoid the bombs. She and Gracie had said a sensible goodbye and Ada had hugged her daughter hard.

Walter and Gracie approached the Jenkinson's house next door only to witness a frightful scene. Sylvia was screaming at the top of her voice that she refused to go to Ripon. Amy was sat at the kitchen table with her eyes closed and her fingers in her ears. Sylvia had in her arms a paper bag of apples and was throwing them at Bill with all her might. Bill was easily dodging them and laughing loudly which only served to infuriate Sylvia more. Poor Joe was standing close to his mother watching Sylvia with his mouth open.

Walter and Gracie stood in the open kitchen doorway, not really daring to enter for fear of being hit by Sylvia's missiles. When Bill noticed them he turned and waved genially. Sylvia took advantage of his inattention and threw another apple. A particularly large Cox's Pippen caught him smartly on the ear. Bill jumped through the kitchen door outside to join Walter and Gracie and slammed the door behind him.

'Should send Sylvia to the front line, that little cow would be more than a match for Jerry.' He gave Gracie a big smile and squeezed her shoulder.

'Watch out for those country bumpkins Gracie, they are going to love you.'

Walter started to look uncomfortable.

Bill notice the change in his expression and quickly let go of Gracie.

'I think I had better take Sylvia and Joe to the station myself thanks all the same Walter old chap. Give Sylvia a chance to calm down. I feel sorry for the beggars who have to live with that crazy mare for the next few months. Mad as a hatter like Amy. I will miss Joe though. Do you have trouble with your women, Walter?'

Walter shook his head and gave Bill a bland smile.

'Right then, we best be off.' Walter decided to hurry along. He was relieved he didn't have to try to bundle Sylvia on a train and he didn't want Bill to change his mind. He flashed a glance at Gracie, standing quietly beside him and marvelled once again at what a blessing she had turned out to be.

Ada and Walter each privately worried that without Gracie's merry presence in their house they would become ill with the weight of their concerns over the boys. They both thought that Gracie would be alright in Ripon. She had a sensible head on her shoulders and even if she did miss her family, she would actively seek out friendship with new people and at least attempt to stay cheerful.

They reached Leeds station and it was once again busy with soldiers in their drab khaki uniforms. They pushed their way through the noisy throngs of people to find the Ripon bound train. Gracie gripped Walter's arm. In her hand was a small neat brown suitcase which contained her cardigans and frocks, underwear and two nightdresses. There was also a large bag of toffees and apples from their tree wrapped in brown paper. She had packed two comics and her beloved copies of Little Women and Oliver Twist.

She breathed in the metallic damp. She wished Sylvia and Joe were travelling with her.

Suddenly an efficient looking girl with a clipboard appeared as if from nowhere out of the great clouds of hot swirling steam. She was very smartly dressed in a green jumper with a diamond on her shoulder and khaki trousers. She had a gabardine coat slung casually round her shoulders. Her clothes almost looked too heavy for her slight body. She had very slim wrists sticking out of the thick jumper cuffs and her trousers were slipping down slightly from her ballerina frame.

She didn't look much older than Gracie.

'Hello there, are you looking for the Ripon train?' she greeted them in a clipped tone and looked enquiringly at Gracie.

'I am Gracie Atwell, being evacuated to Ripon,' she said helpfully.

The land girl scanned her list and ticked her name off with a flourish.

'Right oh. A quick goodbye dearie and hop on the train.'

Walter hugged Gracie tightly.

'I love you, lovely lass,' he said in a gruff voice.

'I know. I will be fine I am only going to Ripon.'

She almost added, 'not to the front,' then changed her mind quickly. They hadn't heard from Edward, Robert or her beloved Ian for a few weeks. Instead she gave him a wide Atwell smile and climbed into the nearest carriage.

The train pulled out of the station a few minutes later with a groan and great big shudder.

Gracie found herself sat next to a bright looking girl of about thirteen. She had a mop of golden hair pinned up tightly in rolls in rather a grown up manner, huge blue eyes and a tiny button nose. She was wearing artfully applied makeup which enhanced her cherubic prettiness. She held out a small plump hand to Gracie in greeting and shook it vigorously.

'Well,' she said in a slightly shrill voice 'this is a rum do make no mistake. I am Ella and it is good to meet you. I am from Otley, you know it?'

Gracie nodded. She had visited the quaint little town when she was younger. They would catch the bus down to the busy market and take a stroll round Titty Bottle Park by the River Wharfe, so named as it was very popular with mothers and nannies with their charges. Otley sheltered under the protective forest of trees of the Chevin Hills which Gracie had explored with other Westridge children when they had tired of exploring their own woods.

'Have you ever had your hair done at En Vogue in the Kirkgate Arcade?' Gracie shook her head and Ella looked disappointed.

'Well that is our shop. Me, my mother and my sisters run it and we all live in the flat above. I am still in boring old school of course but I can't wait to leave and start my hairdressing training, unless this ruddy war carries on, then I want to join the Wrens. I am going to have my own salon one day and make a fortune. I won't need to rely on a boring old husband then. I will be able to look after myself. That's the way Gracie you know, us girls will need to look after ourselves.'

'Yorkshire mixture?' Ella thrust a sticky bag at Gracie. Gracie accepted a large, slightly fluffy humbug.

'What do you think of the name En Vogue?' she demanded.

'Oh very nice, sounds chic,' replied Gracie.

Ella sat back on her seat and nodded approvingly.

'I thought of it. It's got style and flair that's what I reckon and it's French.' She declared looking expectantly at Gracie for further approval.

Gracie grinned at her new friend and nodded back at her. Figuring she would have to take the big humbug back out of her mouth to reply properly.

Ella beamed back, satisfied.

She casually leaned forward and picked up a thick strand of Gracie's hair between two small fingers.

'You've got smashing hair. I could do a lot with that. Should we try and bunk together do you reckon?'

'Well I am not sure it is up to us,' began Gracie doubtfully.

Ella interrupted.

'Well I have heard we will all stand in the church hall or some such place and the people pick whoever they fancy the look of. A bit like at school when they pick teams.'

Gracie really didn't like the sound of that.

'If we stand together we might get picked as a pair, you know. My sister Joycie said I don't want to end up on my own on some farm miles away from anywhere.'

'It might be nice on a farm if they keep animals,' said Gracie somewhat naively.

Ella shook her head firmly, causing any loose curls to bounce around.

'Gracie. You don't want some old farmer's son rummaging round in your draws on an evening, do you?'

Gracie went red and gave a gasp of shocked laughter.

'Because that is what some men are like,' said Ella with authority. 'That is what my Joycie says. Some men are pigs. Joycie took on an evening job at the flicks, you know as an usher, selling the old ices and shining the torch round. She had her eye on a mink and mum said if she wanted it she would have to get an extra job because there was no way she was getting a raise not with there being a war on and such. Anyway within two weeks old Mr Beaumont, the manager, was down her blouse like a bloody ferret. My Joycie was having none of it and kneed him straight in the knackers. That stopped his gallop, rotten old goat. She is still working there, she had got the mink and she is now saving for the matching hat, she looks smashing.'

The two girls laughed loudly together.

Ella chatted on relentlessly for the entire journey. Gracie didn't mind. She had already decided she liked the vivacious girl. Ella was a year younger than Gracie but seemed much older in her both her dress and worldly-wise opinions. She swore copiously and offered Gracie a cigarette. Gracie refused, she had tried them but they made her feel sick and dizzy. By the time the train had pulled into Ripon's small station the girls had agreed to be friends for the duration of their stay. They alighted the train along with a rabble of about twenty other children and looked around.

Two jolly looking girl guides, aged about fifteen were waving madly at the children and trotted purposefully towards them.

'Hello kids,' they shrilled. 'Come along with us, we've been sent to collect you. Follow us, we are heading to the town hall. Just a short walk. Trot on. When we get there you will be organised by Miss Mountshaft, the billeting officer.'

They entered the hall together. It smelt of damp and dust. Great cracks were snaking their way up the walls and large flakes of paint were hanging down from the ceiling.

A collection of solemn looking adults, many of them in rough work clothes turned to look carefully at the children.

'I told you,' whispered Ella piercingly. 'They are picking out the best kids, you know the big lads will be wanted on the farms to help. Remember what I said. Here hold my hand a minute.' Gracie did as she was told. She suddenly felt an overwhelming wave of homesickness. She was glad that Ella had taken her under her confident wing. Miss Mountshaft scurried over to the children. She was one of the schoolteachers. She was young and smiled warmly at the collection of bemused children standing before her.

'Welcome to Ripon. I hope you have a pleasant stay. I am Miss Mountshaft and I shall be sorting out whose house you are going to stay at. I am also one of our schoolteachers so some of you will see me when you start at our school. Right then, line up everyone, this shouldn't take long.' Each one of the children hoped they would be staying with her.

The children lined up along the edge of the hall and a couple of the smaller children started to cry. Gracie began to move towards a tiny boy who was sobbing in a corner. Ella gripped Gracie's hand tightly and shook her head.

'Stay here a minute,' she hissed 'you don't want to get stuck with the little one.'

A twittering woman of about fifty came rushing up to Ella and Gracie. Her body was positively brimming with energy. She skidded to a halt in front of them and clapped her hands.

'Yes, you two I think. We have room for two and you look like pleasant girls, from good backgrounds. Good, good Mr Smith will be pleased. He specifically said he didn't want boys, they were too noisy and what with his nerves you know. He gets these heads you see. You look healthy. You will do nicely.' She was nodding her head up and down while she was talking.

She was wearing a droopy tea dress in a rather violent shade of purple. She had accessorised with lots of strings of beads and had unaccountably added three different scarves around her neck in various sorbet shades. Her hair was wispy and she wore it long, possibly a little too long for her age. She had attempted to pin it up and there also appeared to be a pencil sticking out of the back of her messy bun. She must have stuck it there in a moment of distraction. Her hair was a startling shade of bright ginger and clashed gloriously with her dress.

She spun round and galloped up to Miss Mountshaft who was beginning to look harassed, as she tried to comfort the crying children and organise the older ones.

'I am taking those two' the lady said forcefully to Miss Mountshaft with great finality.

Miss Mountshaft muttered something about ticking off lists but nodded in agreement.

Ella winked at Gracie. 'She looks alright. We are together, what fantastic luck.'

Gracie thought that it wasn't luck and if the hapless adults had tried to separate them, then Ella would have proven to have been an obstinate force to be reckoned with.

Gracie felt herself cheer up.

Ella released her hand and made her way to the small boy who was still squashing himself in the dusty corner of the hall. She put her arm kindly round him and gave him a pear drop.

'Don't you worry little soldier. I will make sure you go somewhere nice. Are you missing your mother?'

The boy nodded and wiped his nose on the back of his cardigan sleeve.

'Do you know what, I am missing mine too.'

Ella was as good as her word. She quickly scanned the room for a kindly face. She wouldn't let him go to any of the old biddies or hulking looking farmers and their great hulking wives. She shrewdly spotted a young woman who had her own small boy in tow. He looked like a friendly little lad and the woman had a nice open face. Ella managed to catch her eye and nodded to her pushing the sad little evacuee toward her. The woman crouched down to speak to him and her son shyly held out a toy car as a present. Ella hoped it would be a good match, there wasn't really anything else she could do for the poor mite.

Ella returned to Gracie who was making polite conversation with their new landlady, as such, Mrs Smith.

She introduced herself to Ella.

'I am Mrs Smith, the proprietor of the finest greengrocer's shop in Ripon.' She make this statement in a loud voice and looked round fiercely in case anyone was daring to dispute her.

'I am Ella and this is Gracie. We are very pleased to meet you.'

Mrs Smith looked delighted. 'What nice names. Oh yes it is all coming together beautifully. I cannot tell you how Mr Smith has fretted over this but we all must do our bit. Lovely manners too. Come along then, let's go and see my shop.'

As the newly formed trio exited the hall. Bill, Sylvia and Joe were coming along the road. Joe and Sylvia waved enthusiastically smiling at Gracie, delighted to see her. Sylvia's face froze when she noticed Ella with her arm linked with Gracie's. She began to scowl disapprovingly.

'We aren't late are we Gracie?' yelled Joe anxiously, even though he was now only four feet away from them. He felt giddy with nerves.

'No it will be fine. Just go straight in. I will see you really soon I promise.' Gracie soothed her friend.

'I will see you soon Syl,' she added but Sylvia was fixing Ella with a gimlet glare.

'Oh yes madam,' thought Ella mischievously. 'A bit jelly of Gracie's new friend are we? Well I shall be on my guard with you.'

The Jenkinsons disappeared into the dark hall.

Mrs Smith was racing along the high street at a cracking pace and the girls had to break into a trot to keep up with her flying feet. They skidded to a halt in front of a smart greengrocer's shop in the centre of the busy street.

Mrs Smith waved her arms expansively.

'This is your new home girls. Welcome to Smith's Greengrocer's Emporium.' she said grandly.

'It is super,' said Gracie in what she hoped was a sufficiently admiring tone.

Mrs Smith bowed her head, seemingly giving her great store a moment of honorary silence.

Gracie and Ella exchanged glances and tried not to giggle.

They trooped upstairs to the Smith's spacious apartment above the shop. It was clean and very tidy with a faint tang of vegetables in the air. Their furniture was old but very well cared for. The rooms would be rather dull if it wasn't for the large bright canvasses hung around the room. They were absolutely enormous and were covered in wild daubs of paint in madly clashing colours.

Gracie turned to Mrs Smith.

'These paintings,' she began.

Mrs Smith clutched her hands dramatically to her chest.

'Girls, girls do you love them? They are my very own little doodles. My creative outlet. So good for the soul. Sometimes I even get up in the middle of the night, I have to warn you, when the urge overtakes my being and I simply have to release my creative energies. I am guided by my wonderful spirits and I paint with my eyes totally shut.

'Do you love them?' she looked eagerly at her new houseguests.

'Mrs Smith they are absolutely wonderful,' Gracie said truthfully.

Mrs Smith turned to Ella with her eyes narrowed, sensing she wasn't quite as enthusiastic as Gracie about her beloved creations.

She gestured towards a particularly startling example. A combination of turquoise and lime green swirls topped with scarlet splodges. It would have been rather jazzy if it wasn't for the slightly off- putting dry apple cores and kipper bones that had been rather inexplicably stuck in the centre with a large amount of Gloy glue. It was emanating a very strong fishy smell. Gracie wasn't sure if it was the glue or the fish bones themselves.

'I call this one, the moon rises over the pool of happy tears whilst collecting my thoughts.'

Ella studied it carefully for a moment.

'Is that the moon?' she asked innocently, pointing to the kipper.

'No dear.' Mrs Smith almost snapped. 'You are required to sense the presence of it, feel its power, as if you were the sea's tides doing its bidding.'

Ella nodded sagely. Winking at Gracie when Mrs Smith was gazing back lovingly at her latest creation.

Mrs Smith clapped her hands, jangling a great number of bracelets on her wrists.

'I thought you would be hungry after your journey so I have made us rabbit stew and dumplings.'

'Lovely,' chorused the girls.

'I have put you in the attic room, just up those stairs.'

She pointed to a small white door in the corner of the kitchen. 'There is a wash stand up there so you can tend to your ablutions. Mr Smith will be along shortly after he has closed the emporium.'

They made their way up the tiny rickety staircase. They had to hold on to the walls with their hands to steady themselves as the climb was almost perpendicular.

The attic room opened out before them. It was a large warm room containing two white hospital- style iron beds each covered in a bright patchwork quilt. There was a large wash stand with a mirror above it. There was a blanket box and a wardrobe for the girls to share. The entire room, including the wooden floor had been recently whitewashed by the ever energetic Mrs Smith. The room also had a lingering smell of white spirit and had been used by Mrs Smith as her studio in happier times, when she would paint in the nude in the dead of night, listening to her guiding spirits and responding with her brushes.

The girls loved it. There was a large window that gave them a splendid view of the old clock in the market square. It let in lots of light. Mrs Smith had displayed a collection of her amateur daubs at the other side of the room. There was no indication of shape or form but she had used various shades of green and blue paint. Displayed against the stark white walls and lit by the sunshine they looked wonderful.

Ella put her bag down on one of the beds.

'I think we have hit the jackpot here, Gracie my girl,' she said happily. 'Not sure if Mrs Smith might be a bit scatty but she seems alright and if she wants to roll around in paint on an evening with her ghosts then that is her business.'

She opened her little suitcase and pulled out a tiny beaded bag. She opened it and showed Gracie the treasures inside. It was crammed full of lipstick, pan stick and mascara block.

'You can borrow all this if you like,' she offered generously.

She saw Gracie hesitate.

'It's only for practice don't worry,' she said quickly. 'I am not allowed to wear it yet either. Me Dad says I am too young yet, in fact he said he would belt me one if he catches me dolled up like a dog's dinner.' She rolled her eyes and grinned.

'Girls.' Mrs Smith's slightly squeaky voice drifted up the staircase.

They climbed cautiously back down the wooden staircase. The dinner smelt wonderful and the girls were ravenous.

At the table sat Mr Smith. A tall morose looking man with thinning hair and a turned down mouth.

'This is Mr Smith, girls, and he was just saying how much he was looking forward to your stay here. Weren't you Mr Smith?' she looked hopefully at him, willing him to reply.

He nodded gloomily.

Mrs Smith smiled delightedly.

Mr Smith cleared his throat a number of times and stared at his knife and fork. They all looked expectantly at him.

After a long pause he said in a dull monotone, 'You haven't seen the paper have you?'

'No sorry. We have only just arrived. If I see it I will pass it on to you immediately.' said Ella helpfully.

'Right,' he said neutrally, avoiding Ella's beady gaze.

Mrs Smith clapped effusively again.

'Wonderful. We are all getting along splendidly.'

They took their seats round the table.

'Blessing, Mr Smith?' prompted Mrs Smith.

The girls put their hands together and closed their eyes.

'Dear Lord,' droned Mr Smith, 'we thank you for the wonderful food.'

'Particularly the asparagus,' interjected Mrs Smith, 'which is really quite superb this season.'

'Particularly the asparagus.' repeated Mr Smith. 'Forgive us our trespasses and keep Gerald in your tender care up in heaven.'

Mrs Smith interrupted once again this time with a loud strangled sob.

Gracie and Ella opened their eyes in alarm.

'Amen,' said Mr Smith, seemingly unmoved.

Ella and Gracie began tucking into large bowls of wonderful aromatic stew. It was mainly vegetables but little rabbit that was contained in the casserole had been marinated beforehand in juniper berries and a dash of gin to enhance its mild game flavour. Mrs Smith's creativity expanded beyond her avant-garde painting and into other aspects of her life.

Gracie looked over to Mrs Smith who was dabbing her eyes with a handkerchief.

'Girls, this terrible war is bringing so much sadness to us all. I hope you will be happy here and not miss your mothers too much.'

Ella smiled at her. 'We are fine. You don't need to worry yourself. The room is really great and this stew is smashing.'

'You must be wondering who Gerald was?' Mrs Smith enquired definitely.

Gracie quickly interrupted her. 'It's alright, you need not tell us if you don't want. You seem upset.'

Mr Smith was solidly eating his way through his stew seemingly oblivious to his wife's distress.

'I will fetch you a photograph.' Mrs Smith said bravely.

Gracie braced herself to admire the inevitable photograph of a hopeful young man looking smart in his uniform. The same as the three photographs that took pride of place on Ada's mantle-piece at home.

Therefore, she was surprised to be gazing upon a picture of a fat cocker spaniel with a jaunty blue bow tied round his neck looking balefully at the camera.

Gracie released the breath she had been holding in relief.

'He is a handsome fella,' said Ella approvingly.

'He was, girls, he was my soul mate. He was only fifteen when he died.'

'That sounds like a good age,' said Gracie gently.

Mrs Smith nodded. 'We all have to do our duty, girls. When Mr Smith built our Anderson shelter he told me that Mr Churchill, God bless him, had decreed no animals to be kept in the shelters. An order directly from London you understand. Mr Smith was most concerned I had to carry Gerald round because he could no longer walk and if he was left in the emporium when the bombs started to drop he would have been ever so frightened without me, his mother. I went to seek the advice of Mr Watson our vet. Mr Watson said it might be the kindest thing to put him to sleep, after all there is a war on and he had a little trouble with his poopsies, Gerald, not Mr Watson, not his fault of course. Girls it was so terrible. If I ever met that Hitler wouldn't I give him a piece of my mind.'

She burst into noisy sobs. The girls jumped up and patted her heaving shoulder soothingly.

Mr Smith continued to masticate, ignoring the hysterical scene before him.

The girls quickly settled into their new lives in Ripon. They really liked the energetic, quick-witted Mrs Smith and her bohemian ways. She was an excellent cook, with an almost magical way with herbs and spices. She made very good use of any fruit and vegetables that were on the turn. She was always brimming with gossip from the shop and over their evening meal would share the colourful stories of the day. It seemed, like in most small towns, alliances between inhabitants changed on a daily basis. Ella in particular enjoyed the gossip, it reminded her of home and the hair salon where slanderous chat was part of daily business.

A lot of the chatter went over Gracie's head, she was used to a quieter life at home. She was never entirely sure which resident Mrs Smith was pronouncing vengeful judgement upon. She decided it was safest to listen politely and always agree. Besides it was almost impossible to interrupt her once she had got the bit between her teeth. She had a keen sense of right and wrong and would deliver her vehement opinions with the relentless force of a tommy gun. Mrs Smith also took great joy from her life as well and loved nothing more than when the children of the town came into their shop. She made it her business to paint an abstract picture for each new baby born to her customers and bestow it as a gift.

The girls never tried to engage Mr Smith in their conversations. The longest sentence he ever seemed to utter was to his wife. 'You know best Mrs Smith.'

Sometimes he would seem to gather all his energies and attempt a conversation. Usually some comment about the weather. He would flash suspicious glances at the girls, regarding them as unpredictable, dangerous creatures and when they would nod genially in agreement he would disappear back behind his paper in relief that he had done his duty.

Mrs Smith spoke on his behalf the rest of the time whilst he would sit in silence, listening to the wireless, hidden behind the protection of the broadsheet. Mrs Smith didn't appear to notice that she never got any response from her husband and wittered at him relentlessly.

She seemed to adore this shy man and sang his praises to the rooftops to anyone who listened.

The evacuees attended a school close by in the mornings. The resident children of Ripon were now having to continue their education on an afternoon. Gracie and Ella would come home for lunch and help Mrs Smith with one or two chores. They would assist in the shop for a few hours if they were needed, which Ella thoroughly enjoyed. They also had plenty of time to themselves. Ripon had accepted evacuees from all over Leeds. Some of the poor mites were thin and pale looking and had only arrived in the clothes they stood up in. Gracie and Ella became inseparable and were popular in the little school. Sylvia and Joe had also managed to be billeted together with a kindly old couple. Joe was having a pleasant time as the old man had a superb train set in his attic and let Joe play with it. Joe and Sylvia didn't have grandparents of their own and were experiencing patient kindness from an older generation. Even Sylvia was starting to relax. The old lady was teaching her to knit and bake, skills Amy never considered passing on to Sylvia.

One such sunny evening Gracie and Ella made a new friend. They were swishing their way through a golden field. The hay had been gathered and was standing in a number of huge proud haystacks. The sky brilliant blue of the daytime had faded to a softer baby blue and was streaked with white clouds that had their edges highlighted in pink and gold. Ella was sporting a little sun top. It was white cotton gypsy style with little puff sleeves and was embroidered with scarlet poppies round the neck. It had been her birthday the week before and her sisters had sent it to her in the post. Her plump arms were a golden brown and her blond dancing curls were bleached to almost white. Gracie was wearing a yellow sundress which contrasted nicely with her black hair.

'God this weather is glorious,' said Ella stretching her arms up. 'Let's go down to the stream and dabble our feet in to cool down.' They wandered down the gentle slope of the field to the little bubbling stream that ran alongside hedging that marked the boundary of the farmers land. They both shook off their sandals and cooled their dusty feet in the silky water.

'Pooh!' came a loud voice from behind the hedge. 'What's that stink? Has someone taken their socks off? They had better not be washing their feet in my stream they will kill the fish stone dead!'

Gracie and Ella looked at one another with wide eyes.

Then Ella shouted loudly.

'Just you clear off Thomas Blackburn. I know it's you. No one else would be so rude to two young ladies.'

There was silence then a small dead fish came sailing over the hedge and landed plum in-between Ella and Gracie. They scrambled out of the stream as fast as they could, screeching, and set off running back through the field with their sandals in hand.

'Well I never,' panted Ella, 'such a ruddy cheek.'

'I know, we should have brought the fish home for Mrs Smith's paintings,' agreed Gracie gasping for breath.

They didn't stop running until they reached the shop.

That night, in their lovely cosy attic room, under the eaves, the conversation kept returning to Thomas Blackburn and his partner in crime, older brother William.

'If he thinks I am speaking to him at school tomorrow he has got another thing coming because I shan't because I have never been so insulted in my whole living days.'

Gracie nodded. 'He is an absolute beast. If that dead fish had hit us we would could have been injured or worse caught some kind of disease, like warts or something disgusting.'

The girls dissolved into giggles without really knowing why.

'You can't catch warts from fish,' snorted Ella with tears rolling down her cheeks.

'I know,' gurgled Gracie.

'Girls please I must have quiet tonight. The muse is upon me and the spirits and I simply mustn't be disturbed.' Mrs Smith's voice drifted up the tiny staircase.

'Sorry Mrs Smith,' yelled Ella.

'I hope she has got her clothes on,' chuckled Gracie, quite beside herself now with laughter.

'I'm going to have to go in the pot now,' protested Ella and reached under her bed for a pretty chamber pot decorated with roses. 'I daren't go downstairs.'

They snuggled down under their eiderdowns both grinning to themselves in the dim light.

'I shall never speak to him again,' whispered Ella one last time vehemently.

Tom continued to tease Ella for the rest of the week of course. He had clocked her on her first day at the tiny school and was transfixed. She valiantly batted him away as if he was a pesky fly pretending to be exasperated by his presence. Tom and William were residents of Ripon and lived on a farm about a mile out of the town. Being two strong boys they were expected by their parents to pull their weight around the farm and as a result were both muscular, healthy and tanned. Like most of the children around they were pretty much free to roam around on an evening and often appeared in the fields and woods where Gracie, Ella and many other children congregated, enjoying each other's company.

Gracie was surprised by their regular sudden appearances on an evening but Ella had spied them both out of the attic window hanging around the clock tower, obviously waiting for the two girls and then subsequently following them.

Their favourite place really was the field with the stream. The boys would bring homemade fishing rods and bring little tubs of worms that would make Ella squeal. The girls would bring books and pretend to read, whilst peeping over the unread pages and try to catch the boys' eyes.

One fine evening there were about ten children all loitering together, chatting and teasing. Enjoying the sunshine. Sylvia and Joe were there, sharing a rug with Gracie. Joe was hanging on to Gracie's words and staring at her with worship in his eyes. Gracie didn't seem to notice and was in deep discussion with Sylvia about her trip to the shops in Leeds when she had returned home for the day.

Tom's attempts at fishing were proving to be fruitless that evening and so he threw his rod down in disgust and went and flopped down next to Ella.

She immediately turned her back on him. His hands were still damp from the stream and he reached round and rubbed his hands vigorously on her pink cheeks.

Ella let out a yell.

'Arrrrgggg you are the most annoying boy I have ever met.'

He put his hands under her gypsy top and squeezed her tummy with his icy hands.

Ella was affronted. 'How dare you,' she gasped. 'I ought to knock your ruddy block off.'

'You will have to catch me first.' Both children jumped to their feet and Tom set off running off down the field. Ella tucked her blue gingham skirt in her knickers and gave chase.

Sylvia rolled her eyes.

'Poor Tom, she is such a flirt, obsessed with the boys,' she said with disdain, her lip curling.

Relations between Ella and Sylvia had never thawed from their first meeting. Ella thought Sylvia's jealousy of her friendship with Gracie was amusing and would always play up by discussing the shop and the Smiths with Gracie, anything to deliberately exclude Sylvia from the conversation. Gracie saw what she was doing and would chastise her for it.

'Don't be rotten to Syl,' she would plead with Ella. 'She is not that bad and you are making yourself look mean.' Ella would listen but it was too much fun to stop teasing Sylvia completely.

Tom's brother William sat down beside them on the rug. He smiled at Gracie. He was much quieter than Tom, but was a fine looking boy.

'We had better go Syl, we have to be home by eight, and you know that.' Joe was tugging at the sleeve of Sylvia's dress.

'I am not going home yet,' snapped Sylvia. 'They can wait. We are guests in their home after all.'

Sylvia had clocked the interested looks William was giving Gracie and she felt cross. She had noticed Tom on her first day of arriving in Ripon. He hadn't noticed the side of the street she walked on. This evening, first Ella had lured Tom to one end of the field and was doing goodness knows what with him, so she was damned if she was going to leave William with Gracie at the other end of the field. Sylvia had no interest in William but thought if she could get his attention, it might very well lead to Tom.

'Syl please,' whined Joe. 'They might be cross with us and I don't want them to be.'

Joe had also seen William position himself in front of Gracie and his little heart ached. Unlike Sylvia, he knew he was helpless to prevent the ways of love and absolutely did not want to witness it.

'Right Syl I am going without you then and I am going to tell Mrs Baker that you are refusing to come along. I might also show her the bruise you gave me this morning when you kicked me.'

Sylvia looked at Joe in surprise. It was unlike him to stand up to her. She was torn for a moment. Old Mrs Baker had said Sylvia could stay up late that night and listen to a programme on the wireless after Joe had gone to bed. Sylvia wanted to stay up late, if only to brag about it the next day at school.

At home, Amy absolutely always insisted her children went to bed early, even though they were older, to give her some peace.

'Alright I am coming then.' She set off after Joe without saying goodbye to Gracie and William.

'I think Ella and Tom like each other.' William observed wisely.

'Oh no,' protested Gracie, 'she is always saying he is a beast and he teases her like mad.'

William smiled. 'Alright if you insist but I think they will be chasing one another for a while yet.'

William was a bright boy and was fond of reading when he got the chance. They discovered they both had a fondness for Charles Dickens. Gracie talked about her family and even admitted her fears for her brothers fighting goodness knows where. After a while William moved closer to Gracie.

'Can I ask you something? Have you ever been kissed by a boy before?' he asked casually.

'Actually, no, I haven't.' Gracie was stammering with embarrassment.

She looked at William. He was the picture of health. His piercing blue, downturned eyes were squinting slightly against the sun. His straight nose was covered in freckles and was slightly sunburnt. The sun had also bleached the front of his floppy light brown hair.

He looked intently at her.

'Gracie you are an absolute peach. I would love to be the first boy you kiss.' He planted a kiss firmly on her lips.

Gracie opened her eyes wide in surprise.

'Would you like another?' he asked with a smile.

Gracie nodded and blushed.

'Yes I rather think I would.'

Ella and Tom returned from wherever they had got to, looking flushed and giggling madly. The four children walked slowly back through the fields towards the town. William slipped his hand in Gracie's.

The brothers bid the girls goodnight and went home. They would have to get up early the next morning to help with the harvest. It was a very busy time.

Ella looked at Gracie with her eyes narrowed. 'Something's up Gracie. You look all kinds of dreamy. Did you have a little kiss with William? I've got lots of older sisters you know, I recognise that dreamy look a mile off.'

'What about you disappearing off with Tom like that, never mind me and William.'

'Don't you change the subject.' said Ella in a comical stern voice. 'I just gave Tom a run for his money that's all. No more than he deserved.'

'What on earth does that even mean?' retorted Gracie full of high spirits.

'All right, I admit, I kissed his face off.' declared Ella in delight.

'Well I kissed William too. It was my first kiss.'

'Oh,' breathed Ella taking in the magnitude of the moment. 'He is a looker for a first kiss. Good stuff. He didn't dribble did he there is nothing worse than a dribbler?' hooted Ella.

Gracie aimed a lazy punch at her and they both skipped into the shop full of the joy.

Much later that same night Ella was woken by a noise. 'Gracie are you awake?' hissed Ella loudly from under her quilt. 'Gracie did you hear that?'

'What?' groaned Gracie, her voice thick with sleep. She turned over to look at the little alarm clock that was balanced on the blanket box. 'Ella it is four in the morning, what is the matter?'

'Listen, can you hear that noise?'

Gracie sat up in the semi-darkness and immediately banged the top of her head on the low eaves. She listened carefully whilst rubbing her head. She could hear a faint rhythmical thudding noise coming from downstairs.

'Oh Lord do you think it's the invasion?' she whispered urgently, unable to think clearly, panic rising in her throat.

Ella let out a snort of laughter.

'No you goose, Mr and Mrs Smith are at it.'

Gracie tipped her head to one side and noted the banging was getting faster. Then she heard a deep rumbling groan.

'Oh no, goodness me.' gasped Gracie in embarrassment.

She rounded on Ella who was looking angelic in her white frothy night-dress and curls round her cheeks. 'I can't believe you woke me up to listen to that.'

'Do you think Mr Smith is still reading the paper?' giggled Ella.

Both girls buried their heads in their pillows in an effort to keep quite. They had tears streaming down their faces, quite hysterical with laughter.

It had been a magical, romantic evening for everyone.

The next morning at breakfast the girls were sat tucking into big bowls of porridge topped with swirls of Mrs Smith's raspberry jam. Mrs Smith was fluttering busily round the kitchen humming 'There will be blue birds over the white cliffs of Dover.'

'You seem very cheerful this morning Mrs Smith,' said Ella politely, her face a picture of innocence. Her curls resembling a halo in the light streaming in through the window behind her.

Gracie shot her a warning glance and felt her cheeks redden.

Mrs Smith looked suspiciously at Ella for a second then gave her head a visible shake. She said dreamily 'I had a very satisfying creative evening. The spirits were abundant and energies were flowing.'

'Have you done some more lovely paintings?' asked Ella.

'Yes dear of course. Yes of course.' Mrs Smith was suddenly very flustered indeed.

Mr Smith shuffled into the kitchen and sat down, face as morose as ever.

'Good morning Mr Smith,' chirped Mrs Smith and looked indulgently at him. 'I have saved you the last egg. You need to keep your strength up.'

Mr Smith nodded solemnly, unfolded his newspaper and began his lengthy perusal.

Mrs Smith brought a large brown teapot to the table. 'I have just freshened the pot girls, would you like another cup to set you up for your busy day. Mr Smith was telling me that he is really enjoying your company.'

'Really?' said Ella. 'Thank you Mr Smith.'

Mr Smith suddenly put down his newspaper and said loudly,

'You know I can't remember the last time I saw a banana.'

Chapter 11

Gracie's days spent in Ripon passed happily enough. At first she had a huge crush on William. They spent many a happy hour in the fields on soft summer evenings. Their kisses dusted with the magic sparkle of youth and excitement. As the weeks passed by though, Gracie realised he didn't have a great deal to say on any subject really. Thomas, Ella's boyfriend, his brother, seemed to have inherited all the personality. It was fine when the friends were spending time altogether but when Gracie and William were on their own, Gracie found, if she wasn't kissing him, she was bored.

Sylvia and Joe also enjoyed one or two brief, gentle little romances of their own and made friends with the boys and girls on the road where they were billeted.

One day Gracie was helping Mrs Smith to pod peas in the kitchen. She was mulling over the thorny problem of how to tell William she no longer wanted to be his girl, when there was a quiet knock on the apartment door.

Mrs Smith fluttered down the little corridor to open it and receive their visitor. Gracie could hear the murmur of low voices. Mrs Smith appeared in front of Gracie with a serious look on her face.

Gracie looked up from the bowl of glowing, fresh, green peas and gave a gasp of joy.

Ada appeared from behind Mrs Smith.

Gracie scraped back her chair and flung herself into her mother's arms.

Ada hugged her tightly.

'I didn't know you were coming, how lovely. Mrs Smith, this is my mother, Ada Atwell.'

Mrs Smith smiled but didn't meet Gracie's eyes. She was blinking quickly and was rubbing her hands together in an agitated way, making her bangles jangle.

'I think Mr Smith may well need me in the shop, I had better scoot down and see.'

She disappeared quietly out of the room.

Gracie sensed something was wrong.

Her eyes filled with tears and she began to feel like she couldn't catch her breath.

'Mother?'

Ada's sweet face was full of sadness.

'Sit down Gracie dear, I need to tell you something.'

Ada pulled a chair round so she was sat next to her daughter and she held her hand firmly. Gracie began to cry. Whatever this news was she absolutely didn't want to hear it. She wanted to put her hands over her ears.

'It is Aunt Clara, there was an accident, darling. She was thrown by her horse. Her neck was broken.'

Gracie let out a long painful wail.

'It was very quick darling, she didn't suffer.'

Ada began to cry along with Gracie. They sat side by side at the table, holding hands as the tears flowed. Ada found she had no words of comfort for Gracie at that moment, her own pain rendering her speechless. Both Ada and Gracie were weighed down daily with the terrible thought that the boys could be killed in war. Clara's accident was a huge shock to them.

Mrs Smith managed to prevent Ella from striding into the kitchen to offer her own condolences.

'Why don't you help me with the potato delivery, Ella?'

Ella began pulling faces. 'I hate messing with those mucky old things. Gracie will need me. I am going up to be with her.'

Mrs Smith snapped. 'Ella why don't you just do as you are told, without argument, for once in your life?'

Ella stared at Mrs Smith in surprise. She had never raised her voice to her or Gracie.

Even Mr Smith looked up from his onions and raised his eyebrows a fraction.

Mrs Smith put her hands over her eyes and took a deep cleansing breath.

Ella looked contrite. 'I am sorry Mrs Smith, you are right, of course.'

Mrs Smith beamed, forgiving quickly. 'I am sorry I raised my voice Ella, it is very upsetting. Gracie needs her mother for the moment. You can comfort her when her mother has gone home. She will need your kindness.'

Ada went back home that night. She had to arrange the funeral.

Gracie was almost silent for the next few days. She had gone round to tell Sylvia and Joe. They were both saddened by the news and cried genuine tears. Joe particularly was fond of Clara. She always made time to greet the children and would offer them boiled sweets. She would ask them how they were getting along at school. She taught Joe to whistle loudly with his fingers in his mouth. Joe's favourite story about Clara had come from Ian. Apparently one day Clara had got into an argument with the vicar at a parish meeting and become so enraged that he was daring to argue with her over some matter regarding the stalls at the summer fair that she farted loudly and at length. 'That jolly well shut him up,' Ian had joyfully quoted.

Gracie carried on with her days that followed automatically. She went to school, helped in the shop and with the chores and saw her friends. William tried to comfort her in the only way he knew how, with kisses and cuddles, but Gracie was not interested and pushed him away. Ella tried to cheer her up and kept up a steady patter of conversation to which Gracie only really replied in monosyllables. She didn't cry again.

Sylvia on the other hand took to her bed and refused to go to school on the grounds of her distress. The sweet old couple that she was staying with were running round tending to her every need.

One night, Gracie lay awake into the small hours of the morning. She heard various clatters and bangs from downstairs in the kitchen and a faint sound of happy humming.

Gracie got up and crept downstairs. She knew Mrs Smith must have got up really early, the muse upon her. Gracie didn't want to disturb her but was intrigued and wanted to see her vibrant host in creative action. Gracie knew that, for all she and Ella giggled at her eccentricities, Mrs Smith was a real artist. She hoped she wasn't naked. Gracie did not want to see that.

She peeped her head round the kitchen door and jumped. Mrs Smith was standing in the centre of the kitchen floor with her eyes closed. She was dressed in a wonderful lilac kaftan, made all the more colourful by the daubs of multi-coloured paint that covered it. Her hair was tied on the top of her head with a lime green scarf. Her feet were bare. She had streaks of orange paint across both cheeks, as if she had grasped her own face in a moment of creative energy. Gracie thought she looked wonderful. Mrs Smith's eyes opened as if she sensed someone was there.

Mrs Smith looked surprised and smiled.

'Gracie, come on into the kitchen. I was just putting down some of my own feelings on canvas. It has been such a disturbing week. For all of us. Especially you my poor poppet. I find painting helps me to make sense of this world we all inhabit.'

Gracie nodded slowly and turned away as if to return upstairs.

Mrs Smith looked thoughtfully at her retreating back.

'Gracie, dear, why don't you have a little try yourself with the paints? Here is a clean canvas. You can use all my paints. Just give it a little try. It is five o'clock in the morning, I don't suppose there is much point in going to sleep now, is there dear?'

Gracie looked sceptical for a moment.

Mrs Smith offered her a brush. 'Just a little try dear.'

Gracie chose a vermilion and tentatively painted in a small corner of the canvas. She sat staring helplessly at the blank canvas and her face was white and set. Suddenly she dashed the brush across it, making a bold red slash across the centre. Mrs Smith deliberately turned her back on her and got on with her own painting.

Gracie continued to paint with fierce energy and concentration for a further half an hour. Great splodges of colour, mixed up vigorously. Mrs Smith passed her sheet after sheet of paper, canvasses being rather expensive after all. The colour was slowly returning to Gracie's cheeks and she found she was breathing heavily.

All of a sudden she let out a howl of rage and threw her brush down.

116

'You see the thing is,' she shouted up towards the ceiling. 'I was so relieved it wasn't my brothers that were dead. For a moment I felt glad it was Aunt Clara. That is a terrible thing to think. Poor Aunt Clara, poor mother.'

Mrs Smith came across the kitchen and put a gentle hand on her shoulder.

'I think you have got yourself a little mixed-up dear. You are very sad about your aunt and you are glad your brothers are still alive but continue to worry about them. They are two separate things. You mustn't feel guilty about any of these feelings. There is nothing to feel guilty about. You love your family very much.'

Gracie looked up at Mrs Smith's kind face. Gracie's young face was a mask of confusion and pain.

'Yes, they are separate aren't they? I think about my brothers every single day. I don't think I can stand it anymore. I want them to come home. I want them to be safe.' Gracie paused as her confused anger began to dissipate slightly. The relief of saying these things out-loud. After a while she said 'I think you would have liked Aunt Clara, she was really bossy and funny.'

'I tell you what, I will make us a cup of cocoa and you tell me all about her.'

'Mrs Smith,' said Gracie. 'You have got paint all over your face.'

Mrs Smith smiled and said, 'that's funny, so have you.'

Chapter 12

1940

Charles Dunne grew up in a tiny cottage in Meanwood very close to Leeds city centre. He was the only adored child of Molly and James Dunne. Molly had been raised by her mother and grandfather.

Molly's mother and grandfather hailed originally from a tiny pit village up North. Molly's mother had worked in a mill and had become pregnant to the mill owners son, out of wedlock. The son wanted nothing more to do with Molly's mother and his wealthy family ensured a shotgun wedding was out of the question so Molly's mother and her grandfather moved down to Leeds to escape the stigma of her carrying a bastard child.

Molly's mother tried to make Molly aware of her shameful parentage from an early age. Regularly using phrases such as 'born the other side of the blanket', which mystified young Molly for a long while. Molly grew up under a shadow of shame without really understanding it. Her grandfather always maintained that Molly's father was dead, which confused Molly even more.

As she grew older Molly finally understood where she had come from but remained perplexed as to why she should be sorry for her arrival into the world. She always tried to hold her head high though and remained suspicious of other people, thinking they could be disappointed in her for some reason, like her own mother.

When she held her own child, Charles, in her arms in the first moments of his life she was absolutely determined to do everything within her power to make him happy and confident. She was filled with pure joy when he was born.

Molly and James didn't have very much money but they made up for that by lavishing attention on young Charles. James had a sister who had three lively daughters and Charles spent a great deal of his childhood playing with his cousins. He was at his most comfortable surrounded by adoring girls. The happy prince.

Charles did very well at school and achieved his school certificate with ease. He was popular and very sporty. He could sometimes bully weaker children, which was not necessarily a strength but his forceful personality was nurtured through the adoration of his mother. She thought he showed determination, which he would need to succeed as a man of the world.

When he left school he found a job immediately working in the bank as a clerk for the Circus branch of the Yorkshire Penny bank on Meanwood Road. On Sundays he played cricket for the bank team where he proved to be an asset with swift accurate bowling and an excellent eye for catches.

He would go to the picture house on a Friday night with his best pals from school, Alf and Ron, usually with a local girl or two in tow. His enormous white cat, Jimmy, would accompany them on their stroll down to the cinema. He would walk at Charles's heels all the way down to the Ritz and sit and wait outside for them. Charles would get fish and chips on the way home, without salt and vinegar, in deference to Jimmy's tastes and share the cod with the cat as he followed him closely home again. Charles loved Jimmy. He actually belonged to the farm up the road where he did a sterling job keeping the vermin population down in the farmer's barn. Jimmy was a ferocious ratter. Although he was a very busy cat, he spent his leisure time at the Dunne's cottage. He would regularly have a snooze at the bottom of Charles's bed.

It was the perfect relationship as far as they were both concerned, a friendship with minimal effort. The only drawback to Jimmy's adoption of the Dunne family was when Charles or his parents hurried down the garden on a morning to use the outside lavatory, they were often greeted by a dead rat, usually without a head, placed reverently on the toilet seat. A generous gift from Jimmy to his favourite family.

By the age of 21 though Charles was beginning to feel a little claustrophobic in the tiny cottage under the ever vigilant watchful eye of Molly. He got on well with his father, who was a lively little man, always ready with a joke. At work in the bank Charles would glance around at the much older, dusty-looking clerks and wonder if they would die at an earlier age just through sheer tedium of working at the same desk for the whole of their lives.

He knew it was time to leave Leeds and spread his wings. The only thing that was holding him back was the whispers of the approach of war.

When fighting broke out in 1939 Charles thought long and hard about his options. He wanted to fight, there was no doubt about that.

One sunny Sunday afternoon he was enjoying his regular game of cricket. He was fielding out on the boundary and as their opposing team had such a poor standard of batting he didn't have much to do. He was looking round the field vaguely when suddenly he seemed to take notice of the beauty of his surroundings for the very first time. The lush green field with its neat little clubhouse painted a smart dark blue. The fellows all pristine in their whites, playing his beloved ancient game with gentle dignity and skill. They had drawn quite a crowd that afternoon as the sun was shining. Girls in pretty flowered frocks and their fellows in casual shirts with their sleeves rolled up and their collars undone. There were children milling round the edge of the fields, dashing about laughing and older ladies and gentlemen nodding peacefully in the deck chairs under straw hats.

A particular couple caught his eye. They were relaxing on a wool picnic rug and the boy was feeding his girlfriend strawberries and chocolate cake from a fork.

Charles suddenly felt extremely angry, he could hardly catch his breath. How dare Hitler, that odious little man, try and spoil all of this. How dare he try to take it away from him, from all of them.

That was the moment he decided to join up himself rather than wait for his call-up papers.

His father James had fought in the trenches in the Great War. Charles had heard the tales of mud, rats, endless noise and endless fear. James had three toes missing and his feet were a source of constant discomfort. A souvenir of the dreaded trench foot. Charles's father joked that he could have done with Jimmy by his side in the trenches to scare off the rats.

'Oh yes,' he would add in a low voice, 'your mother too, she would have given the Hun what for,' as Molly's solid form would enter the room topped with her regular fierce scowl and complaining loudly about some injustice or other.

Charles quickly discounted the regular army, there was no way he was going to be swallowed up in mud. That was a horrible way to die.

He also decided against the RAF. The thought of going up in an aeroplane made him feel quite faint.

He shrewdly guessed his best option would be the Royal Navy.

To join the Royal Navy you had to be educated to a good standard, otherwise it would be the Merchant Navy. Charles had his school certificate which should be sufficient.

He liked the sea and always felt drawn to it. His family always took their annual holiday in Scarborough on the East coast. Charles and his father would go on fishing expeditions and he found the sea thrilling. He thought he might actually have a better chance of keeping warm and dry than if he was in the trenches, as long as his ship didn't sink of course.

Joining the Royal Navy was by no means a safe bet though. Britain was an island, the Nazis would target the fleets. It would dangerous.

Once he had signed up Charles couldn't help feeling a build-up of excitement. He had a very pleasant, ordinary life but he had become stagnant still living at home. He had fun with his pals and there were plenty of girls twittering round, attracted by his golden hair, bright blue eyes and confident manner. All pleasant distractions, but now he had the opportunity to test out what kind of man he had grown into, when faced with a very real and frightening challenge of fighting for his country and loved ones.

When he told his parents they were naturally very concerned. His father in particular was upset. The thought that his only son might share in some of his terrible experiences of fighting at the front in the last war was almost too much to bear.

Molly was effusive with praise over Charles's decision to join up voluntarily, telling him over and over again how brave and strong he was and how very proud she was. Her heart was like ice through fear for him though, fear for her only baby.

Charles was called up quickly and soon made his way down to HMS Impregnable in Devonport. He was a little surprised he would train at a land based camp. He caught his train along with about 30 other chaps all heading to Devonport. He was also surprised to find that the majority of the new Royal Navy recruits were actually boys. Some of them had only just turned 14 and had lied to the higher powers, claiming to be 15, the age the Navy deemed it acceptable to become a sailor. The boys chatted excitedly about the fun they would have giving 'that bastard Hitler a bloody nose.' Many of them boasting about the girls they would pick up in each port and the fruity things they would do to them. Each talking loudly in voices that had barely broken.

Charles managed to get a corner seat in his cramped carriage and spent the journey quietly smoking. He hoped he wouldn't be bunking with the kids. They would be training for 12 months. They seemed like a good bunch of lads but he couldn't stand listening to all that posturing and swank.

On their arrival they were issued with their splendid uniforms, with flared trousers, blue tunic, Trafalgar collar and white cap. Charles had to admit to himself, it looked really smart and was very comfortable. He definitely suited navy blue. It was miles away from the itchy wool khaki of the regular army. Charles secretly thought the Germans had the edge on smart uniform but he kept that thought to himself.

He was greatly relieved to find that he was bunking with men of a similar age and the boys on the train were sleeping in separate quarters. They still trained with the younger recruits though. The days were long and hard and always seemed to include lengthy sessions of climbing up and down rigging.

Charles was having the time of his life. After the first couple of weeks, where every bone in his body would endlessly ache, he became fitter. Not only was his body growing in strength but he was learning mental skills that required a great deal of concentration. Morse code and semaphore he could handle as he had a good memory, but he was struggling to recognise the many bugle calls as he was tone-deaf. He was taught to handle guns which he had to admit, gave him a bit of a thrill.

After a further few months he was given the opportunity to train to be an electrician. He jumped at the chance.

To successfully pass the training the new recruits all had to climb a 175 foot mast of the Impregnable. It was to test both their physical and mental strength. The feat was achieved by climbing up the rigging at a steady pace and pushing through a number of trapdoors. The mast would sway violently and there were absolutely no safety features.

The only advice the chief petty officer gave was to bark 'Climb up as quickly as you can and for God's sake don't fall off.'

The boys went up first, even the little bugle players.

Charles watched them with growing apprehension. He wasn't afraid of heights but this really did seem quite dangerous. The day was very bright and Charles guessed if you looked up to see where you were climbing you would get the sun straight in your eyes. Unfortunately the wind was quite brisk also.

The boys had all descended successfully and seemed none the worse for their adventure.

Charles went up next. He concentrated on his own hands grasping the thick ropes. He set himself a fast paced rhythm. As he reached the trapdoor his shoulder muscles were singing with pain, despite his fitness. It seemed to Charles, on reaching the top that the wind had whipped itself up into a hurricane. The mast was swaying alarmingly. His face was ridged with tension. He repeated the same mantra over and over again in his head. 'Don't look down. Don't look down.'

He had to pause for a minute or two before he began his descent. He couldn't work out how to move his arms and legs in reverse. His body had frozen with fear. Eventually his limbs obeyed their instruction and he made his way back down. Stood back on parade his found his mouth completely dry and his willed his knees not to give way. He could see out of the corner of his eye a fellow recruit had tears streaming down his face. The man didn't dare brush them aside for fear of drawing attention to himself.

The year of training passed swiftly and Charles was assigned his first ship, which was to be his home for the next three years. He had qualified as an electrician and would be putting his skills to excellent use on an enormous landing craft carrier.

The sailors came from all walks of life. Discipline on the ship was just a strict as it was on the Impregnable. Charles thrived in that environment and had no desire to rebel anyway. He was a grown man and if Britain was going to win the war it meant digging in hard and obeying orders. The younger boys were treated with a harshness that made Charles feel uncomfortable on occasion. The Royal Navy still had some rules that were punishable with a lashing if broken. The boys seemed to spend most of their time scrubbing the decks. Charles didn't give them too much thought though. His days were very busy.

He was bunking with some decent fellows. There was George, he was twenty-one, and same age as Charles. He was a lively Liverpudlian with an eye very much for the ladies. There was also Johnny. He was a black young man of nineteen who hailed from Alabama. He joined the

Navy to escape the terrible poverty of his small town. He was an absolute genius on the harmonica and often kept the men entertained with his soulful songs from the Deep South. Finally there was Geoffrey Wicks. He was a hulk of a man, at least six foot seven with hands like shovels. He was the only one of the group who was married, with a small daughter. He came from Newcastle where he was a blacksmith. He worked as a welder on the ship. The four of them got on well and spent their small amounts of spare time playing cards, smoking and swapping stories from back home.

The first time their boat docked they managed to get shore leave together. Charles and George decided to go to the pictures first, then find a pub for a belly full of beer. They got themselves ready, looking forward to the reaction of any ladies that crossed their path.

All the nice girls love a sailor and all that. They were about to get off the ship when they realised that Johnny was holding back.

'Come on,' said Charles impatiently.

'Hurry up you are wasting time.'

Johnny shook his head. 'You go on without me, its ok fellas.'

'Johnny don't you want to get off this bloody boat and walk on dry land for a bit?'

'Yeah sure I do, but they won't let me into the movies with you, will they? Me with the white boys, yeah sure.'

Charles looked puzzled for a moment they his brow cleared.

'God, we don't go in for that kind of nonsense in England. Come on it will be fine.'

Johnny still looked hesitant.

Charles clapped his hands together impatiently. 'Tell you what Johnny mate, you are fighting for our country and if anyone has anything to say about you going to the pictures then they will have to go through me first. Alright?'

'Bang on Charles.' chimed in George in agreement.

Johnny nodded slowly and looked serious.

'I suppose we could give it a go then, thanks fellas.'

They left Geoffrey behind on the ship. He didn't fancy sitting down in a smoky cinema for a couple of hours and he agreed to find them in the pubs on the docks later on.

They all enjoyed the film and later found themselves in a very busy pub, a stone's throw away from where their ship was docked. No one concerned themselves with Johnny and he finally relaxed.

The beer was good and they were approached by a succession of hard-faced painted women offering lonely sailors comfort on the shore, for a reasonable price. The men took it in good part and laughed along with the women and bought them drinks. They didn't take them up on their kind offer though. 'Sorry ladies,' hiccupped George in his singsong Liverpool accent. 'Me da says I've got to keep it in my trousers.'

Charles got up somewhat unsteadily and swayed his way across the pub towards the bar to get the next round in. As he reached the bar and rested his elbow in the beer puddles. His arm immediately slipped and he jostled a huge beefy docker who spilt his pint. Charles took in the sheer size of the man with his ugly bulldog face and angry expression and quickly began to apologise. He frantically patted his pockets to locate some change to reimburse the fierce creature bearing down on him. Even through his slightly crossed eyes Charles could observe that this man was really mad.

The beer had gone all down the man's shirt and Charles dabbed ineffectually at his front with the sleeve of his own tunic, Charles also, unfortunately, found the situation amusing and started to laughing, great snorting laughs.

This served to anger the bulldog further. He grabbed Charles by the neck and shouted profanities in his face. Charles was turning purple, unable to breathe. The pub went quiet most of the clientele leaning forward eagerly, thrilled to witness a ruckus.

No one moved for a second.

George and Johnny, both slumped towards the back of the smoky pub, were too drunk to notice what was happening. In fact the only sound in the pub for that minute was George bellowing in Johnny's ear.

'There was nowhere else to go so I rogered her behind the bins. True story Johnny lad,' and belched loudly. Johnny nodded sagely, wondering whether to be sick under the table.

The docker drew back his fat fist, about to lamp Charles one on the nose when he was tapped on the shoulder.

'Can we have a word?'

The voice was deep and rumbling, with an unmistakable Tyneside twang.

The docker turned his head, spitting with rage and looked straight into the magnificently rouged and lipsticked face of Geoffrey the welder. The docker released Charles's throat in surprise. He looked Geoffrey slowly up and down, taking in the stretched peach tea dress, low cut to reveal a hairy barrel chest. Ropes of pearls enhanced his bull neck. He was wearing high heels and his wide apart legs were encased in real silk stockings, with a seam down each one. The vision was completed with a ginger wig that had slipped slightly to the side. The docker backed away with his hands in the air. 'Alright mate no problem here, no problem at all.'

Geoffrey stepped forward and clouted the docker straight in the face. The docker rocked back on his heels, dazed. Geoffrey followed up with another hefty punch on the side of his head and the giant man slid down onto the floor.

George and Johnny had finally realised Charles might be in a bit of bother and had stumbled across the pub to rescue him. All three friends stared open-mouthed at the glorious sight of Geoffrey dressed in his finest.

'Good Lord.' muttered George.

'Now then lads,' said Geoffrey, straightening his luxurious ginger wig, 'let me get the beers in.'

The sailors nodded in approval. The barman wasn't in the least disturbed by Geoffrey and politely called him madam as he served him. Transvestites were not uncommon round the docks. 'Each to their own,' he would say benevolently 'as long as they buy my booze.'

Back on the ship, they laughed about Charles's near brush with death but no one mentioned Geoffrey's get up.

'It's just his business I guess,' said George thoughtfully later on in the night, referring to Geoffrey 'what ever gets you through this bloody war. Of course who is going to say anything anyway? He is built like a brick shit house.'

Geoffrey kept his make-up and clothes in a small pink satin valise which he hid in the bottom of his kitbag along with a picture of his wife and tiny pretty daughter.

A year later Charles's path finally crossed with Gracie's.

They met at a dance held in a shabby ballroom in Leeds. Charles had got a few days leave and was spending it with his mother and father. He was still dressed in his smart Navy uniform because he quite enjoyed the attention it drew. Charles was leaning on the bar feeling restless. He had tried to look up his old pals. They had both joined the army. Ron was away fighting but Alfie had been killed in action a month or so before. Charles dropped in to see Alfie's mother to try to say some consoling words but Mrs Trewlove was overcome by the sight of Alfie's old friend that she clung to Charles and howled and howled. Charles gently untangled himself and made her a cup of tea. He made sure she drank it, then left.

He was now leaning on the bar, nursing a rum, scanning the room for familiar faces. He didn't recognise many of the young people dancing and wondered sadly who else had been killed.

He knocked back his rum to ease the churning pain he so frequently got in his gut. He was missing his sailor friends and their banter. As the war shuddered along Charles found that if he spent time alone his spirits would quickly lower. Charles looked towards the double doors of the ballroom as they were pushed open.

In walked Gracie dressed in her finest. She seemed to glow with health and was dressed in a very pretty chiffon red tea-dress. She had put a red rose behind one ear and had swept her luxuriant dark hair over one shoulder. She was accompanied by Sylvia, whose curls were dropping limply round her wan face and was sporting a petulant expression when she noticed the attention Gracie was creating. 'It is always the same. She struts in like she owns the place.' she thought with hefty dose of venom.

'Oh do cheer up Syl.' snapped Gracie, unusually short tempered.

Sylvia looked surprised that Gracie had seemed to read her uncharitable thoughts and felt faintly embarrassed. They had both been looking forward to having a drink and a dance.

'Who knows,' said Gracie in a conciliatory tone 'you might meet a chap tonight. You met a lovely young man last month.'

'Well I won't with you swanning around in that dress. It is cut very low, you don't have to put everything on display,' Syl replied spitefully.

Gracie blushed, she also was wondering if the neckline was a little too low and was embarrassed that Sylvia had pointed it out in such a loud voice.

'Yeah well no one will bother with you if you are in such a bad mood will they? Honestly Syl you do spoil things sometimes,' shot back Gracie with spirit.

She took a deep breath as she noticed Sylvia's eyes fill with tears.

'I tell you what, let's just stick together, just us girls, we won't bother dancing with any chaps. Let's go see if there is any gin and orange.'

Syl's crocodile tears cleared up immediately as Gracie knew they would.

Joe bounded up overjoyed to see them, rather like a Labrador puppy. He had managed to secure a job working at the airport close to home so he still saw the girls often.

'Don't know if I can give you a dance tonight,' said Gracie winking at him 'it is just us girls tonight.'

'She in a mood?' asked Joe. 'She will be right as rain if a nice boy whisks her around the floor in a romantic waltz won't she?' He clasped his hands to his chest and pirouetted in a circle.

Gracie giggled and Sylvia gave her brother a look that would make a weaker man cry.

Sylvia cheered up after a couple of gins and the girls and Joe began to have a lively fun evening.

Later on in the evening Gracie became conscious of someone watching her. A tall blond sailor with piercing blue eyes and a determined jaw.

Charles was transfixed by her. She was certainly striking looking but it wasn't her beauty that was sustaining his interest. She was so full of energy and danced with such joy. Admittedly, not the most graceful of dancers but was clearly enjoying herself tremendously. He noticed the easy way she laughed with the drippy girl and the other lad with a merry face.

Gracie had a word with Joe. 'Can you go and tell that sailor to stop looking at me, I don't like it.'

Joe saluted her and dutifully trundled across the busy dance floor towards Charles.

Charles had to crouch down slightly to get to Joe's diminutive height. Even though Joe now was in his late teens, his face still had the look of a naughty boy scrumping apples, with his round rosy cheeks and silly grin.

Joe delivered his message.

Charles looked over at Gracie and raised his eyebrows, he gave a wolfish grin 'You go and tell that lovely lady in red to stop looking at me, she is making me feel very uncomfortable and if she doesn't stop I will go and tell my mother.'

Joe relayed this message and Gracie smiled despite herself.

After a while Charles approached her and asked her politely if she would like to dance. Gracie agreed and they spent an enjoyable evening together. Charles was friendly and joked around but was also courteous. He was nice to Sylvia and Joe, knowing that Gracie would be impressed with that.

When they left that evening, Charles asked Gracie if he could see her the next day. Gracie agreed. She was very taken with this gentleman sailor and like him very much.

Chapter 13

Gracie and Charles had been courting for nearly ten months, Charles was often away, one of his duties was overseeing the transport of prisoners through England, so he managed to return to Leeds more often than before when he was permanently on the ships. The time they managed to spend together was precious to both of them. Charles was welcomed by the Atwell family and enjoyed any time spent with them. Gracie learned that Charles was fiercely intelligent and challenged her so she always found their conversations really stimulating. In turn Charles liked Gracie's careless beauty and lack of self-consciousness. She had a lot of spirit, a quick wit and would immediately argue with him if she thought he was wrong about something. She was also a lady and Charles, using up most of his self-control, behaved like a gentleman.

Charles finally took Gracie to see his own family in their tiny cottage in Meanwood. They took the bus and on the journey Gracie chatted amicably about her week, only to notice Charles was unresponsive and seemed unnaturally quiet. He answered her questions in one word, snappy answers. Eventually Gracie gave up and enjoyed the journey in silence, looking out through the steamy window at the bustling back streets of Leeds. The little streets of back-to-back houses were full of children all happily milling about together, playing with balls and sticks, hopscotch on the rough paving stones. Thin children, dressed in shabby hand-knitted hand-me-downs. Above them fluttered lines and lines of washing, drying in the breeze. Women stood together in little groups, arms folded across coloured aprons, gossiping on their freshly scrubbed doorsteps.

They alighted from the bus and Gracie started to feel a little uneasy. Charles's mouth was set in a grim line. They arrived at the little cottage. It was sweet in its own way. It had a low roof and was built from solid Yorkshire stone. The front garden was neat but unimaginative. There was a small stark border that just contained two

130

tea roses, one pink, one white. Gracie recognized the white one as an iceberg rose.

Charles knocked on the brown painted door and waited. Gracie was puzzled. Her own family door was almost always open in the summer and she wouldn't dream of knocking on the door of her own home. Besides, the Atwells never locked their doors in the daytime, even if they had all gone out.

They seemed to be on the doorstep for an eternity.

Charles gave Gracie a sideways smile.

'Its mother she insists on locking herself in. She is convinced the Germans will come and steal her away. She keeps the rolling pin behind the door along with her umbrella so she can cosh any intruders. It's safer to knock.'

Gracie smiled back at him. Relieved the tension had dissipated.

Gracie still jumped when the door finally opened with a noisy creak.

Charles's mother Molly stood before them with her feet planted wide apart. Her mouth was set in a downturned grimace. Her strong arms were crossed firmly over her solid body. She was dressed in a man's shirt, skirt and cardigan, all seemingly the colour of seaweed. Her thick ankles were encased in brown woollen stockings, covered with neat, visible, darning. She glared at Gracie for a few seconds.

'Best come in then,' she barked and turned and went back inside.

They obediently followed Mrs Dunne into the gloomy front room of the cottage. Everything in the room was spotlessly clean but in an indeterminate shade of brown. A heavy Victorian dresser dominated the room. It was covered in photographs of Charles. As a chubby blonde baby, a serious schoolboy, and of course pride of place was his photo from the Royal Navy.

Charles caught Gracie looking and raised his eyebrows in a comical way, pretending to be embarrassed.

'Sit down then,' Mrs Dunne ordered.

Gracie approached a wing-back chair cautiously. A huge white cat was sitting in the middle of it and was eyeing Gracie malevolently.

'Charles I'm not sure Mr Puss wants to move.'

Charles laughed, the sound seemed unnaturally loud in the silent room.

'Come on old lad, out you come.' The cat hissed and rewarded Charles with a clawed swipe across his hand.

'No need for that Jimmy old lad,' said Charles affectionately and rubbed his huge head. The cat began to purr. 'Have you missed me eh?'

Gracie sat cautiously in the chair conscious that her dark grey suit was about to become absolutely covered in Jimmy's hairs.

Charles wandered into the kitchen where his mother was rattling cups and saucers loudly.

'Need any help, mother?'

From her armchair Gracie could see Charles and his mother talking. She couldn't hear what they were saying but she could see Mrs Dunne's face soften with love as she looked at her only son. Gracie breathed a sigh of relief. She recognized that under Mrs Dunne's tough northern exterior there was kindness and affection. It would remain to be seen if Gracie could win her over.

'What's tha name lass?'

Gracie jumped. There was another arm chair in the room facing the unlit fire in the grate. This chair contained Charles's father.

'Sorry, I didn't see you there,' Gracie's cheeks reddened. 'Sorry I am Gracie, yes Gracie I'm a friend of Charles's.'

'I am James, Charles's father.' He smiled and held out an oil covered hand. He had oil ingrained into the wrinkles round his clear blue eyes. Charles's eyes.

'Gracie you must be special, this is the first time our Charles has brought a girl home. He must really like you.'

'James,' his wife barked as she came back into the room with a tea tray. James dropped Gracie's hand quickly.

'Yes Molly love?'

'We are going to have a cup of tea then we are going to see Granny Dunne.'

'I hope you two have had a good lunch,' said James and winked at Charles, who grinned back at his father.

Gracie looked puzzled.

'James!' said Molly sharply but she managed a smile from behind the big green tea pot.

They spent a pleasant time over their tea. Gracie told them a little about herself. Molly listened politely, but whenever Charles spoke her head swivelled round to give him her undivided attention. Charles's father was a mechanic and was quite chatty. Gracie warmed to him immediately.

Molly frowned fiercely at Gracie. 'Right come on then, if you have finished your tea.'

Gracie jumped up quickly.

Charles helped Molly as she struggled into an enormous grey coat that smelt strongly of mothballs. She waved away his suggestion that the day was warm enough to go without a top layer.

James waved goodbye to the trio from the doorstep.

It was a fine sunny day and they walked along for about ten minutes in silence. Gracie tried to spark up a harmless conversation with Mrs Dunne about the weather.

Mrs Dunne stopped, turned to look at Gracie and said rather inexplicably, 'I shan't be chatting with you until I have got to know you a bit. That's right isn't it Charles?'

'That's right mother everything in its own time,' said Charles soothingly.

Gracie gave up and they arrived at a little through-by-light house.

Charles whispered in Gracie's ear, 'whatever you do, don't take any cake when she offers, just say you are still full from lunch. She gets very upset if you take her food.'

'Has she gone a bit in the head?' mouthed Gracie discreetly so Mrs Dunne couldn't hear.

Charles snorted. 'No she is a penny-pinching old meanie.'

Granny Dunne was a little woman who had never really forgiven her son James for marrying Molly, with her shameful parentage.

When Molly's pregnant mother and her grandfather arrived in Leeds from the pit village they told everyone the baby's father had died in a tragic pit accident. Molly's grandfather was a tailor and managed to establish a small successful business and he trained his daughter and his granddaughter.

As time went by Molly's mother whispered stories of her heritage, swearing her to secrecy and often cried and lamented that Molly should be dressed in the finest silks and be rubbing shoulders with the gentry. Somehow, in her child's mind she took this to mean that she was at fault. It was a stigma that weighed heavily in her little heart.

Molly got to know James who lived round the corner from her, just after her mother passed away. He was such a breath of fresh air. Always so lively and jocular and of course those sparkling blue eyes. He had that terrible limp from being in the trenches but he never let that stop him from doing anything. They fell in love. She told him about the pit owner's son and James said he sounded like an evil cad and he deserved his upper class block to be knocked off. James always made her feel better, about her little worries, about her big worries. Unfortunately James mentioned it to his own mother, Granny Dunne, thinking she would be just a sympathetic to Molly's plight but Granny Dunne took a very dim view of her son marrying a bastard.

Granny Dunne was kinder to Molly after Charles was born, after all he looked just like her James.

Granny Dunne was small and wrinkled with a hunched back. Her sparse hair was pulled back in a surprisingly modern style.

She gave Charles a hug and greeted Gracie genially with a grin that had a fair few missing teeth.

The little gate-legged table had been set up in the corner of the room and there were miniature sandwiches and small raisin cakes. There was also a junket and scones. Gracie looked hungrily at it, then remembered Charles's warning. Granny Dunne had clocked Gracie staring longingly at the food and was staring challengingly at her with her eyes narrowed, as if daring her to help herself.

Gracie tore her eyes away and Charles changed the subject quickly, wisely asking Granny if she had any more episodes of lumbago.

Granny was delighted to take the reins of the conversation, particularly when it was a conversation about her own health.

Apart from that little moment of tension over the gate-legged table the visit also went quite well. Granny and Molly got onto another of their favourite topics, Charles when he was small.

Granny Dunne had had three children, James, Annie and Iris. Iris had had three children of her own, Charles's cousins.

Charles often visited his cousins, they live close by in a large rambling house in Roundhay. Iris had had the foresight to marry a doctor, a good few years older than her. She had produced three vigorous strong blonde girls full of boundless energy, not dissimilar to springer spaniels. In fact Iris would often moan that they needed exercising like dogs. Iris and Molly got along well and in the summer months they would shoo the children out of the door into the jungle-like garden and only let them back in for mealtimes. The children had wonderful times together they lived a stone's throw away from Roundhay Park and took their bikes, with baskets loaded up with goodies and rode for miles. They all loved tennis and played endless games on the shaggy lawn.

Mabel was the oldest, the same age as Charles and when she turned twelve she began to form a fascination with smoking. She would pretend with a rolled up bit of paper, eyes half closed in the manner of a starlet. It would drive Iris and her husband mad, neither of them approved of smoking. Her younger sisters, Hilly and Dotty were most impressed with how grown-up Mabel looked and immediately began to copy.

One slightly overcast Tuesday. Charles and Molly had called in to see Aunt Iris and the girls. The children were unceremoniously ejected out of the house as usual.

Mabel had been feeling the need for a bit of excitement. Charles often had pockets full of change, being indulged by Granny Dunne. He had managed to buy three cigarettes from the butcher's boy and had brought them with him.

'Well?' demanded Mabel, 'have you got them?'

Charles gave a swift glance towards the house to ensure his mother and aunt Iris were firmly ensconced in the lounge. He drew the cigarettes nonchalantly out of his pocket.

'Got em, it was easy.' he said carelessly.

'Crumbs, how did you manage that?' asked Dotty breathlessly, she was only eight and her voice was full of admiration for her older cousin.

Charles tapped his nose.

'Ask no questions, I will tell no lies.'

'Ok.' Dotty nodded sagely, her eyes wide.

'We had better go behind the shed so no one sees the smoke. Mummy will go wild if she catches us. She hates the smell for some reason. I like it.' Hilly, or Hilda as was her Sunday best name, was giggling almost hysterically in excitement.

She then exclaimed loudly, 'Oh what about matches?'

'Shhhhhh.' Mabel and Charles rounded on her fiercely. 'Honestly Hilly can you shout any louder?'

'Sorry,' hissed Hilly, 'I don't even know why I am laughing, it is such a fun wheeze.'

The children pushed passed a clump of nettles and squeezed between the shed and the boundary stone wall at the bottom of the garden.

'Euuuug spiders!' said Mabel shaking her head vigorously.

Charles showed her the cigarettes and matches he had brought.

'Done this before Charles?' Mabel asked challengingly, fixing him with a stare.

'Oh Lord lots of times, I mean who hasn't?' replied Charles with a flick of his hair, returned the stare unblinkingly.

'Mabs, I can't get past the stingers. Help me I want to try the fags too,' Dotty's voice piped up from round the other side of the shed.

Mabel rolled her eyes. 'Go away right now Dotty.' she ordered.

'Please,' Dotty immediately started to wail loudly.

'Dots listen, fags can hurt your throat. They will make you cough. You won't like it.' Hilly tried to reason with little Dotty. Hilly was the kinder of Dotty's older sisters. Mabel usually won her arguments with a kick or a sharp pinch.

Dotty continued to howl.

Hilly had an inspired idea. 'Dotty remember when you had croup last year and father walked you round the garden in the cold night? Well the cigs might bring on croup again and you won't want that, will you?'

'Just shut her up will you,' snapped Charles to Mabel. He was tired of Dotty's wailing. He wanted to get on with the smoke.

'Dotty I tell you what, why don't you have a go on my new bike, go on, see if you can climb onto it. You could have a go with the gears.' Hilly tried once again to get her younger sister to leave them alone for five minutes.

There was silence as Dotty weighed up her options.

'Alright,' she piped, 'but I am coming back in one minute.' She gave a loud sniff and wandered away.

Charles lit the cigarettes and passed them to his cousins. Both girls inhaled deeply and started coughing with watering eyes.

'Delicious,' spluttered Mabel. Hilly nodded in agreement, her face now flushed red.

Charles did his best to lean against the wall in the cramped space and took a controlled puff. He had actually bought the whole packet of smokes from the butcher's boy and had been practicing controlling his cough reflex so he could perfect his swagger in front of the girls.

Mabel and Hilly looked at him, full of admiration. He was such a splendid cousin, so good at things.

'Hilda, Mabel, Charles come out from behind the shed at once.' It was the girls' mother, Iris's voice screeching and she sounded very angry indeed.

The children shuffled out single file but not before throwing the butt ends into the nettles.

'Breathe through your nose then they can't smell your breath,' advised Mabel to Hilly, who was looking a little panicky.

They rounded the shed to be confronted by a stern looking Molly and an outraged Iris. They both had their arms folded in disapproval.

'Dotty tells me you three have been smoking. Smoking,' she yelled 'is not for children your age.'

Mabel fixed Dotty with a gimlet glare.

Dotty burst into noisy sobs. 'I had to tell them Mabs. They thought the shed was on fire. They were about to call the fire brigade.'

'Go to your rooms Mabel and Hilda, just wait until I tell your father about this.' The two girls scurried off towards the house.

Iris rounded on Charles, 'and I suppose you brought the smelly items with you?'

Charles said nothing his face impassive. His chin was jutted slightly in defiance. His aunt glared at him for a few moments then gave up.

'I think we had better go now,' said Molly her face twitching slightly with laughter. She quickly straightened her face as Iris turned to her.

'I will see you next week Molly,' she shouted over her shoulder as she set off marching towards her house. Iris had grabbed Dotty's hand and was dragging her along with her. 'Oh do stop that snivelling Dotty,' she said sharply to the still wailing Dotty.

Molly looked at Charles, he appeared entirely unmoved. She gently shook her head in admonishment at her son.

'I think you have upset Aunty Iris.'

Charles shrugged and gave his mother a winning smile.

She smiled back, indulgently.

'I think we ought to go. The bus will be along in ten minutes.'

Granny Dunne told Gracie the story gleefully and Gracie enjoyed hearing tales of Charles's exploits. He had never bothered to tell her much about his childhood, just because he didn't think it was particularly interesting. It made Gracie feel closer to him.

'Will you drop in on Annie? Go on,' encouraged Granny Dunne when she saw Charles was hesitating. 'She will like to see you.'

Charles's jaw set in a mutinous line and he shook his head but Granny Dunne met him head on with a fierce look of her own.

Eventually Charles dropped his eyes and sighed. 'All right. When we have finished our cup of tea.' Gracie looked longingly at the raisin cakes. Granny Dunne gave a disapproving cough.

On their way out, Charles and Molly were half way down the path when Granny Dunne followed Gracie and tugged at her sleeve, making her pause for a moment.

'Don't put up with any nonsense from his Nibs will you girl? Mustn't let him get the upper hand too often will you, his ma and dad didn't say no very often you know and neither did I for that matter.'

Gracie smiled at the tiny old lady but Granny Dunne looked serious.

Gracie said cheerfully, 'Oh don't worry about me. I shall be alright, I grew up with three older brothers. It has been lovely meeting you.'

Charles and Molly were waiting for her at the end of the street. Charles looked so tall and handsome with his broad shoulders and gleaming blonde hair. He was leaning against a lamppost looking relaxed, smiling at Gracie, his bright blue eyes squinting against the bright sunlight. The picture was spoilt ever so slightly by the dumpy figure, swathed in boiled wool, of Molly standing too closely to him and looking up at him with a goofy, adoring expression. Gracie shivered, then shook off the feeling of disquiet. Granny Dunne was suggesting Charles was a spoilt child but did that translate into adulthood? Gracie wasn't exactly sure yet.

'Do you think Annie will be in?' Charles asked his mother, hopeful of a negative reply.

'She is allus in,' grunted Molly.

Molly turned to Gracie. 'Our Annie is not quite full shilling, alright?' She looked carefully at Gracie, expecting her to display some distaste.

'Right, of course, no problem,' replied Gracie lightly.

Annie only lived round the corner from Granny Dunne. Their houses were similar both being through- by-light.

Molly rapped loudly on the front door. It wasn't locked so they went straight into the house.

'Annie,' yelled Molly, 'it's me. I've brought our Charles to see you and his new lady friend.'

They were met with silence.

Molly, Charles and Gracie crammed into the tiny dark entrance corridor. It was painted with olive green gloss and smelled of a thousand roast dinners. Molly pushed open the wooden door of the front room. It creaked open slowly. Gracie began to feel nervous. The front room was crammed with inherited heavy furniture. There was a wine-coloured carpet and the walls were painted with the same oppressive green as the entrance hall. There in the corner sat a delicate woman. She was very thin and her face was lined and careworn. Dwarfed by an ancient leather club chair. Her feet were clad in boots and didn't touch the ground. She fixed Gracie with a shrewd look.

Gracie gulped then took the initiative.

'Hello, I am Gracie, please to meet you Annie. We have just come from your mother's house.' Gracie spoke slowly and really loudly.

Annie nodded and grunted genially.

Molly elbowed Gracie crossly in the ribs, making her jump.

'She's not deaf you know you don't have to shout.'

'Do you want some tea?' enquired Annie. She had great difficulty forming her words and they came out of her mouth thick and undistinguished.

'No thanks,' bellowed Molly loudly, 'just had a cup.'

Gracie looked at Charles in irritation. He pretended not to notice that his mother was shouting just as loudly as Gracie had done.

Annie actually had excellent hearing and was mentally very sharp. She had been born with a severe cleft pallet. A lifetime of being either ignored or patronised had meant that eventually she gave up trying to have conversations and became one of life's observers. She spent most of her days now sat in her front room.

When she was younger she was actually very pretty. The roof of her mouth was badly damaged at birth but her face was perfectly formed. In her youth, children still shied away from her because she sounded funny. Her sister Iris and brother James did their best to ensure she was happy when she was young and would defend her with great energy when she was teased by some of the more cruel children on their street. She left school at a very young age and with the help of a kindly vicar's wife, she managed to secure a job in a flower shop, where she would make lovely creative bouquets. She had always helped with the church flower arrangements. She had a wonderful flair for colour and form. The vicar's wife was fond of Annie when she was a child, recognised her real artistic talents, she used her considerable influence to ensure Annie had some decent employment. Annie worked at a florist run by a couple called the Bedwins. Annie would work very quietly in the back room of the florists. The Bedwins were kind to her but never allowed her up front to serve customers or discuss the customer's ideas. She knew that they would often pass off her creations as their own but it didn't bother her particularly. She had never really expected anything from her life and was happy to be surrounded by the lush beauty of cut flowers.

Her life took a disastrous turn when she was in her late teens. She had been spotted by a young man, he was attracted by her pretty face and neat figure. She never realised he had taken to following her home and loitering outside the florists shop.

One day he waited until the Bedwins had taken their lunch. They would shut the shop between one and two every day. They would rather lose custom than allow Annie to serve, after all they had some very wealthy clients and it wouldn't do for them to be upset by the poor girl's difficulties. They were doing their Christian duty by employing her and going far beyond it really, they told themselves in self-congratulating, smug tones. The young man entered the shop via the back door. The door lead into the room where Annie worked with her blooms.

He wasn't bad looking really but his presence in her sanctuary from the world made her uncomfortable.

He had closed the door behind him and he introduced himself with a disarming smile as Edgar Jones.

He went on to say that he had seen her around and wondered if she would like to step out with him sometime.

Annie was thrilled. No boy had even looked at her twice. Or if they had, they soon retreated when she tried to speak to them.

She thought she had better save him any embarrassment later and introduced herself.

Edgar looked disappointed when he realised his angel was badly afflicted but quickly hid it.

'Never mind,' he thought to himself, his dull stupid brain working at speed. 'It will make her all the more grateful. I bet she has never even been with a man before. She was a looker alright.'

He preferred women not to talk anyway.

He began to visit Annie on a lunchtime when the shop was closed. He would always slip through the back door. He invented a silly knock so Annie would know it was him and he made her swear to keep his visits a secret. It was easy for Annie to keep quiet.

Edgar Jones was an unpleasant boy whose reputation for the mistreatment of girls was widely recognised. If Granny Dunne had realised he had become fascinated with her shy, sweet daughter she would have come after him with a huge stick and tried to beat the idea out of his thick cruel skull.

Edgar Jones was not without his persuasive charms when he was intent on a conquest and quite quickly he introduced Annie to the delights of the flesh. Annie knew that God was probably looking down at the two fully clothed figures rolling round on the cold floor of the florist's back room on a lunchtime. The florists definitely would be disapproving of the time a whole vase of peonies was knocked to the floor and crushed. Edgar Jones just wanted to get into her bloomers and couldn't care less about God, the Bedwins or the peonies.

Sadly it was only a matter of time before Annie fell pregnant. When she realised she was with child she had a moment of hope that perhaps Edgar and she could make a home together, with a little garden. Annie felt strongly from the moment of realisation that this baby was a girl and had begun to call it, in her head, her little rosebud, to be named Rose when she was born. Annie was overwhelmed and overjoyed.

One day she decided to try to tell Edgar. He was horrified and shoved her away from him. She slipped onto the cold floor. He raged at her, calling her and the baby terrible, terrible names. He said a baby born from her womb would be damaged, just as she was. His temper was violent and just as he was launching into another tirade, fortunately for Annie the Bedwins had come back from lunch early. Mr Bedwin had been served a most unsatisfactory spatch-cock and had left the restaurant in a noisy huff.

When he heard the shop front door opening, Edgar rushed out of the back door, not before charmingly spitting at Annie who lay cowering on the floor, arms wrapped round her stomach protectively. Mrs Bedwin entered the cold back-room, sensing a disturbance and was shocked to find Annie surrounded by flowers lying on the floor, making pitiful whining noises coming from the back of her throat.

Mrs Bedwin, although a spoilt self-centred woman, recognised a girl in real distress and accompanied silent Annie to her home, telling her to have a little rest and come back to work after the weekend.

Annie spent the weekend in torment. She dare not confide in anyone. Her own mother, her sister and her friend the vicar's wife were her whole world and she could not stand the shame of them knowing, yet she loved the beautiful little life inside her.

In despair she bought a bottle of gin from an ale house far from her home. She waited until the household were sound asleep and she drank most of the bottle quickly. Without pausing to think further she climbed on the kitchen table and with arms spread wide she let herself fall onto the stone floor face first. That night she lost her little rosebud in a mess of blood and pain.

After that horrific evening she retreated completely into her own world and never really came back to the surface.

She remained silently in the employment of the Bedwins, until they retired twenty years later, having become fat and rich on the fine reputation Annie had built for them.

Granny Dunne and her husband had little spare money but Iris was quite well off, between them they always made sure their strange silent Annie had everything she needed and never starved when she stopped working with her beloved flowers.

Annie was always grateful for her family's constant kindness.

Charles, Molly and Gracie didn't stay very long with Annie but Gracie was glad to have met her. She didn't speak but looked with affection at her visitors. Annie squeezed Gracie's hand as she left and presented her with a little paper rose she had formed from a piece of newspaper.

Chapter 14

Gracie and Charles continued their courtship as best they could, the war interrupting their romance regularly and for long periods of time. They got along very well most of the time. Charles could be a little moody if something didn't suit him but Gracie usually managed to jolly him along. Sometimes she thought about Granny Dunne's warning that Charles was spoilt when he was a boy and it bothered her. Charles could also be funny, charming and she was in love.

The months went by and eventually they began to hear hopeful whispers that the war just might be drawing to a close. Ada prayed fervently every night for the continued safety of Edward, Robert and Ian.

One fine day towards the end of the war Charles and Gracie were travelling to Leeds train station. Charles had slept over at the Atwell's house that evening, in Robert's old room and was due to return to the navy the next day. Gracie was accompanying him to Leeds train station to wave him off.

Gracie had begun to spend time with Charles's family on a regular basis and enjoyed their company. They were a little different from the Atwell family, brusque mannerisms and an abrupt way of speaking, but she recognised the same deep thread of love that held the Dunne family together.

After Gracie had first met Charles's family they had argued and Gracie caught a glance of a side of Charles's personality that she didn't like. He was a snob.

'I enjoyed meeting your family, Charles, I thought they were really nice. The cottage where you grew up is sweet,' said Gracie in conversation.

'Sweet,' said Charles with some derision. 'Do you mean tiny?'

'Surely that doesn't bother you, does it?' Asked Gracie incredulously. 'Was that why you were so strange and quiet on the way to see them? Don't be silly Charles. I didn't think you were born in a palace.'

Charles took a deep breath, he was about to argue with Gracie but actually she had read the situation correctly. They looked at each other for a moment or two.

'Your cousins sound like a lot of fun. I would love to meet them if they are still around here. It sounded like you had a grand old time with them in the summer holidays when you were little.'

Charles shrugged. 'If you like, Dotty is still living at home and the others aren't living far away. I think Hill has a couple of kids.' He looked slyly at Gracie, 'You will like Auntie Iris's house, it is even bigger than yours.' He looked at Gracie, testing her reaction. She rolled her eyes and dug him in the ribs. Luckily Charles grinned.

At the train station Charles went to the counter to order two cups of tea, the colour of dishwater, in the hot crowded café. It was raining and while she waited, Gracie watched the drops of condensation run down the thin windows. She could see Charles's gleaming golden hair and broad shoulders.

He pushed his way through the throng of people and sat down at the sticky table opposite Gracie.

He presented her with a dry Chelsea bun with a comical flourish.

'Last one I'm afraid, we will have to share.'

They laughed when they found the only currant in the bun and Charles generously gave it to Gracie.

Charles suddenly looked serious for a minute. He reached over the grubby oilcloth on the table and took her hand. She was wearing her best navy kid leather gloves and Charles slowly slid the glove from her hand. Gracie felt a quiver in her stomach.

He looked into her eyes 'Gracie, when I am through with this navy lark will you marry me?'

Gracie gasped and wondered if she had heard correctly.

'You want to marry me?' she smiled teasingly, wanting the moment to last for a few seconds longer.

'Yes,' said Charles slightly irritably thought Gracie considering their conversation.

'Yes I would love to. I love you Charles,' said Gracie quickly and effusively, realising he wanted the moment taking seriously. She looked at his still handsome face, light sandy hair and sparkling blue eyes.

Charles smiled back at her and nodded in approval. He leant back in his chair and put his hands behind his head.

'Good that's that then.'

Gracie blew out her cheeks and nodded in agreement. She looked down and notice Charles had dropped her glove in a pool of brown tea that had spilt on the table.

He looked at his watch. 'We had better get on the platform. I want a window seat.' They walked hand in hand across the station. Charles suddenly put his arm around Gracie's waist and pulled her into an empty telephone box. He held her fiercely. My first kiss as a fiancé thought Gracie happily, that should make up for the disappointing, quickest proposal on earth. She closed her eyes ecstatically and leaned into his embrace. She stopped short as Charles firmly wiped his handkerchief across her mouth. 'If we are to be married I don't want you wearing red lipstick when I am not with you.'

'What!' protested Gracie her face turning red. 'I always were red lipstick. It suits me,' she said defensively. Charles tightened his grip on her arm.

'Promise me,' he said fiercely.

'Alright,' said Gracie crossly shaking off his arm. Charles released her and his face relaxed.

'Good, I need to go. I am not standing all the way to London.' He gave Gracie a chaste kiss on the lips.

'Bye then, write to me.'

'Of course,' said Gracie giving him a bright smile, trying to ignore the feeling of disquiet the moment in the telephone box had given her. Charles pushed the heavy door of the telephone box open and strode away. He was immediately lost in the crowd of soldiers, sailors and their sweethearts and families waving them off. Gracie, after struggling with the door for a moment, tried to follow Charles and push her own way through the throng to get nearer the train. She hoped to see Charles's face at one of the windows. He was nowhere to be seen but she waved enthusiastically anyway. The train pulled away with its usual pomp, ceremony, noise and great clouds of steam. As soon as the train had left, the people all scurried from the platform back to their day to day business, and Gracie was left alone.

It had stopped raining and the sun had come out. She sat down heavily on the hard wooden bench, waiting for her train back home. She felt quite tearful. She patted her pockets in the vague hope she would find a handkerchief. Suddenly a gold cigarette lighter appeared in front of her eyes, making her jump. She looked up, startled, into the face of a rugged looking young soldier.

He was smiling pleasantly at her, displaying white even teeth. He had dark brown eyes and black hair.

'Would you like a smoke miss, you look like you could do with one?' The soldier spoke with a soft American drawl. 'If I am being too bold...?'

Gracie shook her head. 'No thanks. They make me feel sick,' she added.

The solider looked surprised. 'Do they now? How about that then.' He put his cigarette packet back in his pocket in deference to Gracie.

He sat down on the bench a little way from Gracie and stretched out his long legs in front of him. He put his hands behind his head and faced the sunshine. He gave a long relaxed sigh.

The next train bound for Westridge came in and went out again. Neither of them boarding.

As it pulled away Gracie looked quizzically at the soldier. 'Didn't you want that train?'

The soldier smiled a wide easy going grin at her and looked her up and down.

'You didn't get on the train either Miss.'

'Well no, quite,' agreed Gracie reddening slightly. 'Not that that is any of your business but I was just enjoying the peace and quiet of the moment. I like train stations, I like to guess where people are going. Anyway I happen to live quite close and was waving someone off. I have had a very busy morning.' She added, speaking quickly and now feeling quite defensive, almost close to tears.

The soldier held his arms up in a comic surrender. 'I am sorry Miss to have disturbed your musings. I too am seeking some peace. Sometimes, in this war, you have to grab a little time to yourself. Don't worry I will be jumping on the next train and heading off to fight some Germans.'

Gracie gulped, 'Of course I am sorry.'

The soldier laughed. 'You are right about stations, they are interesting. I like this one it is quite pretty if you look close enough.' He flashed a quick look at Gracie's slim ankles then settled his gaze on the purple butterfly bushes that grew in abundance alongside the tracks.

They remained in companionable silence, each admiring the busy butterflies fluttering lightly amongst the violet spires of the buddleias. Another train approached their platform and the soldier sighed regretfully.

'Well my quiet time is up. I had better jump on this next train.' He stood up and turned to Gracie. He was very tall, well over six foot with broad shoulders. His tousled black hair almost covered his friendly dark eyes. He held out his hand. 'I have enjoyed being quiet with you Miss.' Gracie grinned at him and shook his hand.

He held her gaze for a moment and said 'I was looking forward to meeting a real English rose when I arrived in England and now I finally have. When I see a butterfly I will think of you, maybe.'

He let go of her hand and gave her a smart salute. He climbed onto the train and it pulled out of the station.

Gracie still remained where she was and decided to catch the following train. It had been quite a morning. Charles had proposed, he had then left to go to sea for goodness knows how long, yet the foremost thought in her mind was how the soldier's hand felt when it had gripped her own briefly, firm and dry. He had pushed up his shirt sleeves a little and Gracie couldn't help notice his strong tanned wrists, grooved with muscle.

Chapter 15

The Atwell family were full of excitement when they learned of Charles's proposal. Ada suggested a date in April, so Gracie could decorate the church with spring blooms.

Gracie wrote to Charles frequently while he was away, her letters were loving, full of plans for their wedding and subsequent future together. Charles's replies were terse but were always signed with affection, your Charles. The rationing was still on. Gracie had saved her coupons for weeks to bake a fruitcake to send to Charles. She had even begged a few teaspoons of Ada's medicinal brandy to soak into the cake. A week later she received another letter from Charles.

'Thanks very much for the cake. I ate it in one go one night in my bunk. It gave me bellyache.'

It had probably supposed to make Gracie laugh but it had really, really irritated her. Why hadn't he savoured it or even shared it with his pals. During this wretched war, with its strict rationing, everybody spent some part of their day with a dull hungry ache in their tummies. For tea Gracie often had just one slice of bread, a slice of ham, topped with a tomato and a strong cup of tea. Never complaining, of course, but it did get on one's nerves.

Gracie was lost in this thought one Saturday morning. In fact irritation was giving her the strength to tramp back up the huge Mulberry Hill from the village. She had offered to walk down and fetch some potatoes, onions and scrag-end from the butcher's. Ada was making soup.

Gracie found herself marching up the steep road, with her face set in a scowl. She was sick of rationing. Her arms ached with the heavy load of vegetables. She felt tired, hungry and wished she had eaten the bloody fruit cake herself.

A car horn hooted right next to her, making her jump. She dropped one of the bags and the potatoes and onions went rolling back down the hill.

'Blast it,' shouted Gracie in rage. She started scrabbling round in the road collecting up the vegetables and stuffing them back into her string-bag.

She stood up and watched as the onions went rolling speedily back down the Mulberry Hill

The car had stopped in front of her. She stood with her hand on her hip about to give the noisy driver a piece of her mind. The car door swung open and out climbed the soldier from the train station.

He smiled slowly at her, raising his eyebrows, delighted that their paths had crossed so soon, leaving Gracie in no doubt that he was pleased to see her. Then he dashed down the road and rescued the escaped onions.

He brought them back to Gracie.

'I think these belong to you,' he drawled.

'Thank you,' said Gracie smiling back.

'I'm sorry about making you jump with the car horn. I didn't realise it was so loud. I actually startled myself.'

'Oh so it was you making all that unnecessary racket was it,' said Gracie pretending to be cross.

The soldier shrugged.

The car was a Humber Super Snipe, a thing of beauty. The soldier noticed Gracie's appreciative look.

'You like cars?' he asked in surprise.

'Oh yes,' nodded Gracie 'do you mind if I take a look?'

'It's not mine, I wish it was,' he said. 'Staff car. I sometimes drive the big cheeses around. You know much about cars?' he asked looking impressed.

'Not really,' shrugged Gracie 'I have three older brothers who love them so you can help picking up bits.'

'Where are you going with ten stone of veg anyway, not far I hope?'

'Just home, I live at the top of this hill.'

'Would you like a lift?'

Gracie hesitated. The American soldiers had built quite a reputation amongst English girls. The soldier noticed her discomfort.

'I tell you what, why don't I take the veggies. That bag sure looks pretty heavy. They might enjoy it anyway. I might let them toot the horn, see if we can make any more pretty girls jump.'

Gracie laughed shaking her head.

'Oh dash it, I would love a lift in this car. Thank you.'

The soldier held the door open for her and she climbed in as elegantly as she could.

The journey lasted a minute. Gracie couldn't take her eyes of his hands on the steering wheel. They were so strong-looking, the hands of a manual labourer.

When he pulled up in front of the Atwell house he turned to look at Gracie.

'So we meet again English rose.' He scratched his head contemplatively. 'Are you busy on Sunday afternoon? Some of the boys in the platoon were going to drive to Ilkley and have a picnic by the river. There will be about ten of us all together. Some of the guys and their girls.'

Gracie started to shake her head.

'There is a boyfriend, huh? I guessed you had a boyfriend already, a looker like you. Is he away?'

Gracie nodded, wishing for a moment she was footloose and fancy free. Just for a moment.

The soldier smiled in a friendly way.

'I tell you what why don't you come along anyway. I know the score. I can't say I am not disappointed but it is just a nice afternoon by the river, no funny business, I promise.'

Gracie notice the curtains of number ten beginning to twitch so she began to open the car door.

'Alright. A picnic will be lovely, thanks. My name is Gracie by the way.'

'Raymond.'

He held Gracie's gaze. His handsome face suddenly still. His eyes were the colour of treacle toffee, fringed with thick black lashes.

Gracie was transfixed for a second. She felt almost hypnotised. He really did have a beautiful face. She felt like he was looking right into her heart.

She shook her head slightly, breaking the spell.

'Right oh soldier boy,' she said in an overly hearty voice to cover her new wave of blushes. 'I will see you on Saturday.' She jumped out of the car and sprinted up the path of the house.

'What about the shopping?' Raymond called out after her.

'Blast.' Gracie stopped, screwed up her eyes in embarrassment for a moment, took a deep breath and turned round on her heel.

'Of course silly me.' Her voice was still booming. She grabbed the bags from him, not meeting his eyes and scuttled back down the path.

'Bye,' she yelled over her shoulder.

She dived through the kitchen door and slammed it behind her. The kitchen was fortunately empty.

'Oh Lord,' she groaned her face bright red.

'What on earth am I doing?'

Her stomach was turning somersaults. Really he was an absolute dish. She dropped the shopping on the stone floor of the kitchen and ran herself a cool glass of water.

'I love Charles and he loves me,' she told herself firmly but why did a five minute meeting with a handsome American turn her into a dithering idiot.

'Oh Lord.' she said out loud again.

She spent the whole of the working week agonising over whether she should go on the picnic. She thought of nothing else. She made plenty of mistakes at work, even the other girls asked if she was quite well. By Friday she had made up her mind. Raymond hadn't been in contact at all. In fact she told herself he had probably clean forgotten about her and had given another girl and her vegetables a lift and invited her to a lovely picnic by the river. Men as good-looking as that were bound to have a dozen girls running after them. She thought fondly of Charles. Blond and equally handsome in his own solid square-jawed way. Bravely sailing the seas who knows where. She shivered slightly and hoped he was safe.

Saturday morning came. It was a bright sunny day and Gracie was helping her dad pile the soil up over the potatoes to protect them from frost. She was dressed in an old red blouse and a pair of shorts. Her hair was tied up on the top of her head with a red ribbon. It was hot work. Tendrils of hair were escaping the ribbon and her face was glowing.

'Gracie love,' said Walter, 'I think there is someone here to see you.'

Gracie stood up quickly acutely aware of the fact that she had been bending right over the potato crop and her bottom was in Raymond's direction. She quickly folded her arms to hide the circles of dark sweat that had appeared under arms of her blouse.

He was leaning against the wall of the house, smoking in a casual manner. He smiled his slow smile.

'Hi there, had you forgotten our picnic?' He looked her up and down. Gracie felt frozen to the spot. Walter was not frozen by any means and was bristling slightly at the presence of this overly confident young man who was staring with obvious longing at his beloved baby daughter.

Raymond suddenly bounded forward and offered an outstretched hand towards Walter. He smiled broadly at Walter.

'Hello Sir, pleased to meet you my name is Private Raymond Blake, my division is stationed close to the village. Pleased to meet you. There is a party of us driving along to Ilkley for a picnic this afternoon and I wondered if Gracie would like to accompany us.'

'Including our captain, boys and girls together.' He added quickly as he saw Walter begin to look slightly panicky. The idea of Gracie going off with a truck full of soldiers was very concerning indeed.

Walter glanced at Gracie. He questioned hesitantly 'Is this right, lass?'

'Yes dad, it is fine. It will be nice to meet some new lads and lasses for a change.' She smiled reassuringly at Walter.

Walter raised his eyebrows and shrugged. 'Alright then.'

'I will just get changed.' Gracie threw a smouldering glance at Raymond over her shoulder.

She pulled on an old tea dress. It was faded pink cotton, covered with tiny pretty roses. She had other much nicer dresses but felt it might give Raymond the wrong impression if she came back downstairs all dolled up to the nines. Besides it wouldn't be fair to Charles.

She hesitated just before she left her bedroom to go downstairs. She looked at herself in the mirror. She wasn't a particularly vain girl. She knew she had an attractive figure, long slim legs and broad shoulders with all the curves in the right places. She loved Charles but they hadn't seen each other for months. It was only a blasted picnic anyway. Raymond was probably being kind. She felt slightly irritated at Walter's concern. After all she was eighteen and knew exactly what was what as far as boys were concerned. She vowed to tell Raymond about her engagement the first chance she got, so then there would be no confusion. If he still wanted to be her friend then that was a fine. Just because he happened to be gorgeous. She blew a raspberry into the mirror and steamed it up.

There was a hesitant knock on the door. 'Gracie love?' Walter's voice came from the other side of the door.

'Come on in.'

Walter stepped in looking uncomfortable.

He rattled the loose door handle on the wooden door.

'Is this thing still broke. Gracie?'

'Yep,' said Gracie cheerfully. 'It has always been broken. Ian took it apart to find out how it worked do you remember? Years ago.'

Walter smiled and cleared his throat a number of times and looked slightly perplexed.

'What is it?'

'Do you know what time your mother is back from the shops?'

Gracie shook her head.

'What is it, anything wrong?'

'This boy downstairs. He looks a bit….' Walter trailed off, wishing Ada was beside him.

He tried again. 'He looks a bit lively.' He then cleared his throat loudly and went red in the face. 'Well you hear things about the Americans. Offering our girls chocolate and such like….'

Gracie realised what he was trying to say. Gracie didn't want to particularly have this conversation with her father, it was embarrassing.

'It is fine to go off on a picnic of course, you should have a good time, just use your loaf that's all lass. Just use your loaf.'

Walter went back downstairs feeling relieved that he had spoken to Gracie and she had seemed to understand what he was trying to say.

After all he had been young once and enthralled by the fairer sex. It seemed a little different in his day. Nature seemed to run at a more leisurely pace. The young men of today should bloody well slow down and keep their trousers on. Walter suddenly felt old and tired.

Gracie thought for a moment. She knew Sylvia was home, she might want to come along. Gracie didn't particularly want to share Raymond with Sylvia but then decided it might be for the best after all. Walter didn't dispense fatherly advice very often and he was clearly uncomfortable with her dashing off in a car with an American on her own. Of course there was Charles to consider as well. With a pang of regret Gracie knew she would probably have to ignore the heady crush she had just developed on the dishy Raymond.

She ran downstairs, jumping the last three steps, a childish habit she found she couldn't give up.

Raymond looked approvingly at her when she appeared through the door. His face fell slightly when she asked if he minded if she brought her friend along.

Raymond realised that Walter was unashamedly monitoring his reaction from behind his spade. So he gave a cheery shrug and said 'Sure, that would be swell.'

Gracie pushed through the hedge. Amy answered the door looking bemused, like she had just woken up from a snooze. She quickly hid the cut glass tumbler of whiskey she had dangling loosely in her hand, behind her back. She was dressed in a smart linen dress with a matching jacket slung over her skinny shoulders. She had a large run up her stockings though that she appeared not to notice.

Sylvia pushed Amy rather roughly out of the way when she heard Gracie's voice. She like the idea of a picnic and the possibility of meeting a boy or two. Luckily she had just washed her hair and had managed to secure the limp hanks into some rather good rolls. Gracie immediately complimented her hair and her new tea dress which encouraged Sylvia's fragile good mood further.

They walked back to the Atwell's garden arm in arm.

Sylvia said 'Crumbs' under her breath as she absorbed the beautiful Raymond.

He smiled politely at Sylvia and turned to leave the garden.

Sylvia flashed a round eyed look at Gracie and both girls dissolved into giggles. Sylvia's laugh sounded rather like a bath water gurgling down a drain, which made Gracie laugh even more.

Raymond had brought the car. He had the door open and was stood looking slightly perplexed at the giggling girls, although he knew girls often gave lovely nervous laughs around him. He started to preened a little but then started as Gracie let out a laughing snort.

'So where are we meeting the rest of the gang?' Gracie asked as she settled comfortably into the soft leather seats of the car.

'We are meeting them by the river. Just us three for the journey.' There was a slight barbed edge to his voice which Sylvia immediately picked up on and registered with a scowl. Her mood dropped slightly.

'How did you manage to get the staff car for the afternoon?' Asked Gracie.

Raymond gave her a sideways glance.

'Let's just say the Captain owed me a favour.'

'Right.' Said Gracie decided not to enquire further.

'Anyway, I thought we could get to know each other a little better.'

Gracie tried to ignore the flutter of excitement in her heart.

She thoroughly enjoyed the journey to Ilkley. Raymond was a confident driver and handled the car with ease. They chatted about their favourite authors, music. They both loved to dance. He told her about the family farm he grew up on in New Jersey and his plans to renovate the family farm house. The journey passed swiftly and they found themselves parking on the bridge over the river in the centre of the pretty town of Ilkley.

Sylvia remained quiet. Observing the two of them accompanied by the usual jealous tang in her mouth. She was obviously the third wheel, again. How did bloody Gracie do it? She was wearing a really old dress and hadn't even brushed her hair. It was tangled like a bird's nest. Sylvia thought spitefully that when Charles returned she might mention this little trip out to him. He wouldn't be very happy to think his intended was driving out with another man. Sylvia actually liked Charles. He was always kind to her and said she looked nice and he always included her in his conversations. She rather disloyally allowed herself a little day dream of Charles coming round to her house in the dead of night, her in a silk negligee, and him declaring his undying love for Sylvia and telling her he only pretended to like Gracie to get closer to Sylvia and did Sylvia realise she looked exactly the same as Veronica Lake? Sylvia let out a loud sigh causing Gracie to spin round and ask if she was feeling quite well, making Sylvia jump.

They reached picturesque town of Ilkley and Raymond parked the car on the dark stone bridge that stood solidly over the River Wharfe.

Raymond jumped out of the car and opened Gracie's door. He reached in and grabbed her hand.

'Come on woman,' he said in a mock Yorkshire accent. 'We 'aven't got all day.'

Sylvia laughed loudly at Raymond. He gave her a brisk smile but turned back to Gracie and virtually pulled her out of the car.

'Come and look at this view.'

'God, England is a beautiful little county.' His grip tightened on her hand and he turned to look at Gracie. 'Beautiful,' he drawled softly. Gracie was caught once again in his stare for a moment.

Sylvia crossed the road and joined them.

Abruptly his mood altered again and he let go of her hand.

'Right let's go and see if we can see the guys.'

Raymond set off at a quick pace down the stone steps at the side of the bridge and left Gracie and Sylvia behind.

Sylvia scuttled after him, caught him up and breathlessly linked his arm to walk with him. Raymond stiffened slightly, annoyed, but let her arm remain where it was.

Gracie followed at a more leisurely pace, entirely unperturbed by Raymond's sudden departure. In fact she wondered if Raymond used the "beautiful view" line often. She felt the urgency of her crush lessen slightly. She wandered along admiring the pretty riverbank, the stillness of the ancient trees and soft grasses, a contrast to the jaunty pace the River Wharfe itself was setting. She watched a little team of ducks swimming valiantly together across the lively river. Suddenly a vibrant image of Edward, Robert and Ian appeared in her head and her stomach filled with a fearful energy. She shut her eyes for a moment to steady herself and tried to breathe deeply for a moment. She knew that the fearful adrenaline would subside and she would be left once again with the constant helpless worry that lived quietly in the back of her mind.

The town of Ilkley nestled under the protective shadow of an imposing moor. Gracie looked up at the heather covered moor with its huge rocks and it seemed to loom over Gracie, almost as if it would crush the pretty little town and the kindly Yorkshire folks that lived in their dark stone built terraces. She briefly thought of the Pathe news reel shown at the cinema the other week. The sound of the gunfire, so loud and so frightening. The noise of the destructive roar of bullets had stayed with her.

She shut her eyes once more and set up a prayer to God. 'Please keep them safe, please keep them safe, please keep them safe.' Sometimes she would repeat the mantra hundreds of times until she felt the fear dissipate.

She dragged her eyes away from the dark moor and looked once more along the riverbank. It was busy with groups of soldiers, girls in flowered frocks and sun hats. Land girls in their uniforms, stretching out legs in shorts warming in the sunshine. Gracie finally focussed in on Raymond he was already lounging on a picnic rug with Sylvia hovering uncertainly by his side, trying to decide whether to sit down or not. He was laughing uproariously with another young man. He had a shock of white blond hair and a broad face covered in freckles.

Gracie walked leisurely towards them.

'There you are Gracie. Come and sit down and meet my best buddy in England. Tim the bravest soldier I know.'

Raymond pulled Gracie rather unceremoniously down onto the rug. Tim grinned, put down the big brown bottle of beer he was holding and held out his hand in greeting. He had unbuttoned his tunic revealing a surprising amount of blond chest hair. Gracie averted her eyes. Tim's own eyes were slightly out of focus due to the beer but he seemed friendly enough. His other hand was firmly round the waist of rough looking girl whose own dress looked to be equally as unbuttoned. She seemed to be smiling to herself, swaying a little and was taking frequent drags from her own large bottle of beer.

Raymond introduced some of the other soldiers and their girlfriends. It seemed like a jolly group.

Sylvia had sat herself down on one of the rugs when Gracie had arrived and had crossed her arms and legs primly. She was staring disapprovingly at the rough girl, who was called Bernie. Bernie had just managed to spill beer down the front of her dress and Tim was mopping it up most enthusiastically, encouraged by Bernie's raucous laughter and wriggling. Tim suddenly started to lick at the beer and was surprised when she pushed him off.

Bernie was upset. Her eyes filled with easy tears.

'I am a lady thank you very much,' she slurred. 'What do you think you are doing? Do you think I am common or something?'

Tim's face flashed with anger.

'It is only a bit of fun,' he said.

'Don't want to waste the beer eh Raymond?'

Raymond grinned. 'The man is right about that Bernie. Don't be such a spoil sport.'

Gracie felt very uncomfortable. She thought Bernie was absolutely right. Tim was going too far. She looked to Sylvia to see if she also felt sorry for the girl but Sylvia was now laughing along with Tim and Raymond at Bernie's discomfort.

Gracie felt annoyed at Sylvia. God she was mean at times.

Bernie pushed her grubby feet into her sandals. She swayed as she stood up and Gracie offered her hand to help her up. Bernie swiped Gracie's hand away in irritation and flounced off with as much dignity as she could muster.

She yelled over her shoulder 'Your cock's not that big, tank rear gunner my arse'

The party burst into laughter.

Tim grinned round not bothered in the slightest. He shuffled round so he was next to Gracie.

'What do you think Gracie? This is a good way to spend a day's leave eh? Friends, ales, pork pies, chocolate from our good friend Raymond and this lovely river. Don't worry about Bernie, she's a good girl, she knows what's what.'

'I love this place. I am from the Norfolk broads, do loads of fishing with my Pa. Yep me and my Pa.'

He looked wistful for a moment, obviously thinking of home.

He turned to Gracie and tried to focus his eyes. 'Raymond has told me about you.'

Gracie smiled uncertainly.

'He said you have got the best tits he has seen for ages.'

Raymond whacked him across his ear and everyone laughed again.

Raymond winked at Gracie and shrugged his shoulders ruefully. She tried to laugh along but again felt little uncomfortable. It wasn't that she didn't have a sense of humour, she always enjoyed a laugh. Growing up with Edward, Robert and Ian, her brothers were always joking about something but their jokes tended to be silly and they mainly stayed away from coarse humour or bad language.

The subject was changed and everyone settled down. The day continued to pass pleasantly. There was something infinitely precious about such golden afternoons. Everyone was only too aware that the war was rumbling away in the background threatening everything and everyone they each loved. So the laughter, although not forced in any way, seemed to be louder more raucous than usual. The quiet moments had an undercurrent of fragility that was to be absorbed. Raymond had made his way round the group one by one chatting and introducing Gracie to his other friends.

Tim had nodded off briefly but had woken up full of high spirits and had homed in on Sylvia, who was laughing at his wild stories and madly twisting her hair in her fingers and batting her short pale eyelashes. She was excited by his attentions and was looking at him with fascination.

Throughout her early teens Sylvia had had her fair share of male attention. She dressed very well, cajoling money easily from Bill or Amy. Often friends of Joe would approach Sylvia, thinking Joe's sister must be as much fun as he was. They would be quickly put in their place as she would brush them off relentlessly and often cruelly. She didn't want any old village boy she was always waiting for a handsome, rich man to come along and sweep her off her feet.

Tim's pride had been hurt by Bernie's drunken rejection earlier, especially in front of the other lads and he thought it was time to redress the balance. Sylvia seemed a very easy target. The ugly friend, perfect.

Gracie was relieved Sylvia seemed to be enjoying herself. Gracie wasn't entirely taken in by Tim's ready patter. She had seen the rage flit across his face when poor Bernie had refused to let him rummage around amongst her wet clothes. Gracie knew enough about the world to know what could have happened if Tim and Bernie had been on their own. Tim was exactly the kind of boy Walter had tried, in his round-about way, to warn Gracie about. She decided to try to keep half an eye out for Syl. Someone had produced a bottle of whiskey and another of brandy and were passing them round the group. Gracie noticed Tim was encouraging Sylvia to take some very large gulps.

The afternoon gradually eased into early evening with a lovely soft sunset over the river made up of blues, pinks and golds.

The lively chatter of earlier had settled. Couples whispered their love to one another, held hands and exchanged gentle kisses and friends talked quietly about their families, home and hopes for the future.

Gracie and Raymond were laid companionably side by side on a rug watch the river flow by, the sunset making its muddy depths glow and sparkle. They had been talking for a couple of hours. Raymond was a very good listener. He encouraged her to talk about her worries for her brothers. She even found herself telling him about Charles's proposal and how sometimes she had doubts over whether she should marry him. Eventually they fell into silence. Gracie felt drowsy from the warmth, the food and the mouthfuls of brandy she had drunk. Raymond was laid apart from her but had crooked his little finger round her little finger.

Gradually Raymond's friends and fellow soldiers were drifting toward the pub to round off the day with one last drink. Anything to put off tomorrow. Tim was whispering suggestive words in Sylvia's ear and she was blushing and batting him away coyly whilst staring back at him with a look of fascination, fear and excitement.

Raymond turned to Gracie and looked intently at her from his deep brown eyes.

'So, are you happy?' His voice was very deep and the American drawl was very attractive.

He held her gaze.

'I think you are making me happy,' he said quietly.

Gracie wasn't particularly given to deep introspection. She found it all together embarrassing to talk about one's feelings all the time.

She shrugged, spoiling the mood slightly.

'It think it has been a lovely day. Thank you for bringing me and Syl. Most of your friends seem very nice indeed,' she said pointedly with an impish grin referring to Tim.

Raymond didn't smile back but continued to stare at her.

'You didn't answer me, are you happy?'

He seemed to scan her face as if looking for clues. He had moved very close. Gracie breathed in his masculine scent. Their faces were a couple of inches apart. Her lips parted and she began to close her eyes.

Suddenly they were jolted by a loud yell from Tim. They both turned round and saw Tim bending over Sylvia who was laid supine on the grass not moving. He was shaking her shoulders. Gracie jumped up and ran across to them, Raymond sauntering slowly behind.

'What on earth is the matter with her? Asked Gracie in panic.

She put her head to her chest and was relieved to hear a resolute steady heartbeat. Her breathing seemed a little shallow. She also stank of brandy.

Raymond kicked her leg gently. 'The silly cow has passed out, she seems alright though.'

Gracie sat up straight.

'I don't think unconscious is particularly alright even if you do.' she snapped.

Tim and Raymond both rolled their eyes.

Sylvia had her mouth wide open and her tongue was lolling out of the side of her mouth. A thick strand of drool was making its way down her cheek.

Tim hiccupped. 'Look at that, sleeping beauty. Imagine waking up next to that, I've had a narrow escape eh Raymond mate? Waste of that booze though, I thought she was a game old bird. I am never going to get my leg over today at this rate.'

Raymond snorted with laughter.

Gracie decided to ignore them and save her anger for later. She rubbed Sylvia's hands and face vigorously and was relieved when her eyes began to flutter open.

'Come along dear, it's me Gracie, open your eyes for me.'

'It's alright, I am here,' she reassured Sylvia gently.

Gracie looked up to see Raymond and Tim looking on dispassionately.

'Help me to sit her up,' she snapped at them in exasperation. Tim was smoking a cigarette.

'Raymond mate, I think I will join the others in the pub, the dozy mare will be fine.'

Sylvia suddenly turned over and vomited violently all over the grass. Gracie was pleased to observe a large splash of sick had landed in the middle of Tim's boot. He hadn't noticed.

Syl began to cry, muttering something incomprehensible about Amy drinking gin.

Tim turned on his puke splattered boots, snorting 'I have had enough of this, are you coming mate?'

'Raymond, we need to take her home, she is poorly. Could you please take us back home? Or at least help me to the train station?'

Raymond looked mutinous and shrugged his shoulders, like a spoilt child. This was not part of his plan.

'I never even invited her, it was supposed to be you and me. I do know that there is now way I can take a staff car back stinking to God damn high heaven. She might throw again. To be honest Gracie I can't stand women who can't hold their drink, it is so weak.'

Gracie was furious. 'She didn't realise what she was doing. She hardly touches the stuff. It was your friend who was tipping it down her throat, hoping to get his mucky hands all over her no doubt. How can you be friends with such a beast? He is a vile cad.'

Raymond stared at Gracie, his face was still and voice cold.

'I don't know what a cad is Gracie, presumably not a compliment, I am not from your jolly little town. I do know that Tim is the best, bravest man to have beside you fighting in the field. You are making a fuss about nothing. You are not a child and neither is Sylvia.'

'Stay here and play Florence Nightingale with your friend. When she had sobered up put her on a train. She will be fine. I am going to catch up with the fellas.'

'Will you help me to the train station, then, she can hardly stand up, please Raymond?'

Sylvia staggered to her feet.

'I will come with you if you really need me to.' Raymond said rolling his eyes.

'Oh don't bother,' spat Gracie, 'we will be fine on our own. Thank you very much.'

Raymond's voice softened to a conciliatory tone.

'Meet me in the pub later, you are really pretty when you are angry.'

He walked away with a jaunty whistle, with complete confidence that Gracie would appear in the pub later with freshly applied makeup, slightly ashamed of her temper. He would forgive her magnanimously and who knows where the rest of the evening could lead. He was already imagining the tones he would adopt, firm at first because she didn't obey him straight away as he expected, then soothing and forgiving as he accepts her apology.

Gracie was really angry. He could jolly well forget it. Some men were absolute rotters. She didn't need to go crawling back to him to beg for a lift. She had just enough money with her to catch the train with Syl.

Sylvia was crying quietly to herself. 'Don't tell my father will you?'

Gracie private thought that neither Bill nor Amy would even notice if Syl had been on the booze. They had never really bothered what Sylvia was doing or Joe for that matter.

'Of course not, I will come in with you and tell them you don't feel very well. You will need an aspirin and a big glass of water before you go to sleep.'

'I don't like the booze Gracie you know. It spoils things. Don't really like the taste either so I don't bother with it. Besides,' she hiccupped 'Amy drinks it all in our house.'

Sylvia looked really sad and Gracie's heart went out to her.

It took hours to get home and they had to catch two trains. They arrived home after 9 o'clock. She got into her bedroom after making sure Sylvia was safe in her own bed. Bill was out and Amy didn't appear to realise Sylvia had even gone out. Gracie made Joe find a bucket and laid it next to Sylvia's bed along with a couple of towels from the bathroom. She asked Joe to look in on her before he went to bed. Joe agreed.

Gracie thought he would be giggling at the state of his sister, as they didn't get along at all well. But when he realised Sylvia was drunk, Joe just looked sad.

Gracie climbed into her own bed after having a quick wash round in the sink. She felt tired, dirty and if she was honest with herself a bit of a fool. A few minutes later there was a gentle knock on the door and Walter came in holding a steaming hot cup of tea. He set it down on the little table besides Gracie's bed.

'Everything alright lassie?'

Gracie sighed.

'Yep it had just been a long day that's all, I am really tired.'

Walter nodded.

'Alright, are we going to see the American boy again?'

'No,' said Gracie slowly. 'I don't think so.'

Walter nodded again and looked thoughtful.

'Probably for the best lassie, face like a dog's arse anyway.'

Gracie exploded with laughter.

Walter went out of the door.

'Dad,' she called, 'thanks for the tea.'

A week later, Gracie was feeling a bit brighter about things. Charles had managed to get a couple of days shore leave and he had come straight to see her. He had bought a beautiful tiny engagement ring, it was set with three small diamonds on an elegant twist. It suited her slim fingers perfectly. After having a meal at the Atwell's home they had taken a walk through the woods. Charles had held her quietly in his arms for a very long time. He breathed in the soft scent of her hair and detected the faint aroma of the pork chops Ada had cooked them, for a treat. They sat on a fallen beech tree and held hands, still quiet.

'Gracie,' said Charles tentatively.

'Do you still want to marry me?'

Gracie smiled. 'Yes I think I do.'

'Only think?' Said Charles surprised.

Gracie decided to be honest with him. 'I love you. I really do. You are a lot of fun and I can easily imagine spending the rest of my life with you. The thing is, when you proposed I felt a bit let down.

Gracie stared at Charles and began to feel foolish. She decided to press on though.

'I know I sound like a spoilt, silly woman but I always thought my own proposal would be in a room filled with roses and violin music and I would be overwhelmed with the romance of it all. Little girls imagine this wonderful moment, or at least I did. A snappy question over a dry current bun in the smelly station café was slightly disappointing.'

Charles nodded sheepishly.

'I have been a bit bothered about it as well. It was shoddy. I am sorry. I am not used to this proposal business.'

Gracie was about to reply archly that she should think not but as she looked into his face she realised that he was genuinely upset and was speaking from the heart. The war was so full of uncertainties. Why on earth had she become wrapped up in something unimportant?

He suddenly smiled and slid down from the tree trunk.

'Back in a tick.' He disappeared into the woods for a few minutes.

He came back with a tiny posy of early wild violets and soft yellow primroses. He presented them to Gracie with a flourish.

'I can't give you violin music but if you listen carefully I think you will be able to hear my highly expensive organized choir of thrushes, black birds and maybe even a nightingale or two.'

Gracie laughed.

Charles took hold of her hand.

'I love you Gracie Atwell I have done ever since I saw you in that dance hall. I know I am not the easiest man to get along with, as Granny Dunne regularly informs me,' he smiled wryly. 'I knew I had got everything wrong that morning in the café. I was so overwhelmed everything came out wrong. I didn't intend to ask you to marry me in the train station. Believe it or not, some of us boys have ideas of how we would like to propose. Not as soppy as you girls of course, we are tough guys after all'. He grinned again. Then carried on speaking quietly. 'I was suddenly so frightened of leaving you and if I am totally honest frightened of heading back out to fight again. I don't know, that morning, life seemed all the more precious. I don't know, something about surviving for so long, I just wondered for a moment if my luck would still hold out.

'Oh Charles' breathed Gracie.

Charles got down on one knee in front of her and asked her to marry him for the second time.

He slipped the pretty ring on her finger and they kissed, slowly, quietly, lovingly. The kiss of two people in love.

Chapter 16

Gracie was busy admiring the way the little diamonds on her ring caught the light as she typed quickly and efficiently in the large noisy room of an insurance company typing pool where she worked.

Gracie had begun working for the company when she left school. Sylvia had already been working there for a year. She told Gracie of an opening position in her typing pool and recommended her for the job. Gracie had done quite well at school. Her English, and Spanish for that matter, were excellent and she had an aptitude for figures.

Gracie found touch typing mind-numbingly tedious work but the rest of the girls in the pool were pleasant. She liked the banter and enjoyed the shared bits of gossip and tittle tattle. The insurance company was forward thinking and had one or two good opportunities for women. Gracie intended to climb that slippery ladder and not let one minute of her education go to waste. She just had to start at the bottom that's all and, thanks to Sylvia, she had a foot in the door.

Sylvia held a slightly senior position to Gracie and many of the other juniors which suited her down to the ground. They were still friends and managed to get along but Gracie often had to listen to complaints especially from the young members of staff about Sylvia's bullying tactics. Gracie would listen and shake her head sympathetically, then diplomatically suggest they take it up with one of the managers if they were really upset. She absolutely did not want to get involved in the serious office politics that Sylvia took great delight in creating, wielding her miniscule amount of power.

As soon as Gracie told Sylvia about the proposal. Sylvia insisted on being the bridesmaid and steamrolled Gracie into agreeing.

Gracie didn't really mind and agreed to keep the peace.

A little later that day Gracie was in the smoky break room of the office putting her handbag in her locker. It was the last couple of minutes of her lunch break before her busy fingers would be back to work. She felt her usual twinges of indigestion. She went home for a cooked lunch every day. The insurance office was practically next to Leeds train station and there were regular trains to Westridge station. Sometimes she fancied grabbing a sandwich in town or looking round the shops but she was becoming increasingly worried about Ada. Ada seemed very quiet, too quiet.

Gracie had come home one day the previous week and Ada had her hat on in the house. It was her summer straw hat, wholly inappropriate as it was windy and raining outside. When Gracie asked her if she was trying it on. Ada had looked absolutely blankly at her. Gracie took the hat from her and changed the subject and Ada seemed fine and carried on an ordinary conversation. On another occasion Gracie noticed the usually tidy Ada was wearing a cardigan with a large hole in one sleeve.

That lunchtime, Gracie had asked Ada if Robert and his wife Rita were coming over for lunch the next day which was Saturday. Ada had replied she didn't think so. Robert would be boxing as usual. The family knew Robert had given up boxing after he returned from the war. He found he no longer had the stomach for violence of any kind.

Walter said he would walk back down to the station with Gracie. She asked Walter straight out if he thought Ada was behaving in an odd way. She thought Walter would reassure her and tell her he thought Ada was just tired.

Instead Walter shook his head slowly and said after a while

'I just don't know lass. I just don't know. She seems a little bit forgetful at the moment. She has been sick a fair few times recently. I have asked her if she feels well of course but she says she is fine. Let's give it a bit more time, just you leave the worrying to me. You have got a lot on your plate what with planning a wedding and such. I will keep an eye on her.'

His face was serious and Gracie wondered just how forgetful Ada was getting. Walter was still working and he planned to retire at the end of the year. He was now thinking seriously if he could leave Ada to her own devices until Christmas. There had been a number of incidents recently of water overflowing from sinks and potatoes left on the stove to boil dry, filling the house with acrid smoke.

Gracie felt better if she popped back during the day even if it meant the discomfort of digesting stew and dumplings on an afternoon in a stuffy office.

Sylvia scurried in.

'Hi there.' She seemed in high spirits.

'I think there will be an announcement this afternoon in the office.' She said theatrically.

She paused looking round the busy break room.

'Can you tell us Syl?' Asked Milly one of the youngest typists.

Sylvia shook her head grandly.

'Oh no, of course not, you will all have to wait for Mr Banks, he will tell you all when he sees fit.'

Mr Banks was the General Manager of the office. A kindly decent man who treated all his employees with fairness and respect.

Milly nodded, going slightly red.

Gracie gritted her teeth. She was not in the mood for Sylvia's nonsense this afternoon. Why does she have to be so irritating? She had always enjoyed being privy to information that she refused to share but made everyone around her aware that she knew. It was aggravating when they were children and still just as irksome.

Gracie spent a lot of her free time with Ella, who she remained friends with after they were billeted together when they were evacuated. Ella had no time at all for Syl and Gracie was tiring of defending her, there were plenty of easy going fun people to be friends with. She wished she wasn't her bridesmaid. Gracie and Sylvia had had quite a fall out about Raymond and Tim. Instead of thanking Gracie for rescuing her from the vile attentions of Tim and getting her home safely she accused Gracie of spoiling her fun and insisting she was absolutely fine and was having a wonderful time. She told Gracie she couldn't have all of the boys in the world and even suggested she would tell Charles about her dalliance with Raymond the next time she saw him.

Gracie was really angry with her. She already felt guilty about her silly crush on American Raymond and disloyal to Charles so she ended up absolutely letting fly at Sylvia, calling her ungrateful and spiteful.

Sylvia was actually taken aback by Gracie's attack and they had formed an uneasy truce with one another. Sylvia didn't actually want to lose Gracie's friendship and wondered if she had pushed Gracie's easy going nature a bit too far. She would hate it if Gracie said she could no longer be a bridesmaid.

Gracie was absolutely fed up to the back teeth of Sylvia's sniping, it seemed to be all the time now.

She had become unbearable.

Sylvia was currently stepping out with a handsome, helpless lad who worked in their post room called Sidney. All the girls had noticed him when he joined the insurance company and vied for his attentions. Sidney found all this female attention rather perplexing. His parents were a strict, miserable couple who had never praised him once for fear of spoiling him. So he had grown up almost entirely unaware of his fine bone structure and beautifully straight nose.

He was a nice enough boy, rather an innocent. He was very shy and stammered every so often. He never could manage to pluck up the courage to approach any girl himself. Sylvia had decided it was about time she got a proper boyfriend so she asked Sidney to take her to the flicks and then bullied Sidney into stepping out with her. Poor bemused Sidney didn't like Sylvia very much. She spent a lot of their time together gossiping and saying mean things about the rest of the girls in the office. She allowed him a chaste kiss and a cuddle every so often, just enough to pique his interest. Sylvia was thrilled she had managed to bag the best looking fellow around. Sidney had absolutely no idea how to untangle himself from her attentions though and was currently very worried indeed because Sylvia had started mentioning engagement rings.

Sylvia's moment in the lime light had passed so she turned on Gracie.

'Was Ada alright today Gracie?' Sylvia asked.

Gracie looked at her. 'I don't know she seems really distant I think we need to take her to the doctors. It is getting worse, she was really confused this morning.' Gracie gulped as she got a pain in her throat. She felt like crying.

Sylvia sniffed dismissively. 'Actually thinking about it, it is probably just the booze.' Sylvia let out a sharp, silly laugh.

'What?' gasped Gracie.

'It is not. I think she is ill.'

Sylvia rolled her eyes.

Gracie stared at her friend of eighteen years. She was absolutely aghast. How could she be so flippant about Ada? Ada, who cooked endlessly for Sylvia and Joe and allowed them to stay at the Atwell's house when-ever they liked, particularly when Amy was indisposed due to drink. Ada had endlessly listened to Sylvia's troubles and given Joe a hug if he was worried about his mother. When they were children they would run to Ada if they had fallen and scraped their knees and share their good news with her, knowing that even if Amy listened to them she certainly didn't celebrate their small childish victories with the same enthusiasm as Ada would.

Sylvia appeared to ignore Gracie as her eyes filled with angry tears, and changed the subject.

'Is that a new jumper then Gracie?'

When-ever Sylvia asked Gracie about her clothing her voice always took on an accusatory tone, never light hearted fashion chat to pass the time of day. It was the same when they were children. The same old flash of jealous pique. As if each new item of clothing Gracie bought was an affront to Sylvia own style.

Gracie was aware of this and decided early on in their friendship that it wasn't worth inflaming the covetous streak in Sylvia.

'Oh no,' said Gracie 'I unravelled one of my old cardigans, you know the one with the pearl buttons? Dorothy knitted the wool up again into this. She is a wizz with the needles.

Gracie met Sylvia's disbelieving stare with a blank expression. Sylvia was conversant with each and every item in Gracie's wardrobe. Sylvia decided not to challenge Gracie's obvious lie this time because the other girls were looking on in interest, sensing tension.

The stand-off was interrupted when Miss Moles, entered into the room. She was Mr Banks personal secretary and looked after the other secretaries and typists. She was an ancient whiskery female whose wrinkled face was always covered in so much powder that she would have fitted in nicely in the court of Louis the 14th. She clapped her hands with loud authority.

'Back to the typing pool girls please it is almost one o'clock and Mr Banks has an announcement for you all, he will be a few minutes so you might as well begin your work, no time to waste.'

The girls dutifully obeyed and returned to their desks. Flexing their fingers and stretching their backs into rounded arches before they commenced the tedious afternoon of work.

Mr Banks entered the room. He was a diminutive man and he cleared his throat a number of times before some of the girls realised he was there. Miss Moles clapped loudly again and the clatter of the machines ceased.

'Now ladies.' Mr Banks stuttered slightly, then coughed.

He seldom ventured into the typing pool. He always felt somewhat overwhelmed. He politely diverted his eyes from the pretty made up faces and collection of curvaceous figures and always treated his ladies with absolute courtesy. He was all too aware of the concentration of female charms. It was the smell that made his senses really reel. The mixture of talcum powder, boiled sweets, peppermints and aniseed balls, hair setting lotion and sweat.

'Ladies,' he tried again valiantly.

He gulped as he became the focus of tens of bright eyes and took a deep breath.

'As you know it is Miss Moles last working day today and as of 5 o'clock this evening she will be retired. Miss Moles has given the last thirty years to our fine company and will be missed, especially by myself.'

The girls giggled.

Mr Banks looked bemused for a moment and decided to press on.

'We wish you good luck and are sure you will have a super time living with your sister in Whitby.'

Miss Moles nodded sagely.

Gracie smiled as she thought 'look out residents of Whitby, you are about to be organised.'

'We have clubbed together and bought you a gift.'

Mr Banks handed over the garish tea pot, decorated in a loud harlequin pattern, with a proud look on his face.

Miss Moles looked slightly startled at the bright colours of the teapot, she was more of a standard brown tea pot kind of female.

'Thank you everyone I shall miss you all.'

Gracie thought she detected a gleam of tears in Miss Moles' eyes and felt a rush of affection for the older lady who had managed her girls so kindly and firmly.

Miss Moles shook Mr Banks hand and he winced at her vice like grip.

Gracie flashed a quick glance at Sylvia. She looked like she was going to burst in excitement.

'This must be the news. They must be giving Sylvia the job of head secretary.'

'Well good for her,' thought Gracie gamely. It will suit her, bossing everyone around and she has been at the company longer than Gracie anyway.

Mr Banks was still speaking

'There is an opportunity to fill the excellent shoes of Miss Moles and become head secretary. Anyone who thinks they would be fit for the vacancy can see me by the end of the day and I will interview them next week. That is all girls. Keep up the good work.'

Mr Banks trundled out towards the safety of his office.

There was a buzz of chatter until Miss Moles said loudly.

'Carry on with your work please everyone.' She looked fondly round the room, she would miss this place but her rheumatism was causing her a lot of discomfort. She was looking forward to retiring to the seaside and felt sure there would be plenty of committees to join. Her sister was a good sort, Miss Moles would be bringing her two cats, Victoria and Albert. The sisters and four cats in total would be very cosy together in the little cottage by the sea. Miss Moles wondered if there would be room for the vile teapot.

The young ladies all obediently began typing again and peace reigned in the typing pool

Sylvia had a face like absolute thunder. She crashed down on the keys with venom. She didn't understand it. As soon as she had found out that Miss Moles was leaving she had cornered Mr Banks and demanded to know who was going to be her replacement. She had pointed out her own typing speed, short hand skills and splendid time keeping. She had also pointed out to him, politely, that she was the obvious choice as her work was superior to the other girls.

174

Mr Banks did not enjoy being cornered by anyone, let alone Sylvia, who was standing so close to him he could smell on her breath, an unpleasant combination of aniseed and onion.

He stammered that he agreed she would be excellent for the job.

Sylvia understood this to mean that she had the job and had hugged the secret to herself with joy.

She had told her parents and Joe. Bill and Amy were pleased for her. They even took her out for dinner in Leeds to celebrate.

Sidney was thrilled for her too for a moment, until she said they would now be able to save up for a deposit for a house. Sidney felt his blood pressure rise with the realisation he was about to be bossed around by Sylvia for the rest of his life. He felt quite faint.

Gracie thought hard to herself. She quickly gleaned what had happened. Sylvia thought the job was hers and was furious when she was disappointed. But it only meant that she would have to apply along with the rest of them and if Mr Banks believed she was the best person for the job then that would mean she got the job fair and square.

Gracie had been to the Lyons tea house at the weekend with Ella. Ella had been full of news. She had completed all her training in hairdressing and was full of plans to open her own hair salon in one of the other towns or villages surrounding Leeds. She didn't want to set up in direct competition with her mother and sisters of course.

Ella was going to be married herself later on in the year to Tom Blackburn the boy she fell in love with the summer of the evacuation.

They had a lively, tempestuous relationship, full of passion. He adored her and she him.

Ella had met Charles and they had got on well. Ella made Charles laugh. Ella was an excellent judge of character and thought Charles might be a little old school, possibly expecting Gracie to give her job and independence, to be the devoted little wife at home after they were married. Ella didn't want to interfere because she loved them as a couple. She decided she loved Gracie more though and she didn't want to see her lose her independent spirit. She approached the subject as cautiously as she could.

'The thing is Gracie,' she had said. 'You don't want to get yourself completely reliant on your man. Earn your own money if you can. If this war has taught us girls anything it is that we can be independent. I can't wait to marry Tom and have lots of gorgeous babies but I want more than that and you should too. Besides you never know what is round the corner. Tom is a roofer at the moment, the silly sod could fall off any time so then where would I be? Wandering round trying to find another fellow to look after me and buy me pretty things when I beg. No thank you very much.'

Ella might look like a giggling blond bit of fluff with her tight clothes and wiggling hips but she had a very wise head on her shoulders and had always been brave and decisive.

Gracie thought her friend talked a lot of sense.

Gracie decided to apply for the job. She and Charles were going to live with Ada and Walter until they had saved up for their house deposit. Charles had suggested she stopped work as soon as they were married but she absolutely didn't want that. She enjoyed herself and Ella was absolutely right about having one's own money. If she managed to land the role then the extra money would be very useful.

She knew that Sylvia's eyes were boring into her as she made her way out of the typing room to go and have a word with Mr Banks. Gracie ignored her but had an uncomfortable feeling in her stomach.

She felt a bit better about it when she told Ella that following Saturday at their usual table at Lyons.

They had wandered round the shops. There wasn't much to buy as England was slowly recovering from the war but they always had a giggle together. Ella was fond of buying dye. She enjoyed revamping her old clothes. She was wearing a bright canary yellow shirt which had been a drab beige colour the last time she had seen Ella wearing it. 'You double your wardrobe you know Gracie', she would say cheerfully.

Ella was delighted when Gracie mentioned the job interview and was very encouraging when she expressed her doubts. Gracie knew Sylvia would make a terrible fuss and she was also worried that she would no longer be included in the gossip and the fun chatter with the rest of the girls. She knew for a fact that they would always hush when Miss Moles had appeared and never shared the jokes with her, Miss Moles wasn't a bad sort but she was in charge so therefore not part of the gang anymore.

'Look Gracie,' Ella said. 'I am absolutely confident you can get this job, you are efficient and I bet you rub along alright with the rest of the girls.' Let me know when the interview is and I will come up and do your hair for you.

Gracie nodded.

'As for that basket Sylvia, don't you dare let her moods dictate what you do.' Ella snorted loudly attracting the attention of other diners in the tea room.

'You have always worried about her and she has always taken bloody advantage. She is a cat. Go for this job, even if there is trouble, hold your head high and think of the money. You will be fine and dandy.'

Gracie smiled, reassured.

'Good now let's split a scone to celebrate.'

Mr Banks gave Gracie the job. She was clearly intelligent and pleasant. She was also dignified and never caused a scene. She would be perfect. Sylvia quite frankly had terrified him, so she was out of the running and the other candidates just didn't seem as bright.

Mr Banks decided to treat himself after years of time spent with Miss Moles and her whiskery chin and endless references to her sister's bowel trouble. Mr Banks was a happily married man but he also, if he was honest with himself, was quietly pleased with the idea of working alongside Gracie with her dark hair and long slim legs. The other directors would take note. He always kept that thought very much to himself.

Sylvia was absolutely furious with her perceived unfairness of it all.

They were so close to the wedding though that she controlled her rage with great effort and managed congratulate Gracie through gritted teeth. She took out her misery on poor bemused Sidney.

Chapter 17

Gracie was sat at the scrubbed kitchen table slicing tomatoes for the ham and gentleman's relish sandwiches that Ada was slowly making.

'Are you feeling alright mother?' Gracie asked tentatively.

Ada smiled, 'of course dear,' and continued cutting the loaves.

Gracie noticed that the slices were very thick.

It was three days before the wedding. The whole family were descending on the Atwell household at four o'clock. After their tea Gracie and her sister in laws were going to the pub for a few drinks. Charles was also going out into Leeds with his friends from work and one or two childhood friends. Robert and Rita were the first to arrive and burst through the door with their two small children. Bobby, aged three, charged across the kitchen making a loud chugging sound and jumped up onto Gracie's knee. He grinned up at her and fixed her with his round blue eyes.

'I have been a train all day long', he announced 'and I found a dead frog.'

He chuckled in delight as Gracie pulled a comically frightened face.

'How lovely,' she said and gave his chunky body a squeeze.

Rita rolled her eyes.

'Yes lovely,' she said with a grimace.

Bobby began swinging his legs so his feet banged rhythmically against the table leg.

'Bobby,' said Rita in exasperation. 'Pack that in.'

Bobby suddenly jumped down from Gracie's knee. 'I know', he chirped 'I will go and find Grandad.' As he jumped down he deftly swiped one of the ham sandwiches from the plate on the table and crammed it in his mouth before Rita had chance to stop him.

'These sarnies are really big.' He exclaimed, his voice muffled by the bread.

Rita glanced at the plates then looked thoughtfully at Ada, who hadn't really spoken.

Rita locked eyes with Gracie, their eyes mirrored one another's concern.

'It's alright,' she mouthed to Gracie. 'We will talk next week. Come for tea.'

Gracie felt relieved and felt the tension ease from her shoulders for the first time in a while. The changes in Ada's behaviour had been so subtle that sometimes Gracie wondered if she was imagining things. Up until her conversation with Walter, no one else from the family had mentioned anything. Of course the boys hadn't lived at home for a long time now but the family had remained very close still with lots of family meals together at home, all of them crammed into the front room as was traditional.

Ada had always been reserved. She certainly held opinions on the world but expressed her thoughts in a careful, quiet way. Gracie didn't think she had ever heard her raise her voice once. It wasn't the new silence though, or even Ada's sometime lack of attention to her appearance, that had frightened her initially.

Gracie had sped down the stairs, one morning a couple of weeks previously in a fearful rush, she had been out late with Charles the previous night and had managed to sleep in. she thought she might just have time for a cup of tea before she dashed out of the door.

'Morning mother,' Gracie had gasped bursting into the kitchen frantically brushing her hair.

Ada was stood at the kitchen window and Gracie had asked if there was any tea left in the pot that was stood solidly on the table, warm in its yellow knitted tea-cosy.

Ada tuned to look at her daughter.

Her face was completely devoid of expression.

'Mother?' said Gracie uncertainly.

Ada narrowed her eyes, as if she didn't recognise Gracie and a momentary flash of anger passed across her face, which changed to fear and then was gone completely.

'Mother are you alright?' Gracie tried again. Ada shook her head and said in an unusually bright voice 'hello dear. There is tea in the pot if you have time for one.'

Gracie nodded and fetched a cup she felt sick. She watched her mother who was carefully washing one or two items of breakfast crockery. She was staring out of the window again but as Gracie hurriedly put her shoes and jacket on by the door, Ada smiled properly at her and said 'have a good day, don't work too hard,' and the morning seemed just like any other.

Bobby sped out of the room making a piercing whistling sound.

Ada burst out laughing.

'What a little whirlwind. Just like Ian at that age.'

'He is wearing me out,' groaned Rita. 'It is a good job you are a little angel,' she said looking fondly at her baby girl, Anne. Anne was eight months old, a beautiful child with Rita's blond curly hair and rosy cheeks.

Ada wiped her hands on her apron and picked Anne up out of her pram. She sat down and Anne relaxed placidly against her and studied the wonder of her own fingers. Ada was gently caressing one of Anne's chubby legs.

Gracie relaxed again. Ada once again seemed fine.

Dorothy and Edward had arrived along with Ian and Janet. They were all in high spirits. Janet was sporting a large round tummy hidden by a pretty pleated blouse with a round collar. She rubbed it protectively every now again. Janet and Ian's baby was due sometime in the May. Gracie watched Ian, so happy. He will make a wonderful father. When he had returned from the war he seemed to have been the most affected of the three brothers. He no longer laughed so easily and his all-encompassing, wide smile rarely appeared. Now it seemed that his old high spirits were returning as he regaled the table with his recent encounter with Violet Pinkerton. He had been working at her manor house repairing the ancient boiler when she had put a hand on his bottom and suggested she checked his pipework. Ian had stood up quickly and whacked his head on the side of the huge iron barrel of the boiler. 'I saw stars. Imagine if I had knocked myself out, she would have had me for breakfast". He giggled.

They all laughed merrily.

'That woman had always been a menace, She once tried it on with me you know, frightened me to death', said Walter grinning.

Dorothy had brought a huge apple pie, sprinkled with brown sugar and large jug of yellow cream for pudding and the family were tucking in.

They didn't notice Sylvia come in through the back door. She sniffed loudly and everyone looked up.

'Syl', yelled Ian. 'Good to see you old fruit. Looking good.' Rita kicked him under the table.

Sylvia gave Ian a tight smile. She was dressed in an ancient bobbly jumper and an old tweed skirt with a droopy hem. Her hair was limp and greasy and hung round her face. She looked slightly taken a back at the sight of all of the Atwell family crowded together. She had been hoping to catch Gracie on her own.

Ada jumped up and ushered Sylvia gently further into the kitchen.

'Have you eaten dear?' She asked kindly. 'I think all of the sandwiches are gone but there is some pie left. Oh there are some tomatoes. I could make you a tomato sandwich.'

'No I don't like tomatoes', Sylvia snapped. She then had the decency to blush when Dorothy raised her eyebrows at her. 'Thank you Mrs Atwell', she added quickly.

'I have just come to say that I won't be coming on your hen night tonight. Gracie. I have got one of my heads, I shall go to bed with a flannel on my head I think.' Sylvia was pulling an irritating martyred expression.

'Nonsense', boomed Dorothy. She picked up her over large handbag and began rummaging round in it. 'Here you go, extra strong aspirin. I take them for my rheumatics, my joints would give one of your heads a run for their money any day. Go home and take a bath,' she ordered. You will be right as rain in an hour. You look an absolute sight.'

Sylvia's mouth dropped open with horror but she found herself accepting the aspirin and nodding in agreement, helpless against the sheer force of Dorothy's personality.

Gracie jumped up and put a tentative arm round Sylvia's shoulder. 'Please come Syl,' she encouraged 'it will be fun, just us girls for the night.' Ella is coming along, she is always a giggle. Why don't you wear your new blue shantung dress. It really suits you. You were just saying that the other day weren't you Rita?' Rita nodded her head vigorously, feeling slightly guilty at the little white lie.

'Oh yes, a lovely dress, must have cost an absolute fortune. I said to you the other day didn't I Gracie?' Sylvia looked suspiciously at the pair's innocent faces.

'Alright if you insist.' She said ungraciously.

Dorothy rolled her large expressive brown eyes behind Sylvia's departing back.

'Why do you put up with that girl? She is such a pill.'

Gracie sighed helplessly. 'I know Dot. We have been friends for years. She is a tricky girl but she really can be a lot of fun.' Gracie knew she was sounding half-hearted. She couldn't actually remember the last time her and Sylvia had laughed together or even had a good chat. Sylvia would either be pulling one or the other girls down, from work, or endlessly moaning about poor Sidney. One day Gracie had asked her carefully if she thought Sidney was the one for her if he was so irritating and Sylvia had immediately burst into tears and said Gracie was jealous because when Sidney proposes their wedding was going to be twice the size of Gracie and Charles's and it was going to be held at the best hotel in Yorkshire. It was exhausting.

'Well if you ask me,' began Dorothy about to launch into one of her many loud speeches. Edward put his hand gently on her large arm he said in his serious voice.

'Let's leave the subject eh Dorothy, she will cheer up after a few gin and oranges.'

Dorothy look slightly put out but relented and let the subject of moody Sylvia drop.

It was a pleasant mild evening for April and the Atwell ladies waited in the garden for Sylvia. They seldom went into pub without their husbands and were enjoying the novelty of the moment. The garden was full of daffodils nodding their cheerful heads in the slight breeze. Walter had been given a cutting the previous year from a clematis montana and it was now in its first full bloom. Its soothing sweet scent was filling the garden. They chatted together pleasantly as they waited.

Rita was full of tales of the mischievous Bobby Atwell. Dorothy was making them laugh as she did a wonderful impression of her boss at Schofields who was a nervous nasal little man who broke into a sweat whenever Dorothy approached him with her sales figures.

A shadow passed across them as Sylvia appeared at the gate.

'About time,' muttered Dorothy under her breath.

She looked quite pretty, her face spoilt slightly by the mutinous expression on her face but the blue dress really did suit her.

'Come on then ladies, let's enjoy one of my last nights of freedom.' Gracie slipped her arm through Sylvia's in a friendly fashion.

Rita and Janet exchanged worried glances. 'I hope she is not going to be in a mood on the wedding day. She might spoil things,' whispered Janet in concern.

'If she does I will jolly well give that miserable face a slap, it is all for attention with that one.' Declared Dorothy firmly.

Rita and Frieda dissolved into giggles, believing Dorothy would keep her promise.

Gracie's sister in laws caught up with Gracie and Sylvia. They entered the pub, they were immediately hit by a warm fug of smoke and beer fumes. Dorothy wrinkled her nose in distain. The pub was busy and there was a low buzz of friendly chatter. They found a slightly sticky table in the corner and sat down.

A small ratty man approached them rubbing his grubby hands together. Now then, we don't often get such lovely, well built, ladies in this drinking 'histablishment. Would you allow me to buy you a drink? He was leering and directing his question towards Dorothy's, not inconsequential, chest. He quickly jumped back as Dorothy stood up straight and pulled herself to her full height, chest puffed out even further in outrage. 'Certainly not,' she snapped loudly 'and please remove yourself from my presence you horrible little man.'

The man quickly reversed away from the table, raising his hat and winking at Dorothy which seemed to enrage her even further. She shooed him away with her hands.

'Damn cheek,' she exclaimed and sat back down with a heavy thud. Gracie and Rita were helpless with laughter, even Syl permitted herself a small smile.

Ella arrived soon after, in her usual buoyant mood and the first part of the evening passed pleasantly. As predicted, Sylvia did cheer up after she had got herself round a couple of gin and oranges. Janet was drinking stout to benefit the baby.

'Now then Gracie Atwell, let's talk about your honeymoon,' Rita hiccupped with a giggle. 'I have got one piece of advice for you my girl and that is,' she leaned forward with a cheeky smile and whispered loudly 'you need to pee after you have done it or you will get honeymoon cystitis and it is horrible, stings like mad, I should know. When me and Robert went to Blackpool…'

Gracie swiped at Rita. 'Stop, stop, I do not want to talk about your honeymoon with my brother thank you very much and my honeymoon is none of your beeswax.'

Dorothy was nodding sagely. 'She's right Gracie, very wise words,' and suppressed a belch.

'Absolutely,' agreed Ella, 'my sisters told me,' she added quickly with a giggle. Ella and Tom weren't married yet. Sylvia looked disapprovingly at her. Sidney hadn't even suggested anything improper, typical of him, pathetic really. Sylvia was most disapproving of Ella and Tom, who obviously carried on in a vulgar manner but it would be nice to at least turn Sidney down in a moment of enthusiastic passion.

'I am sure Gracie will have a simply marvellous time on honeymoon, she always has a marvellous time.' She smiled but the smile didn't quite meet her eyes.

Gracie considered the luxury hotel on the seafront at Bridlington that she and Charles had chosen to spend their honeymoon. The new Expanse hotel had already established itself as one of the most luxurious hotels on the East coast of England. She thought happily of the two new dresses she had bought for their holiday and the smart travelling suit with a matching hat that she intended to wear on the train. She gave a shiver of anticipation as her thoughts strayed to the collection of beautiful silk lingerie she had purchased for the evenings. It was going to be wonderful.

'Let's have one more eh girls,' sang Rita, thoroughly enjoying her time away from her children. 'We never get the chance to do this.'

Sylvia had spotted her father, Bill who had come into the pub through the back door. He was leaning over the bar counter chatting to Beryl the barmaid, a fifty year old platinum blond with a raucous laugh and too much make up. Bill was gazing lovingly into her deep cleavage talking nonsense and Beryl was visibly preening in front of him, delighted by his attentions.

Bill looked round the bar with a genial expression on his still handsome face and spotted the ladies. His face was reddened and slightly puffy with excesses of drink and late nights but he still looked genuinely pleased to see them.

He wandered across.

'Hello all, what a pleasant surprise. What brings you here?'

'Gracie's hen night,' said Ella.

Bill looked in interest at Ella's pretty vivacious face for a moment, ever on the alert for female attention.

He held her eyes for a moment, then Ella looked away, unabashed.

'Of course Gracie. The big wedding, this weekend isn't it, hadn't forgotten, looking forward to it. What is your chap called, Charles isn't it, Navy boy. He is a lucky fellow. Let me buy you all a drink, what will you all have?' He drew a wad of notes out from his back pocket with a flourish and gave Ella a quick grin.

'No thank you,' snapped Sylvia sharply.

'Go on Syl have a drink with your old Pa.' Bill put his hand gently on her shoulder. She shook him off immediately.

'We should go home now.' She shot a hate filled look at her father. 'I suppose you will be staying?' she spat. 'I think your friend behind the bar is waiting for you.'

Bill was embarrassed. He looked imploringly at his daughter but dropped his eyes when he registered her spiteful expression.

'Come on Sylvia,' said Ella, very uncomfortable. 'He is paying after all,' she joked and tried to smile at her.

'What, Ella? Have you fallen under the charms of the great Bill Jenkinson too. I wouldn't go near him if I were you, you'd catch something. He is disgusting. Mind you, you would be happy to have a quick roll in the hay with him.' Sylvia's voice rose to a screech and her face was twisted with rage.

She pushed the table hard, knocking Janet's baby bump. Janet let out a gasp, unhurt, but shocked.

She scraped her chair back loudly and ran out of the pub.

Gracie got up to go after her. Rita put her arm out to stop her.

'No dear, not this time,' her voice was tight with anger. 'She could have really hurt Janet with her latest bout of hysterics. She is a very mixed up, unhappy girl. I think the root cause of this is the old green eyed monster and jealousy is a poison.

Gracie shook off Rita's arm.

She dashed out of the pub and shouted after Sylvia.

'Come back Syl. Tell me what this is all about and I will try to help. Please Syl, we are friends.'

Sylvia had disappeared. Gracie went back into the pub, making up her mind she would try again the next day.

Bill had sat down at the table. He looked pale and was shaking his head.

'She is just like Amy. I have never been able to make her happy either.' He seemed to be talking to himself.

He looked round and smiled wryly. 'Have any of you met Sidney, that wet lettuce?'

Gracie nodded.

'I am not sure if I ought to warn him what he is letting himself in for, poor soppy sod.'

Bill sighed sadly but then perked up when he clocked Beryl pouting, rather like a fish, in his direction.

'Still life's not all bad eh?'

He got up and ambled off, leaving some money on the table for a round of drinks.

Ella blew out her cheeks. She had been rather hurt by Sylvia's attack on her morals. She might have a lovely rummage round with her beloved Tom but she was absolutely faithful to him. Hopefully when Gracie was married, there wouldn't be as much room for Sylvia in their lives turning the knife left, right and centre.

'Right then let's get this evening back on track. I must tell you about my sister Joyce's twins. Absolute naughty devils. Rita, you will feel much better about your Bobby when I tell you what they did to grandad the other day.' She said with a cheeky grin. Rita perked up immediately.

'He was babysitting for them, had a couple of beers, fell asleep and they decided to play hairdressers and gave him a haircut. He was not best pleased when he woke up I can tell you. Best of all Joyce played merry hell with Dad for falling asleep on the job and blamed him. My word there was a row.' She said in delight.

Everyone laughed and the tension was broken.

Bill was stood at the bar lost in thought. Beryl was twittering at him and thrusting provocatively over the beer pumps but he barely registered her. For the first time in a very long time in his mainly selfish existence, he was worried about another woman, Sylvia.

She had always been such a contrary child, difficult to like, difficult to love even. Joe had always been easy to get along with, cheerful and warm. He still was. He was following in his father's footsteps and had become a salesman, a car salesman, which suited him. His easy, honest, manner was very successful with the customers and best of all as far as Joe was concerned he got to speed around in the brand new automobiles. He had met a girl. She was from the village, a lively, spirited red head. Joe was in love.

He went to the pub with Bill on occasion for a few beers. Bill would point out other girls to him in jocular way, making various ribald comments and Joe would smile but shake his head gently saying 'I've got my girl already Dad, why would I want anyone else?'

Joe's life was brand new and full of hope. It made Bill feel slightly grubby and tired in comparison. Bill was proud of the decent man Joe had become, despite his parents.

A few days before, Bill had returned from working away, he had dropped in to see Beryl who lived in a tiny, grubby cottage on the other side of the village. He was very tired indeed and had disappointed her in his lack of ability to make love.

'Making love,' was Beryl's phrase. Bill laughed to himself, there was nothing loving about their coupling. Beryl had harped on for ages about how he must not care for her if he couldn't even get it up. Bill had defended himself half-heartedly, telling her he was just tired and she was a knock out. Her eyes were full of crocodile tears, making her heavy mascara block run into the wrinkles round her eyes. Bill had sat in her bed, smoking, blocking out her moaning voice. The room was small and smelt strongly of damp. There were piles of underwear hung over a couple of wooden chairs and stockings tossed over the bed head. Ashtrays piled up with cigarette stubs and ladies magazines scattered over the threadbare rugs. The sheets were stained, once white, now a dingy grey colour. At that moment, Bill despised Beryl and despised himself.

The only woman Bill had ever really loved was Rosie Frost. She was also the only woman who had ever broken his heart. A couple of years previous he had taken to driving past her home. The house was no longer a boarding house. He had watched her in her garden one day. Her two sons, big strong looking boys were tearing round the garden. One was practicing his bowling technique and the other was climbing an oak tree and jumping efficiently to the ground from the high branches.

Rosie was hanging out the washing, lots of shirts and trousers. Her curly hair was blowing round in the fierce sea breeze. She was wearing a green jumper which Bill knew was the exact colour of her eyes. Bill was sat in his car, close enough to observe the expression on her face. She was watching her sons with affection, a gentle smile playing on her mouth, utterly unconscious of anything other than a moment of happiness. Bill remembered that smile. He thought that was when she was at her most beautiful.

Bill drove away with a searing pain in his heart.

Rosie had settled with Alec, who had proved to be a loving husband. She had returned to nursing and found she got a great deal of satisfaction from her part time job. She still sometimes thought of Bill though. She had loved his boundless energy, sense of fun and wit. She knew that his love for her was real but was driven by the part of him who was abandoned by his mother so long ago and that Bill would continue to search for a woman to love him unreservedly and wholeheartedly.

In rare and very private moments, Rosie would allow herself to remember laying back on her soft feather pillows, Bill's handsome face looking down at her, his shoulder muscles flexed and grooved, as he supported his own weight, just before he entered her. The brief exquisite pause, the moment when she was aware that every muscle of her body was taut with desire for him.

Bill left Beryl's house that night after making sure she was satisfied with the evening together. He had let himself into his house at about two in the morning he and decided to run himself a bath. His head was aching from the whiskey he had thrown down his throat. His body felt sore but his mind was whizzing with figures and strategies for his next trip. Silverbonds had expanded their market into France and Bill was now travelling to Paris.

He pushed open the bathroom door, fully expecting his family to be in bed fast asleep.

A loud outraged squeak made him nearly jump out of his skin.

Sylvia was sat up in the bath. Their eyes met, Sylvia had been crying. Her legs were folded into her body and she was clutching them tightly, visibly in distress.

Bill could see the tops of her thighs and they were covered in tiny cuts and scratches. Some looked quite deep and were bleeding a little into the water.

Bill stared. 'Oh God Syl, what is this, what has happened to your legs?

'Get out,' Sylvia screeched. 'Stop looking at me.'

Bill stumbled backwards out of the bathroom.

'I wasn't looking sweetheart. I am sorry I didn't know you were in there. It is two in the morning. I wasn't looking. I wasn't.'

Bill tripped into his bedroom. Amy was laid on back in the centre of their bed. She was dressed beautifully in a silk kimono. She was even wearing light make up and her hair was curled. He shook her to wake her. He could see his daughter was in some kind of pain, she needed her mother. Amy turned over in her sleep, releasing a sweet dirty smell of brandy. Her mouth fell open and she snored loudly. Bill could see her teeth, they were stained brown with nicotine and red wine. She lifted her arm slightly and Bill caught another sharp unwashed smell which revolted him. He shook her harder trying to contain the anger that was building. This was her fault, all she ever had to do was look after her children. He had provided the money, he had done his bit. She might as well have not been there at all.

Bill thought Rosie and felt near to tears. She would have known what to do. She understood how to love people, how to nurture them so they flourished. She was only ever really interested in making ends meet. Amy could cover her flaws in silks and satins. Rosie was at her most beautiful naked. He should have been brave and married her. Instead striving for financial success had made him cowardly over affairs of the heart and he lost the only woman that he had ever truly loved.

He climbed into his bed. Bill lay listening to the sounds of Sylvia climbing into her own bed. He felt utterly helpless. He could see that Sylvia was really hurting but had absolutely no idea why and absolutely no idea how to ease her pain.

Chapter 18

Sylvia stared intently at her reflection, in a dusty mirror. She was alone in the house. Everyone had left ten minutes ago for the wedding. Joe was in raring spirits, proud to be an usher at Gracie and Charles's wedding. He was delighted to be asked and had bought a new suit for himself and a treated Bea, his girlfriend to a new dress with his last wage packet. He had even bought Sylvia a little bottle of cologne, she had seemed really down in the dumps recently. When he gave it to her he was most surprised to see Sylvia's eyes fill with tears at the gesture. She spoilt the moment soon after, dashed away her tears and said she didn't really like that scent, but she did say thank you.

Sylvia stared at her face and body and slowly absorbed all she was. She had been on a strict diet for the last couple of months, desperate to have a waspish waist. She had noticed Gracie had put on a fair few pounds recently and was pleased. It never seemed to bother Gracie thought but Sylvia wanted to be thinner than her friend. The diet had only really seemed to have affected her breasts, making them look flatter. Her chest was now concave, ribby and pale, and she had large dry scaly patch of skin on the side of her neck. Her face was white and wan making her carefully applied make up look garish and almost ghoul like.

Her arms and legs felt heavy and tired, her latest collection of scratches on the inside of her thighs stung. She briefly thought of how Gracie would look coming down the aisle, radiant, expectant for a glorious future and felt a bitter twist of envy in her stomach.

Sylvia didn't care much for Charles anymore. He had argued with her too many times recently. She still thought he seemed like a good solid chap. That was all. Charles didn't mind Sylvia's company when they had all first met but in the final year or so before the wedding he noticed how her teasing would always have a particularly mean edge, so mainly kept her at a distance. Sylvia was glad Gracie was finally off the market then maybe they could be friends again properly. She really couldn't have stood it if Gracie had swanned off with Raymond the gorgeous charismatic American soldier, proving that she could land better boys than Sylvia. She was glad that Gracie was settling for the fairly ordinary Charles.

Although she knew Sidney was suited up waiting dutifully for her at the church. She felt nothing but distain for him with his mild manner and staring rabbity eyes. She didn't love him and she knew he didn't love her, he was terrified of her, the pathetic child. She just couldn't stand being left out of the conversations, seemingly the rest of the girls in the world had, about their love lives and plans of houses and babies.

Rita had convinced Sylvia to get ready at her own house. She made a lame excuse something about there not being enough hot water for them all to bathe. Sylvia suspected they didn't want her company but couldn't be bothered to argue. It would have been great if it was just her and Gracie getting ready as she initially thought but she didn't want to spend the morning with Dorothy, the fat cow.

Amy had been fluttering in and out of her room all morning offering to do her hair, lending her some brand new stockings. She seemed happy and eager to help.

Sylvia had enjoyed the attention from her mother at first but Amy kept disappearing downstairs and was beginning to waft the scent of gin along with Chanel no 5. Amy came back into Sylvia's room clutching a striped round cardboard container full of expensive dusting power.

'Isn't this lovely. We never get to do this, getting ready together.'

'We never do this because you are always too drunk.' Sylvia muttered.

'You are right Syl. I will try much harder I am sorry,' said Amy contritely. 'Here let me put a bit of powder on those scabby patches, it will cover them up.' She began to dab at Sylvia's neck with a powder puff, dusting Sylvia's dress with a fine layer of powder.

Sylvia stared at her pretty, feckless mother and felt a wave of revulsion towards her.

'Stop it,' she yelled and caught hold of Amy's fragile wrist, she twisted it and Amy gave a whimper of pain.

'Get out of here you useless bitch.' She spat.

Amy stood her ground for a couple of seconds, her reactions were slowed by her early morning tipple. Her eyes were huge in her delicate face and quickly filled with easy tears.

This enraged Sylvia even further.

She shoved Amy hard against the door jamb.

'You are useless. How dare you try to be all mother, daughter now. You never cared about me.'

'That's not true Syl. I just find things difficult.'

'Everyone finds things difficult.' Sylvia yelled. 'Get out. I hate you the most.'

Sylvia's face was a malevolent mask and she was breathing heavily through gritted teeth.

'I will make my own way to the church.' She made a hissing sound like a snake.

Amy made her way slowly out of the room, leaning against the wall for support. Her legs were shaking.

Bill honked long and aggressively on the horn of his new Ford Sedan, Joe was right, she was an absolute beauty. He drummed his hands impatiently on the steering wheel.

Amy came out of the front door, tottering on her high heels. A piece of hair had escaped the pins and her hat was slightly askew. He rolled his eyes as she tripped slightly apparently over her own feet.

'You look a mess Amy, fix yourself.' Bill said dismissively.

He started the car and coughed loudly.

The smell of his aftershave had filled the car and was making Amy feel sick. She noticed a tiny smudge of lipstick on the cuff of Bill's shirt. It was a garish shade of coral. Amy almost felt sorry for Cynthia, Dolly or Beryl. Whoever it was had appalling taste. Amy turned her head away and closed her eyes. She rested her head against the cool glass of the window.

Sylvia made her way down the stairs and took one of her mother's many gin bottles from the drinks cabinet. She sat on the floor and took several long draughts from the bottle. She felt the dry heat infuse her stomach and radiate out into her limbs. She coughed and shivered for a moment or two then continued to drink. Smaller sips this time, she didn't like the taste but made steady progress down the bottle.

She looked up at the grandfather clock and saw it was 1 o'clock. She raised the bottle to the clock face and laughed out loud. The wedding was due to start at 1 o'clock.

She had felt very miserable for a very long time now. So much so that the black heavy fog now seemed to fill her body, had taken almost a physical form now. She awoke every morning with a weight on her shoulders and an oil slick of unhappiness sitting in her stomach. She watched her friends, her brother, and the girls at work all seeming to be enjoying their time in the world.

She was functioning in an ordinary way, working, stepping out with Sidney, eating. Somehow it seemed that she was watching from a distance, as if it was a play. Why couldn't she just be happy for her friend?

Kitty, their cat wandered into the front room and was staring impassively at her.

'What are you looking at?' she yelled suddenly very angry again. She gulped down the last dregs of the gin and threw the bottle against the wall. The cat spun round and leapt out of the room.

Sylvia let out a heart wrenching howl.

All the vile feelings she had carried around inside her for the last couple of years were multiplying and thrashing round like a storm. Jealousy, pride, avarice and above all disappointment.

She grabbed her own face and scratched her nails deep into her cheeks. She caught sight of herself once more in the expensive art deco mirror above the fire place. Her reddened face was twisted in rage, make up smeared, hair stood on end. The reflection in the mirror a stark contrast to the cool sharp borders the mirror's frame provided.

She gathered up the skirts of the beautifully made lavender bridesmaid dress and ran out of the house, leaving the door wide open. She set off through the unkempt fields behind her mother and father's house. Brambles were tearing at her legs but she barely registered the pain. She ran fast towards the fences at the end of the fields. Sylvia climbed over, her breathing was heavy and ragged. She slid down a steep bank and skidded to a halt in front of the railway line.

Sylvia lay down across the track. Her body heaving and letting out little cries of self-pity.

As she lay there gradually her breathing calmed. She registered the cold metal through her dress with surprise. She vomited violently and the haze of alcohol lifted slightly.

She turned her head away from the sick and found herself focussing on a single forget me not flower. It was the result of one lone seed, growing happily between a sleeper and the rail. The blue of its pretty flower matched the sky perfectly.

The driver of the 1.30 Leeds Central Station to Harrogate via Westridge was a genial young man, not long qualified as a train driver and he loved his job. It had been his dream, man and boy to control one of the wonderful steam trains. He had worked his way up diligently. His father and his new wife Daisy were very proud. The train had a full head of steam and they were making very nice time.

Sylvia felt the rail vibrate and gasped with horror. What on earth was she doing? She tried to push herself up from the railway line but her movements were slowed by the gin and her joints felt stiff. One of the long balloon sleeves of the bridesmaid dress, that she had made such a fuss about, had caught on a rivet. She yanked her arm free. The train came hurling round the corner and hit Sylvia, killing her instantly.

Serge Eymond-Laritaz

Le chemin de l'arbre de vie

L'allégorie de Caïn et Abel

© 2021 Eymond-Laritaz, Serge
Édition : BoD – Books on Demand,
12/14 rond-point des Champs-Élysées, 75008 Paris
Impression : BoD – Books on Demand, Norderstedt, Allemagne

ISBN : 9782322377046

Dépôt légal : septembre 2021

Du plus profond des brumes regarde vers les étoiles

La terre réfléchira leur lumière.

C'est seulement ici, dans la vie terrestre
où se heurtent les contraires,
que le niveau général de conscience peut s'élever.
Cela semble être la tâche métaphysique de l'homme.
C.G. Jung

Introduction

L'arbre de vie se trouve mentionné pour la première fois dans la Bible à la fin du chapitre 3 du livre de la Genèse. Dans ce chapitre, qui nous parle du jardin d'Éden, on n'a souvent retenu que la soi-disant « faute » d'Adam et Ève qui ont mangé du « fruit défendu ». Mais suite à cet événement important *ils connurent qu'ils étaient nus*[1]. Cette connaissance est dans la vie la naissance à la conscience de la « dualité » ; c'est pour eux l'émergence d'une conscience de leur « moi individuel » (leur ego), de la séparation qui existe entre eux et ce qui les entoure. À partir de là les hommes ont la *connaissance du bien et du mal*. Cet épisode nous dit que l'homme doit vivre selon les lois de cette dualité, qui est sa condition d'existence sur la terre, quelles qu'en soient les difficultés. Mais nous verrons que cette loi peut, non pas être anéantie, mais transfigurée.

Dans le récit de la Création il y a une progression, depuis la Lumière indifférenciée jusqu'à l'homme qui se caractérise, par rapport au reste de la création, par le fait qu'il vit dans la *conscience de la dualité*. Mais rien ne dit que l'homme doit s'en tenir uniquement là et ne pas encore évoluer ; et on a largement oublié que, dans ce même Éden, il y a un autre arbre qualifié

---

[1] Genèse 3:7.

7

d'*arbre de vie, symbole de la vie en Éternité.* Mais Dieu chasse l'homme de l'Éden pour qu'il n'*avance pas sa main, ne prenne aussi de cet arbre, n'en mange et vive éternellement.*

Qu'est-ce que l'homme pour qu'il ne puisse avoir accès spontanément à cet arbre de vie et en manger ? Que doit-il entreprendre pour accéder à cet arbre et ne pas, au contraire, en rester éloigné, voire s'égarer hors du chemin qui y conduit ?

Pour y répondre il faut d'abord considérer que dans la Bible la continuité des récits et la logique de leurs enchaînements sont telles, que pour bien comprendre un passage quelconque il faut alors le replacer dans son contexte. C'est pourquoi une réponse à ces questions est donnée en continuité de l'épisode du jardin d'Éden, soit au début du chapitre 4 du livre de la Genèse. C'est – sous forme d'allégorie – le récit de la brève aventure de Caïn et Abel.

Voir que ce récit répond à ces questions et nous parle du *chemin de l'arbre de vie* peut sembler paradoxal tant le sens commun le perçoit comme étant celui d'un tragique fratricide. C'est pourtant à un autre point de vue que nous convie cet essai.

Si nous cessons d'avoir une lecture littérale et historique des textes bibliques faisant de Caïn et Abel des individus séparés et rivaux, nous comprenons que cette allégorie parle de l'homme au plus profond et au plus essentiel de lui-même. Le texte nous présente en quelques lignes ce départ de l'homme vers l'Éden et l'arbre de vie, ainsi que du chemin qu'il doit parcourir, qu'il doit accomplir conformément à sa vocation. Le récit pointe précisément l'obstacle qu'il rencontre en permanence dans cette pérégrination et qu'il devra surmonter, mais sur lequel souvent il trébuche l'empêchant ainsi d'atteindre ce but. Mais ce possible faux pas donnera quand même à l'homme l'occasion d'apprendre quelque chose l'aidant à poursuivre sa route. Ainsi, cette aventure ne se conclura pas par un échec total puisque la rédemption lui est toujours offerte et lui permettra de repartir pour tenter d'atteindre un jour *l'arbre de vie*, et goûter la vie en *Éternité*.

Qu'est-ce que cette vie *en Éternité* ? C'est une dimension bien souvent cachée de la vie sur la terre car c'est avant tout la connaissance de l'Infini et de l'Éternité au-dedans de soi et c'est aussi, comme le dit Swami Ramdas, « la conscience d'être impersonnel bien davantage qu'une personne individuelle ». Dans un langage plus poétique Mâ Sûryânanda Lakshmî sait bien nous faire sentir ce qu'elle est : « La vie éternelle est l'identité entre la création et l'Absolu, entre la conscience individuelle incarnée et l'Âme ineffable d'où toutes choses procèdent. Elle est l'actuel, lorsque pour la perception humaine le temps et l'espace ont sombré dans le néant et que resplendit le jour infini de la Sagesse. Le visage réel de l'Éternité est la béatitude de la connaissance et de l'amour dans la vie qui les illumine de sa sainteté. »[2]

C'est vers cela que l'homme aspire au plus profond de son cœur et qu'il doit s'efforcer d'accomplir ici-bas : sa « tâche métaphysique » comme le dit C.G. Jung, ou son « destin surnaturel » selon saint Augustin. « La vocation de l'homme est de trouver Dieu » disait également Shrî Anandamoyî Mâ[3], ou encore dans ce même registre enseigné par Mâ Sûryânanda Lakshmî : « Nous sommes nés sur la terre pour monter à Dieu. » Aussi après être né à la dualité, la vocation de l'homme est d'*avancer* pour conquérir et

---

[2] Mâ Sûryânanda Lakshmî, *Exégèse Spirituelle de la Bible, Apocalypse de Jean*, Neuchâtel (Suisse) : À la Baconnière, 1975, p. 9.

[3] Sage hindoue (1896-1982).

naître à cette vie éternelle qui est le vécu de l'Unité. En ce sens l'homme peut vivre *en Éternité* dès ici-bas – et pas seulement, ou forcément – après la mort. Et remarquons bien que le texte ne dit pas que le chemin conduisant à *l'arbre de vie* lui soit définitivement fermé ; il dit simplement qu'il est *gardé* par des *chérubins qui agitent une épée flamboyante* (v. 24).

Notre exégèse de l'aventure de Caïn et Abel examine ce cheminement de l'homme et de l'humanité. Plutôt que de commenter l'histoire d'un tragique fratricide, elle tente de nous faire sentir en quoi ce récit est le propre de l'homme. Dans cette perspective elle essaie de nous amener à une compréhension spirituelle et par là une meilleure connaissance de nous-même et de la vie.

Cette exégèse, différente sur bien des points de celle des commentaires habituels, a pu être menée grâce à la conjugaison de plusieurs approches : un recours fréquent à l'hébreu mais sans ignorer l'apport des traductions françaises, une intériorisation du récit et l'enseignement de la Sagesse hindoue, en particulier celui d'une contemporaine en Occident : Noutte Genton-Sunier, également appelée Mâ Sûryânanda Lakshmî[4].

L'intériorisation et la Sagesse hindoue sont comme les deux faces d'une même médaille qui nous aide à pénétrer plus à fond dans la compréhension des textes sacrés. Le Père Henri le Saux a

---

[4] Originaire d'une famille protestante, mère de quatre enfants, elle a vécu en Suisse (1918-1996). Disciple de Shrî Aurobindo elle a vécu au plan mystique l'union entre la foi chrétienne et la spiritualité hindoue. Elle a écrit plusieurs livres et donné de très nombreux cours et conférences pour expliquer de manière approfondie tant les écritures bibliques que les écritures sacrées hindoues. Elle a été aussi « la Mère » pour accompagner tous ceux qui ont suivi cet enseignement.

merveilleusement résumé ce que cette Sagesse peut apporter à l'Occident : « Le secret de l'Inde c'est l'appel au-dedans, l'ouverture au-dedans, toujours plus au-dedans ; non point l'enseignement de quoi que ce soit de nouveau, mais simplement l'éveil à ce qui est, au sein du fond. »[5]

Ce mouvement constant vers le dedans apporte à cette spiritualité le sens de l'Unité de toute la vie – de l'identité entre la création et l'Absolu – que l'Occident a largement perdu au profit d'une optique plus dualiste. Or cette optique a eu tendance à privilégier une compréhension des textes bibliques dans un sens historique et moral, leur ôtant du même coup une grande part de leur saveur et de leur parfum. Le judaïsme et le christianisme doivent s'efforcer de comprendre que ce n'est qu'en intériorisant les textes sacrés qu'ils peuvent être compris au plus haut de leur Vérité, donc en s'efforçant de dépasser une lecture purement intellectuelle et mentale.

L'hébreu à la fois sous-tend cette démarche et en parachève l'harmonie. A. Chouraqui nous en trace les contours : « L'hébreu est la langue de la vision, faite pour évoquer l'image, le mouvement, l'expression concrète du geste – davantage que pour l'analyse subtile des idées. Langue d'un savoir global, d'une révélation concrète – davantage que d'une réflexion abstraite – dont le génie arrache la pensée à l'abstraction pour la livrer à l'impératif de l'acte. »[6]

Mâ Sûryânanda Lakshmî, qui a su incarner à la fois la Sagesse hindoue et une approche spirituelle des textes bibliques, explique dans l'introduction de l'un de ses ouvrages : « Toute chose, tout

---

[5] *Les yeux de lumière*, Paris : Le Centurion, 1979, p. 75.
[6] André Chouraqui, *La vie quotidienne des Hébreux au temps de la Bible*, Paris : Hachette, 1971, p. 61.

événement, tout être comporte d'innombrables significations sur les différents degrés de sa présence intégrale, visibles dans les domaines de l'intellect et du concret, invisibles et impalpables dans le psychisme, le supra-mental et le spirituel aussi bien qu'à l'autre extrémité, dans le subconscient et l'inconscient. Son sens immédiat, son aspect terrestre n'est qu'un faible degré de sa plénitude et non le plus important. La perception spirituelle consomme et révèle sa réalité ; l'extase l'accomplit dans sa valeur impérissable. Tout enseignement spirituel n'est de même véritablement compris que s'il est replacé, revécu dans l'optique de la supraconscience lumineuse d'où il vient. »[7]

Dans le sillage de cette pensée, il nous a semblé naturel de rechercher dans ce récit de Caïn et Abel une signification au-delà du seul plan concret et de comprendre comment tous les personnages rencontrés, toutes les situations vécues, peuvent être vus comme des parties de nous-même, des éléments de notre vie. « Lire les Saintes Écritures, c'est obéir à une priorité de l'écoute »[8], dit Erri De Luca, mais à condition de comprendre que cette écoute soit également intérieure. De cette manière l'homme peut retrouver en lui-même l'écho des textes sacrés et croître vers sa Réalité intime énoncée par le Christ dans l'Évangile de Luc (chapitre 17) : *Le royaume de Dieu ne vient pas de manière à frapper les regards (v. 20). On ne dira point : Il est ici, ou : Il est là. Car voici le royaume de Dieu est au-dedans de vous (v. 21).*

Mais dans beaucoup de nos bibles subsiste une erreur de traduction et un malentendu théologique sur le sens de ce dernier verset qui est ainsi traduit : *le royaume de Dieu est au milieu de*

---

[7] Mâ Sûryânanda Lakshmî, *Exégèse Spirituelle de la Bible, Apocalypse de Jean*, Neuchâtel (Suisse) : À la Baconnière, 1975, p. 9.

[8] Erri De Luca, *Noyau d'olive*, Paris : Gallimard, 2004.

(ou *parmi) vous*. Cela n'est pas fidèle au texte grec qui utilise la préposition *entos* signifiant en premier lieu « au-dedans de » ou « à l'intérieur de »[9]. Ce sens est conforté par la très rare utilisation de cette préposition dans tout le Nouveau Testament où elle n'est employée que deux fois : ici et en Matthieu 23:26 où le sens « l'intérieur de » ne peut être dévoyé, puisqu'il s'agit de *l'intérieur* de la coupe et du plat. Elle se différencie alors de la préposition *mesos* signifiant plutôt « au milieu de » ou « parmi » que Luc emploie treize fois dans son Évangile, dès lors que le contexte requiert son usage. Par ailleurs ce qui est traduit habituellement par « royaume » provient dans la Bible grecque du mot βασιλεία (basileia), qui comporte un suffixe d'abstraction (ia) incitant à le traduire plutôt par « règne »[10] ce qui renforce encore le sens de l'intériorité. C'est dire si la parole de Jésus, et de Luc, en faveur de l'intériorité du Royaume de Dieu est incontestable.

Le même type de confusion existe également dans l'Ancien Testament traduit à partir de l'hébreu. Dans celui-ci Dieu s'adresse fréquemment aux hommes, mais lorsqu'Il s'adresse à eux Il parle au cœur de l'homme, dans sa profondeur intérieure, comme le dit le prophète Samuel : *L'Éternel ne considère pas ce que l'homme considère ; l'homme regarde ce qui frappe les yeux, mais l'Éternel regarde au cœur*[11]. Pour exprimer cette intériorité l'hébreu utilise le terme קֶרֶב (*quereb*) dans toutes les nombreuses

---

[9] De plus traduire *entos* par « au milieu de » contredit logiquement ce qui est énoncé par ailleurs dans ces versets, car un « milieu » se situerait forcément « *ici* ou *là* ».

[10] C'est en grec ce même mot qui est utilisé dans l'oraison dominicale : « …que Ton règne vienne… »

[11] 1 Samuel 16:7.

expressions voulant signifier « *au-dedans de toi* » ou « *dans ton sein* »[12]. Prenons comme exemple Deutéronome 7:21 : *Ne sois point effrayé à cause d'eux car l'Éternel ton Dieu est au-dedans de toi.* Mais beaucoup de bibles ont traduit cela par « *au milieu de toi* » ce qui trahit le sens du texte original[13]. Par contre lorsque celui-ci veut parler d'une localisation ou d'une orientation, par exemple « *au milieu du Jourdain* », « *au milieu de la ville* », « *au milieu du champ* », il utilise toujours le terme תּוֹךְ (*tovek*). Cette distinction mériterait d'être prise en compte dans les traductions, ce qui certainement les rendrait plus justes et plus proches de l'enseignement du Christ, tel que présenté par Luc.

Mais la théologie chrétienne, qui reste très dualiste et séparant Dieu de sa création, a beaucoup de mal à concevoir cette intériorité et cette Unité entre l'Absolu et sa création. Pourtant les grands mystiques à travers les âges, de l'Orient à l'Occident, et quelle que soit leur origine religieuse, l'ont toujours affirmé. Le remarquable Évangile de Thomas le dit lui aussi, citant les paroles de Jésus : *Le Royaume est le dedans de vous, et il est le dehors de vous. Quand vous vous connaîtrez, alors vous serez connus et vous saurez que c'est vous les fils du Père-le-vivant*[14].

---

[12] Que l'on peut aussi traduire par d'autres expressions exprimant l'intériorité : « en ta matrice » ou « dans tes entrailles » ou « dans ton cœur » comme le fait souvent A. Chouraqui.

[13] Dans le contexte de ce verset, les ennemis que nous ne devons pas craindre ce sont peut-être des ennemis extérieurs, mais bien davantage encore nos ennemis intérieurs qui nous empêchent de *monter vers l'Éternel* car il ne faut jamais oublier que c'est Dieu qui parle « au cœur » de l'homme. Traduire ce verset avec l'expression « au milieu de toi » fait de Dieu un chef de clan, le clan des juifs exclusivement. Dieu n'est pas cela.

[14] Marsanne : Éditions Métanoïa, 1975, Logion 3.

La façon qu'ont les hommes de comprendre les textes sacrés et de croire en Dieu est liée à cette connaissance (ou méconnaissance) rapportée par Thomas, au fait de voir (ou ne pas voir) selon les mots de Teilhard de Chardin qui a écrit : « Par le fait même qu'ils sont des hommes, même les pluralistes pourraient *voir* : ils ne sont que des monistes qui s'ignorent. »[15] Saint Jean de la Croix a donné une belle illustration de cette vérité, lorsque après une grande extase dans un face-à-face avec Dieu il a affirmé : « Lorsqu'on revient de là et que l'on jette à nouveau les yeux sur la terre on ne voit plus que Dieu seul. »

---

[15] Les monistes considèrent que Dieu et sa création sont « Un » alors que les pluralistes (ou dualistes) ne voient pas cette Unité. Dans « *Comment je crois* », tome 10. Éd. du Seuil 1969, p. 104.

Présentation synoptique de deux traductions du texte biblique

Le récit est reproduit intégralement ci-après dans deux traductions françaises assez connues qui se complètent et s'enrichissent mutuellement pour mieux faire vivre le sens du texte biblique.

Parmi toutes les traductions existantes ce choix n'est pas anodin – elles sont en effet relativement contrastées : celle de L. Segond (noté LS lors de l'analyse des versets) est dans un français clair et fluide alors que celle de A. Chouraqui (noté AC lors de l'analyse des versets) peut parfois dérouter ou heurter le lecteur par sa liberté sur le plan formel et grammatical. Mais cette dernière présente un autre avantage qui est celui de coller au plus près au texte hébreu.

Les noms du Divin sont également traduits différemment dans le texte ci-après. A. Chouraqui retranscrit littéralement les quatre lettres du nom hébreu « IHVH » avec en superposition graphique[16] le nom « Adonaï » car IHVH est considéré depuis longtemps comme ineffable. Louis Segond utilise le terme « l'Éternel » qui évoque de manière remarquable le sens spirituel de IHVH. Ceci sera expliqué plus en détail dans l'Appendice.

---

[16] Ce graphisme particulier, propre à A. Chouraqui, n'est pas reproduit dans notre présentation et nous écrirons simplement IHVH.

Ces deux traductions apparaissent dans une composition qui recrée, par des retours à la ligne, les principales pauses notées dans le texte hébreu lui-même pour sa déclamation. Ceci présente l'avantage de rendre le texte plus clair et de faciliter ainsi sa compréhension. Un recours à la source du texte hébreu permettra aussi de mieux approfondir notre réflexion. Quelques versets seront exceptionnellement traduits autrement lors de leur analyse.

Livre de la Genèse, chapitre 4, versets 1 à 16

Cette présentation est organisée en quatre paragraphes qui mettent en évidence les quatre thèmes que nous y avons décelés. Ces thèmes qui fondent notre vie constituent des repères dans la démarche de l'homme et de l'humanité vers sa destinée.

– Versets 1 et 2 : une seconde genèse

– Versets 3 à 8 : le faux pas ou l'erreur d'appréciation de Caïn

– Versets 9 à 14 : les conséquences de cette erreur

– Versets 15 et 16 : la rédemption fait partie du chemin

¹Adam connut Ève, sa femme ;
Elle conçut et enfanta Caïn et elle dit : j'ai formé un homme avec l'aide de l'Éternel.
²Elle enfanta encore son frère Abel.
Abel fut berger et Caïn fut laboureur.

³Au bout de quelques temps,
Caïn fit à l'Éternel une offrande des fruits de la terre ;
⁴Et Abel, de son côté, en fit une des premiers-nés de son troupeau et de leur graisse.
L'Éternel porta un regard favorable sur Abel et sur son offrande ;
⁵Mais il ne porta pas un regard favorable sur Caïn et sur son offrande.
Caïn fut très irrité et son visage fut abattu.
⁶Et l'Éternel dit à Caïn :
Pourquoi es-tu irrité, et pourquoi ton visage est-il abattu ?
⁷Certainement, si tu agis bien tu relèveras ton visage, et si tu agis mal le péché se couche à ta porte,
Et ses désirs se portent vers toi : mais toi domine sur lui.
⁸Cependant, Caïn adressa la parole à son frère Abel ;
Mais comme ils étaient dans les champs, Caïn se jeta sur son frère Abel et le tua.

⁹L'Éternel dit à Caïn : Où est ton frère Abel ?
Il répondit : Je ne sais pas ; suis-je le gardien de mon frère ?
¹⁰Et Dieu dit : Qu'as-tu fait ?
La voix du sang de ton frère crie de la terre jusqu'à moi.
¹¹Maintenant tu seras maudit
De la terre qui a ouvert sa bouche pour recevoir de ta main le sang de ton frère.
¹²Quand tu cultiveras le sol, il ne te donnera plus sa richesse.
Tu seras errant et vagabond sur la terre.
¹³Caïn dit à l'Éternel :
Mon châtiment est trop grand pour être supporté.
¹⁴Voici, tu me chasses aujourd'hui de cette terre ; je serai caché loin de ta face.
Je serai errant et vagabond sur la terre, et quiconque me trouvera me tuera.

¹⁵L'Éternel lui dit : Si quelqu'un tuait Caïn, Caïn serait vengé sept fois.
Et l'Éternel mit un signe sur Caïn pour que quiconque le trouverait ne le tuât point.
¹⁶Puis Caïn s'éloigna de la face de l'Éternel
Et habita dans la terre de Nod à l'orient de l'Éden.

[1]Adâm pénètre Hava, sa femme.
Enceinte, elle enfante Caïn. Elle dit : J'ai acquis un homme avec IHVH.
[2]Elle ajoute à enfanter son frère, Hèbèl.
Et c'est Hèbèl un pâtre d'ovins. Caïn était un serviteur de la glèbe.

[3]Et c'est au terme des jours,
Caïn fait venir des fruits de la glèbe en offrande à IHVH.
[4]Hèbèl a fait venir, lui aussi, des aînés de ses ovins et leur graisse.
IHVH considère Hèbèl et son offrande.
[5]Caïn et son offrande il ne les considère pas.
Cela brûle beaucoup Caïn, ses faces tombent.
[6]IHVH dit à Caïn :
Pourquoi cela te brûle-t-il, pourquoi tes faces sont-elles tombées ?
[7]N'est-ce pas que tu t'améliores à porter ou que tu ne t'améliores pas, à l'ouverture la faute est tapie ;
À toi, sa passion. Toi gouverne-la.
[8]Caïn dit à Hèbèl son frère …
Et quand ils sont au champ, Caïn se lève contre Hèbèl, son frère, et le tue.

[9]IHVH dit à Caïn : Où est ton frère Hèbèl ?
Il dit : Je ne sais pas. Suis-je le gardien de mon frère, moi-même ?
[10]Il dit : Qu'as-tu fait ?
La voix des sangs de ton frère clame vers moi de la glèbe.
[11]Maintenant tu es honni,
Plus que la glèbe dont la bouche a béé pour prendre les sangs de ton frère de ta main.
[12]Oui tu serviras la glèbe : elle n'ajoutera pas à te donner sa force.
Tu seras sur la terre mouvant, errant.
[13]Caïn dit à IHVH :
Mon tort est trop grand pour être porté.
[14]Voici, aujourd'hui tu m'as expulsé sur les faces de la glèbe. Je me voilerai faces à toi.
Je serai mouvant, errant sur la terre : et c'est qui me trouvera me tuera.

[15]IHVH lui dit : Ainsi, tout tueur de Caïn subira sept fois vengeance.
IHVH met un signe à Caïn pour que tous ceux qui le trouvent ne le frappent pas.
[16]Caïn sort faces à IHVH
Et demeure en terre de Nod au levant de l'Éden.

Celui qui monte ne s'arrête jamais d'aller
de commencement en commencement
par des commencements qui n'ont jamais de fin.

Grégoire de Nysse

Une seconde genèse

v. 1-a

LS : *Adam connut Ève, sa femme ;*

AC : *Adâm pénètre Hava, sa femme.*

On a trop souvent traduit ce premier verset comme s'il s'agissait de deux individus prénommés Adam et Ève. En fait il commence par le mot *adam* précédé d'un article, (הָאָדָם) soit « *l'adam* ». Il s'agit alors, non pas d'un nom propre désignant un individu, mais d'un nom commun qui signifie « l'homme » au sens générique, c'est-à-dire « l'être humain »[17]. Parfois le texte hébreu met au pluriel le verbe dont il est le sujet (par exemple en Genèse 1:26), ce qui nous indique que *adam* peut aussi servir de nom collectif et qu'il serait alors possible de le traduire par « l'humanité ». Ainsi ce texte nous dit qu'il s'agit, non pas de deux personnes mises dans une situation particulière, mais de l'être humain dans sa nature profonde, intime et essentielle.

Notons également que dès le début du récit les deux traductions citées se différencient par le fait qu'elles utilisent (et vont ensuite utiliser) deux temps de conjugaison différents : passé et présent.

---

[17] Quelques bibles, dont la TOB, le traduisent ainsi.

« Le temps de l'action, qui est l'essentiel pour l'Occidental, n'a pour l'hébreu qu'une importance secondaire et n'est d'ailleurs jamais explicite. [...] Pour les Hébreux la date d'un événement ne ressort jamais que de sa nature et de son caractère : la conception de la durée est globale et concrète. [...] Nulle part mieux que chez eux il n'est inévitable de voir toute chose en Dieu, *sub specie aeternitatis*. Le passé et le futur se rencontrent dans la totalité du réel, dont ils naissent, où ils se confondent et dans une certaine mesure s'effacent dans la transcendance qui les fonde. »[18]

Ainsi le mode verbal utilisé en hébreu pour qualifier une action ne se réfère pas forcément à une notion temporelle. Mais comment rendre compte en français d'un texte hébreu, et en particulier de ce premier verset : au passé ou au présent ? Cela dépend bien entendu du contexte, mais il faut aussi voir qu'en général l'emploi d'un verbe au passé a tendance à nous renvoyer aux horizons de l'histoire alors que le présent facilite l'intériorisation en rendant les événements et les faits rapportés palpablement présents et vivants en nous. Notre texte mérite d'autant plus l'utilisation du présent qu'il n'appartient pas à l'histoire et la traduction de A. Chouraqui éveille mieux en nous sa dimension intemporelle.

Dès lors nous voyons que ce texte s'adresse – ici et maintenant – à tous les hommes, non pas pour leur raconter une histoire du passé, mais pour les instruire sur leur démarche spirituelle dans la vie.

---

[18] André Chouraqui, *op. cit,* p. 170.

L'adam connaît/fait l'expérience de/pénètre/comprend Ève, sa femme.

Le nom des personnages dans la Bible désigne toujours la qualité de celui qui le porte ou la qualité qu'il incarne, qu'il personnifie, car « pour les Sémites le nom est identique à la réalité qu'il désigne »[19]. Souvenons-nous de cela tout au long du récit.

Commençons par examiner ce que veut dire le nom de *Ève*, ou Hava (חַוָּה), *sa femme*. Son nom est identique à celui de sa racine (חָוָה) exprimant la vie ; elle est donc *la vie* ou *la vivante*. L'homme doit connaître, pénétrer, comprendre et aimer cette vie qui est en lui-même, *celle qui est os de ses os et chair de sa chair*[20].

L'adam connaît/fait l'expérience de/pénètre/comprend... Le verbe utilisé יד׳ (*yada*) a de nombreux sens et nous n'avons cité ici que ceux qui s'appliquent à la vie. Le plus souvent il est traduit par *connaître*. Notons que co-naître c'est « naître avec » ou « naître en commun » ce qui renvoie étymologiquement à une gnose intime avec laquelle nous croissons et nous devenons. Il signifie aussi « prendre en considération ». *Faire l'expérience de*, c'est connaître intimement, faire corps avec ce que l'on est amené à rencontrer. C'est aussi accomplir, ce qui engage l'homme dans toutes les dimensions de sa vie. *Pénétrer* exprime à la fois un mouvement vers le dedans et un approfondissement. A. Chouraqui, qui utilise ici ce verbe, précise dans le glossaire de sa Bible que ce verbe est équivalent à *connaître*[21]. Ainsi ce verbe *yada*, bien que

---

[19] André Chouraqui. *Le Coran*, note sur la Sourate 1, Paris : Robert Laffont, 1990.

[20] Genèse 2:23.

[21] Ce sens est bien réel, mais un peu oublié de nos jours.

n'excluant pas le sens concret des relations entre un homme et une femme[22], va bien au-delà en exprimant le fait de connaître intimement la vie, de parvenir à la pénétrer et la comprendre sur tous les plans qu'elle recèle, aussi bien dans le visible que dans l'invisible.

Par cette pénétration l'homme doit épanouir et accomplir cette vie pour devenir ainsi fécond sur tous les plans de l'existence. Cet accomplissement se manifestera concrètement, comme toujours dans la Bible, par un enfantement terrestre, mais « son sens immédiat, son aspect terrestre n'est qu'un faible degré de sa plénitude et non le plus important. »[23]

v. 1-b et 2-a

LS : *Elle conçut et enfanta Caïn et elle dit : j'ai formé un homme avec l'aide de l'Éternel.*
       Elle enfanta encore son frère Abel.

AC : *Enceinte, elle enfante Caïn. Elle dit : J'ai acquis un homme avec IHVH.*
       Elle ajoute à enfanter son frère, Hèbèl.

Enceinte, elle enfante Caïn : c'est la vie qui enfante la vie.

J'ai acquis ... avec IHVH. Ève la vivante perçoit que cette fécondation nouvelle vient avant tout de Dieu beaucoup plus que d'un homme. Autrement dit elle voit au-delà du seul plan concret,

---

[22] Il est regrettable que les traductions les plus récentes, telles la TOB révisée, la Segond 21, la Bible liturgique, voulant sans doute épouser la pensée dominante de notre siècle, n'aient vu dans ce verset que le sens d'une relation sexuelle entre un homme et une femme. Ceci restreint fortement la signification de ce verset et de l'ensemble du récit. Surtout une telle vision du texte ne nous apprend pas grand-chose sur le plan spirituel. Or le rôle d'un texte sacré c'est justement de nous apprendre quelque chose sur ce plan-là.

[23] Mâ Sûryânanda Lakshmî, *op.cit.*, p. 9.

au-delà de l'évidence matérielle, et perçoit que toute vie vient de Dieu. Par cette parole Ève nous invite à considérer que dans la Bible tout enfantement peut être également vu, compris, comme une fécondité de l'Esprit. Ce sera plus explicitement le cas lors de la promesse faite par Dieu à Abraham de le *multiplier à l'infini*[24]. En effet, « la postérité accordée par l'Éternel-Dieu est toujours spirituelle même si elle se manifeste par des formes, des êtres vivants dans le monde. Car l'incarnation n'a pas d'autre sens et point d'autre but que de révéler l'Éternel à la conscience de l'univers. »[25] Cette parole d'Ève éveille l'homme et l'humanité à un niveau de connaissance plus élevé que celui du seul plan moral et matériel.

Et effectivement Ève ne dit pas qu'elle a acquis un fils ou un enfant, comme nous le dirions en ne nous référant qu'à l'évidence matérielle, mais dit qu'elle a *acquis un homme-mâle*[26]. Cette acquisition *avec l'aide de l'Éternel* représente en elle-même une force et surtout une maturité plus grande, c'est-à-dire une connaissance de soi et une connaissance plus approfondie de la vie.

Elle ajoute à enfanter son frère, Hèbèl. Ici le verbe utilisé יסף *(yasaf)* veut dire *continuer à* ou *ajouter*. Ce verbe exprime très bien que Caïn n'est pas un individu pouvant se suffire à lui-même, autre chose doit lui être *ajouté*. Il situe également Abel dans la continuité par rapport à Caïn. Il apparaît comme la suite

---

[24] Genèse 17:2.
[25] Mâ Sûryânanda Lakshmî, *op. cit.*, p. 115.
[26] Excusez cet apparent pléonasme, mais c'est à notre avis la meilleure façon de rendre le sens du texte hébreu qui ici n'utilise plus le terme générique et indifférencié de *l'adam* mais campe cet homme *(ish)* dans sa spécificité par rapport à la femme *(isha)*.

naturelle de Caïn comme s'il n'était pas possible qu'il vienne sans lui et comme si Caïn ne pouvait être pleinement sans son frère. Il s'agit alors non pas de deux enfants nés indépendamment l'un de l'autre, mais d'un enfantement unique avec deux aspects différents et formant un tout.

Sur le plan terrestre on peut aussi les voir comme frères jumeaux car le contexte et surtout le verbe *yasaf* contiennent en filigrane cette notion de gémellité[27]. La tournure de ce verset appuie cela puisqu'elle met en premier le mot *frère* avant de préciser qu'il se nomme Abel. Dans toute la suite du texte ce qualificatif de « frère de » reviendra avec insistance puisqu'en seulement seize versets il est utilisé *sept* fois[28]. Ils sont inséparables et ceci sera confirmé plus loin dans le récit puisque la disparition d'Abel aura des conséquences fâcheuses pour Caïn, et cela non pas au sens moral mais au sens ontologique. Ensemble ne représentent-ils pas l'être humain dans son unité et sa totalité ?

v. 2-b
LS : *Abel fut berger et Caïn fut laboureur.*
AC : *Et c'est Hèbèl un pâtre d'ovins. Caïn était un serviteur de la glèbe.*

Que sont en nous Caïn et Abel ?

Si nous nous plaçons résolument dans une attitude d'écoute du texte nous pouvons comprendre que non seulement leur nom

---

[27] Ayant très souvent en mémoire le récit très connu des deux jumeaux Esaü et Jacob qui sont de manière très explicite qualifiés comme tels dans la Bible, nous avons du mal à concevoir que Caïn et Abel puissent l'être également, tant notre texte souligne moins explicitement cette particularité.

[28] Ce chiffre est, comme nous le verrons ultérieurement, celui de la plénitude.

hébreu nous éclaire, mais aussi que leur activité n'est pas mise là comme une simple indication du décor dans lequel se joue cette scène. Elle a au contraire une signification profonde sur ce qu'ils sont.

La psychologie actuelle reconnaît qu'il y a en l'homme une multitude de niveaux de conscience et la Sagesse de l'Inde le savait également. Elle a identifié sept plans principaux qui sont représentés dans notre structure corporelle par les sept « chakras ». Cela a été fréquemment attesté par les Sages des temps anciens et confirmé, parce que revécu, par les plus grands Sages contemporains, notamment en Occident par Mâ Sûryânanda Lakshmî (voir en Annexe la définition qu'elle en a donnée). Nous allons justement retrouver ces différents plans en Caïn et Abel.

Le nom de Caïn, d'après son étymologie, exprime *la possession* car il vient d'une racine קנה (*qanah*) signifiant *posséder, acquérir*. Par ailleurs son activité est d'être *serviteur de la glèbe/terre*. Ici le verbe utilisé pour cette activité signifie bien plus que le simple fait d'être laboureur ou agriculteur car sa racine עָבַד (*'avad*) veut dire non seulement *travailler* mais également *servir*. Non loin après cette indication, au verset 17 du même chapitre, nous retrouverons Caïn en train de *bâtir une ville*. Il est clair qu'il représente en nous les éléments qui doivent s'occuper des aspects matériels et vitaux propres à toute vie ici-bas. Effectivement la vie de l'homme sur la terre requiert cette activité et ce service sous quelque forme que ce soit. Vivre sur la terre c'est agir, et cela à tous les stades de notre existence de la conception à la mort, ainsi que le dit Swami Ramdas : « Le travail est la forme naturelle de la vie, parce que la vie elle-même est activité. »[29] Il

---

[29] Grand Sage de l'Inde (1884-1963). *Présence de Râm*, Paris : Albin Michel, 1997, p. 69.

29

en est ainsi pour les plantes qui doivent d'abord grandir puis donner une fleur puis une graine ou un fruit, et de même pour les animaux qui doivent croître, chercher leur nourriture, puis transmettre à leur tour la vie.

Ainsi Caïn représente en nous les trois plans de conscience du visible : *les plans physique, vital et mental*. Tous ces plans sont caractéristiques de toute vie sur la terre et sans eux elle n'apparaîtrait pas, ni ne pourrait se maintenir. Soulignons que le mental est le propre de l'homme et que « le mental c'est la perception des sens et l'intelligence relative des dualités. Dans ce sens il fait aussi partie du visible au même titre que le physique et le vital »[30]. Par ces trois plans l'homme partage avec les autres éléments de la création les principes *d'existence, de vie et d'intelligence*. S'il en prenait vraiment conscience il la respecterait sans doute mieux.

Si Caïn vient en premier c'est qu'il représente les fondations mêmes, le socle, de cette vie manifestée sur la terre et que sans lui elle ne serait pas, et qu'Abel ne pourrait être non plus, car « l'action est la base aussi bien que le couronnement de toutes les manifestations de la vie »[31].

De son côté le nom de Abel (הֶבֶל) signifie *souffle* ou *nuée, buée*, ou encore *ce qui est sans consistance matérielle*. Le souffle évoque en premier lieu la vie. La nuée/buée paraît au premier abord immatérielle, impalpable, et ne se perçoit que par ses conséquences concrètes, par exemple la rosée du matin. L'activité d'Abel est d'être un *berger/pâtre* ; il est celui qui conduit le troupeau, le nourrit, le garde et prend soin de lui. Cette référence

---

[30] Mâ Sûryânanda Lakshmî, *op. cit.*
[31] Swami Ramdas, *op. cit.*, p. 74.

au berger en tant que gardien et guide se retrouve à plusieurs reprises dans la Bible, tant dans l'Ancien Testament (par exemple au psaume 23), ainsi que dans le Nouveau Testament (par exemple Jean 10:11).

Abel incarne ce qui ne se voit pas, ce qui demeure impalpable comme un souffle, mais est essentiel à la vie, à l'existence et à l'accomplissement de l'homme, tout aussi essentiel que le berger pour la vie de son troupeau. Sans le berger le troupeau ne serait pas ; ainsi sans Abel l'homme également ne serait pas. Il personnifie les différents *plans spirituels*, c'est-à-dire l'invisible en nous ou, autrement dit, l'âme et l'Esprit en l'homme. Selon Mâ Sûryânanda Lakshmî, par ces plans de l'invisible l'homme a en lui les principes de *la Connaissance, de la Sagesse et de l'Amour*. Son rôle spécifique dans la création – sa tâche métaphysique – est de les faire grandir et ne pas les tuer, ce qu'il a beaucoup de mal à accomplir comme la suite du récit va le montrer.

Caïn et Abel représentent donc tous les plans de la conscience et de la vie que l'homme doit faire évoluer pour monter à Dieu. Leur enfantement inaugure le départ puis la démarche que l'homme doit entreprendre sur le chemin vers *l'arbre de vie*, vers la *révélation de l'Éternel* en lui-même et dans le monde. Il est en quelque sorte une seconde *genèse* pour l'éveil de sa conscience à sa Vérité.

Par cette seconde genèse l'homme *pénètre le mystère de la vie*. Ici nous rejoignons l'un des enseignements de l'Inde : alors que l'Occident explore très à fond toutes les manifestations de la vie, l'Inde s'est penchée prioritairement sur la connaissance (pénétration) de la vie elle-même.

Cette genèse n'est pas un moment historique car ce mot vient du grec *genesis*, traduction de l'hébreu בְּרֵאשִׁית *(berechit),* signifiant « dans un commencement » (plutôt que *au* commencement) exprimant par là un commencement éternel et toujours nouveau. Il est donc de notre nature de vivre ce commencement et ce chemin. Mais sur celui-ci nous rencontrons un obstacle majeur, matrice unique de tous les autres obstacles que nous pouvons à l'occasion rencontrer. C'est précisément le mérite de l'allégorie de Caïn et Abel de bien nous faire sentir la consistance de cet obstacle afin que nous puissions un jour le dépasser. Ce sont souvent les tribulations de la vie qui nous amènent à en prendre conscience, nous montrent la voie et nous poussent plus loin vers cet Infini et cette Éternité au-dedans de nous.

Les Écritures saintes sont difficiles à comprendre,
il y faut beaucoup d'oraison.
Sainte Thérèse d'Avila

Le faux pas ou l'erreur d'appréciation de Caïn

v. 3 et 4-a

LS :　*Au bout de quelques temps,*
　　　　Caïn fit à l'Éternel une offrande des fruits de la terre ;
　　　　Et Abel, de son côté, en fit une des premiers-nés de son troupeau et de leur graisse.

AC :　*Et c'est au terme des jours,*
　　　　Caïn fait venir des fruits de la glèbe en offrande à IHVH.
　　　　Hèbèl a fait venir, lui aussi, des aînés de ses ovins et leur graisse.

Au terme des jours : Caïn et Abel doivent d'abord croître et se fortifier selon la loi de la vie, qui est la loi de l'Éternel, avant de pouvoir faire une *offrande*. Ce *quelque temps* ou ce *terme des jours* il n'est pas dit quel il est, ce qui laisse supposer qu'il n'est pas quantifiable, ni forcément temporel car en général quand la Bible veut indiquer une durée elle donne un chiffre, même symbolique. Ce *terme des jours* indique simplement qu'il s'agit d'une étape dans la vie, étape qui sera justement marquée par l'offrande qu'ils vont faire à l'Éternel.

Chacun *fait venir*... Le verbe utilisé ici signifie : *faire venir, amener, apporter, récolter*. Chaque plan en nous offre à l'Éternel ce qui le caractérise et ce qu'il est capable de faire venir et récolter du fond de lui-même et de sa vie : pour Caïn les produits de la terre, pour Abel ses animaux – les premiers-nés – avec leur graisse[32]. Chacun offre tout simplement le fruit de son travail, ce qu'il a pu faire croître dans sa propre vie et dans le monde, donc en définitive ce qu'il a acquis tant à l'intérieur qu'à l'extérieur de lui-même.

Les deux offrandes sont ainsi l'exact reflet de ce que chacun est car l'offrande faite à Dieu n'est pas quelque chose *là-dehors* comme un cadeau fait à M. X ou Mme Y. En réalité l'homme ne peut offrir à l'Éternel que ce qu'il est. Les offrandes sont alors forcément personnifiées, mais rien dans le texte ne permet de penser qu'une offrande ait plus de valeur intrinsèque ou soit meilleure que l'autre. Elles paraissent également valables bien que de nature différente. Leur valeur aux yeux de l'Éternel est uniquement dans la sincérité de cœur et l'amour avec lesquels elles sont faites, comme le dit le Seigneur Krishna dans la *Bhagavad-Gîtâ* : « Celui qui M'offre avec dévotion une feuille, une fleur, un fruit, une coupe d'eau – cette offrande d'amour venue d'une âme qui s'efforce, M'est agréable » (9:26).

D'autres caractéristiques de ces offrandes nous éclairent un peu plus sur Caïn et Abel en nous-même. Tout d'abord, souvenons-nous que traditionnellement le peuple juif consacrait tout premier-né à l'Éternel ce qui souligne le caractère spirituel de l'offrande d'Abel, alors que celle de Caïn est le reflet du travail matériel (les produits de la terre). Ensuite considérons que les *premiers-nés* d'Abel ce sont aussi les *aînés* ce qui signifie que son offrande est placée sous le sceau de la maturité, tandis que les

---

[32] Cette *graisse,* que nous délaissons si aisément dans nos civilisations repues, symbolisait chez ces populations nomades à la fois la richesse et une promesse de pérennisation de la vie, car seuls les animaux bien gras pouvaient survivre dans les conditions parfois rudes de cette époque.

produits de la terre de Caïn sont ceux de la fraîcheur de la récolte et de la saison. Cette différence de maturité existe également en nous-même entre nos différents plans de conscience. Ici il apparaît que Caïn a manqué de maturité lorsqu'il a entrepris son offrande, ce qui sera confirmé dans la suite du récit.

Remarquons aussi que Caïn et Abel agissent chacun de leur côté, mais il semble, d'après le texte, que Caïn ait agi en premier. Déjà pointe ici une première erreur : les différents plans de vie de l'homme ne sont pas unis dans ce moment d'offrande, ce qui n'est vraisemblablement pas juste aux yeux de l'Éternel. Erreur universelle de l'homme que dénonce Jésus (Mathieu 15:8), rappelant ce que Isaïe avait dit : *Quand ce peuple s'avance, de sa bouche et de ses lèvres il me glorifie, mais son cœur est loin de Moi*[33].

De cette différence de maturité et de ce manque d'union des différents plans de la vie, il résulte pour chacun des deux frères une appréciation différente du regard de l'Éternel.

v. 4-b et v. 5-a

LS : *L'Éternel porta un regard favorable sur Abel et sur son offrande ;*
  Mais il ne porta pas un regard favorable sur Caïn et sur son offrande.
AC : *IHVH considère Hèbèl et son offrande.*
  Caïn et son offrande il ne les considère pas.

Une lecture trop rapide de la traduction de L. Segond pourrait nous induire en erreur sur le sens de ce verset, mais la traduction de A. Chouraqui nous aide à ne pas tomber dans cette erreur. Le verbe utilisé ici signifie tout simplement *regarder* ou *considérer*, et rien n'y est ajouté. Il n'est nullement dit que Dieu porta un

[33] Isaïe 29:13.

regard défavorable sur Caïn et son offrande. Il ne s'agit donc pas ici d'une appréciation ni d'un jugement de l'Éternel s'appuyant sur la qualité apparente des offrandes.

La parole de Krishna citée au verset précédent nous aide à mieux comprendre ce verset. Elle nous dit que l'offrande d'une feuille est pour le Seigneur tout aussi agréable que celle de quelques autres biens apparemment plus précieux, dès lors qu'il s'agit d'une offrande d'amour « venue d'une âme qui s'efforce ». Cette nature différente des offrandes représente la sensibilité et l'attitude différentes que nous pouvons avoir dans telle ou telle circonstance, par exemple l'intelligence mentale peut être bien disposée mais le cœur n'y est pas. Lorsque l'offrande est agréable au Seigneur Il la considère, mais sinon Il ne la considère pas ou ne la regarde pas. Nous verrons plus loin qu'effectivement il y a un manque d'amour chez Caïn.

Même si, comme le dit Maïmonide[34], « la Bible utilise le langage des hommes », ceux-ci doivent toujours être attentifs à se défaire d'une vision anthropomorphique[35] de Dieu. Isaïe, parlant au nom de l'Éternel, l'avait bien dit mais l'homme l'oublie sans cesse : *Mes desseins ne sont pas vos desseins, et vos voies ne sont pas mes voies, dit l'Éternel. Oui, les cieux sont plus hauts que la terre, ainsi mes voies sont plus hautes que vos voies, mes desseins que vos desseins*[36]. Parler d'un regard favorable ou défavorable de l'Éternel montre à quel point l'homme a du mal à comprendre

---

[34] Philosophe, théologien et médecin juif (1138-1204). Il s'opposa à la tendance d'avoir une vision anthropomorphique de Dieu.

[35] Voltaire avait bien compris cette incompréhension des hommes, disant avec humour : *Dieu a fait l'homme à son image et celui-ci le lui a bien rendu.*

[36] Isaïe 55:8-9. Dans cette citation on peut remplacer le terme « desseins » par « pensées », à la convenance de chacun.

Ses desseins et Ses voies. Il a toujours tendance à les ramener à sa propre vision étroite de la vie, plutôt que de s'élever vers ce qu'Il Est.

Cette vision restreinte de la vie est le propre du mental et de l'intellect de l'homme qui demeure souvent impuissant à connaître la Vérité de la vie. Cela a été maintes fois enseigné par les Sages de l'Inde, mais reste en grande partie ignoré en Occident, notamment par la théologie actuelle, comme si n'avait pas été entendu ce que Blaise Pascal avait dit : « C'est le cœur qui sent Dieu, et non la raison. » Il ne s'agit pas ici de dénigrer ce plan mental car il a d'autres facultés nécessaires et indispensables pour l'homme, telles que permettre des progrès considérables dans beaucoup de domaines pour toutes les civilisations. Il s'agit simplement de reconnaître ses limites dans le domaine spirituel.

C.G. Jung a aussi expliqué cela. « La première aberrance consiste à essayer de tout dominer par l'intellect. Elle vise un but secret, celui de se soustraire à l'efficacité des archétypes et ainsi à l'expérience réelle au bénéfice d'un monde conceptuel, apparemment sécurisé, mais artificiel et qui n'a que deux dimensions, monde conceptuel qui à l'aide de notions décrétées claires aimerait bien couvrir et enfouir toute la réalité de la vie. Le déplacement vers le conceptuel enlève à l'expérience sa substance pour l'attribuer à un simple nom qui, à partir de cet instant, se trouve mis à la place de la réalité. Une notion n'engage personne et c'est précisément cet agrément que l'on cherche parce qu'il promet de protéger de l'expérience. Or l'esprit ne vit pas par des concepts, mais par les faits et les réalités. Ce n'est pas par des paroles qu'on arrive à éloigner un chien du feu. Et pourtant on répète à l'infini ce procédé. »[37]

---

[37] Dans *Ma vie*. Éd. Gallimard 1966.

Cette affirmation de Jung corrobore la rédaction des textes bibliques qui n'utilisent pas des concepts, mais mettent en scène des personnages confrontés à des situations et faits concrets. Ce sont bien souvent nos commentaires sur ces textes qui cherchent à « tout dominer par l'intellect ».

Mais ce plan mental de l'homme, ne voyant en Caïn et Abel que des personnages individuels et une dualité entre Dieu et sa création, éprouve le besoin de poser cette question – Pourquoi Dieu préfère-t-il l'offrande d'Abel ? – et de trouver une réponse à son niveau. C'est pourquoi bien des commentateurs ont donné des explications basées sur la *valeur supposée* des offrandes, valeur qui serait ainsi propre à déclencher une préférence ou non de l'Éternel. Mais si nous intériorisons tous les éléments du récit et n'oublions pas que tout cela se passe en nous, rien ne permet de souscrire à cette interprétation. Et surtout la question posée n'est ni juste ni utile car il n'est pas nécessaire de trouver une réponse pour saisir le sens de la suite du récit. Poser cette question c'est ramener à l'homme ce qui concerne l'Éternel et c'est justement faire la même erreur d'appréciation que Caïn, comme nous le verrons au verset suivant. C'est oublier que « pour comprendre l'Esprit de Dieu, la mentalité humaine doit se défaire de la notion de préférence qui est étrangère à la conscience spirituelle »[38].

En réalité dans sa vie de tous les jours, que sait l'homme du regard de l'Éternel ? Rien ou bien peu de choses, même s'il s'imagine savoir ceci ou cela ; mais son imagination le trompe si facilement ! Aussi plutôt que de nous imaginer que notre offrande

---

[38] Mâ Sûryânanda Lakshmî, *Journal Spirituel*, Neuchâtel (Suisse) : Éditions À la Baconnière, 1978, p. 92.

est accueillie favorablement ou non, nous pouvons voir que ce verset reflète, sous une forme condensée, la vie telle qu'elle est. Nous vivons tous des moments qui apparemment nous paraissent propices ou favorables et d'autres qui le semblent moins, des moments où tout semble réussir et ceux où rien ne va, des printemps qui nous offrent une abondante floraison et des hivers où la vie est comme arrêtée. Notre propre projection mentale sur le vécu de ces moments nous fait croire que Dieu porte un regard favorable ou défavorable sur les actions de notre vie. Il ne s'agit pas de cela.

L'Éternel met en scène tous les éléments de la vie terrestre, avec apparemment ses bons et mauvais côtés. Mais en réalité tout est bien, comme le dit le récit de la Création : *Dieu voit tout ce qu'il fait, et voici tout cela est très bon/beau/bien*[39]. En discuter et surtout juger l'Éternel comme le fera Caïn au verset suivant paraît faux. Ici la référence au livre de Job s'impose car cette absence de jugement envers l'Éternel y est merveilleusement présentée. Alors que Job est dépouillé de tout et gravement malade, au lieu de discuter et de juger, il dit : *L'Éternel a donné, et l'Éternel a ôté ; que le nom de l'Éternel soit béni !* puis il répond à sa femme qui lui suggère de maudire Dieu : *Tu parles comme une femme insensée. Quoi ! Nous accepterions de Dieu le bien, et nous n'accepterions pas aussi le mal*[40] !

De ce mal apparent, ou plutôt de cette sévérité de l'Éternel, Rabindranath Tagore dans un de ses poèmes en parle très bien et nous en donne le sens :

---

[39] Gn. 1:31.
[40] Job 1:20 puis 2:10.

« Mes désirs sont nombreux et ma plainte est pitoyable,
mais par de durs refus Tu m'épargnes toujours ;
et cette sévère clémence, tout au travers de ma vie, s'est ourdie.
Jour après jour tu me formes digne des grands dons simples
que tu répands spontanément sur moi :
ce ciel et la lumière, ce corps et la vie de l'esprit,
m'épargnant les périls de l'excessif désir.
Parfois languissant je m'attarde ;
parfois je m'éveille et me hâte en quête de mon but ;
mais alors cruellement Tu te dérobes de devant moi.
Jour après jour Tu me formes digne de ton plein accueil :
en me refusant toujours et encore,
Tu m'épargnes les périls du faible, de l'incertain désir[41]. »

« Cette sévère clémence » de l'Éternel, qui est celle de la vie, nous la retrouvons dans l'événement qui se présente à Caïn à ce moment-là. Ce que Caïn est en train de vivre dans ce verset c'est tout simplement une épreuve, c'est-à-dire un obstacle dans sa marche vers l'arbre de vie, comme nous en vivons tous dans notre vie terrestre, et comme l'a vécu Job de façon beaucoup plus dramatique. Cette épreuve offre à Caïn l'occasion de connaître l'obstacle intérieur qu'il rencontre au cours de sa pérégrination sur la terre. Mais il ne va pas comprendre et il ne va pas suivre cette voie de s'en remettre uniquement à Dieu, car le sens véritable de l'offrande c'est de s'oublier soi-même face à Lui. Ce sera justement l'instruction que lui donnera l'Éternel au verset 7. Mais pour l'instant voici justement comment Caïn perçoit cet événement et ce qu'il en ressent.

---

[41] Rabindranath Tagore, *L'Offrande lyrique*, poème 14, Paris : Gallimard, 1963.

v. 5-b

LS : *Caïn fut très irrité et son visage fut abattu.*

AC : *Cela brûle beaucoup Caïn, ses faces tombent.*

Le texte hébreu utilise un vocabulaire très imagé pour exprimer cela : son sentiment le *brûle* de l'intérieur et son visage est défait – *ses faces[42] tombent.* Caïn n'a pas vécu la situation selon la Vérité divine, il ne s'est pas élevé jusqu'aux *desseins de l'Éternel.* Devant l'événement qui se présente à lui il aurait pu se dire « les voies du Seigneur sont impénétrables », et les accepter humblement sans maugréer. Au contraire de cela il reste centré uniquement sur son moi individuel c'est-à-dire qu'il reste attaché à son ego et son intérêt immédiat, donc égoïste. À cause également de son orgueil qui sera révélé quelques versets plus loin, il n'a pas voulu accepter et suivre *les voies de l'Éternel,* mais les a ramenées à sa propre mesure. Sa réaction se situe alors à la hauteur de son propre désir, de ce qu'il attendait dans sa vie.

Son attitude, outre le manque d'amour envers l'Éternel, peut également refléter un manque de maturité. Dans sa sagesse l'Ecclésiaste (Qohèlet) dit : *Il existe un moment et un temps propice pour toute affaire* (ou *désir*) *sous les cieux[43].* Notons que le texte dit *sous les cieux* et non pas *sur la terre,* c'est-à-dire sous le regard de l'Éternel et non pas selon la volonté de l'homme. Jésus a enseigné la même chose à ses disciples lorsqu'il a dit : *J'ai encore beaucoup de choses à vous dire mais vous ne pouvez*

---

[42] En hébreu le mot traduit par *faces* est toujours au pluriel. Les linguistes voient dans ce mot au pluriel une marque de « superlatif intensif » propre aux langues sémitiques. Ici nous voyons davantage l'expression que l'homme a de nombreux visages, de nombreux personnages en lui-même.

[43] Ecclésiaste 3:1.

pas les porter maintenant. Quand le Paraclet sera venu, l'Esprit de vérité, il vous conduira dans toute la vérité[44]. Ainsi l'homme doit avoir la maturité requise pour bien comprendre la loi de Dieu et entreprendre la tâche qui l'attend, mais Dieu seul connaît en lui si le temps est propice pour le faire. Vouloir s'abstraire de ce *temps de Dieu* qui est ce *temps de la vie* et doit être en *harmonie en toute affaire,* c'est courir le risque d'un échec.

Pour mieux comprendre cela il faut se référer à un autre récit biblique qui se situe en fin du chapitre 14 du livre des Nombres puis est repris dans le Deutéronome au chapitre 1. Après leur sortie d'Égypte les fils d'Israël se rebellent contre Moïse et l'Éternel, puis se rendant compte de leur erreur ils se repentent et veulent alors, sans tarder, combattre leurs ennemis. Mais l'Éternel intervient et dit : *Ne montez pas et ne combattez pas, car Je ne suis pas dans votre sein.* Les Hébreux n'écoutent pas cette voix et partent combattre audacieusement. Il s'ensuit pour eux une sévère défaite. Au retour de cette défaite ils pleurent auprès de l'Éternel, mais Moïse dans le Deutéronome précise que cette fois *L'Éternel n'écouta pas votre voix et ne vous prêta point l'oreille.* À la suite de cet épisode désastreux ils comprennent enfin qu'ils doivent partir vers le désert selon l'ordre qu'ils en avaient, auparavant, reçu de l'Éternel. Après cette longue errance de quarante années dans le désert, c'est-à-dire après ce temps de purification et de maturation absolument nécessaires, ils pourront à nouveau affronter et vaincre leurs ennemis.

La Sagesse hindoue enseigne que *l'offrande* ou le *sacrifice* offert à Dieu signifie *le combat sur le chemin spirituel qui doit être parcouru.* C'est exactement ce que nous venons de voir à propos

---

[44] Év. de Jean 16:12-13.

du combat que doivent mener les enfants d'Israël. Mais ils n'étaient pas suffisamment prêts et purifiés pour obtenir la victoire et c'est aussi ce qui va se passer pour Caïn. Le livre de l'Apocalypse enseigne aussi que cette purification est indispensable pour pouvoir manger de l'arbre de vie : *Heureux ceux qui lavent leur robe afin d'avoir droit à l'arbre de vie*[45].

Dans une perspective d'intériorisation des textes sacrés, qui nous a si bien été enseignée par l'Inde, nous pouvons comprendre que ces ennemis ce sont, pour nous aujourd'hui, avant tout nos ennemis intérieurs qui nous empêchent de *monter* vers l'Éternel, c'est-à-dire de monter vers cette vie en Éternité. Ces ennemis ce sont en premier l'attachement à notre propre ego alors que la vie en Éternité c'est justement « la conscience d'être impersonnel bien davantage qu'une personne individuelle » comme le dit Swami Ramdas. Caïn a voulu « faire une offrande » c'est-à-dire mener un combat contre l'attachement à son ego. Cette offrande engageait une grande partie de sa vie (ce qu'il avait récolté), mais était-il suffisamment prêt pour l'entreprendre ?

La réponse de la vie qui n'est pas négative, mais que Caïn a vécue de manière négative, lui est justement offerte pour qu'il reconnaisse cet obstacle qu'il doit affronter, mais que pour l'instant il ne peut vaincre, ce qui l'a *irrité* et aussi *abattu*.

Si nous sommes un peu attentifs à ce qui se passe dans notre propre vie, nous savons très bien que lorsque nous essayons de dépasser telle ou telle difficulté intérieure, souvent nous n'y parvenons pas tant que le temps n'est pas encore venu. Puis un jour ce temps est là et il nous semble que Dieu a triomphé en

---

[45] Apocalypse 22:14.

43

nous-même de ces difficultés, comme dans les combats que le peuple d'Israël a dû mener, car tant de fois l'Éternel lui dit à propos de ses ennemis : *Je les livre entre tes (vos) mains*. Cela ne signifie aucunement qu'il faille être passif mais que seules la prière, la dévotion et l'adoration constantes nous mèneront à la maturité requise et nous élèveront vers l'Éternel qui triomphera alors de nos ennemis.

Tout cela se passe en nous et il n'est pas difficile de reconnaître ici l'incompréhension de l'homme face à Dieu et face à son propre cheminement sur la terre pour pouvoir un jour connaître cette vie en Éternité. C'est pourquoi ce fourvoiement va entraîner un enseignement de Dieu.

v. 6

LS : *Et l'Éternel dit à Caïn :*
Pourquoi es-tu irrité, et pourquoi ton visage est-il abattu ?

AC : *IHVH dit à Caïn :*
Pourquoi cela te brûle-t-il, pourquoi tes faces sont-elles tombées ?

L'Éternel interroge Caïn sur sa réaction devant les événements de la vie qui se sont présentés à lui. La question de l'Éternel est en fait : ta réaction est-elle juste ?

Cette interrogation est déjà en soi une instruction et elle évoque Socrate instruisant ses disciples de la même manière afin qu'ils trouvent en eux-mêmes la réponse. Puisque c'est l'Éternel qui interroge Caïn, cela signifie qu'il y a quand même en lui un tout début de prise de conscience à un niveau plus élevé que celui de ses seuls plans physique, vital ou instinctif. Et parfois il nous arrive de percevoir ainsi, de manière très furtive au fond de notre cœur, ce questionnement : pourquoi suis-je mécontent ?

v. 7

LS : *Certainement, si tu agis bien tu relèveras ton visage,*
Et si tu agis mal le péché se couche à ta porte,
Et ses désirs se portent vers toi : mais toi domine sur lui.

AC : *N'est-ce pas que tu t'améliores à porter ou que tu ne t'améliores pas,*
À l'ouverture la faute est tapie ;
À toi, sa passion. Toi gouverne-la.

Ici l'instruction de l'Éternel va plus loin et ce verset constitue le pivot central du récit. Il est la réponse de l'Éternel à nos perplexités sur notre rôle ici-bas, car malgré tous ses efforts l'homme ne peut de lui-même répondre à cela. La réponse vient de l'Éternel et de Lui seul.

Bienheureuse instruction pour l'homme qui sait la capter en lui-même, ainsi que le dit le Deutéronome : *Ce commandement que je te prescris aujourd'hui n'est pas dans le ciel, pour que tu dises : Qui montera pour nous au ciel et nous l'ira chercher, qui nous le fera entendre afin que nous le mettions en pratique ? Il n'est pas de l'autre côté de la mer pour que tu dises : Qui passera pour nous de l'autre côté de la mer et nous l'ira chercher, qui nous le fera entendre afin que nous le mettions en pratique ? C'est une chose, au contraire, qui est tout près de toi, dans ta bouche et dans ton cœur, afin que tu le mettes en pratique*[46].

La loi de l'Éternel n'est pas quelque chose d'extérieur à imposer aux autres, elle est au contraire à rechercher au fond de notre cœur car c'est là qu'elle se découvre pleinement et nous éclaire. Cela n'exclut nullement le fait qu'il soit nécessaire de l'enseigner et de l'étudier, mais signifie que c'est en l'intériorisant qu'elle

---

[46] Deutéronome 30:11-14.

révèle sa plus haute vérité et toute sa puissance. Est-ce pour cela que ce verset est si difficile à traduire et que, par exemple, les deux traductions citées sont obscures et ne coïncident pas vraiment, comme si nous avions tous du mal à capter l'enseignement de Dieu ? Dans le livre du prophète Isaïe, l'Éternel avait bien souligné cette difficulté : *Va et dis à ce peuple : Vous entendrez et vous ne comprendrez point ; vous verrez et ne saisirez point*[47].

Toutefois cette difficulté n'est pas insurmontable et sainte Thérèse d'Avila nous donne un conseil précieux pour entreprendre son dépassement : « Pour bien comprendre les Écritures saintes il y faut beaucoup d'oraison. » Par ailleurs un recours systématique à l'hébreu qui est « la langue de la vision, faite pour évoquer l'image, le mouvement, l'expression concrète du geste »[48] peut devenir une source d'autres éclairages pour nous aider à mieux saisir l'esprit de ce texte. Alors oublions ces traductions pour nous pencher sur le texte original traité mot à mot.

1/ הֲלוֹא אִם־תֵּיטִיב שְׂאֵת
N'est-ce pas que si tu agis bien, (c'est) une élévation/dignité ? [49]

Le premier enseignement de Dieu explique le sens de l'offrande et de la vie car, vraisemblablement, Caïn ne l'avait pas compris. Cette instruction, qui est encore une interrogation, s'articule autour du verbe יָטַב *(yatav)* qui signifie : bien faire, bien agir, répondre à sa vocation, faire une chose de façon juste, être bienveillant (étymologiquement bien-voulant), rendre heureux.

---

[47] Isaïe 6:9.
[48] A. Chouraqui. *Op. Cit.*
[49] En général l'hébreu n'utilise pas le verbe « être » pour qualifier une situation, mais nous l'avons ajouté en français pour rendre ce mot à mot plus compréhensible pour ceux qui ne connaissent pas l'hébreu.

À travers tous ces sens on comprend que le « bien-vouloir » et le « bien-agir » selon Dieu n'est pas un paradigme absolu mais qu'il est différent pour chacun et uniquement selon sa propre vocation. La racine de ce verbe se retrouve dans l'adjectif טוֹב *(tov)* qui signifie beau/bon/bien, et si nous enlevons toute connotation morale à ce terme il révèle le sens de ce commandement de Dieu : *Si tu marches en ma présence, avec sincérité de cœur et avec droiture, j'établirai pour toujours le trône de ton royaume en Israël*[50].

La vocation de Caïn, énoncée au verset 2, est d'être un *serviteur de la glèbe-terre*, ce qui situe ce service dans l'action concrète de la vie, afin d'offrir les conditions de développement de cette vie sur la terre. Un serviteur agit bien lorsqu'il agit pour le bien et le plaisir de son maître, sans attendre une récompense particulière en retour. Son offrande a-t-elle été faite dans l'optique juste de ce service, dans un détachement de lui-même et sans arrière-pensée ? Attendait-il une reconnaissance, voire une récompense en retour de son offrande ? Nous ne le savons pas, même si nous pouvons le supposer au vu de sa réaction. Mais ce qu'il demeure important de voir ici, c'est que le sens de l'offrande est d'accepter maintenant les événements tels qu'ils se présentent à lui au lieu de se regimber contre eux. Or le verset précédent nous montre que Caïn ne les a pas acceptés.

Mais si Caïn, non seulement comprend, mais agit selon ce que doit être l'offrande à Dieu, il reçoit alors l'instruction divine sur le devenir de sa vie lorsqu'il *agit bien*. Ici le texte utilise le substantif שְׂאֵת *(se'eyth)* qui provient d'une racine signifiant : porter, soulever, pardonner, enlever, être haut élevé, se lever, se dresser. Il signifie une *élévation/dignité*. Par cet enseignement Dieu donne à l'homme une orientation de vie.

---

[50] I Rois 9:4.

Quelle est cette *élévation/dignité* de l'homme lorsque c'est Dieu qui l'instruit ? Il s'agit, comme le dit Jésus, de l'élévation de l'homme au-delà de *la chair et du sang*. Il explique cela dans Matthieu 16:13-17, lorsque Pierre, répondant à la question de Jésus – *Qui dit-on que je suis ?* – reconnaît en Lui le *fils de Dieu*. Jésus alors lui répond : *Tu es heureux Simon fils de Jonas, car ce ne sont pas la chair et le sang qui t'ont révélé cela, mais c'est mon Père qui est dans les cieux.* Pierre a été élevé de son plan de conscience habituel, qui est celui *de la chair et du sang*, vers un plan supérieur où il peut reconnaître Dieu en Jésus. Cette élévation, c'est en l'homme un chemin vers la connaissance de Dieu et le triomphe de l'Esprit, un pas en avant pour pouvoir un jour manger de l'arbre de vie.

וְאִם לֹא תֵיטִיב לַפֶּתַח חַטָּאת רֹבֵץ /2
Mais si tu n'agis pas de façon juste, à l'ouverture/porte le « manquer de but » étant couché,

L'Éternel vient d'instruire l'homme sur le bienfait d'agir de façon juste. Maintenant Il lui explique quels sont les éléments de sa vie qui peuvent être la source d'une erreur par rapport à une action juste.

L'ouverture/porte fait concrètement référence au passage qui permet de communiquer entre la tente, ou la maison, et son environnement. Elle signifie le lieu d'échange entre les circonstances extérieures et notre intériorité ou l'inverse. En effet la manière dont l'homme voit et vit les circonstances extérieures dépend bien entendu de celles-ci, mais bien davantage encore de ce qu'il est. « L'important ce ne sont pas les situations extérieures mais la manière dont nous réagissons » enseigne Mâ Sûryânanda Lakshmî.

Dans notre vie nous sommes tous confrontés en permanence à cette vérité, même si nous n'en avons pas conscience, et un exemple simple nous permettra de mieux la comprendre. Un prêtre nous faisait visiter sa très belle église romane abritant dans sa crypte une statue très ancienne de la Vierge. Depuis des générations les fidèles de cette région avaient l'habitude de venir dans cette crypte pour toucher cette statue et il nous relatait que certains de ses paroissiens s'en indignaient estimant qu'il s'agissait là de superstition ou d'idolâtrie, souhaitant en conséquence qu'il réprouve cette pratique. Ce bienheureux prêtre leur répondait : « Mais non, moi j'y vois un geste d'amour. »

C'est précisément dans sa réaction par rapport aux circonstances de son action que se situe le *manquer de but* de Caïn, son faux pas. Il voit dans la réponse de la vie qui suit son offrande comme une *préférence* de l'Éternel, au lieu de tout simplement considérer que se présentait à lui l'occasion de connaître la loi de Dieu, de l'accepter et donc de corriger son attitude pour avancer un peu plus vers son « destin surnaturel ». Mais lorsque l'homme reste centré uniquement sur son moi individuel, son attachement à son ego, il commet cette erreur d'appréciation et considère que Dieu a des préférences. Comment pourrait-il y avoir une préférence en l'Éternel ? Aucune, comme le dit le Deutéronome 10:17 : *Car l'Éternel, votre Dieu, ... ne fait point acception des personnes*[51].

Le mot hébreu traduit ici par l'expression *le manquer de but* vient d'un verbe חטא *(ḥata)* qui certes veut dire pécher, mais tout d'abord : manquer une cible ou un but, se tromper, s'égarer, ne

---

[51] Cette vérité est réaffirmée dans Actes 10:34 ainsi qu'à de nombreuses reprises dans les Épîtres (Ro. 2:11, Ga. 2:6, Éph. 2:6, Col. 3:25, Jas. 2:9, Pi. 1:17).

pas trouver[52]. Cette expression exprime mieux une dynamique que le terme *faute* ou *péché* car la vie court toujours vers un but, même si bien souvent l'homme ignore lequel. De quelle cible ou de quel but manqué s'agit-il ? Il s'agit justement de cette *élévation/dignité* relatée précédemment. En outre le texte hébreu utilise le « participe actif » du verbe *coucher* pour indiquer que ce risque de *faux pas* par rapport au but à atteindre est un élément permanent inscrit dans la structure même de notre être. Tout cela a bien entendu des conséquences dans notre vie et c'est ce que l'Éternel va maintenant expliquer à Caïn.

3/ וְאֵלֶיךָ תְּשׁוּקָתוֹ וְאַתָּה תִּמְשָׁל־בּוֹ

Et vers toi son attente, et toi tu seras semblable à lui (le manquer de but).

Dans ce passage il y a comme un dialogue permanent, un lien étroit entre nos réactions et ce que nous devenons. D'un côté ce « *manquer de but* » est toujours en attente de faire jouer sa prépondérance en nous si nous ne sommes pas bienveillant, et d'un autre il a la capacité d'induire le devenir de notre vie.

En effet le premier sens du verbe מָשַׁל *(machal)* est « être semblable à », puis vient en second le sens de « dominer ». Le premier sens paraît plus logique que le second dans le contexte où il est utilisé, et surtout il dépasse la vision moralisante que sous-tendrait le sens de *domination* assortie au mot *péché* dans cette phrase. Ce verbe est très clairement au « mode inaccompli » ce

---

[52] Dans la Septante il est traduit par *amartia* venant du verbe *amartanô* dont le sens est en premier lieu *manquer le but*, puis : se tromper de chemin, s'écarter de la vérité, dévier, s'égarer, se méprendre, manquer de faire, trébucher ; puis (seulement en dernier) commettre une faute, faillir, pécher.

qui signifie qu'à partir de l'enseignement de l'Éternel toutes les possibilités de changement de point de vue sont ouvertes. Les Sages de l'Inde répètent « on devient ce que l'on pense » et énoncent plusieurs paraboles illustrant cela. Caïn a pensé faussement au sujet de la vie et de l'Éternel et, s'il ne change pas de point de vue, il deviendra encore plus faux en lui-même et manquera le but assigné par Dieu. C'est bien ce qui va se passer dans le verset suivant.

v. 8

LS : *Cependant, Caïn adressa la parole à son frère Abel ;*
   Mais comme ils étaient dans les champs, Caïn se jeta sur son frère Abel et le tua.

AC : *Caïn dit à Hèbèl son frère …*
   Et quand ils sont au champ, Caïn se lève contre Hèbèl, son frère, et le tue.

Son erreur d'appréciation, qui est aussi souvent la nôtre, se révèle au grand jour dans cet épisode qui découle logiquement des évènements précédents. Caïn n'a pas suivi l'enseignement de l'Éternel et n'a pas changé de point de vue. L'orientation de son attitude est plus dictée par l'attachement à son ego que par l'amour pour son frère et pour l'Éternel, d'où peut-être un soupçon de jalousie car « le noyau de toute jalousie est un manque d'amour »[53].

Caïn dit à Hèbèl son frère …

Nous ne savons pas ce que Caïn dit à son frère et en contrepartie soulignons qu'Abel ne parle pas. Cette parole inaudible de Caïn et ce silence d'Abel rappellent un vieil adage oriental « Le sot parle beaucoup et le sage se tait ». Effectivement, tel Abel, il

---

[53] C.G. Jung, *op. cit.*

n'est pas nécessaire que l'homme révèle aux autres ce qu'il est en train de vivre dans sa relation à Dieu. Ce serait bien souvent une erreur de le faire.

Et quand ils sont au champ, Caïn se lève contre Hèb̲èl son frère...

Quand ils sont au champ signifie tout simplement qu'ils sont dans l'action concrète de la vie.

Caïn se lève... Le verbe utilisé ici קום (*kavam*) veut dire *se lever contre/se dresser/devenir puissant,* ce qui exprime tellement bien *l'orgueil* de Caïn qui se dresse et veut surpasser son frère Abel. Cette attitude entraîne pour lui, donc en nous-même, une conséquence logique : *...et le tue.*

Cette mort c'est l'effacement dans notre vie de la conscience spirituelle qui doit toujours demeurer le berger et le guide de notre vie. Par cet acte Caïn veut agir uniquement selon ses propres prérogatives et ne veut pas laisser Abel vivre en lui-même pour agir pleinement et en harmonie avec lui. Il ne veut pas laisser Abel être efficace dans une démarche d'*élévation* conformément à l'enseignement de l'Éternel. Or laisser notre âme être le guide de notre vie c'est ne pas penser, ne pas agir, ne pas faire de projet sans que ce soit notre âme qui nous le dicte.

Selon l'enseignement de Shrî Aurobindo, laisser l'âme grandir en nous, c'est aussi la laisser nourrir et féconder les plans inférieurs[54] (Caïn) pour les transfigurer, c'est-à-dire les amener eux aussi à cette élévation évoquée précédemment.

---

[54] Ils ne sont pas inférieurs au sens de la valeur, mais au sens où, comme dans un bâtiment, il y a une succession de niveaux, une base et des élévations, qui finissent par former un tout harmonieux.

Ce verset souligne bien les ravages de l'orgueil et nous renvoie à l'enseignement des grandes religions qui toutes prônent la nécessaire humilité dans le cheminement spirituel. « Il n'y a pas de plus grande vertu que l'humilité, ni de vice plus grand que l'orgueil »[55], disait par exemple Swami Ramdas.

Ce verset est aussi l'exact opposé de l'enseignement de l'apôtre Jean dans son évangile (3:30) lorsqu'il dit à propos de Jésus : *Il faut qu'Il croisse et que je diminue.*

---

[55] Swami Ramdas, Aphorismes, dans *Présence de Ram, op. cit.*, p. 129.

Où va l'âme après la mort ?
Où peut tomber la terre ?
Où peut aller l'âme ?
Là où elle n'est pas déjà ?
Swami Vivekânanda

Les conséquences de cette erreur

v. 9

LS : *L'Éternel dit à Caïn : Où est ton frère Abel ?*
Il répondit : Je ne sais pas ; suis-je le gardien de mon frère ?

AC : *IHVH dit à Caïn : Où est ton frère Hèbèl ?*
Il dit : Je ne sais pas. Suis-je le gardien de mon frère, moi-même ?

C'est à nouveau l'Éternel qui parle : *Où est ton frère ?*

Sur le plan terrestre ceci nous rappelle une ancienne discussion avec un prêtre qui avait l'habitude de rendre visite à des prisonniers. Il nous racontait que les auteurs d'un meurtre lui posaient parfois cette question : « Où est-il celui que j'ai tué ? » Sur ce plan-là, c'est ce que Caïn se dit.

Cette question se pose aussi en nous-même : où est-il celui que j'ai tué en moi-même ? À cette question de l'Éternel Caïn répond qu'il *ne sait pas*. Sa réponse n'est pas une tentative de jouer à l'innocent, mais est au contraire tout à fait logique. Il ne sait plus où sont ses plans de conscience supérieurs, puisqu'il leur a ôté le droit de vivre pleinement en lui-même. La *Bhagavad-Gîtâ* décrit très bien le fondement de cet oubli et de cette ignorance : « La colère et l'envie ôtent la mémoire ». Ici ce texte se réfère, non pas à la mémoire cognitive, mais à la mémoire de ce que nous sommes, tant dans le visible que dans l'invisible. Combien de fois ne savons-nous pas où est Abel en nous-même ?

Qu'est-ce en l'homme que cette ignorance ou défaillance de mémoire ? C'est l'oubli et donc l'ignorance qu'il y a en nous une dimension de notre être qui connaît Dieu. C'est en conséquence l'oubli de Dieu dans notre vie. N'est-ce pas l'une des caractéristiques fortes de notre époque ?

Ensuite Caïn pose la question : *Suis-je le gardien de mon frère ?*

Cette question a fait l'objet de nombreux commentaires qui se sont en général bornés à n'en tirer qu'une perspective morale, qui serait : nous devons nous occuper de nos frères. Certes cette perspective nous invite à nous occuper des autres lorsqu'ils en ont besoin, elle est peut-être aussi un garde-fou contre certains abus de comportement dans la vie sociale, mais est-elle accordée à l'essence du texte ?

Remarquons d'abord que le texte hébreu ne dit pas vraiment cela, puisque Caïn pose simplement la question et qu'il ne reçoit pas de réponse. Ensuite si Dieu avait voulu donner à Caïn une telle instruction sur le plan moral, on peut raisonnablement penser qu'Il l'eût fait avant le meurtre d'Abel. Si cette perspective morale n'est pas fausse, elle nous semble de toute façon très insuffisante car elle ne nous dit pas quelle est la voie pour devenir réellement « les gardiens de nos frères ». Or le rôle d'un texte sacré c'est avant tout de nous apprendre quelque chose sur le cheminement de l'homme en marche vers « son destin surnaturel ». C'est dans ce sens que nous allons tenter de comprendre ce passage.

La question que pose Caïn résonne en réalité comme l'affirmation de ce qu'il est, comme s'il disait à l'Éternel : « *Tu sais bien, Toi, que je ne suis pas le gardien de mon frère.* » Caïn sait cela et d'ailleurs Dieu ne lui répond pas sur ce point, ce qui peut passer pour un acquiescement. Nous avons vu que Caïn et Abel incarnaient différents plans de conscience en nous : Caïn les plans physique, vital et mental, et Abel les plans spirituels. Que Caïn ne soit pas le gardien de son frère signifie tout simplement que les plans inférieurs de notre vie ne sont pas les gardiens des plans spirituels, l'âme et l'Esprit en l'homme.

Si Caïn n'est pas ce gardien, qu'est-ce qui l'est en nous ?

Les sept plans de la conscience et de la vie sont comme les échelons de l'échelle de Jacob qui relient la terre et le ciel et sur laquelle *montent et descendent les anges de Dieu*[56]. Ce sont les sept étapes de notre montée vers l'Éternel. Dans une échelle chaque échelon doit être parcouru l'un après l'autre et chaque échelon est le gardien de l'échelon précédent, sinon l'échelle ne tiendrait pas. Il est aisé de constater que cela est déjà vrai entre les premiers plans de conscience physique, vitale et mentale de l'homme. Le plan vital assure la survie de toute créature vivante et garde le plan physique. Le plan mental de l'homme assure un premier niveau de connaissance de la vie et garde les plans vital et physique. Au cours des âges il a notamment permis des progrès très importants dans de multiples domaines pour l'ensemble des civilisations. Mais il peut aussi être source de bien des dérives tragiques, justement lorsque les hommes ont tué Abel en eux-mêmes.

---

[56] Gn 28:12.

Aussi n'apparaît-il pas en filigrane dans ce verset que si Caïn n'est pas le gardien de son frère, ce sont les échelons supérieurs, c'est-à-dire Abel, qui pourraient l'être ? Rappelons-nous qu'Abel est le gardien du troupeau, celui qui le guide et prend soin de lui, ce qui le présente tout à fait comme le gardien des autres éléments de la vie. Par leur maîtrise d'eux-mêmes et l'amour qu'ils répandent, les Saints et les Sages du monde entier nous montrent bien que l'âme et l'Esprit en l'homme sont véritablement le gardien de tous les éléments de la vie.

Alors la meilleure façon, et la plus efficace, d'être les gardiens de nos frères c'est de toujours faire grandir Abel en nous-même, comme le disait Séraphin de Sarov[57] : « Trouve la paix intérieure et des milliers la trouveront autour de toi. » Ces mêmes Saints et Sages nous disent que le souvenir constant de Dieu nous aidera à y parvenir.

v. 10

LS : *Et Dieu dit : Qu'as-tu fait ?*

La voix du sang de ton frère crie de la terre jusqu'à moi.

AC : *Il dit : Qu'as-tu fait ?*

La voix des sangs de ton frère clame vers moi de la glèbe.

Avant d'aborder les versets 10 à 14 qui tous parlent apparemment de la « terre » il est nécessaire de préciser quels sont les mots hébreux rencontrés pour exprimer cela. Il y a d'abord le mot הָאֲדָמָה *(l'Adama)* qui peut être traduit par *la Terre-Glèbe* ou *la Terre-Mère* car c'est de là que l'homme fut tiré comme le dit Genèse 2:7 et 3:23. Le nom de l'homme *(l'adam)* souligne bien

---

[57] Moine et Saint russe (1754-1833).

cette parenté[58]. *L'Adama* exprime à la fois l'énergie et la matérialité qui président au fondement terrestre de l'homme. Nous retrouvons cet archétype dans beaucoup d'autres traditions[59]. Puis il y a le mot אֶרֶץ (*Eretz*) qui exprime un espace indifférencié sur la terre, une contrée pas forcément bien déterminée. C'est là où demeurent les hommes et donc symboliquement *Eretz* signifie aussi leur façon de vivre et d'appréhender cette vie. Cette distinction est nécessaire pour mieux comprendre la suite du récit. C'est pourquoi A. Chouraqui traduit *Adama* par *terre-glèbe* ou simplement *glèbe* et *Eretz* par *terre*.

Qu'as-tu fait ?

Cette parole engage la responsabilité de l'homme, mais loin d'être une mise en accusation de la part d'un quelconque juge, elle est au contraire tout amour et compassion comme la suite du verset va le dire. On croirait entendre ici la voix d'une mère qui entend crier son enfant qui s'est fait mal, accourt vers lui, le prend dans ses bras et dit : « Mais mon chéri, qu'as-tu fait ? »

La voix des sangs de ton frère clame vers moi de la glèbe.

Rappelons-nous qu'Abel représente les plans spirituels de l'homme et l'Éternel dit en nous : « Qu'as-tu fait de ton âme ? » La *voix des sangs* d'Abel c'est notre âme qui du plus profond de nous-même et de la vie *clame* qu'elle est toujours vivante en Dieu, même si apparemment elle est effacée de la terre.

---

[58] Les deux termes *Adam* et *Adama* proviennent d'une racine commune qui signifie « être rouge » ce qui évoque le sang pour l'homme et l'humus pour la terre.

[59] Par exemple : Nannu chez les Sumériens, la Pachamama des Péruviens, la Tellus Mater des Romains, la Gaïa des Grecs, la déesse Prithvi des Hindous, le dieu Geb des Égyptiens.

Cette voix clame et appelle le secours de l'Éternel lorsque l'homme a agi de telle sorte que son âme semble comme disparue en lui-même, ou même simplement endormie. Le verbe hébreu utilisé ici צָעַק (ts'aq) veut dire exactement « appeler au secours ». Or c'est souvent dans la détresse que sa voix peut se faire entendre le plus vivement, et Caïn est certainement dans la détresse après ce qu'il a fait. L'appel au secours suppose quand même que l'homme a confiance en Celui qu'il appelle, sinon il ne le ferait pas. Il est des périodes de notre existence où la louange à la vie et à l'Éternel jaillit spontanément de notre cœur, par exemple dans une prière ou devant un magnifique paysage ou une simple fleur. Il est d'autres périodes au contraire où cela est difficile et c'est l'appel au secours qui s'avère être notre consolation. C'est pourquoi plusieurs psaumes chantent : *Dieu viens à notre aide, Seigneur à notre secours*. Même chez le plus criminel des hommes cette voix ne se tait jamais totalement et clame vers l'Éternel qui demeure inexorablement en tous.

Le texte nous dit que cette voix clame *depuis l'Adama (la Terre-Mère)* parce qu'elle est inséparable de la création elle-même, elle en est une des composantes depuis la fondation du monde. Elle demeure éternellement vivante et ne saurait s'éteindre, quoi que nous fassions. Ceci est l'éternelle *compassion divine*. L'homme se trompe si facilement dans l'appréciation du but à atteindre que s'il n'y avait pas cette compassion où irait-il, que deviendrait-il ?

v. 11

LS : *Maintenant tu seras maudit*
De la terre qui a ouvert sa bouche pour recevoir de ta main le sang de ton frère.

AC : *Maintenant tu es honni*
Plus que la glèbe dont la bouche a béé pour prendre les sangs de ton frère de ta main.

Toute erreur a son corollaire qui est la possibilité et la faculté d'apprendre ou de comprendre quelque chose. Effectivement Caïn est maintenant enseigné par l'Éternel pour comprendre quelque chose de plus de la vie.

Ce passage et le verset suivant ont parfois été vus comme l'annonce de la peine du bannissement qui était une des punitions majeures à cette époque. Le bannissement est l'affaire des hommes, or ici c'est Dieu qui parle et qui instruit. Tout comme nous avons vu qu'il n'y a pas en Lui de préférence, il faut aussi écarter l'idée qu'Il infligerait des punitions et des récompenses. Il y a là simplement une loi de la vie : toute pensée, toute parole et tout acte ont des répercussions sur notre vie. C'est ce que nous avons déjà vu en fin du verset 7 : *Tu seras semblable à...* N'oublions pas que nous sommes ici dans le livre de la Genèse, un livre qui nous révèle la nature et l'articulation de la vie sur la terre. Il ne s'agit donc pas ici de punition ou de châtiment, mais d'une instruction divine sur la vie de l'homme.

Maintenant... Ce *maintenant* nous indique bien que les conséquences de nos actes ne seront pas rétribuées dans un lointain, et tout à fait incertain, enfer ou paradis après la mort. Il s'agit au contraire d'une réponse immédiate de la vie, dès ici-bas. Nous retrouverons également cette immédiateté au verset suivant qui parle lui aussi de *aujourd'hui*. Ainsi le livre de la Genèse nous révèle, comme le dit Mâ Sûryânanda Lakshmî, que « le jugement de Dieu c'est ce que nous sommes ».

Maintenant tu es honni/maudit, plus que la terre-glèbe...
Dans ce verset les deux traductions citées diffèrent sensiblement. Celle de L. Segond nous semble inappropriée, non seulement à cause de l'ambiguïté du mot « terre » mais aussi du fait qu'elle

n'est pas vraiment accordée à la syntaxe du texte hébreu[60]. La traduction de A. Chouraqui demeure clairement plus fidèle : *tu es honni, plus que la terre-glèbe...*

Dans sa définition des différents plans de conscience (voir Annexe), Mâ Sûryânanda Lakshmî indique que le premier plan de la conscience physique est « entièrement et passivement soumise à la loi transcendante matérialisée en elle ». Nous trouvons là une bonne définition de *l'Adama*. Cette Terre-Mère, qui est passivement soumise à la loi de l'Éternel, ne peut pas être *honnie* ou *maudite* par Dieu qui l'a créée[61]. L'homme au contraire dont la conscience mentale est « le siège de la différenciation » a en lui la capacité de ne plus vouloir se soumettre passivement à cette loi. En réalité il ne le peut pas, mais il s'illusionne de pouvoir le faire et c'est en cela qu'il est infidèle à sa vocation puisqu'il est *l'image de Dieu*. C'est pourquoi après ce faux pas, qui est si caractéristique de la vie sur la terre, l'Éternel instruit l'homme qu'il est maudit *plus que* la Terre-Mère. Les conséquences de cette infidélité de l'homme sont précisées au verset suivant.

---

[60] En hébreu les prépositions et conjonctions peuvent prendre de multiples sens et restent souvent difficiles à traduire. Ici le texte original marque une pose de lecture entre le verbe *honnir/maudire* et le substantif *l'Adama,* ce qui indique que ce dernier n'est pas un complément direct de ce verbe. En outre le mot intermédiaire מן (*min*) reliant ces deux éléments est véritablement « construit » avec ce substantif. Ces deux particularités grammaticales font prévaloir que ce lien מן *(min)* ne signifie pas une relation de complémentarité ou de dépendance, mais plutôt une comparaison dans le sens « plus que ».

[61] Une telle assertion semble être en contradiction avec Gn. 3:17 (*Le sol sera maudit à cause de toi*) mais elle ne l'est pas. En effet en Gn. 3:17 la terre semble être maudite du *point de vue de l'homme* car l'Éternel dit bien : *à cause de toi.* Cette malédiction c'est donc la façon dont l'homme perçoit *la terre* après qu'il eut mangé le fruit de l'arbre de la connaissance du bien et du mal, c'est-à-dire être né à la dualité. Ce n'est pas Dieu qui l'a maudite, ce qui d'ailleurs n'aurait pas de sens.

La terre-glèbe qui a ouvert sa bouche pour prendre les sangs...
Les sangs sont le symbole de la vie[62]. Ils retournent à cette terre-mère qui les a fécondés, ce qui ne renie pas qu'ils expriment toujours la vie. Cette *terre* c'est, selon l'hébreu, l'*Adama* et non pas l'*Eretz*, ce qui confirme qu'il ne s'agit pas d'un exil ni d'un bannissement hors d'une contrée spécifique sur la terre.

v. 12
LS : *Quand tu cultiveras le sol, il ne te donnera plus sa richesse.*
      Tu seras errant et vagabond sur la terre.
AC : *Oui tu serviras la glèbe : elle n'ajoutera pas à te donner sa force.*
      Tu seras sur la terre mouvant, errant.

Oui tu serviras la terre/glèbe, elle ne te donnera plus sa richesse/force. Son rôle de serviteur mentionné au début du récit est réaffirmé. Mais sans Abel, c'est-à-dire dépossédé du berger de sa vie, l'homme s'est coupé de sa véritable richesse et de sa force sur tous les plans de son existence. L'*Adama* ne peut plus les lui fournir.

Cette richesse et cette force, ce ne sont pas seulement les biens matériels issus de notre labeur, mais également la beauté, l'équilibre et l'harmonie de toute la vie[63]. Lorsque les hommes font mourir Abel en eux-mêmes il y a rupture de cette harmonie et c'est sans doute faute de respecter cette loi que l'humanité traverse des crises parfois si tragiques.

---

[62] Pour signifier un meurtre l'hébreu dit : prendre les sangs.
[63] Ceux qui pratiquent le hatha-yoga ou certains arts martiaux savent très bien que s'ils se croient les seuls maîtres de leurs actions, au lieu de s'abandonner et faire confiance à la terre, ils perdent leur force et leur équilibre. Il en est de même dans notre travail : si nous le faisons en maugréant au lieu de nous y donner de tout notre cœur, il devient plus pénible et fatigant car nous ne recevons plus la force de l'*Adama*.

Et tu seras errant, mouvant sur la terre. Ici le terme *terre* renvoie à l'hébreu אֶרֶץ *(Eretz)*. Il ne s'agit plus de la *Terre-Mère* mais bien de la contrée où réside Caïn, contrée prise dans le sens, non pas d'une terre géographique précise, mais symboliquement de l'état dans lequel il demeure. Cet état, consécutif de son faux pas, c'est *l'errance*. Caïn qui a perdu à la fois ses racines et son berger-guide dans la vie, lui qui devait concrètement entretenir la terre, s'appuyant sur sa valeur et ses potentialités, se retrouve maintenant instable et désorienté.

Qu'est-ce que cette errance de Caïn en nous ?

L'instabilité est une caractéristique de la vie de l'homme sur la terre et cela nous le vivons et le savons tous. Un moment nous pensons ceci et l'instant d'après à autre chose, un moment nous imaginons de faire une chose et l'instant d'après nous avons changé. Nos pensées sont constamment agitées et instables. C'est pourquoi en Inde le mental de l'homme est souvent comparé à un singe agité qui ne cesse de sauter de branche en branche.

Nous savons que nous pouvons nous sentir perdu, donc errant, en certaines circonstances, par exemple lorsque nous subissons un déracinement physique, affectif ou psychologique. Ce qui est vrai sur ces premiers plans de la vie l'est tout autant sur les plans spirituels. Lorsque, après une période dans laquelle nous nous sentions en communion avec l'Éternel, il arrive un moment où notre cœur devient froid et où cette communion ne nous habite plus, nous ne savons que faire et où aller, ne sachant plus ce qui est vrai, ce qui est bon, ne sachant non plus comment prier avec vérité. C'est pourquoi à un moment donné le prophète Isaïe dit à l'Éternel : *Nous sommes depuis longtemps comme un peuple que*

Tu ne gouvernes pas[64]. Nous nous sentons vraiment tel Caïn sans Abel son frère, *mouvant et errant sur la terre,* car dans ce monde sans cesse changeant la seule chose qui soit véritablement immuable c'est l'Éternel en nous.

Parce que sa vie lui semble désormais si difficile à porter, Caïn va interpeller l'Éternel.

v. 13

LS : *Caïn dit à l'Éternel :*
    Mon châtiment est trop grand pour être supporté.

AC : *Caïn dit à IHVH :*
    Mon tort est trop grand pour être porté.

Aux versets précédents Caïn avait entendu la voix de l'Éternel l'instruisant de la loi et des conséquences de son erreur. Dans le présent verset et dans le suivant il exprime son ressenti par rapport à cette situation, et ce ressenti est à la fois une plainte et une crainte.

Mon châtiment/tort est trop grand... Ici nous trouvons un terme hébreu עון *('avon)* qui a plusieurs sens et reste difficile à comprendre, ce qui se ressent dans les deux traductions citées qui utilisent des termes très différents : *châtiment* ou *tort*. Ce terme signifie : la faute ou le péché, la peine ou la souffrance, le châtiment, le tort ou l'iniquité. Mais dans sa racine on peut aussi voir le fait de s'abriter ou de se réfugier après s'être « détourné de la route ». Le traduire par « *situation* » nous paraît mieux adapté car ce terme a l'avantage de se situer au centre de cette galaxie de sens et n'a aucune connotation morale, même si parfois cette *situation* peut être ressentie comme un châtiment, tel le vécu de Caïn au verset 5.

---

[64] Isaïe 63:19.

Ma situation est trop grande pour être portée. Cet état dans lequel Caïn se trouve désormais établi en lui-même lui semble difficile à vivre. Et une fois de plus l'hébreu est merveilleux car il est à la fois tout à fait concret et spirituel : il utilise le même verbe נשא (*nacha*) pour signifier à la fois *porter* et *pardonner*. Si nous offrons sincèrement à Dieu nos erreurs, au lieu de les ressasser et de nous en flageller, alors le pardon en nous-même n'est pas loin. Mais Caïn n'a pas encore cette attitude, il ne fait que se plaindre à l'Éternel et reconnaît que cette situation génère en lui une certaine angoisse.

Le verset suivant nous apprend en quoi cette *situation* est en nous si grande à porter.

v. 14

LS : *Voici, tu me chasses aujourd'hui de cette terre ; je serai caché loin de ta face,*
Je serai errant et vagabond sur la terre, et quiconque me trouvera me tuera.

AC : *Voici, aujourd'hui tu m'as expulsé sur les faces de la glèbe. Je me voilerai faces à toi.*
Je serai mouvant, errant sur la terre : et c'est qui me trouvera me tuera.

Voici, aujourd'hui Tu m'as expulsé sur les faces de la terre/glèbe. Tant qu'Abel était vivant en Caïn celui-ci n'avait pas le sentiment d'être coupé de l'unité de toute la vie en l'Éternel, il se sentait dans le sein de *l'Adama*. Maintenant (aujourd'hui) il se voit *chassé* ou *expulsé* de cette unité et se retrouve *sur* les *faces de l'Adama*, soit en quelque sorte dans la dualité. Cette situation si grande à porter c'est la nostalgie de ne pouvoir vivre l'*alliance*[65]

---

[65] En hébreu le terme *(Berit)* traduit par *alliance* est extrêmement fort. Pour les Hébreux, une alliance était scellée dans un cérémonial, marquant l'union des deux parties afin qu'elles ne forment qu'une seule entité.

entre Dieu et sa création. C'est la difficulté pour l'homme de connaître cette Unité et donc l'Éternité[66].

Cette situation travaille le cœur de tout homme au plus profond de lui-même, qu'il en soit conscient ou non. Djalal al-Din Rumi[67] exprimait cela ainsi : « Tout être qui est éloigné de sa source aspire à revenir vers elle. » Or quelle est la source de tout homme, si ce n'est l'Éternel lui-même, comme l'a dit Ève au verset 1 de ce chapitre ?

Cette *alliance* fondamentale et éternelle fut révélée à Noé, à Abraham et à Moïse pour que les hommes la connaissent, puis elle fut tout au long de la Bible rappelée par les prophètes pour que les hommes ne l'oublient pas. Elle fut redite par Jésus car les hommes sont ainsi faits qu'ils l'oublient toujours : *Le royaume de Dieu est au-dedans de vous.* De nos jours où le sens de cette alliance n'est même plus vraiment compris – vu les traductions souvent erronées que donnent nos bibles de cette parole – c'est par la voix de la Sagesse hindoue qu'elle nous est rappelée, telle cette parole de Swami Vivekânanda proclamée au premier congrès international des religions (Chicago 1893) : « Hommes, frères, ayez confiance en vous-mêmes, Dieu est en vous. »[68]

---

[66] Cette unité de l'Éternel est affirmée en Deutéronome 6:4 qui, traduit mot à mot, dit ceci : *Écoute Israël : IHVH, nos Elohîms, IHVH, Un.* Cette affirmation de l'unité divine, de l'unité de l'Absolu avec toute la création, en liaison avec le fait que le terme *faces* appliqué à Dieu soit au pluriel, mérite quelques développements qui seront donnés dans l'Appendice.

[67] Poète mystique et sage du XIIIe siècle en Turquie.

[68] Cette parole rejoint très exactement ce qui a été vu dans l'introduction. À la suite de son discours qui souleva l'enthousiasme de cette assemblée, il fut invité à donner de nombreuses conférences aux États-Unis et à Londres. Ces conférences ont été consignées dans un ouvrage intitulé *Jnana Yoga*, Paris : Albin Michel.

C'est le désir de vivre réellement cette alliance qui pousse les hommes à la prière, à la méditation, à la contemplation, à l'adoration et à *bien agir* comme indiqué au verset 7. Chez certains ce désir est si fort qu'ils se mettent en route pour étancher cette soif et rien ne peut les arrêter, mais chez d'autres il reste à l'état latent et ne provoque pas en eux une forte volonté de tenter d'y répondre. Mais que l'homme le fasse consciemment ou non il est de toute façon dans ce cheminement.

Je me voilerai faces à toi. Je serai mouvant, errant sur la terre.
Caïn admet ce que Dieu lui avait enseigné au verset 12 et il en éprouve une certaine crainte parce qu'il reste centré uniquement sur son ego. Il se sent séparé *(voilé) des faces* de l'Éternel. Sans Abel comme guide, il a mis un voile devant la Lumière divine. Dans cette errance il n'est pas question de la difficulté à s'orienter ou se diriger sur le plan terrestre car ce verset nous parle de *l'Adama* et non pas de *l'Eretz*. Il s'agit donc de la difficulté de l'homme à trouver au fond de soi-même la bonne voie sur le chemin de sa quête spirituelle.

Quiconque me trouvera me tuera.
Nous pouvons donner de cette phrase une première interprétation purement psychologique. Caïn a reconnu son état intérieur, mais au lieu de laisser l'Éternel *porter* son erreur il se centre avant tout sur la lourdeur de celle-ci, se créant ainsi *coupable*. La conséquence de cette culpabilité est évidemment la peur, et cette peur fait qu'il craint d'être tué à son tour.

Plus fondamentalement nous pouvons comprendre qu'étant maintenant centré uniquement sur son ego, donc dans la dualité, il se sente séparé des autres hommes. Il s'imagine alors qu'en toute autre personne un ennemi potentiel pourrait se cacher et le traiter comme il a traité Abel. Cette perception génère en lui de l'angoisse. Ne sommes-nous pas parfois ainsi ? Ne retrouve-t-on pas ici l'angoisse devant l'inconnu ou l'étranger, dont la Bible nous dit cependant qu'il doit être accueilli lui aussi ? Et puisque Caïn a lui-même tué son frère il s'imagine tout à fait naturellement qu'il pourrait subir le même sort de la part de quiconque.

*L'impossible d'aujourd'hui est
le possible de demain.*
Shrî Aurobindo

La rédemption fait partie du chemin

v. 15-a

LS : *L'Éternel lui dit : Si quelqu'un tuait Caïn, Caïn serait vengé sept fois.*

AC : *IHVH lui dit : Ainsi, tout tueur de Caïn subira sept fois vengeance.*

Après cette prise de conscience de Caïn sur son erreur et sa situation, voici l'intervention de l'Éternel et sa miséricorde pour aider l'homme à poursuivre sa marche vers l'arbre de vie.

L'Éternel continue d'instruire Caïn, mais une fois de plus il est nécessaire d'intérioriser cet enseignement pour le bien comprendre. En effet si notre lecture reste au niveau extérieur qui voit dans les personnages de cette allégorie uniquement des individus séparés, avec pour Caïn et Abel leur rivalité jalouse, voilà un verset qui mettrait cette lecture devant une double contradiction. D'une part elle tordrait définitivement le cou, si besoin était encore, à l'idée qu'Adam et Caïn furent les deux premiers hommes, ancêtres de toute l'humanité, comme cela a été parfois dit. D'où viendraient dans ce cas *tous ceux* qui pourraient le trouver et le frapper ? D'autre part, elle nous amènerait à considérer que Dieu fait preuve de partialité. Pourquoi ceux qui tueraient Caïn seraient-ils condamnés plus lourdement (*sept fois*) que Caïn lui-même qui a tué son frère ? Ceci paraît d'autant plus illogique que la suite du récit indiquera que Caïn sera pardonné.

Tout tueur de Caïn peut bien entendu évoquer des individus qui risqueraient de porter atteinte à sa vie, mais il se réfère aussi, et peut-être davantage encore, à tout ce qui en nous détruit les éléments nécessaires à la croissance et au maintien de la vie sur la terre. Nous savons bien que si nous n'avons pas une hygiène de vie équilibrée et malmenons notre corps au-delà du nécessaire nous en abrégeons le cours. Par exemple s'adonner à certains excès dans la nourriture ou la boisson va nécessairement abréger la durée de cette vie.

Tout tueur de Caïn subira sept fois vengeance. Dans la bouche de l'Éternel il ne s'agit pas de *vengeance* au sens dualiste (œil pour œil, dent pour dent…), mais tout simplement d'une loi de la vie : nous portons en nous-même les conséquences de nos pensées et de nos actes. Mais ici ces conséquences paraissent graves puisque le texte emploie le chiffre 7, qui dans la Bible est toujours un chiffre symbolique. Ce chiffre correspond aux sept plans de conscience et de vie évoqués en début de cet essai. Pour A. Chouraqui[69] ce chiffre indique une très grande quantité. Nous pouvons aussi considérer que 7 = 4+3 dans lequel 4 représente les éléments terrestres et 3 l'Esprit, c'est-à-dire l'homme dans toutes les dimensions de son être – visible et invisible. Ce chiffre nous indique que ces comportements, envers les autres ou envers soi-même, sont graves. Il nous dit également qu'ils atteignent aussi l'humanité.

Mais pourquoi transgresser cette loi est-il si grave ? Tout au long du texte nous avons vu que l'homme se heurte en lui-même à des obstacles sur le chemin de l'arbre de vie, et que malgré ces difficultés c'est sa vocation de vivre cette aventure, qui est son

---

[69] Dans son *Encyclopédie de la Bible*.

« destin surnaturel ». Se tromper lors de cette pérégrination est pardonnable parce que toujours corrigible. Mais tuer Caïn, c'est-à-dire tuer la base même de la vie sur la terre, ne peut être corrigé de la même manière et paraît contraire à la loi de la création. Caïn est notre socle de la vie qui permet l'élévation vers l'Esprit. « C'est seulement ici, dans la vie terrestre où se heurtent les contraires, que le niveau général de conscience peut s'élever » disait C.G. Jung. Frapper ou tuer ce socle ne permet plus cette élévation et c'est pourquoi l'homme doit en prendre soin. « Le mal que l'on fait au corps c'est un mal que l'on fait à l'Esprit. »[70] Tuer ce socle est donc grave parce que c'est ne pas respecter la loi de l'Éternel et c'est empêcher que la rédemption puisse avoir lieu. Or, puisque Caïn ne sera pas tué, celle-ci va venir dans la suite du verset.

v. 15-b
LS : *Et l'Éternel mit un signe sur Caïn pour que quiconque le trouverait ne le tuât point.*
AC : *IHVH met un signe à Caïn pour que tous ceux qui le trouvent ne le frappent pas.*

Avec l'habitude humaine de toujours regarder vers l'extérieur nous nous imaginons que ce signe est mis *sur* Caïn, donc destiné à être vu par les autres hommes. Ce serait comme un tatouage-talisman protecteur qu'il porterait ostensiblement et ayant pour but d'empêcher quiconque de le tuer. Mais *l'Éternel ne considère pas ce que l'homme considère ; l'homme regarde ce qui frappe les yeux, mais l'Éternel regarde au cœur*[71]. Aussi c'est au cœur que nous devons nous efforcer de regarder pour tâcher de comprendre le sens de ce verset.

---

[70] Mâ Sûryânanda Lakshmî, conférence du 02.05.1992 à Giez (Suisse).
[71] I Samuel 16:7.

Dans la Bible lorsque l'Éternel donne aux hommes un *signe,* celui-ci est le témoignage d'une révélation. Ce signe-témoignage peut parfois prendre forme sur le plan matériel pour que l'homme puisse s'en souvenir plus aisément et l'intégrer dans sa vie. C'est pourquoi la merveilleuse révélation de l'alliance entre Dieu et les hommes fut à chaque fois accompagnée d'un signe tangible, donné à Noé (l'arc-en-ciel ; Genèse 9:13-17), à Abraham (la circoncision ; Genèse 17:10-13) et à Moïse (l'arche d'alliance ; Exode ch. 25).

L'Éternel *met un signe* pour Caïn.

Ici nous ne connaissons pas la nature de ce signe. Le terme hébreu traduit par signe veut également dire *prodige, preuve, avertissement.* Par ailleurs le texte ne dit pas que « cela » est mis *sur* Caïn, mais *à* Caïn ou *pour* Caïn, ce qui signifie qu'il n'est pas visible par d'autres hommes. Le verbe שׂום *(soom)* qui est traduit habituellement par *mettre,* a en hébreu quantité de significations qui sont intéressantes à noter : placer, mettre, mettre dans une direction déterminée, diriger, établir, faire que, tracer, écrire, instituer, fixer. Ce que l'Éternel place en Caïn n'est pas quelque chose là-dehors mais représente la transformation et la nouvelle orientation de sa conscience, tracée/dirigée/établie par l'Éternel. C'est sans doute pour cela que L. Segond dans son édition originale de la Bible[72] a traduit ce verset autrement :

Et l'Éternel fit connaître à Caïn que quiconque le trouverait ne le tuerait point.

---

[72] Première édition de 1874. La révision de 1910 n'est pas due à Louis Segond lui-même car elle a été effectuée après son décès survenu en 1885, alors que de son vivant il n'avait pas voulu que sa traduction soit retouchée.

En quoi consiste cette connaissance ou cette révélation ?

Caïn *connaît* ce signe/prodige/avertissement et sait également qu'il vient de Dieu. Autrement dit, cette révélation il la vit et en comprend le sens. Rappelons-nous que Caïn n'est pas un individu mais représente les premiers plans de conscience de la vie en l'homme. Cette révélation est alors la connaissance que son faux pas, ou erreur d'appréciation, est aussi celui que peuvent faire tous les hommes. Elle fait partie intégrante de la création. « Ce qui réellement existe ne peut cesser d'exister ; de même ce qui est non existant ne peut commencer d'exister (*Bhagavad-Gîtâ*, 2:16*)*.

Ainsi l'Éternel révèle que cette possible erreur est universelle et qu'elle ne peut donc avoir comme conséquence la mort et la disparition des hommes sur la terre car « le dessein de Dieu n'est pas la destruction de l'humanité mais sa transfiguration » comme l'affirme Mâ Sûryânanda Lakshmî. C'est pourquoi Dieu lui dit que *quiconque le trouverait ne le tuerait point*. Nous trouvons déjà là une annonce du commandement que l'Éternel donnera plus tard à Moïse : *Tu ne tueras point*[73].

Cette révélation, ou nouvelle connaissance, est une grâce donnée par Dieu à Caïn. Elle lui donne une nouvelle orientation possible de sa vie. Cela lui permet de ne plus être enfermé dans sa peur, ni dans sa perception du monde dominée uniquement par son ego comme il l'avait exprimé aux versets précédents. Il sait qu'il est *pardonné,* c'est-à-dire *libéré de l'emprisonnement*[74] de son faux pas, de cette erreur de perception de la vie. Aidé désormais par cette grâce, Caïn est appelé à sans cesse vaincre cet emprisonnement et pour cela il va devoir continuer son chemin.

---

[73] Exode 20:13.
[74] Car tel est le sens étymologique du pardon.

Ce verset rend compte de la miséricorde divine qui ne condamne pas les faux pas de l'homme et de l'humanité mais affermit en eux leur vocation d'avancer vers l'arbre de vie, vers la vie en Éternité. Elle leur donne non seulement la possibilité de poursuivre cette route, mais aussi le désir de le faire et l'énergie pour persévérer dans cette voie. « La vocation de l'homme est de trouver Dieu » disait Shrî Anandamoyî Mâ.

À partir de ce moment, la route de Caïn sera jalonnée par la connaissance de son faux pas. Cela ne signifie pas forcément qu'il ne le commettra plus jamais, car nous savons bien que nous retombons souvent dans le même travers avant de pouvoir vraiment nous en libérer. Cette miséricorde n'est pas sur Caïn seul, elle est en tout homme, accompagne chacun de nous car elle fait partie de la vie.

v. 16

LS : *Puis Caïn s'éloigna de la face de l'Éternel*
       Et habita dans la terre de Nod à l'orient de l'Éden.

AC : *Caïn sort faces à IHVH*
       Et demeure en terre de Nod au levant de l'Éden.

Ce verset qui conclut le texte est très important, car ce qu'il est convenu d'appeler « la chute » par laquelle s'achève un récit est toujours, soit un révélateur, soit une confirmation de son sens. C'est vers ce point d'orgue que tend le texte tout entier. C'est bien le cas ici.

Caïn avait un court moment accédé aux plans supérieurs de sa conscience pour que l'Éternel puisse l'instruire. Maintenant, il *s'éloigne des faces de l'Éternel,* littéralement *il sort* de l'intimité qu'il avait avec Dieu mais doit quand même continuer sa route.

Le ressenti de cet éloignement nous le vivons tous à un moment ou un autre lors de notre quête spirituelle.

Mais cet éloignement n'est qu'apparent car en réalité Dieu est toujours là. Cet éloignement est non seulement un fait mais une aide absolument nécessaire pour que l'homme ne s'égare pas dans des illusions et puisse toujours monter vers le Seigneur, comme l'explique très bien le poème de R. Tagore déjà cité :

« Parfois ... Tu te dérobes de devant moi. Jour après jour Tu me formes digne de Ton plein accueil : en me refusant toujours et encore, Tu m'épargnes les périls du faible, de l'incertain désir. »

Il *demeure en la terre de Nod*. Cette contrée, comme l'indique clairement le terme hébreu נוד *(nod)* est celle de l'*errance,* conformément à ce que l'Éternel lui avait annoncé au verset 12. Dans son encyclopédie A. Chouraqui écrit : « Ce nom symbolique qui signifie *errance* interdit d'y voir une réalité géographique précise. » Plutôt qu'une contrée spécifique sur la terre il exprime la situation ou l'état intérieur dans lequel les hommes sont en général établis, là où ils *demeurent.*

Le texte ajoute que cette contrée est *à l'orient de l'Éden*. Cette précision, qui n'est donc pas géographique, indique à l'homme dans quelle direction il doit regarder et quel est l'axe majeur du déroulement de sa vie, malgré toutes les erreurs qu'il peut commettre.

De tout temps l'Orient ou le Levant désigne le lieu d'où va jaillir la lumière, le renouvellement du jour et, par extension, le renouveau de la vie. L'Orient c'est ce qui apporte la lumière, la lumière physique mais aussi celle de l'Esprit, celle de la connaissance de Dieu, la lumière en nous. *Éden*, en hébreu, vient d'une racine signifiant : délices, charme, agrément. Cet Orient de l'Éden c'est non seulement l'imminence d'un renouveau mais aussi l'espérance et la promesse d'une joie et d'un bonheur que chaque homme est appelé à vivre. C'est la possibilité qui lui est offerte d'accéder à l'arbre de vie.

Souvenons-nous également qu'à la fin du chapitre 3 de la Genèse, c'est à *l'orient de l'Éden* que l'Éternel a placé : *des chérubins qui agitent une épée flamboyante pour garder le chemin de l'arbre de vie.*

Cette *épée flamboyante* c'est la Lumière de Vérité qui tranche l'ignorance de l'homme qui méconnaît sa propre Vérité de *fils de Dieu*[75]. Il doit se confronter de multiples fois avec cette Lumière afin de connaître sa situation, son ignorance et son erreur. Bien que Caïn soit dans l'errance – comme il nous arrive à tous de l'être parfois – il est en même temps toujours à l'orient de l'Éden donc sur le chemin de l'arbre de vie. Quand le moment sera venu il sera prêt pour se confronter à nouveau avec l'épée de ces chérubins et peut-être faire un pas de plus sur ce chemin. Ainsi, même s'il ne perçoit peut-être pas encore que la lumière du renouveau – la rédemption – est possible, celle-ci demeure à tout jamais présente, toujours actuelle en lui comme en nous : *au levant de l'Éden.*

Cette rédemption a traversé toute l'histoire de l'humanité, elle est éternelle et universelle car, comme le dit Mâ Sûryânanda Lakshmî : « Ceci est, depuis la fondation du monde, l'articulation même de

---

[75] Rappelons-nous ici cette parole de Jésus : *Le Royaume est le dedans de vous, et il est le dehors de vous. Quand vous vous connaîtrez, alors vous serez connus et vous saurez que c'est vous les fils du Père-le-vivant.*

la loi de la création. » Jésus, qui est le rédempteur de la vie et des hommes, affirme exactement la même chose : *En vérité, en vérité, je vous le dis, avant qu'Abraham fût, Je suis*[76]. Cette parole nous dit clairement que la rédemption est dès l'origine de la création et pour toujours, en toute Éternité. Le prophète Isaïe avait déjà souligné cela : *C'est toi, Éternel, qui est notre Père, qui dès l'Éternité, t'appelles notre Rédempteur*[77]. L'Éternel est à la fois le créateur et le rédempteur, au travers de nous-même et de l'humanité.

Il peut nous sembler qu'il y ait une contradiction entre cette rédemption éternellement présente, et ce que Dieu dit et fait à la fin du chapitre 3 de la Genèse (v. 22-23) : *Voici l'homme est devenu comme l'un de nous pour la connaissance du bien et du mal. Maintenant de peur qu'il n'envoie aussi sa main et ne prenne de l'arbre de vie, n'en mange, et vive éternellement, Dieu le chasse du jardin d'Éden.* Après sa naissance à la connaissance de la dualité, donc à sa connaissance du bien et du mal, l'homme est chassé de l'Éden pour qu'il n'ait pas spontanément accès à l'arbre de vie pour connaître l'Éternité. Mais de suite après l'énoncé de cette loi de la vie sur la terre, Dieu révèle à l'homme – par le récit de Caïn et Abel – quelle doit être sa démarche pour qu'il puisse un jour accéder pleinement à cette vie en Éternité, à cette dimension plus vaste et plus heureuse de la vie. Il lui donne aussi Sa grâce en soutien de cette démarche.

S'il n'y avait pas ce double mouvement de la vie en l'homme, comment pourrait-il connaître le Bonheur et la Joie de vivre l'aventure du retour vers l'arbre de vie ? C'est pourquoi l'homme a aussi son rôle à jouer. Il doit faire l'effort d'avancer vers cette

---

[76] Év. Jean 8:58.
[77] Isaïe 63:16.

Lumière qui est la connaissance de l'Éternel, malgré les multiples obstacles qu'il rencontrera en lui-même, et quoi qu'il arrive, de toujours poursuivre dans cette voie.

Cette apparente contradiction dans ce double mouvement est en réalité un enseignement. Elle apprend à l'homme que c'est Dieu, et Lui seul, qui le conduit sur ce chemin de l'arbre de vie. La vie des Saints et des Sages nous montre bien qu'ils ont compris cela et dépassé cette contradiction. C'est pourquoi Shrî Aurobindo répétait à ses disciples : « En avant, toujours en avant, au bout du tunnel il y a la Lumière, au bout du combat il y a la Victoire. »

L'âme humaine voyage de la loi à l'amour,
de la discipline à la libération,
du plan moral au plan spirituel.
Rabindranath Tagore

Conclusion

Dans l'interprétation de ce texte la tradition rabbinique a voulu retenir le récit de la jalousie fraternelle et du premier meurtre de l'humanité avec une morale découlant de cet acte. Certains y ont vu le sens de la rivalité entre les peuples sédentaires, représentés par Caïn, et les peuples nomades, représentés par Abel, avec le sentiment d'une préférence de l'Éternel pour les peuples nomades, comme l'était – et se considère encore en grande partie – le peuple juif. Quant à la tradition chrétienne elle a fait sienne la première interprétation. Mais « L'objet, le seul objet, des Écritures sacrées c'est Dieu en l'homme, la progression de l'Esprit, de la Lumière Divine en l'homme, et non pas l'homme sur la terre »[78]. C'est pourquoi nous avons souhaité offrir une autre perspective de ce texte biblique pour l'homme d'aujourd'hui qui cherche dans les textes sacrés une réponse aux questions qu'il se pose sur le sens de sa vie, sur sa propre quête spirituelle et celle de l'humanité.

Si nous cessons d'avoir une perception littérale, historique et morale des textes bibliques faisant de Caïn et Abel des individus séparés et rivaux, nous percevons que cette allégorie parle de

---

[78] Conférence de Mâ Sûryânanda Lakshmî donnée à Paris le 17.05.1987.

81

l'homme au plus profond et au plus essentiel de lui-même. Le texte a mis le doigt sur l'obstacle permanent qu'il rencontre dans sa démarche pour avancer vers l'arbre de vie, symbole d'Éternité. Cet obstacle est source d'un possible faux pas – parfois tragique – mais il est en même temps l'occasion d'apprendre que la miséricorde et la compassion divines sont toujours présentes pour l'accompagner et l'aider dans son cheminement.

Cette nature de la vie de l'homme, faite de la rencontre d'obstacles et de leurs dépassements, est universelle. L'Inde l'a également merveilleusement révélé sous la forme d'un Dieu : Ganesha. Avec son gros ventre et sa tête d'éléphant, son effigie très familière est répandue partout dans ce pays où il fait l'objet d'une grande dévotion. « Ce Dieu représente l'appel à la force spirituelle par opposition à la confiance en la force matérielle, la puissance de la grâce divine par opposition à l'effort humain. Aussi est-il le Guide, le Seigneur des obstacles qui, à la fois suscite ces obstacles pour l'entraînement spirituel de l'homme et enseigne à les surmonter. »[79] Nous voilà devant une même révélation que celle de notre texte biblique, bien que transmise sous une autre forme.

Ce cheminement de l'homme et de l'humanité vers l'arbre de vie, qui a été exposé pour la première fois dans ce chapitre 4 du livre de la Genèse, sera rappelé tout au long de l'Ancien Testament au travers des multiples combats, victoires aussi bien que défaites, et longues errances que vivront les fils d'Israël en route pour conquérir le pays *où coulent le lait et le miel*. Et il existe bien des éléments communs entre le récit de cette grande épopée et celui que nous venons d'examiner.

---

[79] Jean Herbert, *Spiritualité hindoue*, Paris : Albin Michel, 1972, p. 333.

Ce cheminement a été attesté par les Prophètes, il est accompli par le Christ[80] et révélé par l'Apocalypse de Jean. Ce dernier livre de la Bible, loin d'être le récit des cataclysmes et catastrophes qui attendent l'humanité, peint dans une fresque grandiose « *la Révélation de ce combat de l'homme et de Dieu en l'homme* »[81].

Cette Révélation conclut pleinement notre récit du livre de la Genèse. Elle enseigne à l'homme que, malgré ses tribulations, l'issue de ce combat est l'accomplissement de la promesse de manger de l'arbre de vie.

À celui qui vaincra,
Je donnerai à manger de l'arbre de vie
qui est dans le paradis de Dieu[82].

Et en toute fin du texte de l'Apocalypse, l'image qui est donnée de cet arbre confirme ce que la Genèse avait préparé en parlant de « vie en Éternité » :

Sur les deux bords du fleuve il y avait un arbre de vie,
produisant douze fois des fruits, rendant son fruit chaque mois,
et dont les feuilles servaient à la guérison des nations[83].

Ce livre, par le fait qu'il soit aussi le dernier de la Bible, nous indique que ce chemin est long pour l'homme et pour l'humanité. Il demande beaucoup de persévérance tout en sachant que tous les hommes ne le vivent pas de la même manière. Face à cela Jean

---

[80] *Je ne suis pas venu pour abolir la loi ou les prophètes ; mais pour les accomplir* (Mt 5:17).

[81] Le mot grec traduit par « apocalypse » signifie « révélation ». Voir à ce sujet la splendide exégèse spirituelle de Mâ Sûryânanda Lakshmî, de laquelle est tirée cette citation.

[82] Apocalypse 2:7.

[83] Apocalypse 22:2.

nous dit, dans son introduction, que pour y parvenir l'homme ne peut échapper ni à l'épreuve, ni à la persévérance en vue d'un accomplissement dans le royaume. « *Moi Jean votre frère et votre compagnon dans l'épreuve, le royaume et la persévérance en Jésus, j'étais dans l'île de Patmos ....* »[84] Cette persévérance est aussi évoquée à de nombreuses reprises dans la Bible[85].

Si nous nous efforçons de lire le récit de Caïn et Abel avec notre âme, tout en ne craignant point de jeter un regard du côté des autres « Sagesses », nous voyons qu'il institue les prémisses de l'enseignement de toute la Bible. Cette allégorie est un condensé admirable de l'aventure intérieure de l'homme, actuel et en devenir, avançant vers l'arbre de vie, soit la vie en Éternité. En ce sens, elle sommeille au fond de la vie, au fond de nous-même. En partant d'une description de ce qu'est l'humain, elle ébauche le sens de sa vie et de son rôle, tout autant que de ses difficultés et de ses erreurs, tout en laissant place à l'espoir, puisqu'il pourra toujours repartir vers cette « cible » qu'il ne connaît pas, mais vers laquelle il tend inexorablement pour aboutir à cette Transfiguration : *Moi et le Père nous sommes Un*[86].

---

[84] Apocalypse 1:9.

[85] Par exemple : Daniel 6:6 : *Après avoir jeté Daniel dans la fosse aux lions le roi lui dit : Puisse ton Dieu que tu sers avec persévérance, te délivrer.* Év. de Luc 21:19 : *Par votre persévérance vous sauverez votre âme.* Ép. Hébreux : *Nous désirons que chacun de vous… imitiez ceux qui par la foi et la persévérance héritent des promesses.*

[86] Év. Jean 10:30.

ANNEXE

Définition des sept plans de la conscience
selon Mâ Sûryânanda Lakshmî[87]

1 – La conscience physique ou instinct, entièrement et passivement soumise à la loi transcendante matérialisée en elle.

2 – La conscience vitale ou énergie créatrice également subordonnée à la volonté unique du Créateur.

3 – La conscience mentale ou « image de Dieu », siège de la différenciation.

4 – La conscience affective, centre de l'adoration et principe de la perception intuitive qui conduit à la vision supra-mentale.

5 – La conscience supra-mentale ou intuition mystique, début de la vision lumineuse surnaturelle en l'homme. C'est là que commence en lui le règne du Verbe de vérité, une fois que l'agitation du langage mental dominé par les dualités est apaisée.

6 – La conscience spirituelle rayonnante et régénératrice qui enfante le moi individuel à la perfection de sa nature supra-consciente.

7 – La supraconscience éternelle et infinie, silence de la béatitude dans l'authenticité parfaite de l'Absolu.

---

[87] Mâ Sûryânanda Lakshmî, *Exégèse Spirituelle de la Bible, Apocalypse de Jean*, Neuchâtel (Suisse) : À la Baconnière, 1975, p. 82, ainsi que dans de nombreuses conférences données en Suisse et en France.

APPENDICE

J'ai trouvé, oui j'ai trouvé la richesse,
le joyau de Nom divin
MiraBai

Les faces de l'Éternel ?

Dans la Bible en hébreu le terme *faces* est toujours au pluriel. Lorsqu'il s'agit de l'homme on peut y voir l'expression que l'homme a de nombreux visages, de nombreux personnages en lui-même. Mais lorsqu'il s'agit de Dieu que peut-il signifier ?

Dans le texte original Dieu a plusieurs noms. Parmi eux les deux noms en très grande majorité les plus cités sont *IHVH* et *Elohîms* et très souvent ils sont associés, tels que « *IHVH nos Elohîms* » ou simplement « *IHVH-Elohîms* ». La terminaison du nom *Elohîms* exprime un pluriel[88], mais le verbe utilisé avec ce sujet est toujours au singulier dès lors qu'il désigne le Dieu du peuple hébreu[89]. Pourquoi ces deux noms dont l'un est au pluriel associé à un verbe au singulier, et quel est leur sens ?

Les linguistes voient dans le pluriel de ce nom *Elohîms* une marque de « superlatif intensif » ou de « pluriel de majesté », ce qui dispenserait de mettre le verbe au pluriel. Nous voulons bien l'admettre, mais s'agissant d'un texte sacré il paraît normal de s'interroger plus à fond sur cette tournure originale et l'appréhender

---

[88] Ce pluriel est rendu en français en ajoutant un « s », tout comme l'a fait A. Chouraqui.

[89] Par contre lorsque la Bible veut parler des idoles, qu'elle nomme les Dieux des autres peuples, elle utilise ce même mot Elohîms mais avec un verbe au pluriel.

de manière plus vaste que ne le font nos raisonnements intellectuels, si savants soient-ils. Quant à ce double nom, pourquoi ? Là encore nous verrons que s'il existe une réponse des exégètes qui peut paraître satisfaisante, en réalité elle ne l'est qu'en apparence.

C'est dans le fameux passage du Deutéronome 6:4 – profession de foi de tout juif croyant – que nous pouvons trouver une première réponse. Ce passage, transcrit mot à mot depuis l'hébreu, dit ceci :

Écoute Israël : IHVH, nos Elohîms, IHVH, Un.

Voir dans ce « *Un* » le fait que ces deux noms désignent le même Dieu est un premier niveau de compréhension, mais nous pouvons aller plus loin. Il faut y chercher une signification sur la nature même du Divin :

Il est *Un*.

Cela exprime beaucoup plus que la notion très familière d'un Dieu *unique*. En effet selon le sens que le dictionnaire donne à ce terme, cela laisse entendre une comparaison, donc l'existence de quelque chose extérieur à Lui, ce qui serait paradoxal car si Dieu est *Un* Il ne peut être également que *Tout*, logiquement.

En même temps que l'Unité, ce verset exprime la multiplicité du Divin par ce nom *Elohîms* au pluriel. D'ailleurs il n'est qu'à observer la vie sur la terre pour voir concrètement cette diversité et multiplicité de la création dans l'unité. Ceci est confirmé pleinement par les « sciences de la vie ». Ce que la science actuelle nous dit, les anciens Hébreux le savaient déjà puisque la Bible nomme toujours la *vie(s)* au pluriel en associant ce mot à un verbe au singulier. Elle exprime ainsi cette unité et pluralité de la vie(s). Ainsi la multiplicité *des faces* de l'Éternel est en totale cohérence à la fois avec la création et la façon dont le nom de Dieu est exprimé. Là est sans doute le génie de la langue hébraïque qui sait nous faire sentir de façon simple, et en seulement deux mots, quelque chose de la Vérité divine.

Quant à ce double Nom n'a-t-il pas autre chose à nous révéler ?

Pour l'expliquer plusieurs pistes ont été explorées par les exégètes. La réponse la plus couramment admise serait que deux traditions, l'une issue du polythéisme et l'autre plus strictement monothéiste, se seraient fondues dans le texte biblique que nous connaissons aujourd'hui. Cette explication semble tout à fait plausible, mais elle s'interroge sur les conditions de rédaction du texte et non pas sur le texte lui-même. Aussi, si elle apporte quelques satisfactions sur le plan intellectuel, qu'apporte-t-elle à l'âme assoiffée de connaître Dieu ? Elle ne la comble vraisemblablement pas car si Dieu révèle Son Nom c'est pour se faire connaître et pour se faire aimer des hommes. N'est-ce pas aussi comme cela qu'agissent les hommes entre eux ? Par ailleurs cette réponse des exégètes n'explique pas pourquoi dans tel passage c'est *IHVH* qui est utilisé alors que *Elohîms* se retrouve dans d'autres, sans que l'on comprenne bien le sens de cette alternance.

Si nous nous souvenons que « pour les Sémites le nom est identique à la réalité qu'il désigne »[90] nous pouvons envisager une réponse qui nous est donnée dans la vision du *buisson ardent,* au chapitre 3 du livre de l'Exode. Du sein de sa vision Moïse pose, au nom des fils d'Israël, la question : *Quel est Ton nom ?*

---

[90] A. Chouraqui, dans *Le Coran, op. cit.*

La réponse lui est donnée en deux temps. Il est d'abord dit au verset 14 :

Je suis qui Je serai.
Tu diras ainsi aux fils d'Israël : Je suis, m'a envoyé vers vous.

La formule hébraïque utilisée pour exprimer cela (אֶהְיֶה אֲשֶׁר אֶהְיֶה) est difficile à traduire en français. Si l'on s'en tient à une traduction littérale, plusieurs autres façons d'en rendre compte restent possibles : *Je serai qui Je suis, Je suis celui qui suis, Je serai comme Je suis, Je suis parfaitement Je suis, Je serai en tant que Je suis, Je suis en tant que Je serai, Je suis lequel Je suis ...* etc. Aucune prise individuellement n'en épuise le sens, mais prises toutes ensemble elles révèlent, ô combien, l'Éternité de l'Être. Alors peut-être qu'une traduction libre serait mieux à même de rendre compte de l'esprit de cette célèbre formule, par exemple :

Je suis Cela qui est,
ou *Je suis l'Être immuable,*
ou *Je suis l'Être éternel.*

Puis la réponse est complétée au verset 15 :

Tu diras ainsi aux fils d'Israël :
IHVH, Elohîms de vos pères, Elohîms d'Abraham, Elohîms d'Isaac
et Elohîms de Jacob, m'a envoyé vers vous.
Voici mon Nom pour toujours.

Dans cette révélation de Son nom donnée à Moïse par ces deux versets n'est-il pas possible de voir quelque chose de plus que la simple juxtaposition des deux textes d'origine différente ? Ces noms ne peuvent-ils pas nous révéler quelque chose de Dieu ?

Le recours à un éclairage extérieur à la tradition judéo-chrétienne peut nous être une aide très précieuse. En effet, si la nature du Divin est *Une* et si la Vérité divine est également *Une,* il apparaît logique qu'elle se retrouve dans plusieurs textes sacrés de par le monde si on considère ces révélations à leur sommet.

Ce que la Bible a exprimé dans ce passage, la Sagesse hindoue selon le Vedanta[91] l'exprime d'une autre manière : Dieu est à la fois « Le sans-forme (ou Absolu-Brahman) » et « Avec-forme (ou Dieu personnel et Puissances exécutrices) ». Il est tout à fait remarquable de retrouver très exactement ces deux aspects dans le texte hébreu.

Le nom de *IHVH,* formé de quatre lettres en hébreu (יְהֹוָה), représente un arrangement particulier et complexe du verbe *être.* Selon Abraham Ibn Ezra[92] « ces quatre lettres rendent compte à la fois du passé, du présent et du futur ». Ce nom synthétise en quelque sorte le début du verset 14 et se réfère à l'Être ou à l'Absolu. L'Être « en tant que ce qui n'apparaît pas, mais qui se manifeste dans l'étant »[93] est équivalent à la notion du *sans-forme.* Remarquons que dans la tradition juive, comme en écho à cela, ce nom du *sans-forme, IHVH,* est considéré comme ineffable, donc ne doit pas être prononcé car le prononcer ce serait déjà lui donner une forme[94].

---

[91] Doctrine métaphysique issue des écritures sacrées hindoues. Elle était au départ centrée sur la non-dualité, en particulier dans l'Advaïta-Vedanta, donc équivalente au « monisme » en Occident.

[92] Rabbin andalou du XIIe siècle. Il est considéré comme l'une des plus éminentes autorités rabbiniques médiévales.

[93] Hannah Arendt, dans *Journal de pensée*, Paris : Le Seuil, 2005, p. 931. Elle reprend ici la pensée de Heidegger.

[94] Lors de la lecture ou la récitation de la Bible il est alors remplacé par un autre nom : *Adonaï.*

Après ce nom de l'Absolu ou du *sans-forme*, le verset 15 ajoute l'expression *Elohîms de vos pères, Elohîms d'Abraham, Elohîms d'Isaac et Elohîms de Jacob*, qui évoque très clairement le *Dieu personnel*, c'est-à-dire *avec-forme*. Le Dieu personnel est celui que chacun peut prier et adorer, car il faut bien reconnaître que chaque homme a une vision et une compréhension particulière du Divin, d'où ce nom *Elohîms* mis au pluriel.

Cette compréhension singulière des hommes, donc multiple, n'empêche aucunement que Dieu soit toujours le même et demeure à jamais *Un*. Mais pourquoi dans le verset 6:4 du Deutéronome, ce nom de l'Absolu est répété et encadre le nom du Dieu personnel (*IHVH – nos Elohîms – IHVH*) et non l'inverse ? Ceci n'est pas qu'un simple effet de style, ou mis comme cela par hasard, mais porte en soi une révélation. Cette forme particulière nous révèle que rien ne peut encadrer ou limiter l'Absolu : Il est le commencement et la fin de toute chose. Nous retrouvons ici ce que Jésus a dit : *le Père est plus grand que Moi*[95].

Mais, comme l'enseigne Mâ Sûryânanda Lakshmî, l'homme a besoin de passer par le Dieu personnel, car l'Absolu ne peut être connu directement. C'est ce que Jésus révèle lorsqu'il dit : *Nul ne vient au Père que par Moi*[96]. Ici il très important de comprendre que ce « Moi » ne se réfère pas à une personne, donc n'est aucunement limité ni exclusif, comme le pensent trop souvent les chrétiens. Une telle pensée doit être corrigée car « Elle trahit le cœur même du message de Jésus. Donner à Jésus l'exclusivité de la plénitude divine, c'est en priver tout le reste des humains. »[97]

---

[95] Jean 14:28.
[96] Jean 14:6.
[97] Pierre Genod dans *L'Absolu de ma quête*, Éd. Persée p. 199.

Comme, selon le Vedanta, le *Dieu personnel* est également *Puissances exécutrices* nous pouvons trouver là une explication sur la manière dont l'Ancien Testament utilise ces deux noms en fonction du contexte. Pour illustrer cela nous ne prendrons qu'un seul exemple, et non des moindres, mais d'autres pourraient être cités. Par exemple il apparaît logique que dans le récit de la Création (chapitre 1 de la Genèse) seul le nom *Elohîms* soit utilisé puisque ce récit exprime typiquement une action de puissance créatrice et exécutrice[98].

Cette révélation du Vedanta est similaire à ce qu'a dit Edward Leigh dans son *Dictionnaire hébraïque*[99]. Le nom IHVH « marque son Éternité et son existence : son Éternité parce qu'il comprend en Lui toutes les différences de temps, l'avenir, le présent et le passé ; son existence parce qu'il dérive d'une racine qui signifie être, car Dieu est son être en soi-même et par de soi-même, et communique à toutes les créatures tout l'être qu'elles possèdent. » Et puis « Elohîm désigne une certaine relation de Dieu aux créatures, car il marque l'empire et la puissance de Dieu, l'autorité et la force qu'il déploie dans le monde. De là vient que Dieu au commencement de la Genèse, où Il parle de la création, s'appelle non pas Jehovah[100] (IHVH) mais Elohîm. »

Cette révélation du *Nom* donné à Moïse donne une clef pour mieux comprendre cette multiplicité dans l'Unité des faces de l'Éternel. Nous voyons aussi qu'il y a une profonde convergence entre cette révélation, l'enseignement de Jésus et celui du Vedanta.

---

[98] Cet aspect de Puissances exécutrices se retrouve également dans le nom de IHVH-Sabaot, qui est généralement traduit par Dieu-des-armées.

[99] Traduit en français par Louis de Wolzogue à partir de l'original en anglais. Édition de 1712. La première citation est tirée de la préface de cet ouvrage, la seconde de la rubrique sur le nom Elohîm.

[100] Ce terme est simplement une transposition phonétique en français de IHVH.

N'oublions pas cependant que si les textes bibliques et védantiques nous apportent une certaine lumière sur la Vérité de Dieu, cette compréhension reste toujours infime par rapport à ce qu'Il est, comme le dit Shrî Râmakrishna : « Dieu est sans-forme et Il est aussi avec-forme, et encore au-delà de la forme, et de ce qui est sans forme. Lui seul sait ce qu'Il est. »[101]

Il est merveilleux de constater que comprendre de cette manière le texte biblique rend très bien compte de la diversité des religions et sagesses du monde, tout en affirmant leur unité. La multiplicité est parfaitement exprimée dans les religions dites *polythéistes* ; malheureusement l'on ignore trop souvent qu'elles ont en général conscience de l'Unité divine au-delà de la multiplicité des Dieux invoqués. Par exemple, il est un fait reconnu, notamment par les spécialistes de l'Inde, que pour les hindous Dieu est *Un* sous les multiples noms et visages adorés. D'un autre côté les religions dites *monothéistes* se prétendent être les seules garantes d'une vision de l'unité et de l'unicité divine. Toutefois le Christianisme admet explicitement dans sa conception de la Trinité que Dieu puisse avoir trois visages. Dès lors, marquer une séparation, voire une opposition, entre ces deux grandes catégories de religion n'est guère justifié. Prétendre en outre que les religions monothéistes seraient plus avancées, donc supérieures, l'est encore moins. Cela d'autant plus que la Bible elle-même révèle très clairement, et en toutes lettres, cette unité-multiplicité du Nom divin. S'efforcer de le voir ne rendrait-il pas la lecture de la Bible plus féconde et ne serait-il pas, aussi, un levain pour un œcuménisme plus universel et plus vrai, source d'une fraternité plus efficace entre les peuples ?

---

[101] Dans *L'enseignement de Râmakrishna*, Paris : Albin Michel, 1972. Romain Rolland a fait une excellente biographie de ce grand Sage hindou, considéré comme l'un des plus grands Sages de l'époque moderne (1836 -1886).

Sommaire